continued ...

"Wowsa! I liked this book so much, we have picked *Sealed with a Curse* by Cecy Robson as a MUST READ of this winter! . . . Cecy Robson has written about a unique world full of werewolves, wereracoons, a were-bobcat, vampires, and of course the four kick-ass sisters that you will love as your own family!"

— Paranormal Cravings

"*Sealed with a Curse* has just about everything I want in a really good urban fantasy. Strong lead characters? Check. A sexy romance brewing on the side? Check. Vamps, weres, witches, and more? Check! . . . This is an exciting and refreshing debut and I can't wait to see what's next for this series!"   — My Bookish Ways

"*Sealed with a Curse* was impressive. The pace was fantastic, the story exciting, and the chemistry between all of the characters was just great. I loved everyone in this book—even the creepy people. Everyone was compelling and added a lot to the story and to the world Cecy created. I *strongly* recommend this book."

— Yummy Men & Kick Ass Chicks (5 stars)

"It is rare that an urban fantasy book can grab me from the first few pages. . . . But this book, this one definitely got me hooked after the first few pages. There was action, humor, danger, sisterly bonding, witty one-liners, something fun and completely unique and a whole new world just waiting to be discovered and I knew I wanted to discover it."   — My Guilty Obsession (5 stars)

The Weird Girls Series by Cecy Robson

The Weird Girls: A Novella
Sealed with a Curse

A Cursed Embrace

A WEIRD GIRLS NOVEL

CECY ROBSON

A SIGNET ECLIPSE BOOK

SIGNET ECLIPSE
Published by the Penguin Group
Penguin Group (USA) Inc., 375 Hudson Street,
New York, New York 10014, USA

USA | Canada | UK | Ireland | Australia | New Zealand | India | South Africa | China

Penguin Books Ltd., Registered Offices: 80 Strand, London WC2R 0RL, England
For more information about the Penguin Group visit penguin.com.

First published by Signet Eclipse, an imprint of New American Library,
a division of Penguin Group (USA) Inc.

First Printing, July 2013

ISBN 978-0-451-41674-2

Printed in the United States of America
10 9 8 7 6 5 4 3 2 1

PUBLISHER'S NOTE
This is a work of fiction. Names, characters, places, and incidents either are the
product of the author's imagination or are used fictitiously, and any resemblance
to actual persons, living or dead, business establishments, events, or locales is
entirely coincidental.
 The publisher does not have any control over and does not assume any responsibility for author or third-party Web sites or their content.

If you purchased this book without a cover you should be aware that this book
is stolen property. It was reported as "unsold and destroyed" to the publisher and
neither the author nor the publisher has received any payment for this "stripped
book."

*To Jamie, my husband and best friend,
and to our children, who honor me with more love
and happiness than I deserve.*

ACKNOWLEDGMENTS

This story of love and exploding demon parts would not have been possible without the talents of my editor, Jhanteigh Kupihea, and the members of the Penguin team. Jhanteigh, thank you for taking a chance on me, and for your laughter and tears—the good kind, I mean!

To my überagent and friend, Nicole Resciniti. Nic, you hold my hand, you cheer me on, and you always believe in me—even when I don't believe in myself. Where would I be without your heart and guidance? I love and adore you.

To Jamie, who read my pages and said, "This is going to get published," and for his bromance with Misha. Babe, I would have never made it this far without you. Thank you for making my dream a reality, and for loving me and our babies.

To my buds: Kaitlyn Ballenger, Amanda Flower, Kate SeRine, and Melody Steiner—women and authors I've come to know and cherish.

To Katie Davis, Sue Henrikson, Willow Kallop, Natalie Volberding, and my FMC family for reading my work *and* enjoying it! Natalie, I'm sorry I told you about the giant, slimy tongue shooting out of the trash chute . . .

just as you were opening the trash chute. But you have to admit, it was kind of hilarious.

To my parents, Armando and Carmen Galdamez, who encouraged everyone they've ever met in their lives to buy my books. And to my brother, Douglas Galdamez, who I respect more than he'll ever know.

CHAPTER 1

A dead wereraccoon on your doorstep is no way to start the morning.

"I'm bored."

Neither is a whiney vampire dressed like a naughty Catholic schoolgirl.

I raised my brows at her. "Edith Anne, I'm sorry you didn't get to kill anything. If you're this bored, why don't you go home or find someone to snack on?"

Edith Anne's blue-black hair shone like satin in Tahoe's early-morning sun. She swung her knee-high red leather boots over the railing where she sat and—good Lord, I don't think she was wearing panties beneath her tiny plaid skirt—stomped across the wooden floorboards, careful to avoid the blood and pus pooling around the body. "Oh, Celia." She said my name as if she'd caught me eating her shoes. "The master says you and your"—Edith Anne scowled and motioned to my three sisters behind me—"weird-ass family are now under his protection. I can't leave until he knows you're safe." She protruded her fangs, picked something off one with her perfectly manicured nails, and flicked it to the side. "Besides, I ate before I got here."

If I didn't know vampires needed only small amounts of blood to survive and were forbidden from killing humans, I would have staked her. "Did Misha say you had to do anything to keep me safe?"

Edith Anne rose to her full height, which meant her chest was right in my face. Oh, goody.

She pursed her bright red lips. "Why?"

My grin widened. "I'll take that as a yes. Why don't you start patrolling the perimeter of the house—you know, in case the bad guys try to sneak up on us?"

Edith frowned. "Your grass is muddy from the rain and I'm wearing four-inch heels."

I glanced down. "Yes, you are. They'll make a perfect weapon should some scary monster show up. Be sure to aim for the heart."

Edith blinked her large brown eyes at me. "But what if he comes while I'm out back?"

"I promise to yell really loudly."

"But what if—?"

"Get moving, freak," Taran snapped, coming to stand next to me, arms crossed, attitude at the ready. As the second oldest, I could always count on her to have my back.

Edith Anne stuck out her bottom lip before turning on her four-inch heels and storming down the wooden steps. "You guys suck."

She adjusted her bosom beneath her lacy red bra as she sloshed through the mud and disappeared around the house. Edith Anne was all about class.

"Son of a bitch, Ceel." Taran stared at the dead *were*. The wounds gurgled pus like a fountain, deep from where the cursed gold bullets had lodged.

But the pus, and the blood, and the death were not what made Taran clutch herself protectively. I moved a little closer and whispered so our other sisters, Shayna and Emme, couldn't hear. "Did you dream again, about those . . . creatures?"

I didn't want to say "demons." And neither did Taran. Yet the dread surrounding her nightmares over the past few weeks and the way she described those *things*—reptilian bodies, leather wings, and strangely humanoid faces—left us few choices from which to select. Gargoyles didn't exist. Neither did any type of Fae. But demons? If a good, loving God existed, and darkness still reigned in our world, something not so good, not so loving, had also found its place among us.

Taran's petrified blue eyes peered out to the horizon where Tahoe's gentle waves sparkled beneath the warming April sun. The magic within her stirred, causing wavy strands of her jet-black hair to flutter around her stunning Latin features. Either the divination of the lake had stimulated her gift or she'd attempted to lure it to do so. She knew that Tahoe both settled and enlivened my beast—the literal tigress within me, who emerged when the superscaries came out to play. And while she didn't understand how to draw its magic, something happened. A trickle of rising power brushed past me from the direction of the lake and into Taran. Whatever she gathered, though, didn't seem to be enough. She shook her head, disappointment crinkling her neatly shaped brows. "It was the same dream, Ceel, the one where I see them sweeping down on us like locusts. They cover my body and claw at me and . . ." She shuddered. "Shayna's cries are the last sound I hear before I wake up screaming."

She jumped when I placed my hand on her shoulder and scowled hard enough to set me on fire with her power. "Damn it, Ceel. Don't touch me when I'm—" She shut her lids tight and shook it off, swearing a mantra beneath her breath. When she opened her eyes, her scowl deepened, erasing any remaining susceptibility. Taran didn't allow herself to express vulnerability very often. Attitude, yes. Bitchiness, daily. But that's what kept her safe. And in the supernatural world we lived in, a little bit of boldness kept you very much alive.

I reached for her once more, moving slowly to avoid irritating her fragile nerves. My fingers squeezed her arm. "We have a pack of werewolves watching out for us." I smirked when I thought of Misha. "And a guardian angel master vampire who feels indebted to us for saving his billion-dollar backside. We're going to be okay."

I had an inner beast. Taran, an inner bitch. They both worked well to help us through our struggles, just in different ways. She sighed. "Yeah. Maybe." She stomped back to the body, scrutinizing our unexpected visitor from his gushing head to his seeping toes. "When the hell are the *weres* getting here? No offense to this poor sap, but he's making a ridiculous mess."

I tried not to think about the mess. Or the wereraccoon. I'd first found him riffling through our garbage a month or so back. Since then he'd periodically hid, watching us, in the tall, dense firs surrounding our house. Was it creepy? Oh yeah. Did I want him around us? No. But he'd been one of many supernaturals who had shown up since my sisters and I were "outed" to the mystical community. And unlike the other audacious idiots I pounded, this guy seemed . . . skittish.

Streaks of blood and pus ran from the thick brush behind our house and up the porch steps to the body. The *were*'s feet hovered over the threshold while the rest of his naked body lay facedown across our dark chestnut wood floors. Blond curls stuck to his scalp. His head twisted in an odd angle and his eyes stared blindly beneath our couch. He couldn't have been more than twenty-five, like me. Too young to die, especially like this.

Our training as nurses drove us to try to save him. But his throat had been slit where his pulse should have drummed, and the pungent scent of death told me there was nothing left to save. I didn't have many friends. And I had the feeling the wereraccoon hadn't had any.

Shayna played with her phone. She'd taken one look at the body and called her behemoth werewolf boyfriend right away. Since then she hadn't stepped anywhere near the *were* and had kept her eyes averted. She knew as the earth's guardians, her boyfriend and his kind would take care of it. Or maybe it was the pus. Shayna and I delivered babies for a living. While we dealt with other body fluids, pus never reared its ugly head. "Koda says they're almost here . . . and that Aric says not to do anything stupid."

Aric. His name filled me with heat while chills shot down my spine. I wanted to see him. I just wasn't exactly ready. And I especially wasn't ready for him to find me standing over a corpse. Again. "Aric's coming?"

Shayna nodded hard enough to make her silky black ponytail bounce behind her. "He cares about you, Celia. He wants to make sure you're safe."

The cool April breeze swept through the opened door, sending goose bumps scurrying from my arms up to my neck. I wrapped my bare arms around my body. I usually dressed in a tank and jogging shorts when I went for my run; otherwise my inner tigress made me unbearably hot. But standing still did nothing to warm me. She flicked her tail inside me, excited to see Aric's wolf. I only wished my human side shared her enthusiasm. "I doubt he cares as much as you think," I muttered.

"Aric hasn't called?" My sweet sister, Emme, curled her arms around mine. She reminded me of Natalie Portman—pretty, gentle, and soft-spoken. I almost smiled. Against my gold skin tone and lean muscles, her fair skin appeared lighter and her delicate arms more fragile.

A twinge of her pale yellow healing light that matched her hair slowly built until it completely enveloped us. I shook my head. "Don't, Emme." She attempted to soothe my emotions with her healing ability—the way she did my physical wounds. But disappointment was nothing to heal, rather just something to get over. "I'm not mad at Aric. You don't have to calm me."

Emme released me, sympathy further softening her gentle green eyes. She nodded and leaned against the back of our sofa, smoothing the skirt of her long blue dress.

Shayna frowned and stepped toward me, but apparently she was too close to the body. She backed away again and tucked her iPhone into the pocket of her jeans, fiddling with the holster of her sword as she spoke. "But you said Aric's texted you quite a bit."

Shayna's glass remained perpetually half full and often overflowed with hope. I supposed it complemented her perky cheerleading persona. Me? No one would have referred to me as perky, and let's just say my cup didn't runneth over. "Only to tell me he'd call soon, but we haven't spoken since . . . you know." I didn't want to mention the morning I'd woken in bed with Aric's arms holding me tight. Good grief, had that only been a little over a week ago? I was trapped inside a burning mansion with a psycho master vampire. Aric had saved me from being burned to cinders.

My fingertips swept absentmindedly over my lips. He'd kissed me long and hard that morning. And I willingly returned his affections. My heart pounded, my skin sizzled, my body begged for his . . . and then he jerked out of bed and left. Just like that. Without explanation. Without a good-bye. Just a promise to call. The wandering hands I expected never explored, the tongue I wanted to skim along my flesh never tasted past my lips, and the werewolf I expected to stay in bed with me didn't bother. Despite the record-breaking heat between us, we hadn't made love. Maybe it was better. I'd only had sex three times in my life, when I was seventeen. And while the experience could be described as sweet, the words "awk-ward" and "clumsy" also came to mind. I still remained unsure whether the first time even "counted."

Shayna leaned on the cream-colored couch next to Emme, a safe distance away from our deceased guest. "Aric's probably just been busy, dude," she offered.

"Koda calls you every day, throughout the day." And spends every night with you, I didn't add.

Shayna's bright smile and blue eyes lacked their fa-mous sparkle. "Koda's neither a pureblood nor a Leader like Aric. He doesn't have the responsibilities Aric has."

"Nor does he have to answer to his Elders for dating outside his race." I knelt over the body, my anxiety over the wolves' arrival riling my beast.

Taran tossed her midnight waves so they fell behind her shoulders. Since first realizing Shayna called Koda, she'd rushed to change out of the camisole she'd slept in and now donned a chic pale olive dress and silver gladi-ator sandals that added four inches to her five-foot-three frame. She'd dressed for Gemini, Aric's Beta. Taran's blue eyes peered beneath the shroud of thick lashes she'd inherited from our Latina mother. "It could be worse. He could pat your damn head."

Taran's allure crushed men like potato chips. You know those women men ignored their dates to ogle? Taran was one of those. She could have had any male she wanted. Anyone, but Gemini, it seemed.

Emme placed her hand over her mouth. "Oh my goodness. Is Gemini still petting you?"

Taran twirled her platinum and diamond bracelet — a gift from Misha. "Yup. Just last night."

"Do you think perhaps it's a wolf thing?" Emme of-fered.

Taran dropped her hands to her sides. "Does Liam pet you — on the couch, in bed, in the tub — *ever*?"

Emme blushed. "Um, well, no —"

Taran turned to Shayna. "How about Koda? Any head rubbing going on?"

"No, dude. But—"

"Then don't tell me it's a damn wolf thing. I'd give anything for that fine hunk of Japanese ass to kiss me, touch me—*anything* but the damn head pat!"

Emme frowned, making her appear bunny rabbit fierce. "Don't swear in front of the dead fellow. It's disrespectful."

Taran's harsh brows softened as she took in the dead *were* once more. "I really don't think he gives a shit, Emme."

In the distance, my sensitive hearing fixed on three speeding SUVs. I rose and nudged Taran. "The wolves are here." Seconds later the vehicles screeched into our small development, Koda's silver Yukon in the lead, followed closely by a black Escalade. *Aric*'s Escalade. A red four-by-four pickup pulled against the curb last, and three males I didn't recognize stepped out. Koda and Liam raced in, leaping one by one over the body and hurrying to Shayna and Emme. Aric and Gemini jogged out of the Escalade. Gemini reached the door first. His dark almond eyes widened upon seeing Taran, but quickly regained their composure. He held out his hand. "Will you stand outside with me, in case any witnesses arrive?"

A spark of blue and white flame ignited on Taran's fingertips. She nodded. Gem pulled her into his arms and swept her down the steps. A gallant Prince Charming move if only Prince Charming hadn't patted a pissed-off Snow White's head.

Aric's pace slowed the moment he caught sight of me, his light brown eyes bright against his navy shirt and five o'clock shadow. Unlike the others, Aric didn't fuss over me and stopped a few steps in front of the *were*'s feet. "You okay?"

Aric's deep tenor voice tugged at my heart, yet a nod

remained my only response. When I said nothing more, he fell to one knee and examined the body. The *were* who'd driven the pickup—a tall male with military-cut black hair and ebony eyes—hustled to his side.

Commando Guy shook his head after taking a sniff. "Not one of mine."

"Lone?" Aric asked.

Lone were, he meant. I was right, this *were* hadn't belonged to a pack.

Commando nodded. "Yeah. And not from the area. I keep track of the few *lones* around here. Who found him?" He scowled. "And why the hell do I smell vampire?"

I stepped forward. "I found him, and, uh . . ." Hmmm, how to explain why the vampire family of Aric's enemy was here?

Before I could ease Aric into knowing Misha's keep arrived ahead of him, Edith Anne leapt onto the porch in her muddy boots. "Can I go now?"

Edith returned Aric's glare with a smile that clearly said, *Why, thank you, I'd love a bite.*

I groaned. "Yes, Edith Anne, please go." The last thing I needed was another dead thing on my doorstep. Thank God the porch rails and potted plants hid the view from our nosy and evil neighbor.

Edith twisted her body playfully as she twirled the edges of her long hair. She kept her eyes on Aric when she spoke. "Okay, Celia. Be sure to wear something sexy for dinner. The master has arranged for a cozy meal and looks forward to seeing you again." Her smile widened as the burning scent of Aric's shock and anger singed my nostrils. "Oh, I'm sorry, mutt. Didn't you know Celia and the master have been spending time together? Why, just the other night—"

"Good-bye, Edith!" I hissed.

Edith tossed her hair back and strutted to her candy-apple red Mercedes. She blew one last kiss Aric's way and sped off. Where was something sharp and pointy when you needed it?

Aric turned back to me once Edith disappeared. "Paul, this is Celia Wird. Celia, this is Paul Nalis, Leader of the Raccoon Gaze in the area."

Paul stepped over the threshold and held out his hand for me to shake. His grip was strong, yet lacking the challenge Alphas notoriously threw in the faces of unknown preternaturals. So why did Aric's brow knit into a tight frown as he watched us?

"Good to meet you, Celia," Paul said before releasing my hand. "Could you tell me what happened?"

I focused on him, rather than Aric. "My sisters were sitting down to breakfast and I was getting ready for a run. I heard something hard smack against the door while I was tying my shoes. When I opened it, he fell through." My head angled back toward the *were*. "His skin was barely warm when I touched him, and his heart had stopped. He bled out in puddles of blood and pus. I'd never seen anything like it."

Paul huffed. "Yeah, that much gold in a *were*'s system will have that affect." He stuck his black boot beneath the raccoon's chin and lifted it, lolling his head side to side. "The dagger used to cut him was gold, too. You can tell since there's no evidence his body had tried to heal him."

"I'll take your word for it." I'd seen gold mess up a vampire. Preternaturals couldn't even hold the stuff without making them want to hurl. Except I'd never seen damage to this extent. The poor guy had been brutalized.

"Did you hear the shots or see anything suspicious?" I shook my head.

"What about them?" He motioned to my sisters.

"Celia's inner beast is a golden tigress. If she didn't sense anything, the others wouldn't have, either."

Aric didn't typically answer for me. And it would have

bothered me had I not picked up on the underlying protectiveness of his tone.

Paul gave me the once-over. "But she's not *were*."

Aric's tone grew more of an edge. "No. She can't heal."

The corners of Paul's lips curved into a smile. "What a shame."

Judging by the way Aric leapt over the body and wedged his way between us, Paul didn't pity my lack of healing abilities. "Watch it, Paul."

Paul cocked his head to the side. Something he saw in Aric forced the smirk from his face. "Jesus, Aric," he said.

I glanced at both of them, confused about what had transpired.

"Just get him out of here," Aric growled.

Paul leaned against the wall and whistled. Two more wereraccoons appeared sporting thick rubber gloves—the kind I suspected could be found at any local nuclear power plant. We moved out of the way. One of the *weres* grabbed the legs and the other the wrists. On the count of three, they lifted. The air rippled and translucent waves pushed against my face.

And that's when the body exploded.

CHAPTER 2

A sonic boom blasted my eardrums. I landed on the couch face-first, Aric on top of me, shielding my body with his. Something hit the wooden floor and glass shattered. Thick, polluted air tightened my chest the moment I attempted to take a breath. It was like inhaling muddy water through my lungs. And the stench—good Lord, a toxic waste dump smelled rosier. I coughed, the sharp smell stinging my eyes. I tried to rise. Aric kept me down. He adjusted his position on top of me so I didn't bear the brunt of his two-hundred-plus form, allowing me to turn my face enough to see . . . blackness. Or should I say, a solid mass of green?

"Stay down." Aric's voice sounded strained. My sisters gagged and hacked. Someone threw open the windows and the sliding glass doors leading out to our deck. Horrible retching ensued from the direction of our powder room.

Outside, Taran voiced her concerns. "Son of a bitch! What the hell is this shit?"

The good news was my skin didn't melt, my bones remained in one piece, and no funky thing with tentacles attempted to birth through my belly. One never knew what one might have encountered in the supernatural world.

I tried to slow my breathing, not wanting to inhale more of the foul odor than necessary. If only the rising heat between Aric and me allowed it. My tigress, hell, she thought Aric on top was hot stuff and that we should make out with him while we waited for the air to clear.

I didn't agree.

I twisted a little, hoping to ease him off me. All that did was rub his body against mine and send quivers jetting to my already alert girl parts.

Oh . . . crap.

I'd promised myself I'd keep it together the next time I saw Aric—I was tough, strong, formidable . . .

"Try to breathe through your mouth." Aric's instructions came out in panted whispers.

I was in trouble, that's what I was. "Okay," I moaned like an idiot.

Aric's soft growl rumbled against my back. I refused to purr in response. And I didn't.

Until his head fell against mine and his nose nudged playfully against my ear.

Aric froze when my beast purred to come hither. Damn it. Whose side was she on anyway?

Neither of us moved, despite the intensity of warmth we shared. And just like that, the moment quickly turned from unbearably sexy to horribly awkward. My house reeked of swamp butt, and there we were, acting like two unsupervised hormonal teens.

Slowly, like molasses sliding into water, the dense air thinned out. As soon as the first gulps of fresh air hit my lungs, Aric leapt off me, pulling me with him to stand. Except instead of releasing me completely, his arm slid around my body, keeping me close. I didn't fight it, welcoming the affection I'd longed for the past week.

A thin haze lingered around the expanse of our large

open family room. Similar to when something burns in the kitchen and the remnants hang on despite the opened windows. Nothing appeared stained or destroyed—strange, especially since the force of the explosion hit harder than a truckload of sweaty sumo wrestlers.

Emme and Shayna appeared with their wolves, pale with obvious nausea. The toilet flushed. One of the were-raccoons stepped out from the powder room. Thank goodness he made it in time. The other one waited outside with Gemini and Taran.

Paul stood holding two picture frames. "Sorry. I knocked these over when I hit the floor."

I hurried out of Aric's hold and took the pictures from Paul. The only picture we had of our parents remained intact, just chipped at the corner. But the one of our foster mother, Ana Lisa, had a large crack down the center. I carefully placed them on the mantel of our brick fireplace, barely acknowledging Paul's offer to replace the frames as I focused on the faces of the only people who'd shown us love during our childhood.

I cherished the pictures, so much so it scared me that something could irreparably damage them. Yet I never held or admired the old photos much. Sadness bristled inside me when I thought for too long about those stolen from me. Some things hurt forever, I supposed.

My finger slid along the edge of Ana Lisa's frame. Shayna had taken the photo with a disposable camera she'd found abandoned on the street. Ana Lisa's hand rested against Emme's back. My youngest sister was only about seven then, her tiny arms hugging Ana Lisa's robust figure. Tears glistened in Emme's eyes. I remember scolding Shayna for taking the photo. But all I saw was Emme's pain. I failed to see what Shayna did—the compassion and Ana Lisa's silent promise to keep Emme safe. She'd kept us all safe. Until the monsters returned . . .

I moved on, urged by the need to protect what remained of my family.

Everyone had assembled where the body had lain. I casually ambled to Aric's side, surprised by how easily he gathered me into his arms again. I tensed briefly before his comforting presence relaxed me like the feel of a warm blanket fresh from the dryer. It felt right to be with him. If only I knew his feelings mirrored mine.

"What happened?"

Aric shook his head. "I've never seen anything like this." He motioned to the floor with his chin. "Or that, except in magical sacrifices."

A charcoal outline, resembling those drawn in chalk on crime shows, was all that remained of the *were*—that, and the cursed gold bullet slugs. Taran looked around the room at the same time I did, articulating my thoughts beautifully. "For shit's sake. Is this dead guy all over our house now?"

Gemini's jaw slacked, the quiet, reserved Beta appearing stunned by Taran's colorful vocabulary. "Uh, it would seem his remains dissipated in the air and are traveling in the current."

I reached for a throw pillow and took a whiff. The awful smell didn't reach my delicate senses. "I think Gemini's right. What's left of him is on the floor."

Taran sashayed to the back of our kitchen and into the laundry room. She returned with a handheld vacuum and proceeded to suck up the wereraccoon and the bullets. "Not anymore," she muttered. She held it out to Paul, who gripped it by the handle at arm's length. "There you go. *Lone* or not, I expect you to give him a proper burial."

Our friend Bren was a *lone* wolf, my sisters and our other friend Danny his only pack. I couldn't think about losing Bren, but if we did, we'd want him honored.

Paul passed the handheld to the other raccoon. "Do you want us to help you track?"

Aric slid his fingers down my side to rest against my hip. "No. We'll take it from here."

"If I find anything on this guy, I'll let you know."

"Likewise," Aric said.

Paul paused to watch us. Aric's hand tightened on my hip. Paul noticed and nodded my way. "Celia."

"Good-bye, Paul." My husky tone failed to register as superfriendly, not that that was anything new. After a lifetime of being labeled as "weird," I never let my guard down. A strenuous way to live, but as my family's defender, I kept us safe that way. Only Aric had found a way through my defenses.

My sisters and wolves dispersed to the kitchen, leaving Aric and me alone. No, that wasn't on purpose or anything.

Aric faced me, slipping both hands onto my hips. "How are you?"

I straightened to my full five feet three inches, which, when the wolf of your dreams stood a good foot taller, did absolutely nothing. "Considering I woke up to find a corpse slumped across my threshold, only to have the remains pop like a balloon and attempt to suffocate me? Okay, I guess." I shrugged. "My sisters are safe. I'm thankful for that."

Aric gave me a halfhearted smile. "I don't want you to worry. I meant it when I promised to protect you." One hand curled around my waist, while his opposite hand traveled beneath my long chocolate waves to cup the nape of my neck. I closed my lids, relishing the addicting warmth that always accompanied Aric's touch.

I opened my eyes in time to see him lean forward. I turned away before his lips met mine. He dropped his hands and sighed. "I suppose I deserved that."

My hands found the back of the couch. Lack of experience with males made me kitten shy, not tigress fierce.

"I'm sorry I haven't called," he added quietly.

"It's all right." I said it, but Aric could scent I didn't mean it. Still, he humored me.

"No, it's not, Celia."

"You're right. It's not." My fingers drummed against the ridge of the sofa. "So why haven't you called?"

He ran a hand through his dark brown hair. He'd cut it since the last time I saw him. He kept the top long, the sides short. I wondered what else or who else had occupied his time.

Aric crossed his arms. "Things have been more complicated than I'd expected." He glanced over his shoulder to find Shayna, "Miss I Respect Your Privacy," peering around the corner. He laughed when she scurried away. "Take a ride with me and I'll explain."

When I didn't move, Aric bent and kissed the top of my head. "Please," he whispered. "We need to talk."

Aric took my hand when I nodded, and led me to the door. "Celia and I are going out," he called over his shoulder.

The wolves murmured an acknowledgment over Taran's "It's about damn time" remark. Aric grimaced at the comment as he lifted me over the threshold where the blood and pus had oozed. Nothing remained except the lingering memory of a tortured soul. I searched the wide floor planks, the steps as my feet descended, and the stretch of lawn. Nothing. He was gone. Forever. The revelation caused the already heavy sadness pressing against my sternum to intensify. I resisted the urge to lean into Aric for support and shied away from him once more.

Aric's fingers found the small of my back. "I know you're not happy with me, Celia. I'm hoping I can change that."

I didn't answer. I would've circled the world with him, and he probably suspected as much. But despite how he made my insides melt and my breath catch, I couldn't ignore the last week. His rebuff had both stunned and hurt me, more than I dared to admit. I needed to know what happened . . . and if the possibility of "us" still existed.

Aric opened the Escalade's passenger door for me. The tan leather seat chilled my bare legs. Although I didn't react, Aric immediately started the engine and flicked on the seat warmer. He took me to the closest diner. The patrons ceased their conversation as we entered. Aric's commanding presence made them take notice. They settled and resumed their meals once we took our seats. I flipped through the menu. The gore slathered across my front porch had initially erased my appetite. Except the scents of frying bacon and pouring pancake batter quickly proclaimed festering body parts be damned. So I didn't complain when Aric ordered enough food to feed a small village . . . or a wolf and a tigress.

"I flew in from Colorado last night."

"Oh?" I sipped on my orange juice. "What's there?" *Besides the countless droves of weresluts you've bedded?*

Aric smirked. While he couldn't read my thoughts, my tone probably screamed, *Caution: bitchy Latina ahead.*

"My mother, Celia." He glanced out the wide diner windows with a panoramic view of Lake Tahoe. The breeze had picked up, sending a ripple of blue waves to splash against the sandy shore. "It's where I grew up. Where I used to find my peace."

I finished the last bit of my biscuits and gravy and moved on to the eggs. I could relate to what Aric meant. The mysticism of the lake welcomed us like humans never had. I knew my sisters and I had found our home when we visited the area.

I stopped playing with my eggs and met Aric's gaze when he said nothing more. "What did you need peace from?"

"Here. This situation between us."

Sadness filled my lungs like water and drowned my hopes. I thought he was saying good-bye. So his next words surprised me. "Have you been seeing that moron, Celia?"

"Huh?"

Aric leaned back in his seat. "The vampire. Have you spent time with . . ." Aric swallowed hard, barely able to spit the name out. *"Misha."*

I stared at my eggs as if they would somehow give me a clue how to answer. How could I tell Aric that the first time Misha called, I'd scrambled to my phone, expecting it to be him? And when it wasn't, how it made me long for Aric's call more?

Unlike Aric, Misha had called me, every day, sometimes more than once. At first our conversations revolved around our near-death experience on the night of the fire, when we'd taken on a master vampire, his army of ravenous, bloodsucking monsters, and, oh yeah, his psycho gal pal witch. I'd saved Misha's life. And I'd inadvertently returned his soul. And although my sisters and I first became involved with him to help clear him of a crime, somewhere along the way he'd become a friend— a self-absorbed, often arrogant, flirtatious, O-positive-worshipping friend, but a friend nonetheless. And one I felt protective of just then. Misha wasn't perfect, except he also wasn't as awful as the wolves liked to believe.

I looked up from my eggs. "I don't want to discuss Misha with you."

The truth of my words hit Aric hard. He raised his chin and tightened his jaw. The waitress bustled over and dropped off the check. I reached to pay my share. Aric lifted it away. "At least allow me this."

Aric reached for my hand upon catching my crinkled brow. "I'm sorry. I just thought . . ." He sighed. "A few dead males have been discovered scattered around the area," he whispered, out of the range of human hearing.

My tigress sat up in attention—unsure why Aric had changed gears and itching to protect me from the latest evil threat. "Are they leftover food from the vampires infected with bloodlust?"

Aric's thumb teased the center of my palm. "That's what I thought at first. However, they weren't in the same condition as the others. And they were also all male—human males. Not a female in sight."

I took a chance and laid my other hand on top of his—a brave move on my part. I was never this forward. My curved fingers stroked between the ridges of his knuckles. "What do the victims being male have to do with anything?"

Aric watched my movements, surprised, I supposed, that I'd returned his affection. "The infected vampires didn't discriminate—male, female, human, *were*—it didn't matter. Something else killed these men."

Great. Another hungry killer. Just what Tahoe needed. I opened my mouth, just to shut it again, remembering Taran's dreams. My sister possessed the unique gift to generate and manipulate fire and lightning as a weapon. She could also alter memories to some extent. And while she couldn't predict the future, she did have the ability to sense different types of magic—*were*, vampire, and witch. Could she have also sensed something darker? "Aric, could this have anything to do with demons?" Aric's hard stare told me something I didn't really want to know. I rubbed his knuckles harder. "This is the part where you accuse me of being ridiculous."

"How much do you know about demons?" he asked instead.

I shook my head, not realizing at first how hard I'd gripped his hands, until he shifted his grasp and caressed my fingers. "Not much. Just that they're wicked bad and don't belong here. Right?"

Aric lifted my hand to his face and brushed them

against the stubble of his beard as if he'd done it a million times. "You're right. They don't belong. The power of good keeps them in hell. The strongest occasionally surface, except they're never strong enough to stay for long."

"How long is too long?" A millisecond seemed too much to hope for, especially judging by Aric's serious disposition and the way he seemed to beat back a growl.

"Somewhere around five minutes."

The image of someone with a stopwatch and a demon patiently waiting to be dragged back to hell didn't follow evil creature protocol. Something had happened with enough witnesses to gauge the passage of time. My voice cracked, though I'd insisted it shouldn't. "How do you know?"

Aric leaned closer, his tone lowered. "As guardians of the earth, *weres* have encountered an array of evil throughout the centuries. About ninety years ago, a demon appeared in Ireland, called forth by a dark witch seeking more power. My great-uncle had been hunting her. She'd violated several laws and needed to be put down. He and his wolf pack of five found her too late. She'd already called him and another forth."

"Did the wolves kill him?"

"No. It's damn near impossible to destroy a demon, Celia. You can hurt it. You can weaken it. Ultimately, you're just buying time until it's ordered back to hell."

More good news. I cleared my throat. "What happened?"

"The pack found the first demon on top of her."

I shuddered. "Killing her?"

Aric shook his head, his jaw setting tight. "No."

My eyes widened, and I shriveled inward. "Oh my God."

"He vanished when the other revealed itself. They fought the evil for about five long, agonizing minutes. By the time he disappeared, only three wolves remained."

Across from us a group of teens laughed. The one in a

UCLA sweatshirt pushed his buddy in play. Obviously they hadn't heard Aric's tale. I only wished I hadn't, either. "And the witch?"

"She killed herself. The wolves then destroyed the spawn thriving in her dead uterus."

"Oh." I said it as if he'd just explained how to change a tire. What I really meant to say was "Oh, *shit!*"

I glanced at my uneaten food. Something told me my appetite wouldn't return any time soon. I worked up my courage. "You think demons are being called forth?"

Aric shrugged. "There are rumors. The good news is very few beings of magic are able to summon such a strong evil. And like I mentioned, their time is limited. But something appears to have shifted in the demon realm. We just don't know what it is yet."

"Could they have killed those men? I mean, if they'd summoned them with some kind of magical, demon, evildoers artifact?"

Aric smiled at my attempt to lighten our conversation. "No. That shit only happens in movies. Like I said, it takes magical power to call magical power. The one doing the summoning has to possess a certain amount of mojo to get through."

Aric's large hands covered mine easily, stimulating the growing heat. It comforted me, and I wanted to just relax and enjoy it, but I needed to voice my fears. "Aric, Taran's been having dreams. Bad ones. They involve what we think are demons, attacking us."

"How many?"

"Excuse me?"

Aric watched me carefully. "How many demons appear in her dreams?"

"I don't know. Lots of them. She describes them like a swarm of locusts."

The tension in Aric's powerful shoulders built. "I'd never heard of so many at a time. And no one has ever been able to bring forth two simultaneously. That's why the one assaulting the witch disappeared when the second arrived." Aric lowered our hands. "The rumors flying around and the mysticism of Tahoe energizing the air could be affecting her dreams. Try not to worry, okay? I'm here now to help keep you safe." He said it. And I think he meant it. Yet he couldn't hide the underlying concern in his voice.

"Okay, but if these demons didn't kill the men, what did?" Aric didn't answer, but the way he regarded me made me suspicious. "You don't think I had anything to do with this, do you?"

"Of course not, it's just that . . ." Aric's hold tightened. "Tracking is one of my stronger traits. My wolf picks up the scent of death easily. I was the one who found the bodies while hunting the infected vampires and dismissed them as more of their victims. I should have suspected something else at play." He let out a long breath. "My Elders feel I've been distracted lately. They believe if it wasn't for my lack of focus, I would've recognized that a different being had killed the humans and possibly saved lives."

My tigress pawed inside me and chuffed with annoyance. "Aric, you're the chancelor of students at the Den. When you're not teaching your young wolves arithmetic and dismemberment, you're the driving force in helping to protect the area from evil. Of course you're distracted! You carry a great deal of responsibility on your shoulders. They need to back the hell off and—"

Aric's grin cut me off and made my heart pound hard enough to muffle the toddler throwing a set of utensils across from us. He leaned over the table and brushed his soft lips against my cheek, reminding me why the fearless tigress had fallen so hard for the big, bad wolf. "My duties keep me busy, yes, but I've always managed . . . until now." His eyes bored into mine, turning my blood into liquid fire. "You're my distraction, Celia. You came into my life and knocked me on my ass. It's hard to concentrate on anything else."

The portly waitress hustled by to fill our water glasses as our emotions locked us together with invisible straps. "Would you folks care for anything else?"

A cup of your best ice cream, down my pants, please.

Aric slowly released me and pulled out a wad of clipped bills. He shoved a few into the small pleather folder. "Are you ready?"

To straddle you? Sure.

I nodded and half stumbled from the booth, my head spinning from Aric's words. The way he spoke in that deep tenor voice and the terms he'd used to express his romantic feelings shoved back my fear and stimulated my desires. Aric noticed my lack of grace. He didn't chuckle or comment like I'd come to expect. The strong angles of his face held nothing but seriousness—smacking me back into reality more than a dip into the freezing-cold lake.

Aric reached for my hand as we walked to the car. I gripped it tight, wanting to hold on to the moment. For someone who professed his feelings for me, he didn't appear happy. If anything he seemed torn.

Aric settled into his seat after opening the door for me. He peeled onto the road, his voice lowered. "After giving it a lot of thought, I worried my Elders were right, and believed maybe some distance between us might help. That's why I haven't called."

The way back to my house gave the passenger-side view of the woods. The thick firs whirled by me in a blur. My throat tightened with angst. I wasn't sure what Aric might say next. "Did it help?"

Aric stayed silent for several breaths. "No. It just made me miss you more."

I would have thrown my arms around him if it hadn't

been for his ominous tone. It reinforced that our connection might be a bad thing. He didn't say anything else until he parked in front of my house and twisted his body to face mine. I unbuckled my seat belt and crossed my legs, resting the side of my head against the seat. To anyone watching, I appeared calm, possibly even bored, my feline side feigning a state of complete relaxation. But Aric's beast scented my fear, sensed my tightening muscles, heard my racing heart. For the first time in years, I was close to having someone special. And yet he still seemed so far away.

Aric's palm curved against my cheek, and his thumb stroked me gently. The light trickling through the sunroof shimmered in those baby browns. I wanted to touch him, but my natural defenses kicked in, and so did my shyness. So I waited and watched, mesmerized by his rugged good looks and the way his thumb rhythmically passed against my skin.

"Celia, I can't ignore my duties as a pureblood," he said softly. "But I also can't dismiss what's happening between us. I'd like us to try to have something, providing you want to as well."

Aric's hand trailed against my brown locks, lightened with the gold tones of my tigress. I inched away, worry for him preventing me from accepting his caress. "What about your Elders?"

"If I can catch who murdered the men, it would prove to them I haven't abandoned the responsibilities to my pack."

"Then let me help you. I could—"

That oh-so-familiar "you can't help because you can't heal" expression played across Aric's features like a violin, completely cutting me off. "Celia, did you miss the part where I explained that these creatures rape women and are so atrocious the world's power banishes them back to hell within five goddamn minutes?"

I tapped my foot impatiently against the car matt. "Did you, Mr. Leader of Wolves, miss the exploding body in my house? Aric, evil not only knocked on my door, it brought leftovers and displayed them across my threshold like a UPS package."

"No shit. Which is more of a reason you should stay away from this mess."

I narrowed my eyes. Yeah. Like that had any effect on him. "I know you think you can protect me by keeping me out of this—"

"Not if you don't let me. And not if you ignore me when I tell you to keep out of trouble."

"You act like I go out in search of danger."

Aric counted off the error of my ways one finger at a time. "Vampire court. Storming a crazed vampire's estate—*twice*." He added two fingers on that one. "Consorting with the undead. Tracking an infected vampire in a stolen vehicle. And don't get me started on getting trapped in a raging inferno."

I crossed my arms defensively. "I don't *consort* with the undead." He tightened his jaw. "Much."

We glared at each other. *He's really sexy when he broods,* my tigress sighed. *Shut up and focus,* I hissed back.

I cleared my throat. More than once. My beast had a point. "Aric, if the wereraccoon is somehow related to this thing consuming humans, it knows where I live. It knows where my family lives. I get that you don't want me fighting alongside you. Except you need to understand that I have to keep my sisters safe. So if you don't want me with you, that's fine. But you can't stop me from protecting my family."

Aric growled, more with frustration than anger, knowing I'd stomped his argument with my mighty, if not stubborn, logic. *Take that, big shot.*

Aric rubbed his forehead and swore under his breath.

"You have to promise to stay with me at all times. You are not to hunt this thing on your own—that includes going off alone with your sisters. I'm not sure what we're up against, or what it can do. If my Warriors or I are not with you, you are not to engage it. And if anything else wanders onto your property, I should be the first call you make."

I probably shouldn't have smiled considering I just willingly volunteered to go after yet another scary monster . . . who also likely slithered in from hell.

Aric shook his head. "Don't look at me that way, Celia. It would destroy me if you were hurt."

"How could a little kitty like me get hurt with a pack of supermacho wolves on my side?"

Aric didn't find my attempt at humor funny. "Shit. What did I just get you into?"

"You didn't 'get me into' anything. I think the were-raccoon managed that on his own." I sighed. "Look, Aric, I also hate being the source of your problems. If helping you kill Tahoe's latest superbeastie alleviates your situation with your Elders, let me."

"Don't for a moment think you're the cause of my problems." Aric leaned forward, sweeping his lips across my crown line. "What goes on between you and me is none of their damn business. But if eliminating this threat will shut them up, it's more motivation for me to hunt and kill it."

Aric wanted to mean what he said, except distress swept around his aura like a noose. Had I been of his kind, would his Elders have been as upset? Probably not.

"The purebloods are plentiful," Aric continued as if trying to convince us both. "My Elders need to stop demanding that I associate with *were*-only females."

Demand? Aric had practically growled his last statement. As one of the strongest *weres* in history, he didn't like being told what to do. Even by those considered above him. I didn't know much about wolves, or *weres* in general, and feared what the consequences his decision to pursue me might bring. So it only seemed right for me to help him hunt. Maybe he was right. In killing this *monster*, perhaps he'd prove he hadn't lost his focus or abandoned his duties.

Stress further tightened Aric's muscles. My tigress convinced me to comfort him through touch. I rubbed my face against his. "What will happen if they continue to insist that you do?"

Aric groaned, low and deep. His reaction had nothing to do with his Elders and everything to do with our contact. "Let me worry about it." He cupped my face in his hands. "You and me, we can take things slow and see where it leads us."

Aric tilted his head toward mine. This time I didn't deny him. I think he only meant to give me a small peck. But when my lips parted, and the tip of my tongue met his, his beast growled with need. And so did mine.

So much for taking things slow.

Aric's taste sent my tigress into a frenzy, craving more of him in my mouth. The clicking sound of the seat belt release sounded miles away. Aric struggled to free himself from its hold, all the while keeping his mouth hard against mine.

The steering wheel dug into his hip as he lurched his body across the center console, pressing his T-build firmly against me. If it were up to my wild side, I would have ripped his clothes from his body in pieces. But my inexperienced half took over, unsure what to do, and dumbstruck by Aric's immediate effect on my delicate areas.

Holy . . .

Body parts I barely acknowledged pounded; the tips of my breasts tightened. I slumped back against the side window, moaning, my lips pleading for Aric to explore.

My hands swept over his back. His hard muscles tensed beneath my fingertips, and his arms beckoned me closer. I wanted Aric. Then. Now. Fast. Especially when his mouth moved to my neck and found a spot behind my—

"*Celia Wird!* You unhand that boy this instant!"

And that's when the devil in support hose appeared. *Sweet God in heaven . . . no!*

Aric's head snapped up. His face heated. "What the hell?"

I wrenched my neck to face my neighbor, Mrs. Mancuso. Her penciled-in brows angled in a permanent state of pissed-offness, her curlers tightened hard enough to make her scalp bleed, and her neck skin flapped in the wind. "This is a family neighborhood!"

And because having an eighty-plus woman catching me in a major tongue-hockey moment wasn't humiliating enough, my lovely sister Taran came to the rescue. She didn't have supernatural hearing, but she could spot a Mancuso attack a mile away. Taran threw open the front door and stormed down the steps. "Goddamn it, woman, aren't you dead yet? Get back in the house and mind your own freaking business!"

"Whore." Mrs. Mancuso dragged out the word as if she were teaching it to a bunch of preschoolers, accentuating it with two stiff ones. "Trollops, sluts, tramps!" she screamed, waving her middle fingers like flags.

I scrambled out of the car when Aric lifted his weight. Taran's face was inches from Mancuso's, her blue eyes firing with rage. "I am sick and tired of you calling us whores. It's not like we parade shirtless men around here."

As if on cue, Liam jogged around to the front of the house. Naked.

Mrs. Mancuso's jaw dropped down to her Depends at the sight of Liam's overly developed man parts. Fortunately the sight of Liam's studly physique was too much for the old terror. She backed up abruptly and ran indoors, crossing herself to protect herself against the likes of us.

Liam stopped near Aric, oblivious of my own alarm at seeing him naked. "Hey, Aric."

Aric pinched the bridge of his nose. "Liam. Why did you let Mrs. Mancuso see you naked?"

"I was trying to hide my wolf form," he said like it was obvious. God forbid he'd hide his naked form. He shrugged. "Anyway, I tracked the raccoon's blood and pus back into the woods. Looks like he'd been hiding out just below the ridge. Whoever attacked him caught him off guard. There's blood at his campsite and bullets lodged into the trees leading down to the house." He regarded me closely before handing Aric a wrinkled piece of office paper.

Aric unfolded it carefully. Liam's fang marks pierced the top. He'd obviously searched the woods in his beast form. My breath caught at the image printed in gray scale. It was a picture of me and Aric, standing outside my back deck. Dry blood splattered across our faces.

Aric growled with fury. Liam nodded. "He was watching you, Celia."

CHAPTER 3

"What could that wereraccoon possibly want with you, dude?" Shayna sat in the front passenger seat. It was the closest to the driver's side we'd allow her to get. Hell hath no fury like Shayna behind the wheel.

I adjusted my turtleneck. Originally I'd planned to wear a button-down blouse with my jeans, until Aric left quite the memory of our time together just below my jawline. "I don't know, but he was watching me for a while. That picture was from the day the wolves came over for a barbecue."

Emme clasped her hand over her mouth. "Oh my goodness. That was several weeks ago."

"I know. Aric thinks he may have started watching the house even before I first caught him riffling through our garbage. There's no way to tell for sure, I suppose."

Emme's eyes widened. "I suppose not. Did Aric say whose blood was on the photo?"

I shook my head. "He didn't have to. I could smell the *were*'s blood all over it. It must have splattered when the first bullet hit . . . or when they'd tried to slit his throat."

"He must have had the picture open when he was attacked." Taran shuddered. "Shit. You don't think he was doing something funny while staring at your—"

"Can we please not go there?" I growled. "Taran, it's bad enough he'd come around. I'd prefer not to ponder what he did in his alone time."

"Sorry, Ceel. Look, this whole thing sucks. But at least he's not around to hurt you anymore."

"No. But whoever killed him is still out there. So is whatever murdered those men." I adjusted my position. Blood and death made my inner beast restless to protect. I barely managed to keep her still. "I called Bren and Danny. Danny offered his science and research expertise should we need him. Bren wants to help us track. With his nose, maybe he can help us find something."

"Sounds like an awesome plan." Shayna finished pulling up her hair into a ponytail. Spending the afternoon with Koda hadn't given her much time to get ready for dinner with Misha. A little tidbit she failed to share with Koda. "Hey, Ceel. Does Aric think the murders are related to this weredude?"

"He didn't say. But I can't see how. The men were drained of their blood. The *were* was shot and somehow booby-trapped." What he did tell me was not to leave the house unescorted and not to do anything dangerous.

So I didn't. Sort of.

I left the house with my sisters as backup . . . and so I wouldn't be alone in a master vampire's estate. Misha and I had made plans for dinner earlier in the week. Dinner and the diamond earrings he'd given me previously were the only thank-yous I'd allowed. Yes, I'd saved his life. Yes, I'd inadvertently returned his soul. But I didn't want him feeling like he owed me. And I sure as hell didn't ever want to owe him.

Taran tuned the satellite radio to a classic rock station as we pulled into the mile-long drive leading up to Misha's front gates. We chuckled when "Werewolves of

London" was the first song to play. We stopped laughing when an über-size vampire tackled another in front of our car.

Taran slammed on the brakes. It didn't help. Our velocity was so fast that we ran over them like beached whales. The car rattled and our bodies bounced off the seats. "Son of a *bitch*! Are they dead?"

I jerked my head backward. The bigger of the two Plymouth-size giants grabbed the other by the throat and drove his protruding five-inch nails into the other's heart. I recognized him as Hank, one of Misha's bodyguard's, before blood and ash splattered across the back window and plastered our view. Taran flipped on the rear wipers. Hank waved a nasty hand at me. "Hey, Celia. The master is expecting you."

Emme buried her face in her hands. "Do you think we've come at a bad time?"

"They're fighting for dominance," I muttered. It wasn't easy being BFF with the undead.

Taran scowled. *"What?"*

"In killing the other master, Misha took his power and inherited the evil bastard's minions." I pushed my long hair out of my eyes. "Misha's vamps want to stay top dogs and the others want to move up in position. The fighting has been going on all week. Misha assured me it would stop during dinner."

Taran rolled her eyes and started forward again. Shayna's gaze remained glued to the rear windshield. "Dude! That's, like, totally barbaric."

I'd come to accept that the rules among preternaturals had existed for centuries and for their kind's own well-being. As outsiders, my family and I couldn't say or do anything to change that. Still, that didn't mean I liked or encouraged their behavior. "I know. But it's the way of the vampires. They could just concede and accept their new ranks, except vampires are all about prestige and status. Those higher up remain closer to Misha. No way are any of them going to back down."

The wrought-iron gates opened before Taran could hit the intercom system. The cameras hidden within the gargoyle heads lining the stone wall must have alerted Misha's keep of our arrival. Since he'd named himself as our protector, we'd been elevated to our own status within the vampire world. In other words, mess with us, mess with Misha. And no sane vampire messed with Misha. As a rare vampire with a soul, he essentially juggled life and death, granting him unrivaled power.

Taran crossed over the stone bridge and circled the enormous fountain to park in front of the three-story mansion. When we first caught a gander at Chateau Misha, Shayna tried to convince us we'd inadvertently wandered onto a posh ski resort and spa. Misha's home could only be described as a colossal mountain Craftsman surrounded by well-manicured botanical masterpieces. The essence of calm and tranquility surrounded the thirty-thousand-square-foot house overlooking Lake Tahoe.

Usually.

A cluster of vampires spread out in an arch near the man-made river filled with carp the size of alley cats. Two vampires in Catholic schoolgirl uniforms circled each other, their clothes ripped to shreds, their pigtails askew, their fangs out. A few yards away, beneath a white fir tree, two other vampires attacked each other like rabid rats while the fist-pumping crowd chanted, "Fight! Fight! Fight! Fight! Fight!"

In the middle of the chaos stood our werewolf buddy, Bren, taking bets and playing referee. "Hey, Mary Catherine! I told you, no axes allowed! Put the axe down. Down, Mary Catherine. *Down!*" He shook his head like a frustrated camp counselor. "Fuckin' vampires."

I leapt out of our SUV. "What the *hell* are you doing here?"

"Hey, babes." Bren shrugged. "Heard about the smack-down. Thought I'd make a few bucks."

Taran quirked an eyebrow. "And they let you—a wolf—inside Misha's compound?"

"Only after I told them I was with the little missus." Bren winked my way. He whistled through his fingers, ignoring my growls not to call me that. "Agnes Concepción. Let go of his nuts! Fangs and claws, peeps. Fangs and claws."

Emme clutched my arm. After the dead body strewn across our doorstep, the last thing she needed was more supernatural drama. As a hospice nurse, she dealt with end-of-life issues and death, and managed it beautifully. Blood, guts, and flying body parts . . . not so much. I led her toward the house before some poor bastard vampire's ear could smack her in the face. "Come on, Emme, let's find Misha."

"Put me down for fifty on the freak with the axe," Taran whispered to Bren before hurrying to catch us.

We walked across the stone-paved driveway. Edith Anne and Maria approached, swinging their hips hard enough to fan their tiny plaid skirts. More naughty Catholic schoolgirls. Awesome.

Edith Anne grimaced when she saw us. "The master is expecting you. This way." She tossed her hair back and led with Maria at her side. She pointed to her mud-splattered platforms. "They made me march around the house in my new boots," she complained to Maria.

Maria shot me the official hairy eyeball. "Beetches," she muttered in her thick Brazilian accent.

The good Catholics always knew how to lay on the charm. Unfortunately they never felt the need to lay it on us.

"Screw off," Taran shot back.

Before I became acquainted with vampires, my image of a vampire's crib was stereotypical—an old, dank, dimly lit castle—paler than snow creatures lurking behind every turn waiting to eat me. Then I met the so-called creatures of the night. Tanning and admiring themselves seemed to be the Catholic schoolgirls' favorite pastime. As far as Misha's pad went, "dank" remained furthest from the truth.

The warm glow from the wood and iron chandelier greeted us in the mammoth foyer, dimly lighting the blue-slate floors and timber cathedral-style ceilings. Soft browns, golds, and muted burgundies accented the rich wood and stone walls. Misha's decorator accomplished making his estate, a home—a rare feat considering the immense size. It reminded me of Misha: Although great in magnitude, it had a heart.

Taran's high-heeled sandals clicked along the blue-slate floor, and while Emme wore ballet flats, her soft footsteps echoed louder than mine. Even with me in two-inch mules, my predator side barely made a sound.

We crossed the expanse of the long hall, roughly the size of Rhode Island, and into the solarium. Two of Misha's very polite and very hypnotized servants opened the floor-to-ceiling glass doors leading outside. I stepped through first and onto the terrace. The breeze had picked up along the lake, but the six outdoor fireplaces built into the stacked-stone railing warmed the area at least ten more degrees. My thin cotton blouse would have worked perfectly, had I not had werewolf nibbles to hide.

My face flushed slightly at the thought and hoped the heat from the flames would hide my embarrassment. Emme had offered to heal my marks, but I needed proof of my time with Aric. It made our moment real and not simply one of the steamy dreams I'd had.

Misha stood upon seeing us and gave me a wink, strands of his long blond mane falling against the strong angles of his face and clean-shaven jaw. Vampires believed themselves gods who walked among mortals. If that were true, Misha was Ares—to be feared—all the while carrying the masculine beauty of Adonis. Tonight he dressed in all black. A black suit outlined the muscles of his tall, strapping form, an opened black silk shirt buttoned below his collarbone, and black shoes that cost a month's mortgage. I smiled. It was good to see his body completely regenerated after the torture he'd suffered at the hands of his enemies.

He greeted Emme and Taran with kisses to their cheeks. Emme blushed, of course. Taran kissed back. I wondered how our boys would take that. The wolves' dislike of vampires bordered on hate—Aric and Misha especially loathed each other. And while I remained sure each side had its reasons, I couldn't condemn an entire race based on the actions of a few rotten apples.

"I told you to wear something sexy," Edith Anne hissed under her breath. "You look like a dork."

No matter how annoying the apples were.

Misha's gray eyes flickered despite his back facing the flames. "Edith, is this any way to treat our most honored guests?"

Misha's light Russian accent held no hint of anger. Yet his vampire mojo surged enough to lighten Taran's eye color from blue to crystal. Edith and Maria cowered back, bowing as they retreated into the house. Edith's voice shook. "My deepest apology, Master."

My tigress itched to protrude my claws, alert in the presence of a dangerous predator. I calmed her by reminding her how Misha had guarded Emme, and how his family had shielded us from harm under his command. I wasn't naive. And I sure as hell wasn't stupid. With an estate full of vampires at his disposal and the amount of power coursing through his veins, Misha could kill us. But he wouldn't. I'd caught glimpses of his pain, witnessed his heartbreak—a side I'm sure he'd preferred hidden. Yet it was that same side that won me over and allowed me to trust him not to harm us.

Shayna grinned when Misha kissed her and casually returned her small box of toothpicks into the pocket of her slacks. She'd sensed Misha assert himself and whipped out her favorite weapons. My lack of aggression eased her tension. Perhaps Koda's animosity hadn't turned her against the vampires. Yet.

Shayna punched him in the arm. "How's it going, dude?"

"Rather well, my dear." He reached into the inside of his suit as the breeze swept his long hair behind his shoulders. "I saw these and I thought of you." Misha retrieved two long Asian hairpins and held them out for my perky sister to see.

The gleam to Shayna's smile returned. *"Cool."* She lifted them from his palm and stimulated her ability to thicken and manipulate metal. A trickle of light sparked from her belly-button ring as she transferred the element into the delicate pieces of hair jewelry, turning them into small, deadly daggers. She stepped back from Misha and tossed them a few times in the air, getting a feel for their weight. "A girl can't have enough weapons these days, you know?"

Misha's smile faded as Shayna returned the hair jewelry to their original shape and tucked them into the base of her ponytail. "No, it is best to be safe." He regarded me then. "Which is why I am not pleased to hear you are to assist the . . . *weres* in their latest quest."

It probably took Misha every effort not to say "mongrels" or "mutts" or some other inappropriate word to describe our wolves. I crossed my arms. "And how did you hear about that?"

Misha flashed me his famously wicked smile. "I have my ways, kitten. Shall we?"

I shook my head. Misha's wealth went a long way. It

wouldn't have surprised me if his family greased the palms of *weres* in exchange for what could be interpreted as harmless information.

Misha stepped aside, revealing the elegant table setting. White linen covered the large round table while black silk napkins folded into ravens lay over the delicate china etched in silver. The staff appeared to pull out chairs for my sisters. Misha held out my chair himself. He leaned forward and paused, his lips close to my ear. "I see that mindless beast has finally come to his wits and shown you some affection."

My cheeks heated. "Misha, I'm not going to discuss Aric with you." Gee, this conversation sounded familiar. "And don't call him names."

Taran laughed. "You'd better get your groove on, Misha. Otherwise that wolf is going to steal my sister from under your thumb."

"Nonsense." Misha's wickedness returned with a vengeance. "Celia may enjoy what I can do with my thumb."

Just when I thought my face couldn't get any hotter. "Stop it. Both of you."

Taran danced her brows at me. "Aw, come on, Ceel. After years of dateless nights, you deserve a little attention."

I would have slapped Taran upside the head if I didn't think my blow would kill her. "There's nothing between Misha and me."

"That is only because you won't allow it." Misha leaned back in his seat, those gray predator eyes of his sharpening as they zeroed in on my neck. "However, we do have some time before the main course. Ladies, would you mind starting without us?"

My jaw tightened. "Yes, they would. And cut it out."

Misha laughed. He flicked his napkin in the air. His and ours took off like the blackbirds they'd been shaped to resemble. Emme jumped as they circled above us and landed in our laps, unraveling and resuming their cloth forms.

"Damn," Taran muttered. "I wish I could pull that shit off." She didn't just mean the flock-of-birds act. Taran often griped about the strength of her power being mostly limited to fire, lightning, and light. She possessed a rare gift—hell, we all did—but she wanted to do more. Witches couldn't command fire to the extent or ease that she could, but their magic opened up possibilities Taran only dreamed of possessing. While my sister wasn't power hungry—far from it—it almost seemed she craved something more spectacular.

Taran lifted the napkin again and placed it back on her lap after scrutinizing it closely. I poked at mine, half expecting it to peck. "You're getting better at harnessing Tahoe's power, Misha."

"I find it easier now that my soul has returned." He cocked his head. "Is there something you wish to discuss with me, my love?"

I frowned. "So Tahoe's magic allows you to read minds now?"

Misha pulled my wrist toward him and touched the underside of my forearm. "No. But there are advantages to passing you my *call*."

Misha had transferred the mystical equivalent of his phone number onto my arm. Should the superscary bad guys come knocking down my door, all I had to do was think his name and he would come to my aid. Apparently my arm also possessed reverse speed dial—it was how I'd found him when he'd been close to death.

I pulled my arm back. Misha hadn't hurt me, but I didn't want to do anything that might lead him on. And allowing his touch might tempt him in ways I only desired for Aric. "I didn't *call* you today. How did you know something happened?"

The servers brought the first course, some sort of fondue thingy set on fire. Taran lifted the flames with her hands and blew them out with a kiss. Fire flat-out scared me, especially after almost being roasted alive. Taran beheld it like an old friend. The rest of us leaned back so the staff could extinguish our plates with silver covers. My sisters dug right in, dipping the chunks of bread into the thick, creamy liquid.

Misha didn't eat. "I thought I sensed your distress and therefore I sent Edith to investigate. I was not pleased when she returned and told me what you discovered. You should have *called* me."

Maybe I should have dialed 1-800-Misha, except given the pus, blood, and ooze, he was the last fellow with fangs on my mind. "I was distracted, Misha. Especially after the body exploded."

Misha didn't frown much. Scowled, yes. Glared, oh yeah. Smiled wickedly enough to dissolve clothing, yup, that, too. He did frown then, though, his brows knitting ever so slightly. "The werebeast exploded?"

"They have cleaner for that," Edith Anne called out. She and Maria moved around in the solarium like a couple of sinister goldfish in a bowl. I guessed waiting for us to leave so they could apologize to Misha in their own naughty way.

I ignored them. "There wasn't anything left of the *were* to clean, Misha, only a ring of ash where his body had fallen. The body fluids vanished, too. Do you know what could do that?"

Misha's brows returned to their original shape instead of angling farther. Either he didn't know or he was keeping something from me. "No. It is not a magic I am familiar with. Is that all you wished to discuss?"

His tone tightened. My sisters didn't seem to notice. But I did. *Oh, so you are hiding something. Time to poke around.* I draped my arm against the table. "Dead bodies of men have been discovered around Tahoe, drained of blood, but not appearing to be the victims of the infected vampires. What else would quench their thirst through blood? And what could possibly destroy a *were* like that?"

Misha didn't blink. "Dark witches consume small quantities from human sacrifices and some may cast powerful enough to disintegrate a *were*."

His indifference told me he preferred I drop the subject. So of course, I didn't. "This isn't the work of a witch, Misha. But I guess you already knew that." I smiled without humor. "Are you going to tell me what you do know?"

"You are to *call* me if another incident occurs."

"If another body shows up, sure. But—"

"I will send a security team to patrol your home."

"That's not necessary, and that's not what I'm asking—"

"Then perhaps a few bodyguards will be more to your liking."

"Misha, cut it out. I'm not having vampires hanging out at our house, especially with Emme and Shayna's wolves always present. Look, I don't want to fight with you. Just tell me what you know and maybe I'll stop harassing you."

Emme and Shayna eyed us with growing concern. They never understood my friendship with Misha, and I scented the sour aroma of their fear as I continued to force the issue. Master vampires, especially of Misha's caliber, weren't creatures to toy with or order.

Misha shoved his plate aside. A servant appeared and quickly vanished with the untouched food. He bent his elbows against the armrests of the heavy carved chair, regarding me closely. "Celia, there are dark forces in our world that even as a vampire I refuse to engage. I hear things in my sleep. I believe the lake whispers to me secrets and carries the final breaths of those murdered in the wind."

In a movie, the creepy music would start right about . . . now. The breeze silenced around us as Misha spoke, like he somehow commanded the air to do his bidding. Based on the way his spine straightened, the unusual silence surprised him, too.

Taran dug into the fondue like it would add more perk to her bosom, failing to meet my gaze. She didn't need to rehash her nightmares, nor did she need more deets to fuel them.

Emme scooted her seat closer to me. "Wha-what sort of secrets?"

I was kind of glad Emme asked. I considered myself pretty damn fierce. But having fought off psycho monsters trying to eat me over the last several weeks, I debated whether I wanted to know more about the darker side of the mystical world, especially following my demon conversation with Aric. And without his presence by my side, the creatures that bumped in the night bumped harder. My tigress, conversely, sat up, whipped out her iPad, and began taking copious notes. She wanted to hunt. And she wanted to know what prey we hunted.

Misha lowered his voice. "I only tell you this to warn you against joining the *weres*. Something seeks to align those unworthy and forgotten. If it succeeds, it may become unstoppable."

"It?" Taran asked. "Not he. Not she. But *It*?"

Misha nodded.

Taran gave up on her fondue and tossed her napkin on the table. "Oh. This shit can't be good."

I clenched my fists, my inner beast kick-starting my courage. "Isn't that more of a reason to help the *weres*?"

Misha's cold gray eyes drove into me like ice picks. "Not if it comes at the expense of your life." He faced Shayna then. "Or that of your family's. Something is taking shape, Celia," he said, meeting me head-on once more. "When it reaches its full supremacy, it will seek the strongest to destroy. To allow it a chance to view the full gamut of your power is to taunt death itself."

Shayna's slacked jaw and Taran's string of swearwords pretty much summed up how I felt. Emme's grip to my arm tightened, although I barely felt it.

Misha watched me, expecting I imagined a sign that I'd heed his warning and back down. And yet as much as his warning frightened me, running away screaming meant abandoning the *weres* to face whatever was coming alone. I wouldn't abandon the wolves. I wouldn't abandon Aric. I'd promised to help him. And I'd promised to help *us*. My face hardened. I shoved the trembling fear deep within me where it couldn't paralyze me, and once more urged forth my strength and will to survive. I said nothing to Misha. But I did respond in a way he didn't like. I transformed my human eyes to that of my tigress, illustrating that I'd choose fight instead of flight.

Misha let out a huff. "Enough of this, my darling. We've come to feast, not quarrel." He motioned the servants over with a gesture of his hand so subtle I almost missed it. My plate disappeared and was replaced with greens topped with diced pears and slices of roasted lamb. Because nothing said "something wicked this way comes" like a yummy salad.

CHAPTER 4

"Where are we going exactly?"

Aric kept his hand over my knee while he maneuvered the Escalade through a small town just above Truckee. "An old werepossum lives in the area. He called the Den last night swearing he caught the scent of sulfur and anise in the air. He wanted to investigate, but his mate's reaching her hundredth birthday in two weeks and he doesn't want to leave her side."

I squeezed my hand over Aric's. "Oh no. Her time's coming to an end."

Aric nodded, a hint of grief finding its way into his voice. "It sounds like her birthday falls the day after the full moon. It will give them another few weeks together, but yes, she'll pass when the full moon arrives next month. As his mate, he'll join her by the rise of the following moon." He glanced at me. "It's a shame. He's fifteen years younger and they'd only just found each other a few years ago. But when I spoke to him, he sounded ready to follow her into heaven."

"Have you known them long?"

"I actually tracked them with my dad on their honeymoon." He laughed when he caught my slacked jaw.

"They disappeared while camping in Mount Whitney. Her family called us when they couldn't find her. She was strong; she could handle the rough terrain. Being human, her mate didn't fare well. He fell while hiking and crushed his skull. She saved his life by *turning* him."

I cringed. *Weres* pierced human hearts in order to transfer their essence and *turn* a human *were*. It was the only time a *were* could protrude his or her fangs without *changing* completely. The problem was the success rate was rare and ultimately killed both parties. "I'm surprised they made it, given their ages."

"Not as surprised as I was when we found them safe, sound, and very much enjoying their honeymoon." Aric shuddered. "There's some shit a twelve-year-old should never see."

I laughed out loud. "But they're mates, they probably couldn't help themselves." All *weres* had mates, somewhere in the world. The lucky ones found them and spent the remainder of their lives loving each other. I only wished to have something so dear. "It's beautiful in a way to die together, you know? Tremendously sad, but joyous at the same time. They'll always be together."

Aric's stopped smiling and stared straight ahead. "Yeah. They will."

The sudden stiffness in his voice confused me. I angled my head to see if I could interpret his expression. It wasn't cold per se, but definitely masked. I didn't know Aric well enough to judge him. Maybe he didn't like to discuss one mate losing the other. His parents were mated. Yet his mother's love for Aric had kept her from joining his dad when he died. A rare feat from what I understood. Then again Aric had been so young, and a mother's loved seemed to hold no limits.

Aric kept his hand on my knee but didn't say anything for a while. After a few minutes of silence, I spoke for me and my beast. "The anise, being an herb, is associated with witch magic, correct?" Aric nodded. "What's associated with sulfur?"

"Anything evil a dark witch helps create."

Fantastic.

Aric didn't miss my eyes widening, despite my efforts to squelch my surprise. "Celia, you don't have to be here. I can take you back home." He groaned. "In fact, I'd rather."

I placed my hand on his shoulder when he attempted to turn the SUV around. "Home's not safe anymore, Aric. If it was, I wouldn't have carcasses falling through my front door. I meant what I said about protecting my family. And about helping you." I stroked him a little. "Besides, don't you think I'm safer being with my wolf than home alone waiting for some slobbering monster to show up?"

Aric's sideways glance melted my toes. "You think of me as your wolf?" A blush crept its way into my cheeks, answering for me. He caressed my knee, his fingers skimming just a little bit upward. "Good," he whispered. "That's how it should be. I'll protect you, Celia. I swear I will."

I'd shared brief moments of physical intimacy with Aric, but I never felt as close to him as I did now. I curled my arm around his and left it there until he pulled into a spot in front of a small antique store. He reached for a pack filled with extra sweats strewn across the backseat. "Koda, Liam, Shayna, and Emme are headed to the old *were*'s house, just in case they pick up a scent from a different direction. They'll *call* if they find anything."

I wouldn't have typically allowed my youngest sisters to track an unknown danger without me, but considering that Liam could eat glass like popcorn and Koda was roughly the size of a tank, I figured they were in safe hands. I stepped out into the crisp air and waited near the door to the shop. Chips cut into the cream-colored paint, adding to the charm of the quaint little place. Ordinarily I would have liked to look inside. But evil didn't allow time for browsing.

Taran and Gemini parked a few lanes down. Aric motioned to them as they walked toward us, trying in vain to hide his smirk. We'd donned long-sleeved tees and old jeans to make for an easy *change*. Gemini wore his classic pair of slacks and a sweater. My sister? You'd think she was set to catwalk for Prada's winter line instead of hunting supervillains. Her black knee-high leather boots clicked along the cracked sidewalk, and her long gray pencil skirt hugged her curves. I'd have teased her for wearing boots to march into danger, but Taran could probably climb trees in four-inch heels. I'd end up with a nosebleed after falling on my face.

Gemini's eyes locked on to her strut, but he kept his distance. Aric at least held tight to my hand. As sexy as Taran dressed, she remained one step away from another head pat judging by how awkward Aric's Beta seemed around her.

"Shit, it's cold." Taran adjusted the silk scarf around her neck before digging her hands deep into her cropped leather jacket. "Is this damn place far from here, Aric?"

Taran's enthusiasm always made her endearing.

Aric shrugged. "I don't think so. We just need to follow the path. It will lead us in the direction of where the old possum said he'd scented the magic."

"If we need to go off the path, I'll carry you," Gemini told Taran quietly.

Taran's vixen smile reddened Gem's face. A sweet move if he hadn't taken a step away from her. Then another. Taran's shoulders dropped and she let out an exasperated sigh. Most males would have humped her in public just for breathing in their direction. She puckered an eyebrow my way. Other than a sympathetic glance, I had no clue how to respond. Gemini's aroma didn't suggest fear or intimidation of Taran. It suggested something my tigress nose couldn't quite figure out.

"Are we ready?" I asked.

Aric led us through the small brick-laid alley between the antique shop and its neighboring café. A young couple sat in metal patio chairs sipping hot chocolate and discussing their upcoming rafting excursion along the Truckee River.

"Where you headed?" the guy asked as we passed. His casual tone suggested he hadn't taken a good look at the two wolves and the tigress. Our predators' side sparked a sense of danger and fear, although we didn't consciously project either. Most humans kept their distance. Far distance.

"Just for a walk," Aric answered him. He pulled me closer. "You girls want anything from the café?"

The chilly and breezy fifty-degree afternoon felt more like a hot beach day in August around Aric. The closer he drew me in, the more the warmth accelerated between us. If anything, I needed a cold drink to squelch back the intensity. "No, thank you. I'm fine, wolf."

"How about wine with dinner following our walk?" Taran suggested.

Aric's hand skimmed down my back. "Even better," he murmured.

We reached the end of the alleyway and stepped onto the worn, frozen path. The snow had melted, but it seemed the grass hadn't quite recovered from the winter's bashing. The rain and warming sunshine of April would soon resuscitate it. Come summer, the shop owners would struggle to maintain the large section of lawn. For now it lay asleep. Parts of it yellow, other parts balding. Only a few shoots of green daring to make an appearance.

The path widened as we traveled up a small incline leading into the forest. "Would you like to have dinner with me?" Taran asked Gemini. She tried to sound casual, but I recognized the underlying hope. He hadn't, after all, responded to her suggestion.

Gemini gave a stiff nod but didn't speak. And his silence wasn't due to his shyness. His entire demeanor changed as the thick-pined forest swallowed us whole. His dark watchful eyes took everything in. Except he wasn't the only predator reacting to unknown territory. Aric's touch turned from affectionate to protective once the trees shadowed the path and blocked out the faint afternoon sun. My tigress stepped forward, sharpening our sense of smell, sight, and hearing. Even Taran knew better than to speak. Chitchat didn't allow the full use of our senses.

My ears focused on the sounds of the forest, ignoring the way Taran's boots passed along the hard ground. Ravens cawed in the distance and a few chipmunks and rabbits scampered along the crisp pine needles. As we drew farther in, the sounds of the forest reduced to the brush of branches in the wind. Nothing moved. Nothing breathed. Just us.

The world of the living vanished in one gradual space of time. "Do you feel that?" I whispered to Aric.

Aric nodded. "Yeah. Stay close to me."

Funny. That was usually my line to my sisters when evil was afoot.

The path curved to follow along the Truckee River. The melting snow from the mountains had caused the river to rise to the edge. Chunks of ice slid over the roaring rapids. I shuddered, dreading an accidental soak. Swimming remained a skill I'd never mastered. And by the looks of the raging stream, it wasn't an optimal place to learn. *Note to self. Avoid having some scary evil thing take you for a dip.*

The firs along the river dwindled. Benches fashioned from tree trunks rested between the more open spots. A beautiful place to enjoy, I supposed, minus the intensifying creepiness digging a hole into my chest.

The growing heaviness forced Gemini to escort Taran next to me so he and Aric could flank our sides. But then something stirred in the wind, like the heavy sweep of an invisible sail. Pained howls blasted my ears, and the gallop of massive paws shook the ground beneath our feet, sending pebbles to roll like marbles along the trail. Taran instinctively reached for me. The wolves didn't possess her ingrained response. Then again, they never had my unique ability to rely on. I grasped their wrists and *shifted* the four of us far beneath the ground. My rare gift broke down our bodies into tiny molecules, minute enough to pass across the packed earth. We surfaced in the thickness of the woods just as a herd of black bears raced past us along the path.

We probably could have sprinted out of the way, but I would have risked contacting one of the bears. Animals and my "weirdness" didn't play nice. With my protective shields down, I'd fall to the ground in a massive seizure and emerge as Celia the Bear. Considering that I'd have no way to *change* back to Celia the sort-of-human or Celia the formidable tigress, *shifting* us from harm seemed like the ideal way to go.

Aric's and Gemini's mouths parted as they examined their forms. I'd never *shifted* them before and they seemed surprised all their important parts remained intact. "Sorry. I didn't have time to warn you." My face heated, but my unease kept me from experiencing the full range of my humiliation.

"It's all right," Aric said. We stepped back onto the path cautiously, unsure what lay ahead. Aric didn't finish watching the bears disappear around the bend. Instead his preternatural side searched where I searched, in the direction they'd run from. "Gem," he said, his voice bordering close to a growl.

Gemini slipped his sweater over his head, revealing the muscular T-build common of all wolves. Taran's jaw fell open and I think she might have drooled. "Will you hold this?" he asked.

She nodded. This time it was her turn to fall speechless. Gemini cracked his neck from side to side. A large black wolf punched his head through Gemini's back, sniffing the air. Like solidifying ink, he slid his powerful form onto the hard soil and sped off in a blur of black. The human half of Gemini that remained blinked his dark eyes. "Come. I'll let you know if I find anything."

Gemini's ability to split into two remained, hands down, the coolest supernatural feat I'd ever seen. Taran squeaked when he whisked her into his arms and raced after Aric and me.

My tigress made us fast, faster than wolves. Common sense, and the realization that "danger lurked, Will Robinson," kept me from bolting ahead. Aric still felt I moved too quick despite being a breath behind me. "Don't get ahead of me, Celia."

"I found it," Gemini's low voice said behind us. "This way."

The path veered in two separate directions. One led deeper into the woods. Gemini kept us on the one paralleling the river.

The sour stench of death stung my nose just as Gemini's other half appeared before us, baring his teeth. We followed behind him. Our pace slowing as we ambled down a small, steep hill where an abandoned mill hugged the edge of the river. The large broken wheel sat in the water, moving just enough to squeal. The rest of the large structure dented inward where the moss-covered roof had partially collapsed. A death trap in the making, and one long forgotten. Someone should have demolished it decades ago, but the small town didn't strike me as possessing funds to see its destruction through.

The closer we neared the mill, the more the foul odor increased, its acidic scent sharp enough to make my eyes water. "Son of a bitch," Taran muttered. Her blue eyes blanched to clear. Something skulked inside. And it didn't want us there.

Aric whispered into his phone. "We found something. Track us."

"On our way," Koda said on the other end.

Gem eased Taran onto the ground as we crept onto the rickety porch steps. A few good tigress strikes and the moldy and graffiti-lined brown building would collapse inward. Too bad we had to investigate before sending it, and the malevolence lurking inside, to hell's trash heap.

A padlock the size of my palm lay discarded on the mud-splattered floor, its hook twisted as if broken off. Slowly, Aric opened the creaky door.

Foot marks cut into the thick layer of dust. Drops of dried blood splattered like raindrops alongside each step. My growl rumbled in sync with the wolves. My tigress didn't like it here. But she hated what waited even more.

Pockets of light trickled through the holes in the wall, illuminating sections here and there in the otherwise pitch-black room. The increasing aroma of death forced my claws and fangs to shoot out. I barely kept my tigress from emerging.

A set of stairs led up to the second floor. A small office with a door opening to another room sat to our far left. The vast room on our right housed bent and broken pieces of metal office furniture. This must have been the area where the administrative staff worked back when the mill had still struggled to stay open.

We abandoned the small sectioned-off area without so much as a sniff. After all, the revolting fragrance of sulfur permeated stronger to our right. A few folding chairs leaned against the dirty 1960s wood-paneled walls, and a tattered armchair lay tucked in the corner. The calendar push-pinned into one of the panels remained opened to February of many years past.

We followed Aric through the large room, trailing the footsteps, and of course, the blood. I bit back a gag, the smell of decay threatening to bring up my lunch. Taran swore beneath her breath. She didn't have to possess an inner beast to sense the death. Death slapped at our faces and demanded respect.

The roar of the river echoed from the back. Likely a section of wall had caved in based on how loud the sound of rushing water carried through the mill. We passed through a small room where the branches of firs poked through the busted sections of moss-eaten walls. Despite the growing Grim Reaper aroma, I thought we'd have to cover more of the building until we found our quarry.

I thought wrong.

The mill opened to one enormous area strewn with burlap sacks, broken rakes, and, oh yeah, a stack of corpses. Most girls got flowers, or maybe chocolates on their dates. I got dead bodies. Lots of them. Lucky me.

Taran stumbled away, choking back her sickness and burying her face into Gem's chest. Aric gripped my arm, offering me comfort. He didn't need it. He witnessed death as often as I witnessed life as a labor nurse. And yet as much as I wanted to mirror Taran's actions, my tigress kept us in place and took in the horror.

Four males lay slumped like a deck of cards toward our right, their bodies rigid, but no obvious signs suggesting cause of death. The lack of decomposing flesh and the few flies circling their forms suggested they'd met their demise fairly recently.

And yet as gruesome as I found them, they didn't compare to the naked woman left abandoned in the center of the room. My hands trembled. Perspiration slid like ice against my chilled skin. Her clouded eyes stared blankly at the ceiling while an expression of sheer terror and agony froze the features of her young face. Her entire abdomen appeared chewed open from the inside out and her half-eaten bowels lay over her hips like wet ropes. Flies swarmed her and took their fill. Small water bugs crawled along her bloody nails. She'd clawed at the splintered floor. God only knew the pain she'd endured before her heart had mercifully stopped beating.

Part of me wanted to run screaming. The other part struggled not to release my tears. Humans generally feared me. Their fear often manifested into dislike and more than often hate. I'd been mistreated to the point of cruelty throughout my life. But as horrid as others had often behaved, no one deserved to die like this. No one.

Aric pulled me into him, his voice harsh yet gentle all at once. "You don't have to look, Celia. And you don't have to be brave. If you prefer, Gemini can escort you and Taran outside."

I shook my head, unable to rip my gaze from the poor soul in the center of the room. "No. I'll stay."

Aric gave me one last hug before releasing me and stepping forward. He said I didn't have to be brave. So I wasn't. I stayed put as he and Gemini's wolf examined the bodies. They inspected the males first, circling their forms and drawing in their scent. I stopped trying to work so hard to smell. It remained my last-ditch effort to keep from hurling. All the dead men had their mouths open. They probably had screamed until their last breath. A cricket crawled out of one whose tongue hung open. That's when I stopped looking as well.

I heard Aric and Gem's wolf tread toward the woman. They paused. "Do you see what I see?" Aric asked, rage clipping his words.

"Yes," Gemini's human side answered. He clutched

Taran close against him with his head lowered. I supposed he could see with his other half. "Two burrowed out in separate directions."

I forced my mouth open. "Two what?"

Gemini raised his dark almond eyes. "Demon children," he answered.

CHAPTER 5

Taran's shakes turned into full-out convulsions. She jerked when I touched her, burying herself deeper against Gemini. I didn't want to scare her further, especially now that it appeared her dreams were transforming into reality. Nor did I care to frighten myself more. As it was, I wouldn't sleep until roughly the following spring. And yet I asked. Despite my reservations and the aching pain claiming my belly, I asked. "What are demon children?"

Gemini stroked Taran's hair, probably debating whether to explain in Taran's presence. Aric's body heat warmed my back, preventing me from jumping when his arm circled my waist. "They're the extremely rare offspring of a demon and a human female."

"How rare?"

"Very. The last one we'd heard of was the one my great-uncle prevented from being born."

"So then, how did this happen?"

"A witch likely called the demon forth and used that poor woman to incubate the spawn."

I took a chance and glanced over at the men. Bad mistake. More hungry bugs had found them. "That doesn't explain the men."

"No. It doesn't. Something else ate them."

I swerved my body to face his. "Ate?"

Aric nodded. "Their bodies are drained of blood."

"But not from infected vampires?"

"No. Definitely not. Vampires lick their fang marks to seal the wound when they're done feeding. It's an ingrained response. Infected vampires aren't in a frame of mind to maintain their practiced habits. All they care about is quenching their thirst."

I wasn't a racist. But I hated infected vampires. All of them. They were big, green, mean, and hard to kill. On the plus side, they didn't *breed*. I straightened to my full height. Yeah. Like that made me tougher. "Do demons drink blood?"

"As they consume flesh and organs, yes, but they would have left bite marks."

The image of the woman's body hit me like a sack of rocks. She'd been gnawed on by her babies. Okay. I was officially done with my questions then.

The wolves and I whirled around, growling at the sound of approaching steps. "It's just us," Koda snarled from the front. Our not-so-happy feelings and the aroma of mutilated-demon-consumed body parts had peeved his wolf. And he'd yet to get a gander at the bodies. Good times.

"Keep the girls there," Gemini ordered. "We'll come to you."

That was Taran's cue to storm out of the house of decomposing corpses. I chased after her, more out of worry than anything. The presence of the four wolves eased my tigress's fury, but not her vigilance. And every sense I possessed told me my sister needed me. "Don't go outside without us," Koda warned.

Taran did anyway, followed by Emme and Shayna. Taran didn't stop until she reached the center of the path. She bent forward, placing her hands on her knees as she took in huge gulps of air. The air continued to carry the heavy scent of death, but paled in comparison to the bowels of the mill. Shayna knelt in front of her, her blue eyes wide as she took in Taran's pallor. "Dude. Are you okay?"

Taran's glare knocked Shayna back on her butt. "No, *dude*. I'm not okay. Fighting evil is horseshit!"

Emme covered her mouth and glanced over her shoulder. She probably worried Taran's oh-so-accurate description would offend the wolves. They'd all returned indoors with the exception of Gemini's furry half. He sat on the porch, his coal eyes bright as he watched over us. Shayna stood and dusted off. I placed my hand on Emme's elbow and nudged her forward. "There are a few dead bodies inside. Try healing Taran's emotions; it was a lot for her to take in." Hell, it was a lot for me to take in. But bless my tigress's heart, she had a way of helping me through pain, and in this case, revulsion. My urge to bolt and shriek lessened with each passing breath. Still, that didn't mean I desired to hang with the wolves within the confines of the mill.

Emme cautiously stepped forward. She continued to watch me as she placed her palms on Taran's back. "A *few* dead bodies?"

I nodded. Shayna veered toward the porch, fast enough to make her long black ponytail whip behind her. "Koda probably won't let me see." Her grimace trained on Taran. "Not that I really want to. How many were there, Ceel?"

"Four men drained of blood and a young woman . . . naked with her uterus torn open."

Emme's pale yellow light receded from her hands as she took in my words. Her power sputtered as she took a breath. She closed her lids tight. "D-d-did you say her uterus was torn open?"

Taran dropped her head lower. "She'd given birth,

Emme. To twin demons. They freaking ate their way out of her belly."

Shayna unzipped her blue jacket and alternated fanning each side out like a cape. Her fingers skimmed over the hilts of the eight daggers fastened around her leather belt. Shayna often counted her weapons to soothe her. Or in this case, to make sure she had enough to kill whatever could burst a stomach open like a rotten tomato. "Um. Uh. Did you kill—you know—the twins?"

I only told them because I wanted them to stay sharp. "No. We didn't find them yet."

Once more she counted her weapons. This time, she unsnapped the holsters keeping them in place for easy access. "So, what do you want to do about dinner?" she asked with an underlying tone of hysteria to her voice.

Taran homed in on her like a hawk on a band of bunnies with broken legs. "I'm seriously trying not to puke all over my new shoes. Do you really think I want to talk food right now, Shayna?"

I stepped in front of Shayna. If Taran had the ability to shoot laser beams from her eyes, poor Shayna's body parts would have littered the forest floor in diced chunks. "Stop it, Taran. Shayna's just trying to think about other things." Taran didn't have a beast or possess a power like Emme's to soothe her. She hated being scared. So when terror showed its face, her protective instincts called anger and attitude to the surface, unleashing her emotions like a rising inferno. It's how she rolled. But that didn't make it okay to sick her hyenas on Shayna. She needed a distraction. I stroked her black waves and tried to sound encouraging. "It's not such a crazy idea, you know? I think the wolves plan to hang out with us tonight, including Gemini. I couldn't help noticing how he tried to comfort you in there. It's like his shyness dissolved. All he cared about was seeing you through your trauma."

Taran's menace erased, softening the criticism lining

her face and bringing out her beautiful exotic features. My sister didn't fall for men. They fell for her. Hard. This time, though, she'd met her match. I turned my head to Gemini, knowing he'd heard me.

He stood with Aric and the other wolves. "We need to track the demon children," Gemini said. "The scent of the woman's death is too fresh for them to have gone far, and they'll need to feast soon."

"We'll need more noses," Aric said. "Call Paul and the other team."

"I can *change* and help, too." It's not like I'd forget that festering smell soon.

Aric sighed, moving toward me. I tried to meet him halfway until an odd sense of cold shoved at my chest like a pair of enraged sports fans. Gemini the wolf leapt to his feet, snarling at the same time my tigress snapped to attention. An earth-shattering scream cut through the silence. The twins had found their next meal.

I charged toward an overgrown path leading deeper into the woods only to be yanked back by Aric. *"Stay here,"* he growled.

He released my arm and *changed*, joining the rest of his pack already jetting into the dense forest in beast form. Only the original Gemini wolf remained. His hulking body blocked mine when I ignored Aric's request. "Damn it, Gem!"

"Celia?"

Emme's shaky voice kept me from barreling through Gemini. I didn't want to leave Aric to fight this thing alone. I glanced back at my sisters. Shayna already palmed two daggers. Taran's blue and white flames danced along her fingertips. No, I didn't want to leave Aric. But I also couldn't abandon my family.

"Wh-what is it, Celia?" Emme stammered.

"I don't know." I paused. Something dropped onto the roof of the mill from one of the overhanging branches.

One. Two. Like softballs . . . with feet. My ears perked. Whatever it or they were pushed between the splintering shingles and scrambled into the building. Gem crept toward the door. He'd heard it, too.

"Stay here," I muttered.

"Like hell," Taran shot back.

Gemini's tail batted against my stomach as I followed him back into the dust-filled and moldy building. The nauseating stench returned, this time with greater potency. We passed into the first large room, the one with the broken office furniture. I froze. Something scurried across the second floor. Just above where we stood. It scratched the battered wood with sharp little nails as it scampered from one side to the other.

"A squirrel?" Emme asked hopefully.

I really wanted it to be a squirrel. But squirrels didn't move as fast as this thing did. Nor did they hiss. Gemini tore pass me and up the stairs. Garbled screeches followed angry snarls. Dust and pieces of mold pelted us as Gemini's powerful paws pounded the ceiling above. He'd found one of the demon children.

So then, what the hell was Aric hunting . . . and where was the other twin?

A dark blur the size of my shoe scuttled like a crab above our heads. Then to the right. And then quickly down the wall and behind the armchair in the corner. I couldn't make out what it was. Just that it had wings. Bat wings.

"Oh, Jesus," Taran whispered.

Emme clutched my arm as I inched toward it. "Celia, *don't*."

Gemini's paws continued to beat down more dust and his roars shook the building. The thing was fast enough to keep him busy, and small enough to fit into cramped spaces. Like underneath the chair. "We need to kill it, Emme. No telling how big this thing will get. Shayna, Taran, knife or blast it as soon as I move the armchair."

I didn't dare avert my stare to see if they nodded, but their hard swallows affirmed they'd heard me.

I stalked my way to it, slowly. Considering that the bulky piece of crap rested just a few feet from me, it seemed to take a long time for me to reach it. Not that I was in a rush, mind you. Creepy crawlies from hell had that effect on a gal.

The *swoosh* from Taran's fire signaled her readiness to burn the thing to cinders, if Shayna's daggers didn't find it first. Shayna slid the blades she held against each other—her way of challenging the thing, and urging her inner mistress of all things sharp and deadly forward.

They were ready. I was ready. And now I'd reached my destination. My shaky hands extended toward the armrests. Dust poofed out in brown little clouds as I gripped the thick and torn fabric. I took a breath to steady myself and lifted.

The other twin poked its head from the bottom.

And clenched its mouth around my instep.

My lids peeled back and I screamed. Boy, did I scream! But only on the inside. I watched in shocked horror as this sickly gray creature pierced its yellow fangs through my sneaker and into the bones of my foot with a hair-raising crunch.

It hurt like the stab of hot needles, but I could handle a great deal of pain. What I couldn't handle was a *demon child* biting through my shoe and slurping my body fluid like a thirsty dog. My blood ran cold. I dropped the damned chair and jerked my foot in my own freaky version of the Elaine dance.

"Did you get it, Ceel?"

I whirled around to show Shayna that no, I didn't get it. *It. Had. Me.* My sisters screamed. The demon child held tight, flapping its long leather wings as it continued to feast.

"Get . . . It . . . Off . . . Me!"

They screamed once more, because that was *really* helpful. Finally Shayna came to her senses. Sort of.

"Keep still, Ceel." She lifted one of her blades. "I don't want to cut your foot off."

Neither Shayna's comment nor the fact that the demon child continued to suckle motivated me enough to stop prancing around. I kicked out hard, flinging the thing off me. It bounced off the wall, using its thick little frog legs to propel itself toward where my sisters huddled.

They jumped. But then it vanished. Shayna spun around, daggers out. "Where'd it go?"

Taran's head jerked in all directions. "Goddamn it. Do you think it has the power to disappear?"

My eyes scanned the room as my heart continued to make my rib cage its bitch. "I don't know. Aric said their time on earth is limited. Maybe it got summoned back to . . ." My voice trailed off as I caught Emme's blanching skin. She stood still, staring blankly at one of the metal chairs leaning against the wood-paneled walls. "Emme. What's wrong?"

Emme failed to answer, at least with words. She pirouetted carefully until her back was to us, revealing the demon child digging the claws of its hands and feet into her red wool coat, its tail whisking back and forth. It zipped up her back, tangling into the strands of her honey-colored locks before I could blink.

Taran jumped back. "Holy *shit*!"

I lunged at Emme, only to freeze when the demon child's ears perched back and it reeled its head to face me. Quarter-size red eyes narrowed over a toadlike head and mouth. It screeched, protruding and elongating its serrated yellow teeth.

I didn't know what to do. I didn't know how to fight it. But Shayna did.

The blade of her knife caught a trickle of light filtering in as the gamut of her power rose in one tremendous sweep. She elongated the cutting edge of her dagger with her *gift*, manipulating the metal until it lengthened into a giant sword.

Before I could shout a warning to Emme, Shayna two-hand-gripped the hilt and brought it straight down Emme's back, slicing a large chunk of her hair along with the demon child's appendages. Four sets of claws remained attached to Emme's coat and hair. One of them crawled along her shoulder and caressed her cheek before dissolving into a maggot and falling at her feet. Emme's eyes rolled into the back of her head just before she crash-landed into Shayna.

The demon child hissed and lurched onto the ceiling. Taran blasted it with a jagged bolt of lightning, then another, and another, as it flew from one section to another. Gemini yelped above us. He nudged his head through one of the holes, his powerful jowls holding the limp body of the other twin.

The remaining demon child swooped down, clutching an old wall calendar with mutilated limbs as a rapid beat of paws arrived on the other side. Taran gathered her magic and screamed, hurling a tremendous ball of fire at the wall.

I roared, *"No!"* The side of the building exploded, the force knocking us back. Taran's great ball of fire took out the entire section, missing the demon child and thankfully our wolves. One by one they poked their human heads through the cindering edges. "What the *fuck*?" Koda growled.

I didn't have time to explain. The creature dove at Taran's neck, its fangs exposed. I caught it midair, piercing its toad body with my protruding claws. Its slimy, cold-leather flesh made my skin crawl. Emme came to in Shayna's arms, just in time to join my others sisters screaming as they watched the demon child writhe beneath my grip. Its strength surprised me, especially given its small size. My hand jerked and shuddered as it tried to escape. And yet the more that I stared at it, the more the little bastard pissed me off. Not just because it bit me, or attacked my sisters, but because it lived. Something this evil didn't belong in my world.

"Shayna. Wanna play pin the wings on a demon child?"

Shayna stood slowly and answered in a tone that clearly meant she'd prefer a round of Monopoly. "Okay, Ceel."

I pitched the demon child against the wall. Hard enough that its little body indented into the paneling. *One. Two*. Shayna's daggers found each wing. The demon child hissed, its forked tongue extending past its mouth.

The wolves charged in. Naked. My eyes widened as the full breadth of Aric's heat licked my body in teasing strokes. I spun away, barely catching a glimpse of the perfectly cut muscles layering his broad chest, shoulders, and powerful arms.

Aric paused behind me, his voice a soft rumble. "Are you okay?"

No. I wasn't okay. I'd fought a demon child following the discovery of four carcasses and a half-eaten woman. And now there stood Aric in all his hotter-than-hell glory making my female parts tap-dance to "Eye of the Tiger." "Yeah. Totally."

Large hands covered my shoulders, turning the temperature in the chilly building up to a sweltering ninety degrees. "What's wrong?" he murmured.

My body shuddered. Of course he hadn't believed me. He didn't have to possess the ability to sniff lies to detect my blatant dishonesty. My heated body, speedy pulse, and all my girl parts waving hello proclaimed loud and clear that my self-assured tigress had torn from the building and left the inner, awkward, socially inept girl in charge. Thanks a ton, old faithful inner beast.

"The girls aren't comfortable around naked beings," Gemini offered. "In their defense, they haven't associated much with our kind."

Aric stiffened behind me, although not in a good way. "I'm sorry, Celia. I thought since we were together now . . ." He sighed, the warmth of his body rising. "I didn't mean to make you uncomfortable. I'll use more discretion in the future."

Oh God. I buried my face in my palm. I'd embarrassed him. And myself. I hated not knowing how to behave, or what to say, to a male, especially now when it mattered so much. Aric caught a pair of sweats thrown to him. I wanted to turn around and watch him dress, to prove that yes, I wanted to see him. All of him. He needed to know—to *understand* how much I wanted his touch.

But I didn't say or do anything. Instead I waited until I heard the elastic of his pants slip above his legs and snap onto his waist. My tigress made us strong. And yet she stood no chance against the dorky female who ruled on the other side.

The squeals of the squirming demon child beckoned Aric forward. I followed close behind him and stood on his right side as he and the other wolves snarled at the sinful creature. Aric glanced my way, appearing surprised I'd join him and dared to stand so close. *Way to go, Celia. Maybe you should nut-punch him for an encore.*

My sisters kept their distance. Koda winked over his shoulder at Shayna. "Good job snagging it, baby."

"Eh," remained Shayna's sole response.

The little bastard continued to skeeve her out. Me, I just wanted it gone. I touched Aric's arm lightly with my fingertips. He tensed beneath my caress. And it damn well nearly broke my heart. I cleared my throat. "Why hasn't it returned to hell? I thought you said its time is limited."

"Because he's not from hell. He was created on earth through a human vessel. The human side gives him unlimited time on earth."

I said a silent prayer thanking God Almighty these damned things were rare. "He? How do you know it's male?"

Koda's jaw tightened. "They're all male. That way they can impregnate a female if given the opportunity."

I exchanged glances with my sisters following another thank-you to the Big Man upstairs. Their slacked jaws and paling skin told me we shared the same collective thought. *Eww.*

Liam pointed between the demon's legs. "This one hasn't reached sexual maturity yet. Look. Only one of his four balls have dropped."

My sisters' gags announced that they, like me, had enough of Demon Child 101. "Can you please get rid of it?" I asked.

Aric yanked it off the wall by its throat, ripping the wings clean from its body. The wings almost immediately shriveled to resemble dry leaves. I followed Aric, but not before Koda wrenched free the daggers and handed them to Shayna. She seemed hesitant to hold them. "Don't worry, baby. Nothing of that thing will remain. I swear to you."

She shoved them back in her holsters and clicked the snaps closed. "How do you and the others know so much about demon children? Especially since they're so rare, puppy?"

Koda cupped her pixie face. "Mostly from scriptures confiscated from dark witches throughout the centuries."

Shayna bit her bottom lip. "So a dark witch is involved?"

Koda paused. "Maybe at first. But if she raised anything strong enough to impregnate a woman with twins, I guarantee she didn't live long enough to see them born."

CHAPTER 6

Gemini's wolf carried the other demon child, clenching his jaws tighter when it stirred. It still lived. I growled at it. Man, I hated these things.

Aric leaned down on one knee when we reached the path. "You may not want to watch this," he said without glancing up.

I knelt beside him to assure him that I didn't want to leave him, and that I'd had my fill of being scared. "I've seen this much, Aric. I'd rather know what to do. In case more are out there."

He nodded.

And ripped the demon's head off like he was cracking a lobster.

The demon child's innards spilled like tiny maggots. Aric tossed the body onto the hard ground. Almost instantly the parts dissolved in the sun. I cringed. "Do they need sunlight to die?"

"No. Just air once you decapitate them. I did it out here because the added breeze helps."

As the leftover bits of demon child floated away in the light wind, the stench around us was cut by half. In the silence that followed, the urge to explain myself compelled me to speak. "I didn't know how to kill it. Sorry I wasn't more helpful."

Aric shot me a halfhearted smile. "You didn't die. That's good enough for me. But the general rule of thumb is, when in doubt, destroy the brain or heart." He brushed his hands on his black sweats. "If you can't, rip off the wings to render it flightless until you're able."

His voice sounded more didactic than warm, lacking the usual affection I'd grown to adore and crave. So I kept discussing the demon child because I didn't know what else to say. And if we stopped talking, I feared we'd never speak again. "He was fast. It took us a while to catch him."

Aric stood when I did. "I suppose they're born fast to increase their chances of survival."

"Have any ever survived?"

"Not that we've heard." He wiped his large hands against each other. "Yet anyway." The demon child screeched like a mini-pterodactyl and wriggled inside Gemini's mouth like a mound of snakes. "Do you want to kill it?" Aric asked him.

The wolf turned his massive four-hundred-plus-pound body to where Taran stood with her arms crossed. Gemini, the human half, had his arm draped around her. She curled against him when she saw the little booger start to flap its bat wings. "I'd better do it," Koda said, jogging up to us.

The wolf tossed the creature in the air and rushed back to merge with Gemini. Koda yanked it out of the sky when it attempted to flee, tore it in half like a French roll, dropped it on the ground, and walked back to Shayna as if he hadn't just ripped evil in two. It took a lot to ruffle a werewolf's feathers. A Wird sister's feathers? Not so much. Aric should have done the honors. Shayna's skin mimicked the color of my butt.

Aric's eyes widened as the air cleared and his gaze shot down to my foot. "You're bleeding," he growled.

Blood soaked through my tattered running shoe, staining the white laces crimson. My survival instincts naturally forced me to ignore pain. Though that didn't mean my injury didn't throb, especially when the white leather chafed against the bite marks. I shrugged. "Yeah. The little evil bastard bit me when—"

Aric yanked me in his arms and growled some more. "*Emme.* Celia's hurt!"

My tigress circled my arms around his neck, allowing me to cuddle and draw in the scent of water crashing over stone. "It's no big deal, Aric. I'm fine. I just need some antiseptic."

Aric sat on the edge of the porch, draping me across his lap. His strong chiseled arms curled around me. My cheek fell against his bare chest and our bodies melded and relaxed into a state of tranquility. The breeze lifted strands of my long hair, teasing his smooth skin and carrying the scent of budding tulips to my nose. His wolf murmured something softly. My tigress responded with a gentle purr. It was all so beautiful, sensual even. Until Koda pulled my sneaker and sock off in one hard tug.

Gasps, muffled shrieks, and rumbling chests dragged me back into reality and kicked me in the face. The demon child's serrated fangs had sliced my instep and peeled the thin layer of skin away from the bones. Veins spluttered like tiny hoses, releasing my body's precious fluid in squirts. Blood dribbled between my toes and discolored my nails.

Okay. Maybe I needed more than a little Neosporin.

The 3-D view clenched my stomach like an iron vise. Bile bubbled against my throat, and the stinging pain I'd shoved back returned with a nauseating vengeance. I no longer had a foot; I had a mangled piece of meat with digits at the end. I curled farther into Aric, focusing on his strong, clean scent and not my raw flesh. "Son of a bitch," Taran muttered. Soft cotton enclosed my foot. "I'll hold pressure. Emme, start healing."

Emme's soft healing light brightened Aric's golden skin. My eyes centered on his dark pink nipple, stiff from the soft wind, I supposed. He growled again. Okay, maybe just tense from the anger surging through his well-muscled physique. Concern for him beat back the preoccupation with my injury until it no longer mattered. After all, Emme's gift would mend me. But in no way did it spare Aric from worry. "Shhh," I whispered in his ear. "I'm okay, wolf. I swear it."

And I was. Against Aric's body, I definitely was. His presence allowed me to abandon the disturbing images of the day and erased the thoughts of my skinned flesh and oozing vessels.

Aric stroked his stubble cheek against mine. "I shouldn't have left you."

My lips met his briefly as my fingertips slid lightly against his chest, itching with the need to play with that perfect nipple. I withdrew, wondering if the other was just as delightful. Yup. Absolutely. My tigress rolled her eyes, reminding me I could have witnessed more than a little areola action if only my inner nerd hadn't marched forward waving her geek banner with all the grace of a two-year-old on roller skates.

Aric's honey-colored eyes searched mine. They always spoke of power and strength. This time they whispered with more intensity, and a hell of a lot more fire. "I won't leave you again," he promised.

My arms fastened around him, returning his embrace. "Thank you . . . for caring about what happens to me."

My words carried a great deal of emotion. Most beings demonstrated little to no sympathy for me. Then I'd met Aric. Initially I presumed his wolfish impulses caused him to assume a protective role. Altercations with other wolves stomped that theory to bits. Wolves in general didn't feel compelled to protect—*Aric* did. Despite not belonging to his pack, he cared about me. For some bizarre reason, he cared more than it seemed possible.

Taran's hard wipes to my foot forced me to acknowledge that Emme had completed her healing. Aric lifted me, his pace quick as he returned to the path. My head whirled around to my family as we disappeared around the bend. "Where are we going?"

"I need to get you home. My wolves will keep your sisters safe."

I wiggled my foot. Wine-colored splotches painted my smooth pink skin. "But I'm fine now. We need to tend to the bodies."

"No. You don't. The *weres* we have in the local homicide unit have been *called*. They're on their way and will take care of matters inside the mill."

The matters he spoke of no doubt involved identifying the victims and notifying their families. I nibbled on my bottom lip. "Do you think they're local?"

The wind picked up, and so did the roar of the river. "Hard to tell with the number of tourists Tahoe gets."

"I guess." I wiggled against him so he'd put me down. He didn't. "You realize I can walk."

"You're not wearing shoes."

"Aric—"

A throaty, frustrated growl found its way out of Aric and heated his face. "Celia, my wolf failed to keep you safe. Cut him some slack and allow us to care for you now."

My narrowed eyes slowly softened as I absorbed the extent of Aric's culpability. My tigress took protecting my sisters seriously. When she failed, guilt dug hard enough to rupture my spleen. As a beast, I understood. As a female, I also recognized Aric's need to be chivalrous. And yet had any other male carried me then, I'd have *shifted* him into the ground, kicked him in the head, and stomped back to the car. But because it was Aric, I relaxed against him, allowing both him and his beast to tend to me. I kissed the edge of his jaw. "All right. But just this one time, wolf."

Aric huddled me closer. "I was convinced the danger lurked outside the mill. And I believed the sour stench was related to the woman's violent death, not the presence of demons. I wanted to protect you by keeping you away from the fight and thought Gem's wolf would be enough to keep you safe."

"Well, now we know for next time."

Aric tightened his jaw. He didn't say it, but he left me the impression there might not be a next time. My tigress wasn't so sure about that. The evil I'd witnessed terrified me, more than any other magical entity I'd encountered. And yet it triggered such hate and anger that even now my fangs begged to protrude and tear out the throats of those who threatened to shadow the world with darkness. Hell existed for creatures like that. My tigress yearned to send them back, and my faith demanded they never return. I wasn't *were*, but at that moment I understood their loyalty to the earth.

Aric slowed as the trees thinned out and we reached the grassy knoll near the bakery. Human voices pricked my ears. "Where the hell is your brother? He and Beverly were supposed to meet us hours ago!"

A man wearing jeans and a thick jacket loomed over a young woman on her cell phone. She disconnected the call and glared at him. "For the last time, I don't know. Tara and Bill said they haven't heard from them, either."

"We're going to lose the damn deposit on the raft ride!"

The woman's growing annoyance and underlying aroma of fear made her smack her partner's arm. "Will you shut up about the damn deposit! What if something happened to them?"

My eyes widened, but I kept my mouth shut until Aric placed me in the passenger seat of his Escalade. I motioned toward the alley. "Could the screams you went after have come from those missing people?"

Aric watched the storefront of the antique shop as if he expected someone he knew to step onto the cracked walkway. "It was that same couple we passed before we entered the forest. I recognized the man's cologne the closer we neared where they'd been taken."

I stilled. Taken. As in gone forever. Aric clasped my hands, sensing my anger and sadness. "What took them?"

Aric shook his head. "I don't know. When we left you with Gemini at the mill, we picked up a bizarre scent. I've never smelled anything like it. It stank of dark magic and death, but the prominent aroma was human. We tracked it, and the couple, until they vanished."

My brows knitted together. "It didn't rain, though. How could so many fresh scents vanish so quickly?"

An odd sense of gloom filled the car and shadowed Aric's light brown eyes. "My guess? Something with wings carried them away."

CHAPTER 7

Aric slipped into the driver's side and cranked the engine while I absentmindedly clicked my seat belt in place. I thought of the demon children twins, small enough to stomp, yet hard to catch and equipped with a mouthful of sharp incentives to discourage anyone from trying. The wolves had killed them before they'd grown too big. But had others managed to venture into adulthood? "You think there are grown demon children out there?"

Aric pulled onto the road, passing all the quaint little shops that had withstood the passage of time. "My nose tells me the scents are too distinct to be the same creature, but I can't come up with another reason that couple disappeared without a trace."

"And yet the demon children don't explain the deaths of the men."

Aric rubbed his five o'clock shadow, his eyes narrowing when they glimpsed my foot. "No. What they did to you and how they tore that woman apart reinforces the theory that they're cannibalistic creatures."

I swiveled my foot a few times. The skin felt a little tight due to the dried blood and the freshly healed muscles. "Yep, definitely like piranhas with wings."

Aric reached for my hand. "More of a reason I don't want you involved in this shit."

My fingers interlinked with his. Considering that I'd been chomped on like a bucket of chicken, now wasn't the time to argue that he needed my help more than ever. I'd wait until his wolf calmed before I made my argument. Aric's reason stood no chance against his riled beast, especially since my injuries remained on the forefront of his mind.

Five SUVs passed us on the way out of town. Aric gave a stiff nod to the first one. I recognized the last truck as Paul's. "Why did you call Paul here? Is he a homicide cop?"

"He's actually a forensics specialist, but not a cop. His eyes and sharp nose pick up things even most *weres* would overlook. I'm hoping he'll find something we missed."

I crinkled my nose. "I find it hard to believe you'd miss anything, wolf."

Aric's hand released mine to find the nape of my neck. I rubbed my cheek against his arm, seeking more of his touch. He smiled softly. "I didn't search as hard as I could have, knowing I'd left you alone. But when Koda heard Shayna scream, none of us were sticking around to continue the hunt."

I straightened, unease and guilt making me think twice. Maybe Aric's Elders had a point about my presence distracting him from his duties. He stopped the car at the town's only traffic light and pulled me to him. He kissed me deeply, groaning almost as loudly as I did when an impatient driver and his very loud horn alerted us that the light had turned green. Aric released me, winking before resuming our trek out of town. "Don't even think it, sweetness. No way in hell was I not going back for you."

I gripped the edges of the leather seat, panting softly

and trying to regain my composure. Aric planted one hell of a smooch, laced with a great deal of sizzle and emotion behind it. I believed his caring for me was genuine, although I still marveled as to why. Regardless, I couldn't help wondering whether maybe the wolves would have found the couple if they hadn't abandoned their efforts. A thought I couldn't bear to contemplate. We didn't speak again until we passed the exit for the Stampede Reservoir on 89. "Aric, if there are demon children—grown ones, I mean—wouldn't they have left a royal mess long before this?"

Aric placed his hand over my knee, the knuckles relaxing and tightening as he massaged. Good Lord, so much had happened since we first touched in his car. "Celia, over two thousand people go missing every day in the States. Most are never found. They could very well have been abducted by demons and devoured somewhere obscure. Yet the demon's rarity should make it impossible. And so should their vile stench. They can't hide that shit from a human nose, let alone one of my kind."

Aric had a point. About a lot of what went down. Yet still so much didn't make sense. The distinct smells. The leeched men. The missing couple. And the mutilated woman. How were they all connected? "Is it possible the couple and the dead bodies are somehow related, you know, as in from the same family?"

Aric let out a long breath. "I doubt it. The men all appeared of different ethnicities and their clothes suggested varying socioeconomic backgrounds. But the *weres* investigating will look into it just in case." He glanced out the side window, where the lush forest appeared to be greeting the arrival of spring. "You know, Tahoe is a great area. But when you consider its vastness and that three million people visit the area each year, it makes it hard to police when a new threat arises."

I took in the sea of green firs and leaves. Every critter, vine, sprout, even the occasional dead tree with crumbling branches had a place among those that thrived. Malevolent dead things with serrated knives for teeth? Not so much. I lived in the northeast section of the lake in a small, mostly quiet and uneventful cul-de-sac. Yet I considered the entire region home, sweet home. I only wished I could keep it to myself and all the malicious bastards out.

Aric's shoulders dropped and he breathed a small sigh of relief when we entered Dollar Point, probably thankful to reach my hometown with all our limbs still intact. "If you're still up for it, I'd love to take you to dinner."

"Don't you have duties to attend to?"

Aric brushed his knuckles against my cheek. "I passed them to Gemini. I don't like what happened to you, or what I exposed you to. My wolf needs to ensure that you're safe before he can fully settle." He grinned. "So how about you help us out and have dinner with us?"

My growling stomach responded for him and made him chuckle. I met his grin with one that would trump any tween meeting Gaga. "I'd love to go out. What are you in the mood for?"

Aric pulled onto the small incline leading into my neighborhood, humor dissolving from his face like an ice cube in boiling water. "Vampire on a stake."

"What?" I thought I misheard him until I took in our Colonial.

I jumped out of my seat like I'd sat on burning tacks. The very naughty Catholic schoolgirls draped their long legs against the white porch railings like a bunch of lazy monkeys waiting to bite, pull hair, or sling poo. Misha and Danny were also there, standing at the bottom of the light blue wooden steps engaged in conversation. Neither appeared happy. Danny's brows shot up over his

Coke-bottle black-framed glasses when he caught sight of Aric's Escalade . . . and his not-so thrilled expression.

Aric parked along the curb. Right behind Misha's Hummer limo with the BYTE ME plates. "Please don't do anything, Aric." I leapt out of the SUV, and even though my side was technically closer to the sidewalk, and my speed was generally faster, Aric reached Misha first.

"What the hell are you doing here?"

A glint of annoyance flickered in Misha's cold gray eyes when he caught my hands clasped over Aric's. Aside from that, Misha ignored him to face me. I only wished the good Catholics had disregarded us, too. Instead they soared off the porch, over the rhododendron bushes, and landed in crouches hissing at Aric. "Oh, shut up!" I snapped. I glanced between Aric and Misha. "I don't think I need to remind either of you about the treaty forbidding you to tear out each other's throats." Both ignored me. The tension between them bitch-slapped the air, so yeah, a gentle reminder appeared worth mentioning. I cleared my throat, adding as much force as I could muster considering that I stood between two of the world's deadliest preternaturals. "No bloodshed allowed—*especially* on neutral territory."

I said it. I meant it. Too bad I was dealing with a pair of hothead Alpha males who hated each other.

Danny backed away, tripping over the steps in his haste to reach the front door. He swung it open, yelling at the top of his lungs, "Bren, *Bren*. Get out here. We got trouble!"

A deep voice called from inside, "Keep your panties on, Dan, I'm coming." Bren sauntered down the steps barefoot, wearing a stained white T-shirt and black basketball shorts. Potato chip flakes stuck to his dark, scruffy beard as he munched. As a *lone* wolf, he and Aric weren't exactly pals, but his dislike of vampires made him take a position on Aric's other side. He shoved his hand into the Lay's bag tucked under his arm and reached for more salty goodness. "Hey, Ceel," he said between bites. His laid-back disposition suggested indifference, but in the end, *lone* or not, Bren was very much a werewolf. His beast nature would attack if provoked, and so would the loyal friend within if the vampires threatened my safety.

Misha's long blond hair draped against his high cheekbones, eclipsing his already hard stare. "Where were you today, Celia?"

"She was with me," Aric answered.

Misha continued to watch me, which was very much a good thing. Treaty or not, had he met Aric's glare, his wolf would interpret it as a challenge and I'd spend the next week scrubbing fur and blood off my walkway. Misha's tone hardened, not a good thing considering that it hadn't started as cheery to begin with. "Then why did I sense her distress?"

Aric leaned back on his heels. "How did you—?"

It probably took every last bit of control Aric had to hold back his beast when Misha snatched my right wrist. He held it in the air while the middle finger of his opposite hand traced a line down my forearm. "I gave Celia the ability to *call* me."

Aric turned his glare from Misha to me. *Oh, goody.* "He gave you his *call*?"

He wasn't really asking. He was more telling me he didn't like—no, he *despised*—what I'd allowed Misha to do. I jerked my hand away from Misha as if he'd taken a bite. "I, ah . . ." I looked to Bren and Danny, unsure how to respond. Bren, good ol' Bren, choked on his chips with how hard he laughed. I failed to see the humor. Especially then.

My eyes narrowed at Misha, certain he'd somehow screwed me. When he'd first given me his supernatural digits, he'd said, "Should you ever need me, *call* my name and I shall thunder through hell itself to reach you." At the time, I considered it a generous offer. Now, not so much. There was no thundering through hell, just a lot of gloating. And judging by how Aric's heart pounded like a racing Thoroughbred, I started to believe I should have asked for a gift card instead. "Um" remained my only response.

Misha flashed his famously wicked smile. "What troubles you, mongrel? It's my understanding Tahoe's head witch passed you her *call*."

My jaw fell hard enough to scrape against the sidewalk. Genevieve, Tahoe's head witch, was supermodel stunning. We're talking waist-length ebony hair that cradled perfect and perky breasts, large blue eyes, fair skin that had never seen a zit, full luscious lips, and a magical whoop-ass staff capable of turning weregorillas into krill. Genevieve was smart, powerful, tall, wealthy—and did I mention *stunning*?

I crossed my arms, this time, my turn to raise an eyebrow. At Aric. "Did she, now?"

Aric didn't blink. "Our relationship is strictly business."

"Your relationship? Oh. I'll. Just. *Bet*."

Slapping Aric across the face with a dead fish wouldn't have earned me the same expression of shocked confusion. "Why, are you jealous?"

Agnes Concepción whispered in my ear, "Don't worry, Celia. I'm sure some males find small boobs attractive."

"Just because my boobs aren't man-made doesn't mean they're small," I growled back. I ignored her, Bren's snorts, and even Aric to address Misha. "Just so you know, we encountered demon children today."

A small gust of wind spun bits of leaves in the air. Other than that subtle sound, silence ruled my front steps. The Catholic schoolgirls straightened in their neck-breaking shoes. Despite their perpetually petty demeanors, they weren't fools. Some things you just didn't laugh at. Misha raised his chin. "Demon children."

I clenched my fists. "Was this what you were talking about last night?" The strain that immediately formed in the small space between Aric and me told me he figured out I'd spent time with Misha, and that the knowledge didn't please him. I kicked myself on the inside. It's not that I intended to lie to him. But I did want to spare his feelings. Still, we had more pressing matters. I met Misha's stare. "Look, Misha. I know you don't want to think about what's coming. But it seems like it's already here. I'd appreciate it if you would help us out."

Aric clasped my elbow, pulling me slightly away from Misha. "Don't bother, Celia. The only thing this asshole cares about is himself."

Maybe. But I hoped the friendship between Misha and me, or his commitment as my protector, would make him reconsider. "Please, Misha. We need to know what's happening."

Misha examined me closely, like a small diamond that couldn't possibly be real. He cut his stare to Aric. "Very well, but I only do this for you." He lowered his lids and slowed his breathing. I listened carefully until the deep thrum of his pulse dawdled to a point of nonexistence. The breeze picked up from the lake as he called upon Tahoe's magic. The air stirred as if charged, blowing my long mane upward until it fell in a cascade of flowing locks against my shoulders. Flashes of blue light similar to fireflies appeared from the direction of the lake. They swirled as if following the coils of an elongated Slinky and ebbed into Misha's chest. He shook his head, his jaw clenched. "I sense the dark ones. . . . However, what hovers is a different entity."

Misha's words verified what we already believed, the demon children and the creature who'd taken the couple were different beings. In a way that was a good thing. But still not knowing what "it" was made it difficult to hunt and ultimately destroy. Aric pulled me closer to him. It would have comforted me if it hadn't been for the stiffness in his voice. "Is it a demon or not?"

Misha's gray eyes clouded until a silver film encased his scleras. "Demon's kin," he whispered in a sinister voice that erased the traces of his Russian accent.

My husky voice cracked. "Misha?" Something stood in front of me. And it was no longer my guardian angel master vampire. Bren threw his bag of chips on the ground and roared along with Aric. My claws and my fangs shot out, and every nerve in my body shrieked a warning. Misha stumbled forward, grimacing as if in pain before his knees gave out.

Instincts had me reaching for Misha. Aric yanked me behind him at almost the same moment the good Catholics surrounded their master.

"Soon," an inhuman voice whispered in my ear.

My head jerked in all directions, searching for who'd spoken. I'm not sure what my expression held, but it was one that whitened Danny's face and made him fall backward. Poor guy, I'd forgotten he'd hid behind me. I hauled him upright as I scanned the area. No one appeared, and my tigress couldn't sense anything—*anything*. When I looked to the others, all sights were locked on Misha.

Agnes Concepción bared her fangs. "What did you do to our master, mutt?"

Aric's keen sight swept from the schoolgirls to Misha. "Nothing," he answered. The absence of the evil kept his deep tenor voice casual. "If I had, he'd be bleeding and missing a head."

Misha righted himself, pride forcing him to tear from his family's hold. They fell to their knees, heads bowed. His irises had resumed their normal cold gray tone, but his anger blistered worse than when he'd seen me holding Aric. "Did you hear that?" he asked me.

I nodded slowly, fear and hatred causing my bones to stiffen. That *voice* sounded neither human nor animal, more otherwordly—deep and distorted as if the one who spoke gargled shards of glass. "It said, 'Soon.' "

Aric whirled me around to face him, his anger suddenly returning. "What did?"

"I don't know." I let out a long breath, still shaken. "I guess whatever inhabited Misha."

Aric's phone rang, and rang. He didn't release me until the second set of rings. He watched me as he reached in his pocket for his phone. "It's Aric."

Someone, raging with fury, bellowed on the other end, "You fought demon children, and yet you failed to report the matter directly to your Elders!"

Aric stormed toward the driveway, meeting his caller with equal fury. "Gemini is my Beta. As his Alpha I put him in charge of reporting off to you—"

"Is it because you're with *her*? Is *she* with you?"

Aric's spine stiffened so hard I feared it would snap. "Celia is none of your damn business, Anara."

Apparently this Anara guy thought I very much was. He growled something on the other end. I didn't understand it, but Bren did. "Asshole," he muttered, coming to stand by me.

"Don't you *ever* talk about her like that again!" Aric hollered. The cold menace Aric expelled made me shiver. Had he just threatened his Elder because of me? He disconnected, panting so hard I feared his wolf would unleash and take his rage out on the vampires. I rushed to him only to have Misha block my path.

"Forget the wolves, Celia, and heed my warning. Whatever this creature is, it now recognizes who you are. I heard him speak to you. He wants you, and he will come for you."

CHAPTER 8

Aric and I spread out on the couch, his arm draped around me holding me close. Danny sat on the floor, carefully turning the pages of a leather-bound text two days shy of completely disintegrating. Bren lay back in our recliner sipping a beer and watching, of all things, the Angels play. Irony never seemed to be lost in the Wird household.

Vampires, furious Elders, and demonic possession had a funny way of interrupting dinner plans. Aric and I never made it out. Instead we waited for the others to return and collectively devoured all the leftover lasagna, fried chicken, and pot roast. Taking on evil worked up quite the appetite.

My sisters huddled out on the deck with their wolves, speaking in hushed voices and drinking hot chocolate. Their conversation lacked the usual lighthearted humor and laughter. And while the wolves hadn't commented directly, I had the impression their link to Aric alerted them of the unrest within their pack.

I cuddled closer against Aric. He hadn't discussed his Elder's call with me, but I guess he didn't have to. Anara didn't want Aric with me. And that's all there was to it.

Whether Aric would defy his pack remained to be seen. For the moment, I thanked God for his company and the comforting warmth that accompanied our closeness.

Bren took a long swill of his beer. He seemed engrossed in the game, but I knew better. Sports always brought the crazed fan lurking beside his wolf. If he wasn't commenting, screaming at our tiny TV, or accusing the umpire of being a shithead, his head wasn't in the game.

The others had ventured outside shortly after cleanup. After my demon child encounter, I craved the warm glow and security of the house. Aric stayed with me, but neither of us had spoken much.

"Bren and Danny have a key to your place?" Aric asked, breaking the silence.

The question caught me off guard. And at first I meant to respond with an "Of course. Why wouldn't they?" except the subtle bitter scent of jealousy that wafted into my nose null-and-voided my response. "Aric . . ."

Bren turned his head, his scruffy brown beard brightening his jovial grin. "Celia and I are very close." He danced his brows. *"Very* close—*shit!"*

The plastic tumbler I nailed him with bounced off his head and rolled across our dark wooden floors. He was lucky I'd finished my water. "Stop trying to cause trouble." I rubbed my forehead when I caught a whiff of Aric's rising jealousy. "Danny and Bren are our very dear friends. Danny keeps a copy of the key." My eyes narrowed at Bren. "Otherwise Bren would eat all our food."

"Hey, that just happened one time. Besides, you needed to go grocery shopping."

Bren knew two ways to deal with stress. Either kill whatever bugged him or have fun at someone else's expense. Bren, by far, was the annoying big brother we never had. But we loved him despite his faults and he loved us right back.

Aric's frigid glare in Bren's direction told me he suspected Bren and I had shared more than friendship. In all actuality, it was Danny and me who had once been involved. He was the first and only male I'd had sex with. Granted, we were seventeen, and neither of us knew what we were doing. But his caring nature and his kind soul kept our friendship going long after the physical intimacy ended.

Danny glanced up from the frail and stained pages. His black frames slid down his nose, and his unruly curly hair stuck out in too many directions to count. "Um, Shayna called us after you and Aric left them. She thought maybe I could dig something up in one of my texts, so I came right over." He pushed his glasses up, but they slipped back down anyway. "Misha and his family arrived shortly after us, looking for you, Celia. He said he could feel your unrest, but didn't say much more. I didn't know much, either, but even if I had, I wouldn't have told him—you know, unless he used hypnosis or torture or something."

I wouldn't have put it past Misha to use his vamp mojo to extract information. He wouldn't, however, hurt Danny. No decent soul would. Torturing Danny was the equivalent of snapping a kitten's neck. As it was, his stick-thin limbs barely held the oversize book. And yet despite what I believed about Misha, Aric thought the exact opposite, and always would. "I wouldn't let that prick hurt you, Dan," Aric assured him.

Aric's protectiveness made me smile. He felt the need to defend those smaller and weaker than him. I wasn't sure if that would've changed had he known how close Danny and I had once been. So I kept my mouth shut and allowed him to see Danny as he was, a good person and one worthy of our protection.

Aric motioned to his book. "What is that anyway?"

"It's an old witchcraft book I picked up in France, one

with different chants to vanquish demons back to hell. It's considered useless by supernatural standards since by the time the spell works, the demons are already back where they belong." He flipped to another section. "There are, however, a couple of passages describing different types of demons. I brought it along thinking it might be helpful."

"Where in France did you get it?"

Danny glanced around, appearing surprised Aric would continue to show interest in what he had to say. "In a small town outside Montpellier."

Aric frowned. "Were you touring the country?"

Danny's face reddened. "Ah, no."

"Then why were you so far south?"

Bren rolled his eyes. "Because the little turd travels the world searching for old magic books he finds on the Internet. Instead of trying to get laid by hot European chicks, he's banging toothless librarians."

Danny scowled at Bren, something he'd never pull on another werewolf. "She was twenty-five, and it's not her fault her town didn't have a decent dentist."

Aric barked out a laugh and so did the wolves outside. Bren shook his head with disgust and took another swig of beer. All the blood pooled in poor Danny's face, compelling me to draw attention away from him. I adjusted my position to face Aric. "How do you know so much about France?"

Aric coughed into his opposite shoulder, trying hard to muffle his laughter. "After the wolves and I graduated from the University of Colorado, we spent almost two years learning different fighting techniques throughout Europe and Asia. We stayed in Paris for about nine months learning savate."

I perked up. "Did you learn French, too?"

Aric shrugged. "A little here and there."

"Just enough to get some tail, Celia." Liam spoke casually as if merely stating common knowledge. He'd walked in to grab a pack of mini marshmallows from the pantry. Too bad Emme hadn't done so in his place. I didn't need to know more about Aric's sexual past. The females who flaunted and threw themselves at him were enough evidence of his prowess.

Liam did a double take when he caught my open mouth and almost dropped the small package. His hand shot out as he realized his mistake. Sort of. "Don't worry, Celia. All those one-night stands didn't mean anything to him, right, Aric?"

Aric's glare had Liam backing into the sliding glass door. Koda stuck his head in, his brows set deep and his long black hair descending to his thigh-thick arms. "All you had to do was grab some damn marshmallows. Shut your trap and get outside before Aric eats you." He gave me a stiff nod before disappearing outside.

Aric's light brown eyes softened when they met mine. "That was a long time ago, sweetness," he whispered.

I supposed it was his way of offering an explanation or attempting to apologize. I nodded but found myself inching away from him. It hurt too much to think about other hands caressing Aric, especially when my own had barely touched him. No matter how hot, his tempting heat stood no chance against my raging insecurities.

"Baby, I—"

"Did you find anything, Danny?" I spoke to Danny, but by that point I'd twisted enough to face Bren. Bren could've laughed, or joked, or asked Aric for details about his indiscretions. But he didn't. He sensed my hurt, and he didn't like it. That was the great thing about Bren. All kidding aside, he really cared about me.

"You okay?" he mouthed.

My clenched jaw screamed *no*, and that I was in over my head with Aric. Bren made a motion to stand, but it was Danny who actually saved me. He cleared his throat hard enough to make him cough into his hand. "There is something here. *Daemonium consanguineis* loosely translates into demon kin from Latin to English." His finger traced along the passages as his mind worked to translate the words. "It's believed a new breed of demons will arise from hate and dark magic. These demon lords, for lack of better terms, will possess the ability to cross between hell and earth without limitations, but that's all it says."

Oh, is that all? Every muscle in my body saluted in tribute to our impending deaths. One by one, the wolves entered the house and took a seat around Danny. Emme squeezed Liam's hand. "What is it, Lee?"

Aric swore beneath his breath as the wolves explained what Danny had just surmised. He leaned forward, resting his elbows against his knees. "Does it say anything about how you stop them from rising?"

Danny's finger continued to travel along the page. He stopped suddenly and shot his finger back to where he started, his eyes widening as they darted back and forth. "No. But it does say the rise of these demons follows a significant change in the supernatural world."

"Like what?" Koda asked.

Danny slowly met my stare. "Such as a vampire becoming whole once more."

Taran threw her hands in the air. "For shit's sake, Celia. Why the hell did you have to go and return Count Hotness's soul?"

I stood, growling. "If I had any clue that biting Misha would bring about the rise of freaking unstoppable demons, trust me, I would've have gotten defanged."

Every head shot in my direction. Aric rose, his anger permeating through our family room like a tidal wave. He spit his words out like flaming arrows. "You returned that asshole's *soul*?"

"How the hell did you do that?" Liam asked, his amber eyes round with apparent shock.

"Forget how," Koda growled. "*Why* the hell did you do it?"

I wanted to scream. "Oh my God. It was a total accident. He pulled a piece of railing impaling me. It hurt, and I reacted by biting him. Apparently I'm some kind of . . ."

"*Dantem animam,*" Emme clarified. "A-a-according to the vampires, it's a rare ability to stimulate the return of a vampire's soul."

"We know what it is," Aric muttered. His fists clenched at his sides. "Why didn't you tell me?"

I shrugged, not comprehending why Aric appeared so betrayed. "In balancing life and death at once, Misha becomes more powerful, and therefore a threat to other masters. We agreed not to say anything so he wouldn't become a target."

"But Dan knew."

Catholic guilt had a way of pointing a chastising finger at the most inopportune moments. "Yes, Aric. He and Bren both knew."

Shayna tugged Aric's sleeve. "We didn't really know you guys yet when it happened. Danny and Bren were the only ones we could turn to to make sure nothing dangerous had happened to Celia in the process. It wasn't anything personal, Aric."

Aric's features tamed as he took in the hurt settling across my face. He lifted my hands and kissed them. "I'm sorry. I'm not angry at you. That leech is one we watch closely. I like knowing everything he's into . . . and anything that can make him more powerful."

"Especially if he's the one bringing forth the demons' rise," Koda rumbled. Koda didn't waste any time to turn the tides on Misha. I didn't like getting ganged up on. And I didn't like Misha being the go-to bad guy. "Misha is not involved in the shift of the demon realm. He's not, Aric," I insisted. "You saw him today. That thing that possessed him left him drained and vulnerable. No way would he risk his soul by associating with hell's minions."

Aric gathered me to him. "I know. As much as I'd like to find the source, I know it's not him." I tensed against him. "What's wrong, Celia?"

"What if I did it, though? What if I somehow caused this mess to occur?"

"You couldn't have, sweetness. Your heart's too pure to cause something so vile."

I wasn't so certain.

Gemini rubbed his goatee. He hadn't liked Taran's "Count Hotness" reference, but his response had nothing to do with Misha. "Celia, you didn't cause the demons to rise. Things have been brewing in the dark realm for quite some time. And from what Dan said, it preceded such an event. Correct, Dan?"

Danny nodded hard enough to make his curls bounce. "Oh yeah, absolutely."

Aric slipped his arm around my shoulders. "The supernatural world we inhabit is also changing rapidly. We have more *lones* now than ever, and Genevieve's coven has reported a rise in dark witches. My guess is that it started with the shift in the demon kingdom."

I fell against him. Knowing I wasn't the cause of an apocalypse made me feel better. I'd screwed up more times than I could count. But kick-starting Judgment Day and revving it into high gear trumped the list of major "F" ups.

Liam ambled slowly to Aric's side, his features set deep with regret as they took me in. "We should contact the Elders," he said quietly.

Aric nodded. "I'll call Martin." He walked outside to stand on the porch, the weight of protecting the earth tangible against his shoulders.

Bren slung an arm around me. "Listen, Ceel. I don't

like this shit going down. And I really hate you girls getting involved. But if I can help, you let me know, okay?"

"Okay, Bren. Thank you."

Aric's Warriors watched him carefully. As a *lone*, Bren wasn't well received by pack *weres*. But as our friend the wolves had shown him some respect. Gemini gave him a stiff nod. "Your offer is appreciated by our pack," he said quietly.

Other than a nod in return, Bren failed to answer him. "Come on, Dan. You ready to roll, or is there more fun news you'd like to share?"

Danny shut his book and stood, waving good-bye to everyone as he exited. I followed them out to the car, passing Aric, who was leaning against the porch beam. His tone was serious yet respectful, lacking the anger he'd demonstrated when speaking to Anara.

Bren tossed Danny the keys to his 1971 blue Ford Mustang. "You wanna drive?"

"Sure, I do everything else for you. Why not be your chauffeur, too?"

A slow grin eased across Bren's face. "What are you so pissed at, princess?"

Danny shoved Bren's arm, stumbling when the contact threw him off balance. Aside from Koda, at six-five, Bren was the biggest wolf I'd ever met. Danny might as well have shoved the Sphinx. He frowned. "You weren't very nice in there. If it weren't for that sweet toothless girl, we wouldn't have the knowledge about the demons we do. She's the one who, um, suggested the book. You know, afterward."

"You mean after you banged her against the Encyclopedia Britannica?" Bren threw back his head with laughter at Danny's mortified face. He patted his best friend's back, careful not to send Danny flying. "I'm sorry, Dan. I shouldn't have made fun of that toothless chick."

Danny's scowl relaxed. "Well, thank you because—"

"She must've given the best head ever."

Danny's deep blush told me that yes, maybe she had. I hugged them both good-bye and watched them pull away from the curve. Something clicked in the thick brush behind my neighbor's house, and I thought I caught a flash of light. I angled my head and took a whiff to see if I could sense anything. But the tap against the phone screen alerted me that Aric's talk with his Elder had ended.

I walked back to my house, where he waited at the top of the steps. He watched me as he shoved his iPhone into his back pocket. Gemini had brought him a pair of jeans and a black T-shirt upon his arrival. I wished then Aric had kept his sweatpants on, and nothing more. I longed to see the rippling muscles of his chest and to lie against him. I also wished I could have told him so, but of course I didn't have the guts. "Hey."

"Hi, sweetness."

We said nothing for a few beats, yet I wasn't ready to return inside. After all, we hadn't been alone since we'd arrived. So I walked up the steps and took a seat on our wide porch swing. Aric lowered himself beside me and gently pulled me to him. I sensed his hesitancy. Perhaps he couldn't anticipate how I'd react given Liam's oh-so-honest recollection of his love life.

"Your conversation with your Elder seemed to go better this time." The rhododendrons rustled beneath us, and a small bird returning to his nest chirped as it flew from the back of the house. Twilight had long since come and gone. Now nighttime ruled the land.

Aric nodded. "That was Martin, the Alpha of our Elders."

I leaned against his hard chest. My nose took in his scent of water crashing over stones and how it blended into the soft cotton fabric of his shirt. "So there's an Alpha of Alphas?"

Aric chuckled. "I guess you can say that. Native

American and *were* traditions require each pack to be governed by Elders. They consist of an Alpha, a Beta, and an Omega. Martin is a strong and righteous Leader. I've known him my whole life. He was my father's Warrior and one of the few non-*pures* powerful enough to hold the position of Elder."

I stilled. Martin came from a family of humans and wolves. The knowledge gave me hope. "Is he more understanding of . . . us?"

Disappointment broke through Aric's typically confident tone. "No. He's encouraging me to sever all contact with you."

I squeezed my lids tight, preparing for the brunt of the pain and the holding back of the tears that threatened to fall. "Does this mean things are over between us?"

Aric straightened in his seat and cupped my face with his hands. "You asked me before if I spoke French." He smiled softly at my nod. "Then I'd like you to hear me now. *Tu es belle. Je ne te laisserai pas partir.*"

My gaze dropped. The language was lovely and heated my cheeks. But I still didn't know whether our time had drawn to end. "Tell me what it means."

The shadows caused by the dim porch light strengthened Aric's features, yet his expression remained soft as it took in my visage. His light brown irises flickered, giving away the intensity behind his words. "It means you're beautiful. And that I won't let you go."

There were certain moments that would forever be ingrained in my mind. In my soul. In my heart. This was one of them. And I knew then my life would never make sense without Aric. Our lips met. Our bodies touched. And something ignited deep within me . . . and within him.

Aric gripped my hips and lifted me to straddle him. We kissed long and deep, our lungs shrieking for air as we broke apart. I dared to nibble across his jawline and, urged by my beast, to feel him. He groaned, his hands slipping into my hair. His head fell back as my teeth found a new spot to play. *"My Celia,"* he growled.

I reached the perfect little groove, just behind his left ear. It throbbed and begged me to taste it. My tongue listened and—

Aric jerked beneath me, fully aroused. I didn't know what I was doing, but it worked. So I abandoned my inhibitions and listened, really listened to what his body begged mine to do. My lips traveled against his neck, sucking, taunting, leaving little marks that faded too quickly and demanded more of my time. My hips, oh *God*. They swiveled and circled over his lap, pleading with his body to respond to mine. It did. The hard bulge of his erection pounded through his jeans, making me whimper and quickening my motions. He grunted and arched his back. It was all I could do not to unbutton his pants.

Aric tugged my T-shirt free of the waistband. A hand wandered beneath my shirt and latched onto my breast, rubbing, pulling, pinching. I wanted to scream. The ache he caused within me seemed unbearable. But when he unfastened my bra and his hot palm touched my burning flesh, I wrenched back as if scorched. No, not scorched . . . *stimulated*.

"*Aric.*"

Aric yanked me to him, driving his tongue deep in my mouth. His heart pounded against my chest. A sharp, stabbing pain hit my groin, and I started to imagine him touching me in all the right places. Never had I wanted anyone more.

I tried to stop from groaning, but I couldn't. Every time my tongue met his, waves of pleasure consumed me. My sound effects drove him wild. He growled, lifting me and stumbling across the porch with my legs fastened around his waist. The swing slammed against the siding, cracking it, but I could give a damn.

We fell against the wall, barely able to keep upright, besieged with the urge to lie down. My nipples hardened against his muscular chest as he rubbed his body harder against mine. "I want to be inside you," Aric murmured between intakes of breaths. "I want to wake up with you naked in my arms."

His arousal was so strong I could taste it. I couldn't speak. I couldn't catch my breath. All I knew was Aric and how much my body needed him.

CHAPTER 9

Aric fumbled to open the front door. I briefly heard Taran yell, "Holy *shit*!" just before he raced us upstairs.

I slammed my bedroom door shut behind us. Aric released me slowly, letting me slide against his body, letting me feel how much he wanted me. I took a step back and batted at the light switch, surrounding us in darkness.

Aric flipped the lights back on. "No," he muttered. "I want to see you. All of you."

For a moment, we just stared at each other while our chests continued to rapidly rise and fall. A scraping sound from under the door forced my gaze away from his incredible eyes. Taran swore as she shoved a roll of condoms through the crack. I bent to retrieve them and held them up for Aric to see. "We'll need these," I whispered.

Aric grabbed them from my hand and tossed them onto the bed. "Not yet." He slipped off my T-shirt. He stared at my chest, but wouldn't touch me. I reached for my unsnapped bra to tempt him. Slowly, I removed each strap, letting the whole thing fall to the floor. I then grasped his trembling hands and placed them on my breasts. My nipples hardened as he grazed them with his thumbs. I tilted my head and rolled my shoulders to encourage him. He swallowed hard and tugged on the areolas, causing a deep whimper to break through my lips.

I couldn't wait to return Aric's touch. I yanked off his shirt and dragged my nails in a soft caress across his chest. He released my breasts to unfasten my belt. I kicked off my shoes. He knelt to the floor and removed my jeans. With one finger, he hooked the crotch of my thong. I gasped when his knuckle teased the sensitive area. His eyes, heavy with want and longing, locked with mine as he tugged off my panties. I swallowed hard, shaking, unsure I'd survive the experience.

Aric remained on his knees. He placed me against the door, draping my right knee over his left shoulder. I screamed when he pushed his fingers inside me, and his tongue found the perfect spot. What had started out slow and seductive swelled into a frenzied combination of lust and eagerness. His hungry tongue circled while his fingers moved in quick ramming motions. I was helpless. All I could do was urge him on with my moans as I dug my claws deeper into the doorframe.

Aric knew when my arousal peaked and crashed in one mighty wave, but he wouldn't slow down. He intensified his motions, prolonging the experience until I collapsed limp in his arms.

Desire sparked his irises as he carried me across the room and placed me on my king-size bed. My fingers clenched his rock-hard shoulders, pulling him aggressively to meet my lips. His taste mixed with mine drove us both insane. But when he tried to lie on top of me, I wouldn't let him. I dragged myself away from his voracious mouth, rolling him onto his back and tugging off what remained of his clothes. He watched me intently as I stripped him down to his bare flesh. I licked my lips.

And then buried my face in his lap.

The length and girth of Aric's virility made it hard to

take him in my mouth. I'd never done this before, so I used his groans and growls of pleasure to guide me as I savored him. He repeatedly screamed my name, willing me to go farther and faster.

By accident, I grazed him with my teeth. My heart clenched, believing I'd hurt him. I hadn't. He went wild and crawled backward up the bed. But I wasn't done. I needed more of him, so I grabbed his hips and towed him back. Faster and faster I went, his pleasure driving me mad, and fueling my own.

All at once, he gripped my arms and hauled me away. I might have finished him, but we were both covered with sweat and couldn't slow our breaths. Yet as I looked in his eyes I knew we weren't done. No. Not yet.

Aric placed me on my back. He fumbled with a condom wrapper as we continued our deep ravenous kiss. I couldn't believe he was ready again so soon, but then again, I was, too.

My hands fisted the comforter when Aric tried to enter me. He glanced down when he was unsuccessful and adjusted my hips. He tried again, but once more, was ineffective. He regarded me closely, confusion wrinkling his brow. I turned away, worried and frightened my lack of experience would ruin our moment.

Aric touched my chin and moved me back to face him. He smiled softly but didn't say anything. He kissed me, gently at first, then more seductively. As I responded to him, the fire we'd had during our foreplay caught and electrified our skin once more.

I tried to relax, but it was difficult. I didn't want to disappoint Aric. He tried once more and was able to enter. Slowly, he pushed into me, driving me over the edge with anticipation. The more he advanced, the more my body accepted his. My sharp nails pierced through the covers and into the mattress. My heart threatened to explode. My God, I needed him so much.

Aric struggled for breath once he finished filling me. As he withdrew, deep groans escaped our lips. I was already tender, but the ache mixed with bliss momentarily blinded me.

Aric gasped. "Am I hurting you?"

"No, please don't stop," I begged.

Aric gradually increased his rhythm. The yearning as we explored each other's bodies became all-consuming. He moved us in countless positions. I welcomed them wholeheartedly, desperate to learn, desperate to indulge, wanting so much to enhance his revelry and mine.

Finally Aric placed me on my hands and knees. Maybe it was a wolf thing. Whatever it was, I didn't care. I just knew it intensified the experience and made me scream. He pleased me so intensely, but I wanted to please *him*. I pushed my back against his chest, turning my hips in circles against his lap.

Aric kissed and licked my neck. His left hand reached around to play with my nipples. His right traveled down my stomach to rub that entrancing spot. I screamed again, and clamped down. A long deep grumble vibrated hard in his throat. He liked me tightening around him. So I repeated my motions again and again.

Ecstasy had already claimed me multiple times, but I didn't want to stop despite my exhaustion. So I forced myself to continue while Aric urged me on with his hips. And then it happened; complete and utter rapture cloaked us one last time.

Aric fell on the bed, dragging me with him. I was glad my back was still to him as stupid tears trickled down my face. I didn't understand why I cried. I thought it was from all the pleasure we'd shared. Whatever the reason, I wished I could stop. My vulnerability completely embarrassed me. I clasped my hand over my eyes, praying our heavy breathing would be enough to distract him.

Aric swept my sweat-soaked hair behind me and kissed my shoulder. "Are you ready?" he panted.

I didn't want him to separate us, but I nodded regardless. He withdrew, forcing our bodies to shudder. My lids closed tight. Our parting had affected him, too.

Aric lifted me and tucked me beneath the cool sheets, joining me once he put out the lights. I turned to face him when my tears finally ceased to fall. But he knew. Of course he knew. He kissed my eyelids sweetly and rubbed the last drying tear away with his thumb.

"You okay?" he whispered.

"Yes."

"Are you sure?"

I leaned in and kissed him, then laid my face and arm across his broad chest. He held me close and stroked my back with tenderness unbefitting such a powerful male. I discovered the reason for my tears before I drifted off to sleep.

I love you, Aric.

Sunlight hit my face from the crack in the blinds. I slowly opened my eyes to meet Aric's grin. He'd gotten his wish; he'd awoke with me naked in his arms. I returned his smile, still amazed he lay in my bed. His messy hair hung over his light brown eyes, and his five o'clock shadow had darkened into a thin beard. He looked sleepy.

He also looked sexy as hell.

"Good morning, sweetness."

"Hi, wolf."

I climbed on top of Aric, our lips immediately meeting. Good heavens, he tasted so good.

The rising pressure between my legs made me jerk. I tilted my leg and peeked below our covers. Turned out, Aric was extremely happy to see me. He smiled with slight embarrassment before reaching for a condom. I took it from him and disappeared beneath the sheets.

*   *   *

"Sorry about last night," I told him.

We lay facing each other as he played with our intertwined fingers. "I don't want you to be sorry about anything you did last night. I know I'm not."

I smiled and gave him a small kiss. *My God. I really do love you.*

"I don't mean to be an asshole," he said after a moment, "but can I ask why you're not on the pill?"

I hadn't expected this talk so soon, and I supposed my rising temperature announced that loud and clear. "Aric, I'm not—well, I mean, I wasn't sexually active. I've only had two lovers. There was no reason for me to be on it."

Aric lifted his head from the pillow. "I'm only your *third* lover?"

I squirmed against him to hide my blush. "I meant two, counting you."

Aric gripped my shoulders and pulled me away from him. He seemed to piece the puzzles of the night's events together—my timidity, his difficulty penetrating, and likely my tears. Understanding spread across his face, softening his features until his brows knitted into a deep frown. "Why didn't you tell me? We could have taken things slow." He huffed. "And I sure as hell would have been more gentle."

I shook my head, perspiration building between my breasts. "You were gentle. And trust me, I didn't want to take things slow."

Aric's voice deepened. "That makes two of us."

He drew me to him. I traced a line along the ridges of his muscles, smiling diffidently when I focused on his nipple. I'd finally gotten to taste it, and more, last night. "I thought we were going to, you know, make love sooner. But things always seemed to stop before they could get going."

"Like the first night we slept together?"

I tilted my head upward, surprised he brought it up. "Yeah. Like that night."

Aric's hand slipped down to my backside, sending goose bumps across the length of my back. "I was already getting a lot of shit from my Elders about associating with you. But when they scented your aroma and our passion on the night we first kissed, Martin told me to keep my distance. I didn't like it. As my Alpha, though, I felt compelled to heed his words." He kissed the top of my head. "Except things weren't so simple. You got hurt and almost died. And even though Emme healed you, I couldn't bear to leave you that night. So I stayed. I kept telling myself I'd leave when you woke. But the longer I was with you, the more I wanted you, and the more Martin's orders haunted my thoughts." He sighed. "My loyalties to my pack tell me I should obey my Alpha. But I can't. You've been impossible to resist, Celia."

I bit my bottom lip, trying to keep from crying. I'd finally fallen in love, but it wasn't enough, and wasn't so easy. "My selfless side wants to tell you to obey your Elders. But I can't."

Aric's jaw tightened. "Then don't."

My arms slipped around his waist. "What will they do to you for being with me?"

"There's no law saying I can't be with you."

But from what Bren had once explained, pack loyalties and blood bonds ran deeper than laws. I rested my head against him, and asked God to keep him safe from his kind.

Aric's hand massaged my backside. "You know, I was starting to think you didn't want me."

I blinked back at him. "You can't be serious."

Aric tugged on my bottom lip with his teeth. "Celia, when you wouldn't look at me yesterday after I *changed* back, I questioned whether you even found me attractive."

"Mmm. You're right. Your dreamy eyes, sexy grin, and eight-pack abs never did it for me. Neither did your rock-size muscles and long, powerful legs." I failed to mention his fine ass, tight enough to snap twigs, but that was a given. "Are you crazy? How could you not know how bad I wanted you?"

Aric flashed his sexy grin. "Then why didn't you ask me to spend the night sooner?"

My smile faded. "Because I didn't know how."

The humor dissolved from his face. He cuddled me closer. "Now you do," he whispered.

I guess I did. But the evolution of our relationship brought up other issues. Issues I suddenly didn't feel so bashful addressing. "I can start taking the pill if you want me to."

Aric stilled as the aroma of his arousal claimed the air around us. "It would be nice to feel you completely when we make love. But I don't want to pressure you. I'll let you make that decision." He climbed on top of me. I moaned when his lips tickled me across the jawline. "Last night was the best night of my life," he murmured when he reached my ear.

With that, we made use of our last condom.

CHAPTER 10

My pace slowed as I reached the bottom of the stairs and approached the kitchen. Silence in a house occupied by women yappier than Shih tzus was always a bad sign. Despite the comforting smells of eggs and bacon filling the house, I knew I was doomed before I entered the kitchen.

Shayna bounced with her arms crossed, grinning ear to ear. Her long black ponytail swung behind her like a puppy dog's tail. Taran sat at the table smiling wickedly as she stirred her tea. Emme waited next to her. I hadn't even said anything yet, but there she sat, blushing away.

Shayna flung an arm around me and erupted into a fit of giggles. "What's wrong, dude? Up all night?"

"Apparently he was, too," Taran added, her siren grin exceptionally wide.

I rubbed at my crimson face. "I guess you heard us."

"Damn, girl, of course we did." Taran laughed. "It sounded like you were watching Animal Planet." She leaned her chin against her palm. "Did you do it as beasts? Please tell me, I must know."

"Of course not!"

"Well, you could have fooled us." Shayna affectionately punched my shoulder. "Taran activated a silencing spell around your room so we could get some sleep." She threw her arms in the air. "It was like you were watching porn—well, the good kind anyway. I swear, Ceel, all you needed was the boom-chooka-boom-boom sound track!"

I rammed a muffin in her mouth when I heard Aric coming down the stairs, knowing he heard her. Good Lord. I put sewing her lips shut on my to-do list. *"Zip. It,"* I hissed.

Shayna spit out a large piece of muffin in time for Aric to appear. "Hi, Aric," she and Taran sang.

Aric blushed slightly but walked over to embrace me. He then led us to our large wooden table and pulled me onto his lap when he sat, no doubt so I could shield him from my sisters.

He cleared his throat. "Good morning, ladies."

"We have breakfast for you guys," Emme said quietly. She wouldn't look at us when she brought over our plates. I guessed she feared we'd have sex on the table or something.

I dug into the food, feeling the heat creep into my cheeks. "Where are Koda and Liam?"

The sparkle vanished from Shayna's grin. "Hunting. They left early this morning."

My grip tightened around my fork. "Oh?"

Aric finished swallowing and wiped his mouth. "Paul picked up on a trail west of Truckee. They have to cover a thirty-mile radius. Koda and Liam were to relieve them at dawn. Gem and I are taking over at noon."

"Can I go with you?"

Aric shook his head. "After what happened yesterday, I don't think it's a good idea, sweetness."

I started to protest, but Shayna cut me off. "I was all set to go, too, Ceel. But Koda wouldn't let me." She shrugged. "We had our first fight about it."

Aric leaned back in his chair, keeping his hand tight

against my hip. "Shayna, you didn't see the big guy's re-action when he heard you scream. He totally lost it and I need his head in the game." He smiled at her softly. "Try to understand. He doesn't want to see the woman he loves get hurt."

Tears welled in Shayna's beautiful blue eyes. She played with the ties of her tunic. "Koda loves me?"

Aric pushed the eggs around on his plate. "Yeah. He does."

Shayna rushed to sit on the chair next to him and scooted closer. "Did he tell you that?"

Aric shook his head. "I know him well enough to see it. Look, I shouldn't have said anything. I'm out of line."

Too bad for Shayna, Aric wasn't Liam. He would have sung like a werecanary. She latched onto Aric's wrist when he tried to take another bite. "Dude. You can't tell a girl the wolf of her dreams loves her and then go back to eating waffles. If it's true, why hasn't Koda told me?"

Aric rested his arm against the table as he contem-plated what to say. "Life hasn't always been this good to Koda. It's easier for him to be hard and silent than to express what he's feeling on the inside. He'll tell you soon enough."

Shayna pursed her lips. "And if he doesn't?"

Aric's voice grew quiet. "Just give it time."

The seriousness that replaced his pleasant demeanor signaled an abrupt end to their conversation. And as much as Shayna liked to tease and taunt, she never meant any harm. She released his wrist. "I'm sorry, Aric. I didn't mean to put you in the middle."

The corner of Aric's mouth curved into a grin. "It's okay. Just know he's only watching out for you."

His eyes cut to me then, but he didn't say anything. I bent slightly to whisper in his ear, "Are you all right?"

Aric kissed my cheek. "Yeah. Just hungry, baby, and I have a long day ahead."

Taran sat next to me. "Not to mention the poor bastard hardly got any shut-eye."

I threw my fork down when Shayna burst into giggles. "Don't make me kill you in front of Aric."

Taran flashed me another siren grin, yet was kind enough to cut me some slack. Aric surprised me by chuckling. We finished our food and had two more helpings, but then it was time for him to go.

Aric held my hand as I followed him out to the Escalade. The sun brightened the late morning, bringing forth a clear and warm sixty-degree day. Birds sang, and the first orchestra of crickets played their sweet song. A lovely spring day, only to be polluted by a nasty scowl from Mrs. Mancuso. 'Cause God forbid she'd let me bask in my post-making-love-to-Aric glory.

She knelt, tending to the red tulips she'd planted between her creepy lawn gnomes. A wide-brim hat covered her tight curls, a yellow jacket fell over her paisley muumuu, and stiff middle fingers lurked beneath bright pink gardening gloves, waiting to strike. Mrs. Mancuso had accused my sisters and me of "besmirching" the neighborhood, but I think the gnomes and the lawn jockey with the lazy eye had done that long before we moved in.

Aric laughed when he saw her and led me to the driver's side of his SUV. "Come on. We'll use my car to hide behind so I can give you a proper good-bye."

And he did, with a long, deep kiss. "Will you come back tonight?"

Aric kept his hands on my hips. "I want to. But depending on what happens, and what we find, I might not be able to." He kissed me once more. "I'll call you later, okay?"

"Okay. Be careful."

I stepped onto the sidewalk and waited until Aric's Escalade disappeared out of the development. I turned to go back in the house, just to come face-to-face with Mrs. Mancuso. For a woman in her eighties, she moved like a shadow. Normally humans gave me ample space, sensing my predator lurking beneath. Cataracts, apparently, were my tigress's kryptonite. Since Mrs. Mancuso couldn't see well, she probably couldn't detect my formidable beast. I smiled as best I could and tried to be nice. "Good morning, Mrs. Mancuso. Your tulips look beautiful—"

"I saw what you did to that boy, Celia Wird." She pointed her dirty little hand shovel in my face. "You ought to be ashamed of yourself."

My body heated, but no way was I going to let the old crow make me feel bad. This was love, damn it. I lifted my chin so we were at eye level. "Aric is my boyfriend now, Mrs. Mancuso. He was just kissing me good-bye."

Her droopy lids narrowed over hazy blue eyes. "I meant on the porch. Last night."

On the porch . . . ? I clasped my hands over my mouth, trying to muffle a scream. Mrs. Mancuso had seen me straddling Aric. Oh. *God.* Okay, maybe her vision wasn't all that bad. I swallowed hard, gathering my courage. If I were Taran, I'd accuse her of being jealous, and insist she find some guy in a walker to hump and leave me the hell alone. But I wasn't Taran. I was very much me. So I raced into the house, trying not to shriek.

So much for my formidable beast.

Taran glanced up from her tea. "What the hell's wrong with you?"

"Nothing."

"Harlot!" Mrs. Mancuso screamed from outside.

"For shit's sake, lady, just die already!" Taran hollered back without missing a beat. She rolled her eyes and took a sip of her tea. "If only the good die young, that old fart is going to live forever."

Emme poked her head out the window. "My good-ness, I can't believe arthritis hasn't claimed her middle fingers by now."

Taran huffed. "That's because she gets so much damn use out of them." She flipped Emme off a few times. "See, it keeps them flexible."

Emme frowned. "That's not a nice gesture, Taran." She glanced out the window, her eyes widening. "And neither was that one."

I poured myself some chai tea and took a seat next to Taran. Shayna and Emme grabbed two more mugs and followed suit. Shayna grinned. "Celia has a boyfriend," she sang.

I held the mug tightly in my hands, wishing so much hostility didn't surround my new relationship with Aric. "Aric is going against his pack by being with me."

The good humor my sisters demonstrated at seeing Aric with me faded quickly as reality sank in. Romeo and Juliet had it rough. But Romeo didn't face the wrath of fangs, fur, and magic.

Shayna draped her arm around my shoulder and gave me a one-arm hug. "Koda told me. He also said Aric has no intention of turning his back on you."

"Did he mention what could happen to Aric for dis-obeying his Elders?"

Shayna turned her head. "Not exactly."

I frowned. "What did he say?" Shayna slipped her arm off me but didn't answer. "Shayna, please tell me."

Shayna regarded me closely, appearing torn. "Being with a non-*pure*, especially one who's not even *were*, sort of soils his reputation."

My insides twisted. "I'm *soiling* Aric's reputation?"

Shayna reached for me. "Ceel, this is not your fault. Aric's pack doesn't know or understand what we are, and I think it scares them. Koda, Liam, Gemini — it's different for them. They're not of pure blood; they don't have to follow the same rules."

I gawked at Shayna, not knowing what to say. Aric openly defied his Elders by being with me. That was bad enough. But to know his status had plummeted because of me broke my heart. I buried my face in my hands, hating my "weirdness" more than ever. "I can't stand anyone looking down on him. And I can't stand being the cause."

Shayna's thin arms embraced me, the extent of her concern showing through the way she clutched me. "Ceel . . . you've waited so long for someone like Aric. Don't let those haters take that away from you. Just be with each other, enjoy each other. The other stuff, it's just not worth it."

Emme's soft hand stroked my hair. "They just don't know you, sweetie. I'm sure with time they'll see how wonderful you are and accept you completely."

Emme's head consisted of cotton candy houses and kittens wearing pajamas.

Taran slammed her palm on the table. "You know what? *Screw. Them.* If Aric doesn't give a shit what his Elders say, then damn it, neither should you."

I didn't agree. Aric's anger at Anara demonstrated he very much cared. While he didn't hold Anara in the same regard he held Martin, Anara's remarks had affected him. So had Martin's insistence that he break all contact with me. Except instead of listening to his Elders' commands, Aric had chosen to spend the night with me. In words, and the way his body had moved against mine, Aric had pledged his commitment to me. I thought of Aric's touch, his grin, and how he had so easily found his way into my heart, despite the walls my beast had secured to protect us. If Aric faced danger at the hands of his pack, he would do so with me at his side. I loved him. I did. And I'd be a fool to let him go.

The ceramic yellow mug cooled in my hands before I spoke again. "You're right. If Aric wants to be with me, I'm not going to stop him."

"That's our girl!" Shayna lifted her tea. "To Celia, and her hottie big, bad wolf."

Taran winked my way. "It's been a long time coming, Ceel."

Emme hit her cup against mine. "And to good times ahead."

I hadn't quite taken a sip of my tea when Shayna's cell phone rang. She grinned when she saw who called. "Hi, puppy," she answered cheerfully.

Koda's voice lacked the same enthusiasm. "We located the couple."

Shayna's eyes swept to me, knowing I could hear. "Are they all right?"

"No. We found them in pieces."

CHAPTER 11

Pitbull's music usually made me want to dance. Not tonight. I barely registered the beat, despite how the heavy bass thrummed hard enough to shake my seat. My eyes wandered toward the front doors of the club, searching for any signs of Aric.

Gemini's calm voice drew me back to our booth. "Don't worry, Celia. He'll be here soon." Gem sat next to Taran, close, but not quite touching. An amazing feat on his part considering the tiny red dress she'd squeezed her perfect curves into.

Koda and Shayna had taken advantage of the open area on the dance floor. It was still early in the night. The club hoppers had just slowly begun to trickle in. Yet the anticipation of Aric's arrival slowed the minutes, slowed the seconds. He'd promised to show tonight, just like he had every night for the past several days. But every night I'd arrive home from the hospital expecting him to be there, only to be disappointed.

"I'm sorry, sweetness," he'd called last night to say. "Every time I try to leave, we get a new lead I have to act on."

"It's all right," I answered. But each day that passed

made me think things were definitely not all right. It had begun with that mutilated couple. Slowly, more and more bodies of men were being unearthed from desolate locations in both California and Nevada. The packs from each respective state had banded together. Giving Aric's prestige, he led or organized the majority of the hunts. Yet every decaying corpse they found had perished over a period of weeks. No fresh leads. No survivors. Nothing to explain what was happening.

My eyes scanned the area, taking in a group of males ogling three young women at the bar while their shy, awkward friend focused on her drink as if it somehow had the power to make her prettier, wittier, or maybe just a little more desirable. Before we met the wolves, I was frequently the odd gal out on the town—ignored by the hunky guys drooling over my sisters and left to chat with the designated driver about his ongoing bout with acne, if he bothered to speak to me at all. I knew how the young lady felt. It was all I could do not to collectively slap the little punks upside their overly gelled heads. She probably had a lot to offer, if they'd just give her a chance to see the real her.

I tugged at the bottom of my chic little pale blue dress, a recent purchase to look nice for Aric. So much had changed since I'd met him. Yet despite reaching a deeper level of physical intimacy with him, I remained that girl. And as I saw her glance hopefully at the male closest to her, maybe I always would.

The males of "Bad Dates Past" snubbed me out of fear, and their collective desire to lure my sisters to bed. The wolves didn't snub, and they sure as hell didn't fear. They embraced me as part of their group, though I couldn't comprehend why. Was it due to their pack mentality, my connection with Aric, or just the fact that they were kind despite their preternatural instincts to maim and kill? As I watched the behemoth Koda embrace

Shayna with total adoration, I smiled and leaned toward the latter.

My smile faded as more minutes passed. I hoped Aric wasn't having second thoughts or that his Elders weren't overworking him to both punish and keep him away from me. The wolves must have sensed my worry and longing. Koda bought me another beer. Gemini included me in their conversations, and Liam—well, he tried.

He adjusted his arm around Emme. His opposite hand rubbed the top of his head, spiking his short blond tips to frightened porcupine proportions. "Did Aric tell you we're hunting elk this summer?"

I shook my head, both because he hadn't and, well, because I didn't want to hear the deets.

"We're heading to Idaho." He grinned like a kid posing for his Little League picture. "There's nothing like feeling the vertebrae of a seven-hundred-pound bull crunch like popcorn between your fangs."

"Mmm." I nodded. "I'll bet."

"And you know what the best part is, Celia?"

No. And please don't tell me.

"We can snack on one all day and still bag more to bring home!" He jutted his chin proudly. "Blood makes good gravy."

Emme stiffened against him. I couldn't be sure because of flashing club lights, but something told me her skin hadn't been green when we'd first walked in. Liam gave her a wink. "Don't worry, angel. I promise to bring you back the heart."

"The *heart*?" Taran's tone sounded more annoyed than sickened. "What could she possibly want with a goddamn elk heart?"

Liam frowned. "Sandwiches."

Emme inched her way out of the booth. Yep. She was definitely green. I leaned forward. "Are you okay, Emme?"

Her lips puckered into a grimace. "I just need some air."

I started to follow, but Liam slipped out. "It's okay, Celia. I'll go with her."

Because that's what Emme needed—more tales of blood and entrails. "Hey, Liam. Have you asked Emme about her day?" Liam shook his head. "Maybe you should." I smiled when he gave me the thumbs-up. Good thing for Emme it didn't take much to distract Liam. I watched them until they disappeared through the side emergency exit. Patrons weren't allowed to step through the door, but only a masochistic bouncer would confront Liam. Like me, the wolves naturally leaked the "don't make me eat you" vibe and pretty much ran whatever territory they occupied. I stared at the door as it closed behind them, hoping Aric would magically appear.

Gemini quietly interrupted my thoughts. "I don't think Aric is going hunting."

I rolled the beer bottle in my hands. "Why? Liam makes it sound like a good time."

Gemini's dark almond eyes brightened as he rubbed his goatee. "Because he doesn't like being away from you. He's had a difficult week without you."

My gaze dropped. I'd killed things. Lots of things. Most times, quite brutally. But I wasn't cold-blooded. And I carried remorse like a second skin. Humans found me intimidating—scary even. Yet those few who knew me—really knew me—would not have been surprised by my blush.

"I hope you're right," I said almost silently.

Taran placed her hand on Gemini's shoulder, igniting a blue spark beneath her fingertips. Her irises blanched from blue to white, then back again, affected by the strength of Gemini's wolf. "What about you? Are you going?" Her smile and tone carried a spark of their own.

I thought for sure Gemini would beg to bask in her awe-someness.

I thought wrong.

Gem gawked at her palm like she'd slapped a dead rat on his shoulder. "Ah . . ."

Taran dropped her hand, and slumped her typically ideal posture. Aric had made Gemini his Beta based on his strong leadership skills and his ability to make thought-provoking statements.

Yeah. Right.

I took a sip of my beer and almost choked on it when Emme screamed. I bolted across the dance floor toward the side exit, Koda and Gem at my heels. The door flew off its hinges as I crashed through. The alley extended into the next lot, where a new restaurant was currently under construction and where Emme's screams turned from terrified to pained.

Gemini and Koda rushed toward her cries. "Stay behind us!" Gem ordered.

Screw that!

My hair whipped behind me as I bolted through the alley, my claws and massive fur-lined body shredding through my new dress as I *changed*. My tigress form skidded around the corner and into the half-erected building, taking everything in in a single glance. A pile of vampires slashed into Liam near a freshly mortared brick wall. He wasn't fighting back. His four-hundred-pound wolf form curled around Emme, shielding her from the vampire's razor-sharp nails.

My paws dug into the concrete, propelling my body into a wide leap to tackle three of the vampires skewering Liam. Blood spewed as I clawed out the first one's heart and the wolves dismembered the first of their prey.

I faced the other two, my fangs snapping and itching to bite. Something flew past me, severing their heads before I could strike. Shayna had flung a razor-sharp sphere she'd converted from a metal trash lid. She spun with a dancer's grace, driving Misha's elongated hairpin into the chest of a vampire leaping from the second story.

I nudged her back with my rump and knocked a she-vamp's head clear from her shoulders just as a wave of electrified energy stroked my fur in the opposite direction. Taran had stumbled through the opening in her ankle-breaking shoes, throwing streams of blue and white lightning like javelins and jolting three vampires to cinders.

The skeleton frame of the building rattled as Koda collided with an enormous vampire. His large red wolf sank his fangs into a vamp's neck, tearing his jugular open. The vampire's blood splattered like rain against the support beams before converting into ash as the droplets dribbled down the thick metal.

My claws had burrowed into the stomach of another vamp when I caught sight of one stalking toward Emme. I chuffed loudly to draw attention, but she failed to acknowledge me, crying as she cradled Liam's limp human form against her. I abandoned my kill and rushed toward her. Before I could reach her, Emme slammed a forklift into the vamp with her *force*, crushing his chest inward and instantly destroying his heart. She'd used her anger to react, all the while whispering to Liam that she loved him and begging him not to leave her.

I edged backward, my animal instincts alert for the next attack. Two more vampires circled Gemini. But when his wolf sprouted a second head, and a new wolf leapt from his body, the odds evened and body parts flew through the air like hail. To anger a two-wolf being was to meet a bloody and painful death.

We formed a circle around Emme and Liam as the scent of vampire saturated the open area. Dozens more leapt down from the support beams, hissing. My head jerked around. Where were all these vampires coming from? But there was no time to question, only to act.

Shayna lifted a discarded shovel in her hands. As she twirled she transformed the scoop into a deadly blade and sliced off the head of the closest vampire. Liam howled, his pain resonating through his fury. I roared and attacked—his injuries were severe. We needed to get him to safety to give Emme and his wolf time to heal him.

I leapt onto two vampires, my urgency to help Liam making me exceptionally vicious. My back paws held one while my fangs severed through the other's neck. His blood and remains mixed to form a nasty paste, temporarily blinding me and giving another vampire time to jump onto my back. My body was stronger and tougher than an average tiger's, but it didn't make me invulnerable. The vampire hacked into my hide while another carved into my chest.

I surrendered to my tigress and set free the beast that didn't recognize remorse—only survival. She clawed and chewed, ripping several vampires completely in half. The legs of one kicked sporadically in the air until I dug out the heart of the body it belonged to.

Two other vampires surrounded Shayna. Both attacked at once. She stabbed one through the heart at the same time she flung a spike into the eye of the other. We fought hard, but there were too many vampires and not enough of us. I knew this. And thankfully, so did Taran.

Blue and white flames encased Taran as her magic built into a small inferno. Her irises went white as she fell into a deep trance. I roared to get the others' attention. This time it was Emme's turn to shield Liam. She clasped her hand over his eyes and curved her body against his.

The explosion of light was more nuclear bomb than flash of lightning. Spots danced before me when my lids finally blinked open. Only clumps of ash remained. Taran's magic-born sunlight obliterated the vampires, but it cost her. She collapsed to her knees, all magicked out. Gem's two halves rejoined as they raced to her. The moment he reached her, Gem *changed* back and lifted her sagging body in his arms. "Don't worry. Nothing will hurt you," he promised her softly.

Taran's lids fluttered. She was safe. Liam conversely looked like hell. Chunks of shredded muscle exposed the bones of his back. It would take his wolf several hours to heal him. That is, if he didn't have Emme. My youngest sister's pale yellow light surrounded Liam, healing and knitting his ravaged flesh closed until only shiny, new skin remained. He stumbled to his knees and yanked her to him. "I love you, too, angel," he stammered hoarsely.

Flashing lights alerted us to the arrival of South Tahoe's finest. A crowd had gathered where the restaurant opened to the street. I couldn't blame them, really. Shattered bricks from the building, piles of ash, broken boards and bolt fixtures strewn the concrete floor. And let's not forget the six people covered in blood, three who were naked, and—oh yeah, the three-hundred-and seventy-pound tigress.

We all tensed except for Taran. She moaned a little as a wisp of blue and white smoke trailed from her core toward the now screaming crowd of onlookers. The mist expanded, permeating through the crowd just as the police drew their weapons.

"There's nothing to see, there's nothing to see," Taran mumbled. "Go about your business, there's nothing to see."

The clicks from safeties releasing and the barrels aimed at me had me backing into the wall. Taran turned up what little energy she had and mixed it with a whole lot of royal pissed-offness. She tipped her head in Gem's arms, clenching her pearly whites. "There's nothing to see. There's nothing to see. For shit's sake, go about your business, there's nothing to see!"

Slowly, the crowd dispersed. A police officer radioed to report a false alarm. We were in the clear, yet Taran's cover did nothing to squelch the scent of anger and fear rising in the wolves. Koda took Shayna's hand as he hurried to Gemini. "Do you feel anything?" he asked him.

Gemini's grave face hardened. "Nothing."

Shayna's head whipped back and forth between them. "What's wrong?"

Koda sighed, his deep brown eyes darkening. "Something's happened to Aric."

CHAPTER 12

I *changed* behind a stack of cinder blocks, quickly yanking on the long cardigan Shayna tossed me. "How do you know? Is he hurt? Is he—"

My words caught in my throat and squeezed. Koda placed his hand on my arm, but I jerked back, feeling the confines of the demolished room closing in around me. Koda scented my alarm and spoke quickly. "Liam *called* for Aric in his howl. He told him we were under attack— and that you were with us. There's no way he wouldn't have come knowing you were in danger." He closed his eyes and shook his head, his long black hair swaying against the length of his broad back. "Even now I don't sense him anywhere near us."

Gemini stroked Taran's hair away from her face as he held her against him. "We have to find him. I'll take the girls and Liam back to the house and join you as soon as I'm able."

"I'm going with you." My half growl, half psycho Latina tone left no question I meant business. The wolves surprised me by not arguing. Gem nodded with approval while Emme rushed to heal the gashes on my back already soaking through Shayna's white sweater.

"I'm coming, too," Liam insisted.

Gemini's voice remained calm, but resolute. "No. You're too weak from the speed in which Emme and your wolf healed you. You're to stay with the girls. Let Emme care for you. When you've regained enough of your strength, you can help us search for Aric." Gem looked to Shayna, his voice growing softer. "May I count on you to watch over Taran?"

Shayna squeezed Koda's hand as she answered, "You know I will."

"Go with them," Gemini said.

I wasn't sure who he meant until his black wolf sprang from his back like the pull of a wax strip.

Gemini the wolf stared out one of the darkened windows, his gigantic black form taking up most of the length of Koda's leathered backseat. I'd raced half-naked down the street to retrieve Koda's silver Yukon. Upon screeching to the stop near the alley, I quickly slid into the passenger seat and let Koda take the wheel, knowing I was in no condition to drive. My body shook, despite wearing the extra pair of sweats Koda had given me before tugging on a pair of his own.

Koda raced around the streets of South Tahoe's club district, his window cracked in hopes of picking up Aric's scent. "We'll find him, Celia."

I noticed Koda didn't state how we'd find him. But wolves weren't known for lying or for false reassurance. I tried to slow my breathing. It didn't work. My panic for Aric's safety beat my heart against my ribs, threatening to call forth my beast. The thought of losing him accelerated my racing pulse and forced my claws to protrude and retract, over and over until the tips of my fingers ached from the effort. We'd become so close in such a short period, it couldn't all end now.

After a few more sweeps and some swearing, Koda

abandoned the streets and jumped on 89. Gemini growled with equal frustration. I stared out toward the lake, and prayed silently for Tahoe's power to somehow guide us to Aric. The lake didn't answer. I wasn't Misha. I hadn't learned to harness the lake's power. But since in a way I viewed it as a friend, you'd think the watery bastard would have tossed me a bone.

I rubbed my hands together. "Does your link to him as his Warrior tell you anything?"

"Only that he still lives. His death would destroy a piece of my heart."

I wrapped my arms tight around myself, knowing exactly what he meant.

Koda's phone rang, making me startle. "We found him," a voice announced on the other end. "It's not good. Trace my signal—"

Koda's eyes cut to me. "I'm on it."

Koda stayed on 89 until he veered sharply onto the abandoned housing development Whispering Woods. I'd read about this place in the paper. The contractor had purchased it and then lost all his money in a bad investment. Only a handful of houses had gone up before the owner had abandoned ship, leaving his employees out of work and his investors demanding his head on a platter. I rolled down the window, trying to track Aric's scent and unable to keep still. Mud smeared the new road in streaks, and weeds had started to overtake the lots. In the nearing distance, I heard Aric's enraged snarl.

Koda's grip to my wrist kept me from leaping out. "Celia. There are other *weres* present. Don't go off without us."

My head jerked from him back to the open window. "I don't care about them."

"We do. Our presence will keep them from attacking you. I can't make that same promise if you show up without us. Aric's hurt. They'll sense your predator side as a threat to him."

I nodded but barely managed to keep my tigress from leaping out the window.

We passed through four more blocks before a row of SUVs finally came into view. A *were* with a long beard and sporting a leather jacket waved us in to where a mob of *weres* stood with their backs turned. They didn't bother to face us. Either they knew Aric's Warriors had arrived or what held their attention was far more important.

The headlights of Aric's Escalade illuminated a two-story Colonial littered with pine needles and clumps of ash. The driver's-side door was wrenched open, evidently left the way it had been found. An overturned EMT vehicle rested to the left of Aric's SUV, the back doors barely attached to the hinges and smeared with gray wolf fur and blood—*Aric*'s fur and blood.

And that's when my heart stopped beating.

Koda and Gemini sprang from the Yukon. The scent of spilled gasoline burned my nose, and the cool night breeze slapped my face as I shoved the door open. But it was the thunder of Aric's growls that had me jetting behind the wolves.

The crowd of *weres* that easily parted for Koda and Gemini became an impenetrable wall of bodies the second I neared. "Let me through." My voice should have spewed all the anger and terror coursing through me. Instead it softened and shook, revealing nothing but my fear for Aric.

"Not your business, cat," the same leather-clad *were* spit the moment he caught my scent.

"But I'm—" What? The girl he'd slept with? I cleared my throat. "Aric's friend."

A werecheetah dressed in a slinky gold dress quirked an eyebrow. "Aren't we all?" she whispered in a breathy tone that told me more than I wanted to know.

I scanned the area for a possible opening, only to fix on the pale skin of the very still and very dead human to my far right. Droplets of blood stained his white T-shirt. His jeans and underwear had been ripped off. Only a tattered piece of denim remained attached to one ankle. He lay spread-eagle on the asphalt near the driver's-side door of his blue Ford Focus—well, had the door remained attached. The dented clump of metal dumped on an empty lot was all that remained. Claw marks caved the roof in, and clumps of blond extensions littered the passenger-side seat.

What the . . . ?

Another howl of agony had me lunging at the crowd of *weres*. I managed to bust through the cheetah in the gold dress and another female, only to be forced back by the rest of the group.

Koda's deep voice shouted over my growls, *"Let her through!"*

The *weres* abruptly released me as Koda appeared, his glare parting the crowd like the slice of a machete. He extended his hand. "Come, Celia. Aric wants you."

Koda was offering me more than his hand. He was making it clear I was to be left alone, or else. I took it quite willingly and allowed him to lead me through. I hurried behind him only to stop short when I caught sight of Aric.

He lay on a makeshift bed of particleboards elevated by stone pavers, an old army blanket covering his naked and writhing form. My free hand clasped over my mouth to suppress my gasp. Aric's normally golden skin had darkened to a sickly gray, and a waterfall of sweat cascaded down the muscles of his back. About six gaping holes punctured along the length of his spine. I felt my head spinning and I barely grasped onto the realization that he still lived.

Koda's hold barely kept me upright. What could only

be described as a gold, two-pronged meat hook with barbs pierced through Aric's right shoulder and out his back. Blood and pus oozed from the openings where the cursed gold poisoned his body. No wonder he suffered; the gold mimicked acid coursing through his veins. I tore away from Koda and dashed toward Aric, falling to my knees before him.

My hands pushed his sweat-soaked hair from his clouded brown eyes. My God, his skin was on fire.

"Celia," he panted.

"I'm here. Don't worry, we're going to help you."

His lids shut tight with pain, but he inhaled deep to take in my scent. "You're hurt. I can smell your blood."

I stroked his cheek with my thumb. "We ran into trouble, but it's taken care of." Aric jerked his head, and tried to rise. I held tight to his arm. "I'm fine, Aric. I swear it. Please lie down." Aric slowly lowered, groaning with each small movement. My eyes fixed on Koda. "Tell me what to do."

The moment Koda approached, Aric let out a growl that sent every hair on my arm to quivering beneath my skin.

Koda stepped back. "Aric was shot with six gold bullets through his chest. They've been cut out." He motioned to Aric's shoulder. "The barbs go through the length of the hooks, making them harder to remove. The curse from the gold is rushing through his bloodstream. His beast is, well, *pissed* and trying to protect Aric from further harm. If you can keep his wolf calm long enough, we can wrench out the damn hooks."

I blinked back at Koda as Aric released another toe-curling growl. Our recent sexual encounter aside, Aric barely knew me. And his beast barely knew mine. Could I keep him calm? I wasn't so sure. But I'd meant what I said when I promised to help him. My arms fastened around Aric's neck, immediately silencing his growls. My lips teased over his enough for me to taste the salt from his sweat. "I didn't think our next kiss would be like this," I murmured.

Aric's lids peeled back briefly before Koda and another *were* jumped on his arms. Two more grabbed his legs while a werebear donning black rubber gloves up to his armpits straddled him and yanked on the hook.

Aric didn't take it very well.

Aric bucked Koda and the other *were* off and *changed* into his giant gray wolf. My legs lifted from the ground as I hung tight to the tuff of his neck. "Oh, *shit*," the werebear grunted. "Hold him. Hold him now!"

A cluster of *weres* piled on top of him, swearing and growling through Aric's snarls, while I stuck to him like duct tape. I tried to whisper words of comfort, but my voice trembled with fear—fear I was doing more harm than good. Finally I turned to begging, seeing how short of knocking him out, it remained our only option. "Aric, *stop*."

Aric instantly stilled, shocking the hell out of both me and his fellow midnight streakers. He sniffed my hair, as if suddenly realizing his actions could have harmed me. "I'm all right," I assured him. "But I need you to stay calm and not move."

Aric let out a throaty growl, hard enough to shake everyone still attached. I didn't speak wolf, but I took it as a *"Fuck that."*

"Please, baby. They're only trying to help you . . . and so am I." My face rubbed against his as I continued to whisper low enough so only he could hear. "I want to take you home with me. Let's get through this so we can make that happen." Aric's furry head fell against my shoulder and he licked the side of my neck. In that simple gesture, he'd promised to behave. I smiled against him before clearing my throat and addressing the *weres*. "It's okay. You can release him." No one moved. Not even Koda. I wanted to bang my head against the board. "Look, I managed to assure his beast for the moment. I can't guarantee what will happen if you don't let go." The *weres* exchanged glances. At Koda's nod they slipped off one by one. I motioned to the werebear, but the moment he adjusted his grip on the handle, Aric let out a warning growl. "Aric, please. Someone needs to remove the hook."

The werebear examined Aric's back as Aric quieted. "Aric's *change* dug the barbs deeper into the flesh of his beast." Around us, the crowd groaned, but silenced when the werebear held up his hand. "It might be a good thing." He addressed me. "See if you can get him to *change* back. It'll hurt like a mother, but as the muscles revert, it should loosen the holes and be easier to pull out. Go on, now," he said when he caught my "Are you out of your goddamn mind?" expression.

I didn't want Aric to hurt. He probably only managed to stand because his wolf's strength surpassed his. Yet soon even the power of his beast wouldn't be enough. The curse poisoning his blood would bring him down as it found its way to his heart.

I adjusted my body so I could pull his fuzzy ear toward me. "I know you're scared, Aric. And I know you're in a great deal of pain. I also know you don't want to hurt me. But I'll be honest. It's killing me to see you like this." I swallowed hard to choke back the aching truth of my words. "So please, *change* back so the pain can stop for us both."

Even through his fur, I could feel the rising fever. At first, I thought he wouldn't listen, but then he *changed*, collapsing at once when his human form crashed onto the particleboard. I landed hard on my butt. Yet Aric's horrid howls had me throwing myself on top of him when the werebear yanked at the hook.

Aric panted and grunted against my shoulder as the

were twisted and pulled. I kissed his lips, his eyes, his cheeks, all the while reassuring him it would soon be over. After what felt like a lifetime, droplets of blood sprayed my hair. Aric released one last growl of torment and dropped his head. I barely kept his jaw from smacking against the wood. We both gasped for breath—Aric from the torture session and me from the stress. I rose slowly, keeping my hand over his uninjured shoulder, while attempting to wrangle in my beast.

My tigress wanted to punch the werebear in the head for causing Aric so much agony. Fortunately my human side stayed reasonable.

"Get me out of here," Aric rumbled.

Gemini had arrived donning only a pair of slacks. His wolf leapt onto his back and disappeared, merging with the man once more. He and Koda slipped Aric's arms over their shoulders while I tucked the blanket around his waist. The moment I finished, the wolves began to lead him toward Koda's SUV.

Aric stopped short. "Where's Celia?" he choked.

A film of white clouded his eyes. He couldn't see me. And as the gold made a mess of his circulatory system, he couldn't scent me, either. "I'm here, Aric. I'm not leaving you."

I ignored the *weres* watching me. Whether they liked me or not remained of little importance. So long as Aric needed me, I would stay with him.

CHAPTER 13

I briefly recalled hearing the sound of a key fob and the trunk of a nearby car pop, as we reached Koda's Yukon. The werebear appeared with a giant container of sea salt in his hands. He shook the container over Aric's body like he was seasoning meat. Aric threw back his head and snarled, clenching his jaw tight enough to stretch the cords of his neck.

I smacked the container out of the werebear's hands. The salt particles flew out in a stream of white and the cardboard container bounced twice on the asphalt before rolling beneath a nearby car. "What the *hell* are you doing?"

The werebear regarded me like *I* was the sadist. "Keeping his wounds open."

"I can see that, asshole—"

Gemini leaned into my ear. "Now that the hook has been removed, Aric's wolf is trying to seal his wounds. They need to stay open to draw out the gold poisoning his system. Otherwise it will take longer for the body to excrete it."

Heat flooded into my cheeks. "Oh."

If I hadn't felt foolish enough, the werecheetah made sure to dig the Dagger of Shame a little deeper. She smirked. "But how could you know our ways, sweet-heart? You're not one of us."

"Back off, Jennifer," Koda snapped.

The werebear retrieved the container from beneath the car and doused Aric with more salt. I placed my hands over one of his, cringing as the salt sizzled and bubbled against his flesh. The edges of his skin that had started to seal closed ripped open with a loud tear. It was all I could do to stay vertical. I'd seen a great deal of suffering. But never like this. And never involving Aric.

The *were* didn't stop until he emptied the entire container. He gave him the once-over and nodded. "Okay. I think we're good."

Thank you, Jesus.

I hurried into the backseat of Koda's SUV, wanting to be close to Aric, and knowing he was in no condition to sit up. The wolves laid him so his head rested on my lap. I cradled one arm across his chest while the fingers of my opposite hand stroked his hair gently.

"Hold on to him as I drive," Koda instructed.

I nodded, and pulled Aric closer. He didn't complain, and nuzzled against me. Gemini tossed the keys of his Infiniti to another wolf and slipped into the front passenger seat. Koda drove off, his speed fast yet showing care around the bumps and curves. "We'll get you back to the Den."

"No." Aric cleared his throat. "They won't let Celia in. I want her with me. She's a nurse. She can take care of me." He tilted his head up. The film around his eyes swirled like moving clouds. "Is that all right with you?"

I brushed his saturated hair away from his hot brow. "You know it is." He squeezed my hand. I couldn't help noticing the weakness of his grip. God, his condition terrified me. I borrowed Koda's phone and rang my sisters, telling Shayna everything I'd need to care for Aric—bandages, towels, antiseptic—

"Salt," Koda interrupted.

He had to be kidding. "Excuse me?"

Koda's grasp tightened on the steering wheel. "Salt water will continue to keep the wounds open, but will also help irrigate the gold's impurities. If done right, Aric should be functioning by tomorrow."

I chewed on my bottom lip. "Then let's hope I do it right."

Gemini gave me a quiet smile. "We'll talk you through it," he promised.

I disconnected with my sisters and caressed Aric's arm as he shivered. "Can you tell us what happened, Aric?"

Aric coughed, his throat obviously dry from the fever. "I was on my way to meet you when I saw an ambulance and an EMT truck driving toward me in the opposite lane. The windows were down. I caught the scent of the vampires as they passed."

Koda's storm-dark gaze narrowed in the rearview mirror. "What the hell were vamps doing in service vehicles?"

"Hunting." Aric cleared his throat again. Talking seemed to be getting harder. "They were dressed as EMTs. I turned around and tried to follow them but initially lost them. I finally caught their scent and tracked them into the development. That's when I heard the girl scream."

Gemini turned around, his almond eyes sharp. "What girl?"

"A young teen. She and her date appeared to have pulled into the development looking for privacy." Aric sighed and swallowed several times. "There were four vampires, draining the male from the vessels of his wrists, neck, and groin. The girl sat huddled in the car, screaming."

"Shit," Koda growled.

I never thought I'd miss the days when only infected

vampires lurked the streets of Tahoe. "They were healthy vampires, weren't they?"

Gemini nodded when it appeared Aric drifted off. "The bite marks were sealed, just like the bodies of the men inside the mill. The amount of blood they took suggested they'd gone long without feeding." He rubbed his goatee, his dark eyes registering something he'd miss. "And if they overindulged to the point of draining a human, they probably expected more time would pass until their next feed."

Koda let out a string of swearwords. "Those goddamn leeches are in league with the demons."

Yup. I'd figured as much. I smoothed back Aric's hair, slicking my palm with his sweat. I knew what I had to say would piss off the wolves, but I also realized it wouldn't be right to ignore Koda's suspicions. "There may be a vampire-demon party, but no way is Misha or his family involved."

Koda's jaw snapped as he clenched it. I thought my defense of Misha had angered him, and that I'd have to argue his innocence.

His comment threw me for a loop. "You're right. That asshole is definitely not involved. He isn't stupid enough to risk aligning with dark beings, especially now that he risks his soul."

My spine ached from my rising tension. Evil flat-out sucked eggs. "So another master—one without a soul—summoned the demons?"

"I'm not sure it's that simple, Celia."

I rubbed my eyes as my brain thudded hard against my skull. "Believe me, Gem, I'm not suggesting any of this is easy."

Gemini turned to face me once more. "What I mean is the vampires who attacked Aric may not have a master. If they're left over from the dismantled clans, and masters in their own right, collectively, they could be strong enough to resist Misha's pull." He thought about it. "But given Misha's power, any resistance would be temporary. And the longer they defy him, the more they risk destruction at his hands."

I crinkled my brow and grimaced; even that small effort hurt. "Are you suggesting those vampires are . . . homeless? I've never heard of that."

Koda shrugged. "Like Gem says, their true master usually kills them for trying to run or sends us after them. Otherwise there's no one to keep them in line while they're out on their own."

Gem stroked his jaw. "I wonder if it's possible for the demon lords Dan spoke of to take the role of a vampire's master."

Koda's head jerked in his direction. "It could explain the vamps' actions."

"And also the attack on Emme and Liam," I added quietly. Aric groaned beneath me. I brushed his hair again, wanting so badly to kiss him.

Gemini adjusted his position. The growing tension between the wolves thickened the air. "If our theory is correct, and a demon lord does exist, he could be sending the vampires to hunt for his food."

Aric shook beneath me, this time from the growl that formed deep within his core. "I should have been there tonight to protect you . . . and every night before this."

My shoulders slumped. Aric resembled nothing short of death on wheat toast and still he wanted to account for my safety. That was my wolf, protector of all. I leaned close to his ear. "No worries, baby. I managed to kick a little ass without you." I kissed his lobe. "I'm more concerned about you and your wounds." My fingers skimmed the length of his arm before I righted myself and stared out the window. The smell of the cursed gold hit my nose with every breath and fueled my urgency to reach the safety of my home. But then a disturbing thought occurred to me. "Aric . . . what happened to the young girl?"

Aric stirred, keeping his lids shut. "One of the vamps was armed with gold bullets. He shot me the moment I charged. When he realized what I was, he shot me a few more times. The vamp in the EMT truck hauled the girl out of the car and drove off with her while the others tried to immobilize me. I told the first *weres* who arrived. Hopefully they'll reach her in time."

We drove in silence for several long seconds. I supposed everyone needed time to come to terms with the not-so-fun parts of the night. No one said it, but we all realized the *weres* wouldn't find the girl in time. Especially if the demon lord was hungry . . . or seeking to breed. Koda accelerated as we reached the long, straight stretch of 89. "What was up with that damn gold hook?"

"There were two welded into the side wall of the ambulance. They tried to fasten me to them." Aric paused. "I didn't let them."

The acid in my stomach rose to volcanic proportions. "The gold hooks anchored inside the ambulance . . . the vampires wouldn't have needed them for a human."

Gemini clenched his fist against his leg. "No. They were probably prepared to catch a *were*. Our blood regenerates faster. Four vamps could feed on a *were* for several weeks— months even if they provided the *were* proper nourishment. All they would have to do is clean out the gold from his system and tranquilize him to keep him subdued."

My mind latched onto the dead raccoon on my doorstep. "Is it possible the wereraccoon was a victim of a botched hunt?"

Gemini leaned back in the seat. "Perhaps. But it still doesn't explain why he exploded. Or what he was doing following you."

No. It didn't. Good Lord, what a night. I leaned over Aric, protecting him with my body as growing anger tightened my chest. He could have been food. My hand clutched his. But then his stomach lurched.

"Koda, pull over!"

Koda veered to the side of the road. I pushed open the door and hauled Aric over my lap. I wanted to rub his back, but not enough skin remained. The salt had expanded the bullet wounds into gaping craters. The sight would have sickened most. Yet it only made me feel deep sadness, mostly because I hadn't been there to save Aric like he had saved me.

I wiped my tears with the back of my hands. Thankfully, Gemini and Koda gave me the courtesy of turning away. Aric gulped deep breaths of air, but nothing happened. "I'm all right," he said after a few moments.

No. He wasn't. I'd have preferred him to hurl. Vomiting would have expelled some of the poison. I hoped Aric hadn't fought the nausea on my account. But something inside me told me that's exactly what he'd done. I pulled him back into the car and shut the door, wrapping myself around him as he trembled. I fought the urge to *change*. My tigress wanted to enclose him in our warmth. Except my beast was too big and the last thing Aric needed was a fur blanket with legs on top of him.

"Hang in there, baby. We're almost home."

Koda couldn't get back to my house fast enough. The minute we pulled into the driveway, my sisters and Liam rushed out to meet us. "Son of a *bitch*," Taran muttered when she saw Aric.

"Yeah. Pretty much," Aric mumbled.

That was bad enough. But then Emme and Shayna screamed when they saw his coloring. In their defense, his gray tone appeared worse in the light of the family room. I ignored their shrieks. "Is the tub ready?"

Emme nodded while keeping her hands clasped tightly over her mouth. I hurried upstairs as the wolves lifted Aric off his feet. I burst into my bedroom and through the double doors leading to my five-piece bath. The steam from the hot water slowed my steps, signaling the torture to come. I stopped next to my Jacuzzi tub, filled to the brim with water. Salt water.

Koda tugged off the blanket around Aric's waist and he and Gemini lowered him into the water.

And that's when his roars began.

CHAPTER 14

The water boiled from the effects of the cursed gold leaving Aric's body. Eventually Aric's body gave out. He stopped thrashing and fell limp. It scared the hell out of me, but it allowed me to clean his wounds with a scrub brush Koda handed me while Gemini kept his head abovewater. My hands moved quickly, wanting to be thorough yet desperate to be done.

"What would have happened if Aric hadn't been found?" I didn't want to ask except it remained a passing question that continued to gnaw at my skin.

"With the hook and the bullets out, and no intervention, it would take his wolf a few weeks to excrete the poison."

"What if the hooks and the bullets remained?" I asked quietly, wondering whether I truly wanted to know.

Koda tightened his jaw. "The gold would have stopped his heart over time."

My throat tightened. "How much time?"

Koda shrugged. "Two, maybe three weeks."

I stopped scrubbing just to take a few slow breaths and rub my face against Aric's. His stubble scratched my cheek and moistened my skin, but I needed a moment—just one moment. Not caring who saw me have it. Two to three weeks—violently ill and in pain. Only to ultimately die. I sighed. Death by cursed gold seemed the most nightmarish way for a preternatural to go.

Aric's lips opened and closed briefly. I interpreted it as him urging me on and returned to my work, saving the gaping holes from the hook for last.

Koda handed me a toothbrush straight from the package. I closed my eyes as he gave me instructions. "Scrub and twist all the way through. Don't be afraid to be too rough. It will only help him."

I kept my eyes closed when I asked my next question. "Do I—" I beat back my nausea, but just barely. "In order to clean the bullet holes, do I have to dig the brush through his chest and out his back?"

"No. Aric dug the bullets out fairly quickly. The salt water should be enough."

I opened my eyes to catch Koda watching me carefully.

"The gold hook was lodged in his shoulder for more than two hours. It's what did the most damage and kept his wolf from healing him."

I thought I heard wrong. "Aric dug the bullets out . . . himself?"

"The others found a long screwdriver with Aric's blood on it when they arrived." Koda turned his back, facing away like he was afraid to continue. "He used it to push them through his body."

I pictured the six bullets hitting Aric's chest and getting lodged within. It made sense to push them through rather than to attempt to dig them out. The gold would have burned a path straight to the other side. I understood the logic. And the desperation. But that didn't mean I liked it. I made a silent promise to Aric. If I found the surviving vamp, I'd kill him myself.

I let the water out of the tub with shaking hands when Gemini felt the wounds had been thoroughly cleansed. Gold had no effect on me. But I had the feeling even the residue would have sickened the wolves. They stayed loyally by Aric's side. My sisters waited in the hall. I'd ignored Liam when he insisted that Aric wouldn't have minded their presence.

"Should I bring your sisters in now? They're worried about Aric."

I ran the sprayer over Aric's body. "Not until he's dried and covered, Liam."

Liam cocked his head. "Celia, I'm telling you it's no big deal. Plenty of females have seen Aric naked."

I paused my rinsing, praying to Saint Patrick to keep me from strangling Liam with the damn metal hose. I didn't need reminding of how many females Aric had exposed himself to, whether through innocent *changes* before his pack mates . . . or in more intimate settings. Aric's stature, his rippling muscles, his startling eyes, his deep tenor voice—everything about him screamed sex appeal. *Were* babes wanted him. And they would continue to want him despite our relationship. But sure, thanks, Liam, for the update.

I grabbed the stack of chocolate brown towels and spread them over Aric, using one towel per section, drying him carefully. I wished we were alone. And that he wasn't so sick. Over the last week, I'd dreamt of seeing his naked body, of feeling his flesh slide over mine, of exploring him through taste and touch. Just like we'd done our first real night together. But not like this. Not while his injuries debilitated him, and definitely not while the pain froze his features into an agonized grimace. The next time Aric and I faced each other unclothed, it would be to make love again. There would be no pain, no worry, no hesitation.

"I think he's dry enough, Celia," Gemini stated.

His words snapped me back to reality. I hoped the leftover steam excused my blush. I went to lift him, but then thought better of it. I didn't want to hurt his pride, so I moved aside so Gemini and Koda could reach him. "Please get him out of the tub fast. When his fever breaks, the sudden cold may be too much for him."

I tossed the thick cotton towels on the rust-colored tiles, forming a giant pile. The wolves pulled Aric from the tub and wrapped him in a soft blanket, fresh from the dryer.

"Where do you want him, Celia?"

"On my bed please, Koda."

"Are you sure? He might ruin—" Koda stopped arguing when he saw my sisters had padded my bed with cotton hospital pads.

I reached for the bandages on my dresser. "They're waterproof, too." Fear made my voice crack. There was still more to do. I took a deep breath, hugging the packages of gauze against me. Aric's skin shone like alabaster and just as white—sadly, a tremendous improvement from that deathly gray. "What's next?"

Liam opened the door. Emme entered carrying a metal bowl filled with, oh, fantastic, more salt water. The scent made me cringe. I was grateful when Gemini motioned me over. "This won't be as bad," he assured me. "The majority of the poison from the gold's curse has been excreted. All you have to do is pack his wounds and then bandage them tight."

My large bedroom allowed plenty of space between my king-size sleigh bed and the picture window, so the ample berth Gemini gave me surprised me. "What are you doing?"

Gem cocked his head as if I missed the point. "Keeping our distance from Aric. His wolf remains protective and may lash out if we disturb him too much."

I didn't quite understand. "But he's been fine with me."

Koda's eyes reminded me of the center of a twister, so dark and menacing I barely managed to keep his stare. And yet for once, they didn't appear so threatening. "That's because he would never hurt you, Celia."

I touched the hard muscles of Aric's uninjured shoulder, knowing Koda was right. Aric would never hurt me, physically. But I feared that one day he'd break my heart. I sat on the edge of the mattress. The bullet wounds had begun to seal shut, but the damage from the hooks still needed a great deal of care. My stomach clenched. "I have to slip the gauze through the holes ... don't I?"

Gemini nodded. "And make the dressing changes as they soak through." He placed a hand on my arm, but jerked it away when Aric snarled. He remained unfazed, despite Aric's sudden outburst. "Don't worry, Celia. It will be a long night, but he'll be much improved by morning."

"We can take turns," Shayna said. "Ceel, you look beat. Why don't you take a nap and I'll take the first watch ... ?"

I shook my head but wouldn't speak to her. Any normal, sound being would have taken her up on her offer. How could I logically explain Aric was mine alone to take care of?

"What's wrong, dude?"

Koda put his arm around her and led her to the door. "I think Aric would prefer Celia's touch. Come on, baby. Let's go to bed. We'll be down the hall if they need us."

The room emptied out as I went to work on Aric's shoulder. The moment I was done, I wrapped him in another warm blanket and took a quick shower. I tugged on a pair of panties, pausing when I caught his body convulsing from the breaking fever. I dropped my robe and crawled into bed with Aric, abandoning the shirt I'd originally planned to wear. I pulled his chilled body against my bare skin. His hand gripped my hip and squeezed before exhaustion finally claimed his weak body and mine.

"Thank you," he whispered.

I dreamed of flashing lights just before my cell phone jolted me awake. I rolled to the opposite side, searching blindly for the small, sleek rectangle. My eyes burned as I focused on the blaring glow of the screen. Almost four a.m. I slipped the blankets from Aric's shoulder. Only an hour had passed, but his blood had already saturated the surface of the dressings.

I shimmied out of bed and gathered my supplies while my iPhone continued to ring, insisting bandages be damned. "Hello?" I mumbled.

"Why did you not inform me you were attacked?"

There were many advantages to having a guardian angel master vampire. Before-the-crack-of-dawn phone calls were not among them. "Misha, you really shouldn't call at this hour. You're only reinforcing the creature-of-the-night stereotype your people have tried hard to avoid."

"Celia."

"You know, considering your fanged butt woke me, you're awfully testy." I yawned. "Besides, I'd figured your spider sense would tell you eventually."

Misha's low, deep hiss informed me comic book humor was lost on Dracula's BFF. I sighed and tried not to bang my head. "Aric was attacked by vampires draining a human."

"My vampires did *not* assault that mongrel."

Aric growled behind me. He'd heard Misha's voice. And he wasn't happy. I covered him again with the blankets. "Don't call him a mongrel. Look, I need to ask, are your vampires all accounted for? Even those new to your family?"

"The play for dominance is over. Those who survived are under my complete control and carefully managed."

"I figured as much, Misha. But thanks for letting me know." The planes on Aric's face had softened, now that his pain had significantly decreased. Relief flooded me down to my toes. If Gem was right, his wolf had started to accelerate his healing. Perhaps by early evening he'd be able to eat.

"None of my keep would have dared to attack you," Misha said, reminding me our conversation wasn't over.

"I know." I smiled into the phone. Despite my natural distrust of vampires, I did trust Misha. I just hoped that trust wouldn't come back to bite me.

"Tell me more about the attack."

I tucked the phone against my chin and opened more packs of bandages, lining them carefully along the bed. "There were close to thirty. I'd never seen so many vampires outside the presence of their master. They also dressed like . . . foreigners." I hadn't thought about it until I verbalized it, but most of them resembled the European tourists who visited Tahoe. They'd also donned similar clothing—simple dress slacks and shirts. The vamps from Tahoe only wore original designer creations . . . or Catholic schoolgirl uniforms.

I had a thought. "Any chance your master is after me?"

The subtle sound of sliding sheets suggested Misha also had company in his bed. "No. My master credits you with helping to save him. He would not insult you by asking for your heart."

Misha meant that literally. I pushed my long waves from my face. "In a way I wish Uri was after me."

Misha paused. "Why would you desire such a peril?"

"Because at least then I'd know what we were dealing with. Misha . . . the wolves have a theory. They think— well, we think, a demon lord may somehow be controlling the rogue vampires."

A female voice squealed just before I heard a thump

on the other end. I gathered Misha had sat abruptly and, well, caught his companion off guard. Poor, dumb, iron-deficient bimbo.

"No demon in history has ever managed such a task."

"I don't think we're dealing with an ordinary demon." I explained Danny's interpretation of "demon kin." Misha took it as well as I had.

"Demons. Who pass equally through hell and earth. Following events—*such as a vampire regaining his soul!*"

I threw my hand out. "I know what you're thinking—I thought it, too, but this is *so* not our fault."

"No, no, of course, many changes have occurred as of late." He paused. "I take it your band of wolves now know?"

"I know we pinky-swore not to say anything, but it sort of slipped out."

The silence that followed suggested Misha wasn't happy at the news. Except his hard tone wasn't one of anger. In fact, it was downright cocky. "The mongrels know better than to spread such news. Especially if their Leader's bedmate was who caused my rise in power."

I hadn't thought of it that way. Crap. Way to score more points with Aric's Elders. I fell against the wall. My God, I was tired. "Misha, do you think a demon lord exists, one that could also serve as a master to vampires?"

"I would be a fool to dismiss the theory so easily."

I bit my bottom lip. Very few things scared a vampire, especially one so strong. And while Misha's voice didn't quiver with fear, I sensed his trepidation, no matter how much he tried to hide it.

Aric stirred in the silence and attempted to sit. I leaned forward and tried to settle him back down. "Misha, I have to go."

Misha's voice sharpened in severity just before he disconnected. "I will find what did this to you."

I placed my phone on the nightstand and gently

pushed my hand over Aric's uninjured shoulder when he sought to rise again. His skin remained as cold as a marble. "Where do you think you're going, wolf?"

"I need to drink."

The haze in his eyes continued to spin. He failed to see the giant water bottle beside him, and probably failed to scent it, too. I lifted the straw to his lips. "Here. Drink. When you're done, I'll change your bandages."

The liter of water disappeared within moments. In reward, I swept my lips across his when he finished. His fingers reached out and held my chin, allowing our kiss to linger. The soft pecks weren't deep, but as sweet and addicting as always. His fingers slid down my neck and chest, stopping just above my nipple. He closed his eyes. "You're not dressed," he murmured.

I dropped my head, slightly embarrassed by my boldness. "You were cold. I wanted to warm you. If you prefer, I'm sure I could throw a Florence Nightingale ensemble together."

"I'd rather see more than just your sexy ankles." He rubbed his eyes. "Shit. If I could see at all."

"The water should help detoxify your body from the gold's curse. Lie down and I'll change your bandages." I took off the dressings, cringing as I rinsed the wounds with more salt water. "Am I hurting you, love?"

Aric's cloudy gaze focused hard where he heard my voice. "It burns my skin, but just a little. Nothing like before." His hand found my shoulder. "You're pretty good at this, sweetness. Maybe you should stick to nursing instead of taking on demons."

"I do prefer to deliver babies. But I also think other things are more important."

Aric clasped my arm. "I don't want you involved in this anymore."

Aric's grip didn't hurt, but it did emphasize the concern behind his words. "It's too late for that, wolf."

I continued to tend to him. Aric held me, but he remained weak. Slowly his hand relaxed as his body sank into the mattress. When I tried to redress his wounds, he shook his head. "Leave them open to air for a moment."

"Okay." I slipped on my robe and took his water bottle downstairs to refill. When I returned, Liam was there. He stood watching Aric as he slept.

"Hey, Celia. I heard you get up and thought I'd check on Aric. He looks way better."

I placed Aric's bottle on the table and tightened my robe. "Yeah, but he's exhausted."

Liam leaned over him. "That's because his beast is working hard to heal him. See?"

Liam stuck his two fingers through the holes in Aric's shoulder. Aric scrunched his brows but kept his lids shut. Liam pulled back his bloody fingers and wiggled them at me. "Look. No pus. Great job, Celia."

I didn't see, so much as *feel*, myself go white . . . then green. I beat down my gag reflex and choked out my words. "Liam. Please don't ever do that again." *Or I will beat your ass to death.*

"Liam?" Emme stood in the doorway, dressed in one of Liam's T-shirts. "Is everything all right?"

I gripped the edge of the table, still feeling faint. "Fine. Everything's fine. Emme, the poison seems to have left Aric's system. Could you please help him heal?"

Liam blocked Emme's path when she advanced, shaking his head. "Aric's wolf could still be on the defense. I don't want Emme near him just in case." He patted my back. "Give a holler if you need me. He'll respond better to me since I'm one of his Warriors." Seeing how Aric hadn't bitten Liam's hand off when he poked through his skin like a skewer, I tended to believe him. Still, I'd rather have called the Catholic schoolgirls.

"Oh, and, Celia?" Liam paused with one foot in the hall. "Aric's going to wake up very grateful to you for taking care of him—*very* grateful. He'll probably want to have sex for a few hours, so be sure to get some shut-eye. Night."

I nodded, stupidly, though his back was now to me. In his own, boyishly naive, unfiltered, inappropriate way, Liam meant well. Knowing that kept me from launching the water bottle into the back of his skull. I locked the door after them and bandaged Aric's shoulder, then crawled back into bed with my wolf.

CHAPTER 15

I rubbed my eyes. They remained sore from lack of sleep and from the strange flashes of light that had haunted my dreams again. Aric had woke feeling better, and, as Liam promised, extremely grateful for my care. He'd kissed me when I tried to check his bandages and whisked us into the shower for one hell of a good morning.

I sighed contently. Aric's dark brown hair curled, still wet from our romp in the shower. It tickled my belly as I lay against the fresh sheets. "You really scared me last night, wolf."

Aric brought my knuckles to his lips. "And you scare the hell out of me for wanting to take part in the hunt." He focused on the tiered ceiling painted in alternating tones of deep creams and antique whites. "The Leader of the Bear Clan on the Nevada side is taking over my duties for the next few days."

I breathed a sigh a relief. "Good. It will give you time to recover."

"I'm recovered enough." Aric turned a little to nibble on my belly. "Or didn't you notice?" A playful grin swept across his face. If his "gratitude" hadn't worn me out, I might have pounced on him. His palm stretched across my skin to massage my shoulder. "The crisis has kept me from my duties as chancelor of students. The young wolves at the Den are behind on their studies. With my Warriors and me gone all the time, the staff has been stretched thin. Already the term will continue way into the summer."

I hated Aric searching out the demon lord without me. And I hated the demands his Elders placed on him. At least in returning to teaching duties, he would be safe. My fingers swept over his moist strands. "You miss teaching, don't you?"

Aric smiled fondly when he thought of his students. "I do, but I won't be returning to the classroom just yet. I'm to prepare our senior students to assist in tracking the demon lord."

"They're so young," I said quietly, more thinking out loud.

"They are. But they're also not average students. The predators in them are enlivened by the idea of stalking prey. They'll travel with seasoned *weres*. It will give them a taste of their duties without putting them in harm's way." Aric's voice grew distant. "At least that's what I'm hoping. The demon lord is starting to feast on the men before he abandons their remains."

My back tensed. This was news, and not the post-lovemaking conversation any gal ever wanted. "Is he taking their blood?"

"No. He craves meat—lots of it. The last set of bodies I'd found had all the muscle stripped from their thighs."

I grimaced. "And it's not demon children feasting."

Aric rubbed his forehead. "No. The bite marks suggest something bigger, with fangs that mimic more an angler fish than werebeast or vampire."

Damn it. "I wished you'd let me hunt with you."

Aric rolled onto his stomach, supporting himself on

his elbows. "You heard the leech, Celia. This thing has already threatened to come for you. To bring you along would be like handing you to him on a platter." He shook his head. "You're the best thing in my life. I won't risk losing you, sweetness."

Aric feared that the demons, the monsters, and every other thing that bumped the night and shadowed the earth would come for me. Maybe he was right. But my ignorance wouldn't protect me; knowledge and vigilance would. "I'd rather meet him head-on than risk running into him unprepared. But it's not just that, is it?"

Aric frowned. "What do you mean?"

Maybe I shouldn't have discussed it just then, except it was a concern that continued to gnaw at me. "I think you're worried I'm in danger just by being with you."

Aric's expression softened so that the remorse in his features matched his tone. "Yeah. I am. It's something I wrestle with all the time."

"Don't." *And please don't leave me,* I didn't say. His arms encircled my waist. I mused over the way his soft breath drifted across my bare flesh. It just felt right to have Aric against me. It's how it should have been. For me. And my sisters. "Is this why Gemini is so afraid to become close to Taran? He fears what his presence could bring?"

Aric turned his head again and buried his face against my stomach. He jerked once, twice. At first I thought he was coughing, but then I realized he was full-out laughing. "No. Gemini is just trying to be gentle. He worries about scaring her since she's a virgin and all."

"Oh—wait, *what*!" I pulled Aric off me and covered my mouth. "You can't be serious. Taran is many things . . . but a virgin is not one of them. Why would he think that?"

Aric slipped out of bed and clasped my wrists, pulling me to him. "You have to know Gemini. He's shy around females. He's never been openly affectionate in public. Even with women he's been intimate with. Gem's behavior toward Taran is extremely aggressive for him. Since she's not responding to what he feels is obvious interest on his part, he's convinced Taran is untouched."

Aric led us into the bathroom. "Oh no, she's definitely been touched." My sides had started to ache, but it felt good to laugh "Aric, most males are more straightforward when it comes to pursuing Taran. I was starting to think something was wrong with him. And what the hell is up with the damn head pat?"

"It was his way of touching her. I told him there are other things he could do." He winked and cupped his hand over my backside, gripping it for emphasis.

I gave him a gentle shove, though I liked the attention. "Do you think I should say something to Taran?"

"Someone sure as hell needs to." Aric put on a fresh T-shirt and sweatpants the wolves had brought him. He huffed. "I'm tired of scenting his sexual frustration all over the damn place."

I paused before slipping a cashmere sweater over my head. "Is that what the scent is?"

Aric grinned. "I thought for sure you'd recognize it from all those times I almost jumped you. Especially that night you flashed me your breasts."

I yanked my jeans on over my thong. "You forget, I'm the one without much experience." My face heated. "And I didn't flash you on purpose."

Aric backed me into the wall and grasped my hips. "I wasn't complaining, sweetness." He kissed me deep. I thought he meant to play more, but then he pulled away and let out a long, controlled breath. "I have to head to the Den. But I promise to be back to take you out to dinner."

My hands rubbed against his stone-hard abdominals. "You haven't eaten in so long, though. Aren't you hungry?"

"No. The gold did a number on my digestive system. I'll be famished later."

We walked hand in hand down the backstairs and into the kitchen. Koda, Liam, and my sisters were finishing breakfast. Their mouths collectively parted when they caught sight of Aric.

"What the hell happened?" Taran threw her hands in the air. "Damn, Aric. Last night you looked like shit with gravy on it."

Aric's pulled me to him so my back rested against his chest. "I had a nurse take care of me."

Liam nodded. "Oh, we know, Aric. We heard you having sex in the shower. We just didn't expect such a full recovery this fast."

I buried my crimson face in my hand. Aric cleared his throat. "Any news on what happened last night?"

Koda scrolled through his phone. "Paul's Beta and his team found the EMT truck on the Nevada side just before dawn. Though it would have been hard to miss since someone torched it. The girl was gone, but they tracked her and the vamp to Washoe Lake."

My brows shot up. So much for hoping they'd located the secret demon lord's hideout. "There's nothing there this time of year."

Koda placed his phone down. "Except the vamp's leftover EMT uniform. The Beta was the same raccoon who accompanied Paul the other day. He said the scent around the uniform matched the one of the exploding body."

Aric swore under his breath. "What the hell is happening?"

Koda rose, lifting Shayna as easily as a long-stemmed rose. "I don't know. But Liam and I are going to take a look after we check in at the Den." He paused. "Anara wants a full report on your altercation last night."

Aric clenched his jaw. "Then he'll get it. Come on, let's go."

We walked the wolves outside where, hip-hip-hooray, Mrs. Mancuso was busy tending to her garden. I stayed on the porch with Aric. Call me chicken. Call me yellow-bellied. But call me safe from the wrath of Mrs. Mancuso. Shayna wasn't so lucky. She waved as she passed her. "Looking good, Mrs. Mancuso."

No. She wasn't. Mrs. Mancuso's neck skin dragged a path between the tulips. "Go to church and get some morals, hussy!"

Taran adjusted her cleavage just to piss her off. "What's the matter, Mancuso? Did the aliens forget to remove the probe rammed up your ass?"

"*Taran!*" Emme abandoned Liam to haul Taran in the house using a combo of her puny arms and her teleki-netic *force*. Mrs. Mancuso rewarded Emme with another middle finger in addition to the one she was swinging at Taran. There must have been a two-for-one special at her church.

Shayna was busy pulling Koda away. He liked Mrs. Mancuso as much we did, but generally ignored her. Not today, and especially not after she called Shayna a hussy. He snarled and took a step toward her as Shayna dug her heels into the walkway.

"I love you."

Shayna's words froze the big guy in place. He turned his head slowly until he met Shayna's beautiful smiling face. "What did you say?"

Shayna continued to grin. "I said, 'I love you.' "

Koda took a deep breath to inhale her scent and rein-force the truth behind Shayna's declaration of love. His dark eyes widened briefly before he gathered her to him. My sister's willowy frame disappeared beneath the thickness of his arms and the sheet of long black hair that draped around her like a protective cloak. "I love you, too, baby," he whispered.

Aric stiffened against me and I felt his spirit pull away

from mine. My thumbs skimmed the back of his hands. "What's wrong?"

Aric kissed my forehead but failed to meet my gaze. "Let's allow them time to have their moment. I'll see you tonight." He jogged down the wooden steps, giving Koda and Shayna plenty of space before stepping into the Yukon, where Liam waited. I backed into the house, wanting to give Shayna and Koda their privacy, all the while trying not to react to how quickly Aric's demeanor had changed.

Taran was still fuming when I walked into the kitchen. "That old bag needs to get laid. It's the only thing that's going to save us. But who the hell is going to want to bang a woman with a saggy vajayjay—"

"Taran, *please*." Emme stopped in the middle of filling her mug with tea. "I realize Mrs. Mancuso is very . . . unpleasant. But even she deserves some kindness. Perhaps if we made more of an effort to be nice to her, her attitude might change for the better."

Taran took a sip of her tea. "I'd rather photograph her saggy vajajay."

I wouldn't.

Emme sighed and resumed tea pouring duties while I placed a basket of fresh-baked sweet breads in the center of our wooden table. I'd just finished setting napkins and small plates beside each mug when Koda's Yukon roared out of our development. Shayna sprinted into the house, tears streaming down her cheeks as she threw her arms around me. "He loves me, Ceel. Koda loves me."

I held her against me, careful not to crack her spine. Shayna didn't throw the "L" word around. If she'd said it, it was because she meant it and Koda seemed the perfect guy to mean it to. "It must have been something to hear it," I told her honestly.

Her ponytail swayed as she shifted her hips back and forth. "Has Aric told you that he loves you yet? I mean, it's so obvious the way he looks at you. And gadzooks, the chemistry between you is the stuff of legends. . . ."

Her voice faded as my smile took a hike off my face and landed somewhere between my toes. "Things are still new between us. I'm not sure how either of us truly feels." That was only a half-truth. I knew exactly how I felt, and while I believed Aric cared for and was passionate about me, his reaction on the porch suggested our feelings weren't as mutual as I'd wished. "You're the best thing in my life," he'd said. But that wasn't quite love, was it?

Emme walked to my side and squeezed my hand. "Give him time to know you more, Celia. And then he'll have no choice but to fall in love with you."

Emme's soft, encouraging words of hope usually made me smile at her sweetness or gape at her naiveté. This time, they made me a little sad. "I hope so," I said quietly.

I led her and Shayna to the table where our celebratory Koda-loves-Shayna feast awaited. Taran quietly buttered the zucchini bread Emme had baked. The lack of sarcasm and noise revealed she wasn't the only Wird sister feeling insecure. Luckily, I had just the ammo to blast her buns back to the planet Bitch-Assness.

I sat next to her and reached for a blueberry muffin. "Any word from Gemini?"

She stopped midbutter spread and clenched the knife in her hand. "No."

"Really? He hasn't called?" I took a bite of my muffin.

Taran slowly lowered her bread onto her plate while static shocks of blue and white snapped, crackled, sizzled, and popped above her head. "No. No calls. No texts. And in case you're wondering, no Pony Express packages, either."

I nodded. "Mmm. That's so strange."

Emme's mouth popped open. My little sister was evidently shocked by my sudden and very suicidal verbiage. Provoking Taran was like ripping a rabbit out of a dingo's mouth. Shayna shook her head, fast. When I grinned and winked, she waved her hands like she was landing a lunar jet in our family room.

I leaned back in my chair and crossed my arms. "So, any head pats lately?"

I just narrowly missed the bolt of lightning she flung my way. It split the wooden chair down the center and buckled the legs. I landed in a crouch on the table. Taran stood hard enough to tip her seat back, the length of her fingernails streaming with fire. She circled the table, her irises clear as glass from her rising power and the wide-awake, pissed-as-hell, premenstrual Latina within. "Just because you finally got laid doesn't make it okay to make fun of the head pat. Gemini—"

"Thinks you're a virgin," I finished for her.

It was as if we were all in stereo and someone pulled the plug on the surround sound. Emme's pleas to Taran not to barbecue me and Shayna's panicked pulls to my arm ceased. Silence, followed more silence, until a nervous "Heh . . . heh-heh-heh" escaped Shayna's lips.

I leapt off the table and met Taran face-to-face. Her scowl, in addition to her heavy breathing, just sent me into a fit of giggles. You'd have thought I made fun of her footwear. Taran jutted out her chin. "What. The hell. Did you. Just say?" I laughed harder. "Celia. In exactly three seconds I'm going to scorch the living shit out of you. Do you *want* your ass to burn? Well, do you?"

This was harder than I had thought. I threw my hands in the air. "Taran, Gemini thinks you are, and I quote, 'untouched.' "

"Untouched where?"

Emme clasped her hands over her mouth to suppress a gasp. Shayna didn't. Her "heh-hehs" turned into full-out guffaws. She fell to the floor holding her sides, snorting uncontrollably.

Taran paced the room. Her four-inch sandals dug into the hard wood as she marched. "Why the *hell* would Gemini think *I'm a virgin*?"

"Because you haven't responded to his advances."

Taran rounded on me. "What advances? Oh, I get it. Was it all those brotherly hugs? Oh no, let me guess, it was the head pats because we all damn well know that's sexy."

Emme smoothed the skirt of her floral dress. "Goodness, Taran," she said meekly. "I'm actually surprised you haven't tried to, you know, entice him."

Taran turned her glare on Emme. "I'm not used to the shy types, Emme. I've only held back because I'm afraid I'll scare him shitless." By this point, my eyes watered. "Damn it, Celia, stop laughing. While you've been getting it on with Aric, I've been taking cold showers." Bits of flame shot out of her hands like confetti. She gritted her teeth, stopping only to glower at me. "You have *no* idea how bad I want him."

"Aric says all the attention Gem's shown you is a lot for someone as reserved as he is." I grabbed her shoulders. "He likes you, Taran. Aric flat-out told me. It's up to you to show him you like him, too."

I could see the hope and excitement building as Taran withdrew her flame. Her wicked smile easily returned and so did that sultry gleam to her stare. "He likes me."

"Yes."

"And he *wants* me."

"Apparently so." I didn't mention Gemini's sexual frustration. Taran had been tortured enough.

Taran's full lips puckered with anticipation and her aura sizzled with enough heat to scorch my sweater. "I'm gonna knock that wolf right out of his pants."

Yup. No doubt. I played with my nails. I wanted to do

the same for Aric, except I needed an expert's help to do it. "There's something else I have to discuss with you."

Taran crossed her arms and leaned back, curiosity about my sudden awkwardness making her angle an eyebrow. "Yeah?"

"Aric and I, um, have been having a lot of, ah, you know—we're engaging in intimacy."

Taran laughed. "Celia. I wouldn't call all the gorilla sex you've been having with him 'engaging in intimacy.' Girl, you better get on the pill before he knocks you up."

"I'm already on it. It, um, actually took full effect last night. But I, uh, took added precautions this morning just in case." I cleared my throat for all the good it did me. "I was wondering if, uh, you'd go lingerie shopping with me today?"

A devious smile crept across her face. "Why don't we all go? I need something to be devirginized in."

CHAPTER 16

After breakfast, Taran drove us to a South Tahoe boutique that specialized in designer lingerie. When the salesclerks greeted her by name, I knew we'd come to the right place. After a brief consultation with the staff, Taran had us custom-fitted for bras. Turned out, I was a 34-C, not a 36-B.

Taran wandered the aisles, picking out lingerie she determined would best fit our tastes. Her view of me, however, was sexier than I believed myself to be. I'd always worn feminine undergarments, but they were cute and cotton, not lacy, silky, and enticing. After all, before Aric, there'd been no one to seduce. After a rather revealing and embarrassing hour in the dressing room, I was prepared for my night.

When we returned home, Taran laid out the plans like the diva of seduction she believed herself to be. "Okay, everyone put on your choice of underwear for the evening with the shoes you'll be wearing. Celia, I think you should wear the pink bra and panties with the black lace. Here." She shoved a pair of strappy sandals high enough to make my nose bleed. "No mules, UGGs, or running shoes allowed."

I gawked at the shoes and the lingerie she handed me. The thong alone could have fit in a lipstick case. It was one of the more risqué items Taran had selected. I'd hoped to start off slow and ease my way into that little number. "But this one comes with a garter belt and thigh-high stockings."

"No shit." Taran glowered when I continued to gape. "Celia. You're the one who begged for my help—"

"I didn't beg—"

"Now run along and get dressed. Just make sure whatever outfit you wear for dinner hides the lingerie." She hustled us out the door. "Hurry up, we're running out of time."

Emme and I arrived in Taran's room wearing very casual but pretty print dresses. Shayna wore gray leggings under an off-the-shoulder white tunic. I was stunned to find Taran in nothing but red lace and four-inch heels. She threw her hands in the air like we'd committed a major slutty lingerie faux pas. "What the hell are you guys doing? I want you in only underwear and shoes. Take the rest of that shit off."

"Why?" I asked.

"Because we're going to practice posing."

"Huh?"

Taran tapped her heel and huffed like we'd exhausted the last of her patience. "You have to learn which pose works best to enhance your bodies in your lingerie." My blank expression only pissed her off further. "It adds to the seduction process!"

Taran sighed when the rest of us exchanged what-the-hell glances. "Watch and learn." She folded her arms and leaned over her dresser. Emme jumped when Taran threw out her butt like some sort of weapon. Taran continued, unaffected. She flipped her dark hair, pouted her lips, and propelled her cleavage forward like missiles targeting terrorists. I learned two things then. One, Taran had missed her calling as a Victoria's Secret model. And two, I must have been on crack when I asked her for help.

Taran pushed off from the dresser and placed a hand on her hip, clearly presenting herself as the ruler of the overexaggerated backsides. I thought she expected us to bow, or at the very least applaud. We did neither. Nor did we move. Except for Emme, who eyed the door like she might bolt.

Taran ignored her and held out her hands. "Are you ready to try, my young grasshoppers?"

I nodded slowly, surprised by how much work went into seducing a werewolf. My tigress reminded me Aric was worth it, so I stepped forward and began my crash course in posing. I don't know if we were seductively inept or what, but we had to work on our poses all afternoon.

"Shayna, what the hell are you doing? I told you to stick out your breasts!"

"They are out!"

"Oh yes, they are. Sorry, girl."

"Damn it, Emme, flip the hair! More, more, more—*oh, shit.* Not that much!"

"Ow! Oh no, now I have to heal."

"Dude, is this posing stuff supposed to hurt?"

"Quit whining, Shayna. You won't be doing it for long, trust me. One of two things will happen. Either he'll jump you right away or he'll watch you completely entranced. If it's the latter, try to bend over a lot. It drives men wild." Taran turned to me and ran her fingers through my hair, making it fuller. "And for shit's sake, don't forget to work the mane as much as possible. Celia, you have that whole porn-star-hair thing going for you. Milk it for all it's worth. Also, incorporate the furniture somehow. Guys like that."

*   *   *

"Gimme your money and a little affection, *bitch*, and maybe I won't hurt you."

The universe hated me. I was honest-to-God convinced of that fact. Any other gal could have had a nice romantic dinner and gone home to have sex with her werewolf lover. Anyone but me.

Aric pulled me against him protectively. If the gang of delinquents facing us in the parking garage knew what was good for them, they would leave—now. Damn, I was *pissed*. Aric had been telling me how beautiful I was all night and barely kept his hands off me during dinner. My confidence soared, my sexuality bolstered. I was set to seduce Aric via Taran-esque posing. But if these little maggots forced me to *change* and rip my skimpy and expensive lingerie, I was going to beat the unholy crap out of them.

The leader meandered away from the Escalade and glared at Aric. Wrong move against an Alpha werewolf. Aric growled louder and deeper than a hound from hell. The stupid teenager had inadvertently challenged my wolf.

A kid flashed a gun. "Hey, mama. Come over here, I'll give it to you real good."

One by one, the rest pulled out knives. Aric stepped in front of me. His growl deepening as he headed toward the teen brandishing the gun. The others panicked as he advanced. I'd be scared, too, if some crazy guy pretending to be a dog was coming at me.

Before I could say, *We need to get home so I can seduce you*, all but one kid had either run off or lay unconscious. The last idiot waved a knife in my face, clearly terrified. "I'll cut her, man," he told Aric. "I'll cut her if you get near me!"

I snatched the wrist holding the knife and crushed it as I yanked him to me, *changing* my face to that of my beast. The knife hit the concrete. I roared and snapped my fangs an inch from his nose. He didn't take it well. The kid's eyes rolled into the back of his head just before he crashed to the ground. I released him, trying hard not to kick his sorry ass into the wall. He and his friends could have hurt someone. I'd let him off easy with a broken wrist and a mild concussion.

Aric ushered me to the Escalade. "Come on, sweetness. I'll call the *weres* on the force on the way." He opened the car door for me, but something near the dark corner of the garage alerted my senses. I couldn't smell it or hear it; I only *felt* it. And it felt cold, unearthly, *wrong*.

I inched away from the car. "What is that?"

He peered in the same direction. "Stay here."

I ignored his order and followed behind him. Aric kept his arm out near me, but his focus remained ahead. We found nothing in the corner when we reached it, but the sense of wrongness continued to linger. Aric bent to take a whiff. His nose wrinkled in disgust. I inhaled as well, hoping to understand what had stalked and watched us.

An awful, sharp and sour stench burned my nose and made me want to flee from it. My inner beast cringed. Our saving grace was that whatever had lurked was gone, and that its scent faded quickly.

"Demon," Aric said.

I hoped he was joking. "You mean demon child?"

"No. This was one of those damned to hell that can't remain on earth."

I straightened, my blood turning into clotting chunks of ice. "But who summoned it?"

Aric focused on the corner as he stood. "Sometimes demons appear on earth when there's a strong collection of evil. Those damn kids probably attracted it through their shared thoughts and actions." He shrugged. "And with all the attacks and the presence of evil lately, it was probably easier for one to present itself."

My eyes scanned the area. "Should we search for it,

just in case it's still here?" Although I asked, meeting a demon was high on my list of things I never wanted to do. Their offspring had been kicks and giggles enough.

"No. There's no trace of him left. I'm certain he's back in hell where he belongs."

I wrapped my arms around myself. "Glad to hear it."

Aric's eyes shimmered with ferocity when he drew me to him. "I swear to God, I won't let anything hurt you, Celia."

In his arms, with that heat, I believed him. He led me back to the car, holding me close. I didn't like being coddled. I was tough, strong, and capable of protecting myself and those I loved. But something about Aric made it okay for me not to be the hero for once.

Aric's constant touch on our drive back to the house dissolved the unease the demon had created. He kept rubbing my knee and reaching across the seat to stroke my cheek. The scuffle and momentary threat of danger had excited his wolf. I could taste his longing against my tongue and looked forward to exciting him more. But when we entered the house, my confidence took a nose-dive.

Emme and Shayna, both wearing bathrobes, slouched on the couch while their wolves tended to them. Misery and humiliation shimmied like well-endowed burlesque dancers across their faces.

"Bend over a little more, angel." Liam tucked the fan knotted into Emme's hair beneath his arm. His right hand manipulated the scissors, cutting Emme's hair free in large, uneven chunks. "Why did you shake your head so close to the fan, sweet girl?"

Emme's bottom lip pouted down to her toes. "I was flipping my hair, Liam." Her blush could have set off a sprinkler. "Oh, never mind. . . ."

Poor Emme. And Shayna? Good grief. Koda held an ice pack to her neck. He tilted her chin as he examined her head carefully. "I still don't understand why you were lying on top of your dresser like that, baby. You could've gotten hurt a lot worse by the way you fell."

"I'll explain after Emme heals me, puppy," she grumbled.

The wolves seemed so distracted by my sisters' injuries, they'd missed the point entirely. I tugged at my skirt. My tigress made me more graceful and coordinated than my sisters, yet their sexual expertise far exceeded mine. I second-, third-, and fourth-guessed my posing abilities. "Um. Are you guys all right?" Shayna nodded. Emme tried, but the fan impeded her movements. "Ah. Okay. Where's Taran?"

Shayna jerked a rather irate thumb in the direction of Taran's bedroom. "She called Gemini to her room and asked him if he'd like to deflower her. He slammed the door shut behind him. We heard a lot of grunting and screaming, and they haven't come out since." Shayna thought about it. "I think they broke her dresser."

"Oh." Something told me no falls or fan fiascos lay behind Taran's closed door. I hoped none would transpire in my room and made a mental note to avoid the window and anything pointy. I slapped my hands against my sides. "Well, I guess we should head up ourselves."

Emme clasped her hands over her lap. "Yes, good luck with that." Liam had finally set her free. And not to judge, but I think a two-year-old sugared up on Pixy Stix could have done a better job on her hair. For her sake, I prayed her hair would grow back fast.

Aric covered his hand with mine and led me upstairs to my room. He sat on the bed and pulled me onto his lap. "What the hell was up with that?"

"Oh, you know girls." I stood and patted his back like an idiot. "Why don't you get comfy? It's been a long night."

Aric angled his head, scenting my nervousness. Thankfully he didn't push and began to remove his shoes. I gathered my courage and moved to the dresser, watching as he loosened his tie and unbuttoned his collar. I sighed. The disheveled look totally worked for that wolf.

"Aric, could you help me unzip my dress?"

A hint of want sparkled behind his grin. "Yeah, I can do that for you, baby."

The way he gradually pulled down my zipper told me he was ready to make love. I stepped away from him before he could take off my dress. Damn it, I'd worked hard on my ridiculous posing all afternoon. I couldn't spoil the big reveal now. "Thanks, Aric. I'll get the rest."

"All right. . . ."

I turned my back and waited by the mirror as he returned to the bed and removed his clothing. When he was down to his briefs, I let my dress drop to the floor as loudly as possible. I tried not to glance at him for fear I'd be too embarrassed to continue, but I felt his eyes lock on to my body.

Aric swallowed audibly when I thrust out my bottom in the exaggerated way Taran had taught me. He growled when I bent over to pick up my dress and tossed it aside. I rose and flipped my hair back, causing his sound effects to intensify. Then, slowly, I ran my hands down my body.

Aric stood before me at once, his voice several octaves lower. *"What are you trying to do to me?"* His hands gripped my hips, his breath hot and ragged teasing my flesh. I groaned from the evidence of his growing need pressing against my body. "Celia, what are you trying to do?"

My hands slid up his chest as I forced my eyes to reflect an innocence his body had vanquished from its first touch. I licked my lips. "Seduce you," I whispered.

Aric's passion ignited mine. What happened next was a frenzied exploration involving lips, tongues, teeth, and hands. Our cries echoed loud enough to bash down the door, our movements forceful enough to collide the dresser into the wall.

When foreplay wasn't enough, Aric carried me to the bed. He lay on top of me, our sizzling skin sliding against each other, our kisses wild and deep.

I clasped his wrist when he reached for the box of condoms on the nightstand. "You won't need those anymore."

The already burning fire in Aric's eyes intensified into an inferno. He threw the condoms across the room. His head fell against my shoulder and he seized me tight, struggling to stay controlled. With a hard yank he pulled off my tattered thong. He entered me and began to move.

"Do you want me?" he asked between grunts.

"Yes," I whimpered.

"Can I have you?"

"Yes."

"Then you're mine."

Aric's cell phone alarm woke me from the best sleep of my life. He didn't make a move to turn it off. Instead he continued to lie where he'd fallen asleep, with his face buried between my breasts. I maneuvered enough to shut it off, but even my movements failed to wake him. He looked so peaceful and content. I hated to disturb him, except I knew he couldn't be late for work.

I stroked his long dark hair off his forehead. "Baby," I whispered. "It's time to wake up, love." He still didn't move. I glided my hands around his hard shoulders, but instead of his eyes opening, something else perked in attention.

Part of me was scared what we had wasn't real and that it would end too soon. It was that same side of me that wanted as much of Aric as possible while I still had him. So I continued to caress him, triggering my excitement in the process.

My breath came out in quick bursts. Aric stirred. His nostrils flared once before he opened his eyes. My touch hadn't succeeded in wakening him, but it seemed the scent of my arousal had.

He repositioned himself on top of me and kissed my neck. "Good morning, sweetness," he murmured.

My back arched with pleasure. "Good morning." There was no foreplay this time, but it wasn't necessary. Aric hooked my leg over his shoulder, and we began our day.

CHAPTER 17

Emme's pale yellow light receded. "Did I get all of them, Celia?"

I examined my neck in the foyer mirror, trying my best to avoid facing Emme. She knew Aric and I regularly engaged in sexual intimacy. Still, I had to work up my courage to ask her to erase the evidence of his exploration. June in Tahoe didn't allow for scarves or turtlenecks, and my scrubs hid very little. "Yeah. I think so. Thanks, Emme."

Shayna fell into the sofa. Her droopy ponytail matched her mood. She wasn't herself when Koda had to leave her to hunt. "Can I drive us to work today?"

"No," the rest of answered.

I didn't care at that moment how depressed she appeared. Shayna wasn't allowed to drive us anywhere. Ever. If we had somehow slipped into comas and a tribe of cannibalistic pigmies were about to sacrifice us to their volcanic god, and Shayna behind the wheel was our only escape? I'd take my chances with the lava.

Shayna blew out a breath hard enough to flutter her bangs. "Did Aric give you any indication how long he and the wolves would be gone?"

I sat next to her. "No. I just know things aren't going well. Every scent they pick up leads to a dead end."

"Or a dead body." Taran scrolled through her iPad as she paced. "Three more women missing. This time near Carson City."

Shayna lifted her head. "Do you think they were with those three men Koda and the others found near Lake Tahoe State Park?"

"It's possible. Considering the vamps, or whatever, continue to target couples on dates." I rounded up my thick hair and attempted to tie it into a twist. It took a few tries since my hands couldn't seem to work right. "And women out on their own."

Emme helped me fasten my clip. "What do you think is happening to them? We know they're draining the men, but . . ."

Taran shut the cover closed over her iPad. She brushed her hands over her arms as if something crawled along her skin. "I'd rather not think about it, Emme."

There was a lot I didn't want to think about. The fate of the women. The last few breaths of the men. How I'd fallen in love with a werewolf who hunted the supernasties of the world. And how his Elders held him responsible for it all.

I grabbed my purse and huge lunch sack, pausing when I caught Taran continuing to hug herself. "Are the nightmares back?"

She stared blankly out the window. "They haven't left, Celia. They're just getting more vivid."

I moved to stand next to her. "Do you talk to Gemini about them?"

"Not really. They don't happen much when he's around." Taran wiped the crease of her lid, removing a bit of eye shadow that had smeared. Makeup seemed like too much work. That's why I never bothered. She examined the charcoal color on her fingertips. "I'm not looking forward to the night without him."

"He makes you feel safe, doesn't he?"

Taran snatched the keys off the table. "Yeah. Even when I dream of demons raping me."

I stepped in front of her and held out my hand, trying to ignore Emme's and Shayna's gasps. We'd suspected what her nightmares entailed. But Taran hadn't confirmed our fears until now. They must have worsened in the past few weeks. "Why don't you let me drive today?"

Her glare prepared me to argue. Instead she nodded and handed me the keys to our Tribeca. I didn't like seeing Taran so shaken. Thank God Mrs. Mancuso was around to lift our spirits.

"Whores!"

I leaned my head against the car. We'd almost made it safely into the cabin. Taran stepped into the car and leaned her arm against the opened window. "You got that right, Mancuso. By the way, your grandson sends his love."

For a woman in her eighties, Mrs. Mancuso was quite agile. She chased after our car all the while flipping us off. Emme clutched the headrest of the backseat. "Oh my goodness. Celia, slow down before she breaks a hip."

I didn't care what Emme said. A glance at the mirror told me slowing down ranked up there with mooning a weregator. We might as well have kicked our own asses. Mrs. Mancuso was a woman possessed by fury and ill-fitting support hose.

Taran threw back her head, laughing. "That's not funny, Taran," Emme insisted. "I know you'd feel terrible if she did break her hip."

No. She wouldn't. I pulled out of the neighborhood. My last image of Mrs. Mancuso was of her standing at the top of the incline like the Statue of Liberty, minus the torch. "Crap, I hope she doesn't detonate the house."

My eyes narrowed at Taran through the mirror. "You haven't been leaving retirement home brochures on her doorstep again, have you?"

Taran fluffed her hair. "I only did that the one time. And she deserved it after spraying me with her damn hose."

Shayna wiggled in her seat. She hadn't kept still since saying good-bye to Koda. "Ceel. How do you feel about hunting demons? I mean, I know we were a little unprepared last time, but . . ."

"A little unprepared? Shayna, we took on a demon child—*child*. And it chomped on my foot like a taco. I get the feeling a demon lord might be a tad tougher." She fumbled with the silver pins in her hair Misha had gifted her with. Since our showdown with the vamps and our twisted slapstick routine with the little evil bugger, Shayna was constantly armed and ready for the next brawl. I sighed. I could relate. "I want to hunt with the wolves, but Aric flat-out refuses to take me with him, especially following Misha's possession on our front lawn."

Her head snapped up. "I get why Aric is afraid for you. I am, too. But it doesn't seem right for us to sit around. We're not exactly helpless, you know." She blew out a breath, hard enough to make her lips vibrate. "I hate Koda out there without me. I know he's big. I know he's tough. And I know he has more fighting experience than I do. But I want to help keep him safe. Does that sound screwy?"

"No. It's not screwy." Everyone grew quiet, probably thinking of their own wolves. I knew I thought about mine. "I wrestle with two sides of me. When Aric talks about tracking and what he finds, it excites my beast. Both because of her need to hunt, but also because of our need to protect. My mortal side, the one that knows I could die, is scared senseless."

"You get scared, Celia?" Emme asked quietly.

I smiled without humor. As my sisters' defender, I'd learned to charge first and deal with my terror after. Way after. "I'm scared a lot, Emme."

"Sorry," she responded meekly. "I guess that was a stupid comment."

"It's not, babe. I just have a good game face." I slowed the car as I took the turn down a steep hill. It gave a stunning view of the water. Tahoe summers were gorgeous, but the demon lord's unknown whereabouts and killing spree wouldn't allow us to enjoy it.

"Are the runs helping you deal with some of this shit?"

"What? Oh, sorry, Taran. The running helps to a point. My tigress has been hard to control. It's all I can do to stop myself from *changing*, especially once night comes. The air alters come sundown, I think because Tahoe gets energized by the moonlight."

Emme leaned in from the back. "I'm surprised your runs don't help you more. You seem so relaxed when you return with Aric, sweetie."

"It's only because he's with me." I stopped behind a log truck. The driver stepped out fast and adjusted the orange flags before rushing back inside, but it was the dark blue sedan driving in the opposite direction that caught my eye. I recognized the driver as that wereweasel Aric and I had encountered several weeks back. We'd taken a moonlit walk along the beach when the supernatural equivalent of a paparazzo jumped out and snapped a photo of us. I scowled when he waved. *Asshole*.

"What is it, Celia?" Emme asked.

"That stupid weasel that photographed me and Aric just passed us." My scowl deepened. "He has a lot of nerve waving like we're pals."

"Just ignore him, Celia. Someone like him isn't worth your time or energy." Sometimes Emme didn't need her mojo. Her soft voice worked its own magic. "Now, what were you saying about Aric?"

I followed the log truck. "Just that his beast has a tendency to settle mine. When he's away from me, it's a lot harder." I shrugged. "Mostly, I think my tigress longs to fight with his wolf."

Shayna swiveled in her seat. "I want to talk to Koda about going out with him again. Will you talk with Aric?"

"I can. The problem is I think my presence makes matters worse for him with his Elders. And he's already under enough stress." I pulled on to the road leading to our hospital. Like with many of the buildings and restaurants in the area, the stacked stone and wood exterior blended in with the environment and gave it a more mountainous appeal.

"This sucks, Ceel. But you know what? I bet if they saw how tough you are, they'd see past our, you know, uniqueness."

"You mean 'weirdness'?"

Shayna smiled with all the sympathy she could muster. "Yeah, dude. That, too." She curved her fingers and bounced her hand in front of my face. "They have to accept you. You're his sea horse."

"You're such a spaz." I laughed and pushed her hand out of my face. "What do you mean by that anyway?"

It was Taran who answered, though her tone lacked Shayna's good humor. "Sea horses mate for life, Celia."

I flipped through my patient's electronic chart before entering her room. Sandra Conchita Espinosa-Valdez. Spanish-speaking only. Fourth baby. Desiring a nonmedicated birth. This patient was right up my alley. I entered her room. The labor rooms all mimicked one another: one patient bed, a guest bed beneath the large windows, and a crapload of medical equipment secretly stashed behind the inconspicuous wooden panels on either side of the bed.

I smiled. "Good morning. Are you ready to have your baby?" I asked her in Spanish.

The raw scent of fury stopped me from approaching the bed. A wolf in human form leapt across the room and landed in front of me, his hands out, the muscles of his arms bulging. "Get away from my mate," he said in broken English.

My tigress didn't like his posture or his threatening tone. I had to work hard to pull back a growl. I took a breath, trying to relax my stance. When I felt somewhat certain I wouldn't lunge for his throat, I dropped my hands to the sides and slowly retracted my claws. "It's okay, I won't hurt her. I'm here to help her have your baby."

His nostrils flared and he growled forcefully enough to shake his form.

The woman in bed sat up, clutching her large stomach. "*Papi*, no," she said when he took a step toward me.

"She's not normal, not human," the wolf said in Spanish.

I returned to speaking in Spanish, hoping to connect with him and to keep my fist from connecting with his jaw. "No, I'm not human. But I also mean no harm."

A pained grimace wrinkled the woman's face. A contraction had begun. She curved into her belly, unable to speak and barely able to draw a breath. "How long has she been contracting like this?"

The wolf wouldn't answer me.

"How long?" I insisted.

"Almost an hour." The wolf backed away, moving protectively to her side. He muttered animal sounds I couldn't comprehend, all the while keeping his attention on me. When the contraction faded, the *were* sniffed the air again. "You smell like a feline and a wolf at the same time. How is that possible?"

He continued to assert his dominance. His problem

was, no way in hell would I allow myself to be dominated. "Let me help your wife, and then I'll tell you about it."

The wolf tensed further and took another step closer. My muscles tightened enough to tear from my bones. I watched his hands, his posture, and searched for any subtle twitches in his features. His next move would decide whether our beasts would clash. Or whether he'd submit and allow me to do my job.

The sour aroma of sweat and fear scratched at my nose. "Please, *Papi*," his wife begged. "Don't hurt her."

The *were* finally nodded and ambled slowly to his wife's opposite side as I advanced. I adjusted the woman's monitor belts. To anyone entering the room, it appeared as if my full attention focused on her. That's what separated preternaturals from humans. My tigress sensed any faint movement of air around us and searched for the burning smell of rising anger that would precede his onslaught. If he chose to attack me, I would be ready. Still, I needed to work fast and gain his trust.

I pulled the paper tracing from the monitor and held it out for the wolf and his wife to see. "Look. I want to show you how happy your baby is."

He stalked around the bed slowly. His steps shuffled with hesitation and his breath had lowered to that carefully controlled breathing supernatural beasts practice to keep their wilder sides in check. He hadn't decided yet whether he should kill me. Oh, goody.

He examined the paper and glanced up. I gave him, and my tigress, the courtesy of not meeting his eyes. He'd come to me like I'd asked, but his position remained protective. He angled his body so he stood between me and his wife, and so he could sense my movements.

I pointed to the lines on the paper. "You see all these jumps in the heart rate?"

He nodded. "Is that bad?"

"No, that shows me a healthy baby. Her contractions are three to five minutes apart. I think you'll meet your baby within a few hours. I'd like to do a vaginal exam to be sure the head is down and that she's dilating."

Again, he nodded.

After I checked her, I explained my assessment. "Your wife is five centimeters dilated. The amniotic fluid is stained, so we'll have to have the NICU staff present for the delivery."

"Why so many people?"

"The baby had a bowel movement inside the bag of waters. Sometimes they can breathe it into their lungs. The NICU nurses will help clean out the airway to help prevent it from going into your baby's lungs."

The woman stroked her belly. "Will my baby be okay?"

"This is a common occurrence, and most babies do just fine. But we require additional staff in case there's an issue." I knelt before her and extended my hand, knowing better than to touch her directly in the presence of her husband. When her fingers touched my palm, I squeezed her hand gently. "I promise to take care of you and your baby."

My explanation and the truth behind my simple gesture seemed to satisfy them both. "I'm Sandra." The woman panted. "This is Miguel, my love."

"And I'm Celia. Sorry about not introducing myself sooner." I winked. "I was worried your husband would tear out my kidneys."

Miguel dropped his eyes. "Sorry."

When I returned from updating the doctor, I began to aid Sandra through her labor. "Here. Let me help you get on your hands and knees. It will give you some relief from your back pain." I adjusted her in bed and covered her backside with a sheet.

Miguel stood on her opposite side, watching me with renewed curiosity. "Tell me about your scent."

I rubbed Sandra's back. Her contractions had intensified and they returned in shorter intervals. "I don't think now is the best time."

Sandra spoke between sharp intakes of breath. "No, please tell us. It'll be a nice distraction."

I braided Sandra's long dark hair and swept it over her shoulder so the strands wouldn't dangle in her face. I didn't like talking about me but did so to help Sandra. "Well, okay. I'm a tigress."

"But not *were*," Miguel said.

I shook my head. "No. Definitely not *were*."

"Then what?"

"Your guess is as good as mine, Miguel." Hell, we'd managed to bond, but we weren't exactly buds.

Miguel motioned at me with his chin. "What about your other aroma?"

"My boyfriend is a werewolf. We live together." My admission made me blush. While Aric and I hadn't officially discussed it, or announced it, we did live together. Hunting evil expeditions aside, Aric and I were always together and hadn't slept apart since the first night we made love.

Miguel frowned. "Is he a *lone* wolf?"

"No."

"Are you mates?"

His question upset me, mostly because I wanted it to be true. "No. We're not mates."

Miguel and Sandra exchanged confused glances. Miguel leaned my way. "Then why do his Elders allow him with you?"

Allow? It was a strong word, and not one I completely comprehended. I answered as best I could. "I think Aric's Leader status allows him more freedom."

Sandra, who had saturated her gown with sweat, gawked at me like I'd asked for dibs on the placenta. "A *Leader*? The male who shares your bed is of pure blood?"

Many females believed the pains of childbirth granted the laboring woman the freedom to say whatever she wanted. Sandra, it appeared, was one of these gals.

Miguel's suspicious frown returned. "Aric? You're romantically involved with *Aric Connor*?"

Sandra was one centimeter shy of spitting out a human being. Yet I was the one growing increasingly uncomfortable. "Ah. Yes."

Miguel took a deep breath, trying to sniff out what he pretty much perceived as a blatant lie. His aggressive demeanor turned to shock the moment my scent reached his nose. "You speak the truth."

Sandra reached for Miguel's hand, tears streaking her cheeks in tiny zigzags. "Miguel, the love of Aric Connor will deliver our baby."

My voice cracked. "Um. I don't think Aric would necessarily refer to me as his 'love.' "

My statement had little effect on dissolving their obvious idolization of Aric. For the first time since we met, Miguel smiled.

Sandra, thank the Lord, started to grunt. "I think I have to push."

I paged the doctor to the room. Twenty minutes later Sandra gave birth to her and Miguel's first daughter.

I said a quick good-bye following the recovery and headed for the locker room. Sandra's delivery had been the messiest of my career. So much pea-soup-colored amniotic fluid had spewed, I half expected Linda Blair to come crawling out of Sandra's vagina. Our third-year resident physician had gagged, but at least when the baby came out, and Sandra hemorrhaged, he managed to keep it together. It didn't matter that he threw up in the hall afterward; the important thing was mommy and baby were now fine.

Good grief. I examined my overly soiled scrubs. Sandra's body fluids had seeped through the fabric. Rather than attempting to pull the top over my head, I tore them off and called it a day.

I grabbed the emergency shampoo and body wash Shayna and I kept in our locker and headed for the shower. As I scrubbed Sandra's DNA off my body, my mind wandered back to Miguel's comment. He had asked how Aric was "allowed" to live with me. Although I had said Aric could do whatever he wanted, I couldn't be positive that was completely true.

When I finished washing, I reached for my towel to dry my face. But it was gone.

"You don't call on me anymore, kitten."

I slammed backward against the tiled wall. *"Misha! What the hell are you doing here?"*

He tilted his head; an amused smile lifted the edges of his mouth. I ripped the towel from his hand and wrapped it around me before he could answer.

Misha's smile turned from amused to downright wicked. "I came to see you. Is this any way to greet an old friend?"

"Are you out of your blood-sucking mind?" I stumbled out and scanned the locker room. "Anyone could walk in here!"

"Do not fear, my love. Edith Anne and Agnes Concepción are guarding both entrances."

The Catholic schoolgirls were here, too. Awesome. "Oh. Okay, Misha. Now I feel better." I stomped behind the row of gray lockers and slammed my door open. My hands yanked on my clothes as if Mother Teresa's soul depended on it. The moment all the important girl parts were covered, I stormed around to the other side and jabbed my finger into his chest. "Do *not* let those two munch on my coworkers. And I'm not *your love*!"

"No, not currently." Much to my annoyance, he continued to smile and took a seat on the wooden bench. His long legs bent at an angle as he leaned forward to rest his forearms against his knees. Misha's light blue silk shirt gave his gray eyes an added glint, or maybe his amusement. Whatever it was, it bugged the hell out of me. "I see by those marks between your breasts the mutt continues to show you affection. Now, had you been in my company, the only evidence of our time together would be a smile that would never fade from your face."

I adjusted my top and narrowed my eyes. Emme must've missed a few spots. "How long were you watching me?"

"I arrived somewhere between the cucumber body wash and the juniper and olive oil conditioner."

My hands dropped to my sides. "I don't believe you. And for the love of all things holy, wipe that smirk off your face."

He didn't. In fact, it widened. "You seem angry with me. Why is that?"

"I'm not angry with you, Misha. I'm *pissed* at you! Aric would freak if he knew you just saw me naked."

"Why? After all, I have seen you without clothing before." He chuckled. "Or did you fail to inform him?"

I picked up my wet towel off the floor and tossed it into the hamper next to him. "I'll have you know I tell Aric everything." Excluding the part where his archenemy had held me against him naked. "Now tell me what you're doing here."

"My master Uri is visiting my residence. I came to invite you to join us for dinner."

"Am I on the menu?"

Misha considered me quite the comedian. His shoulders shook when he laughed. "No. I assure you, you are not."

I paused. Something didn't seem right. "You could have called me or texted me. There was no reason to stop by. Especially here."

Misha's wicked smile faded. The fingers of his right

hand drummed against his knee as he regarded me. "I know," he answered quietly.

I gestured around the room. "Then why all this, Misha?"

His stare continued to pierce through me. "I supposed I desired to spend time with you."

My mouth parted with surprise. Not just because of what Misha said, but how he said it. The ever-present arrogance in his voice had vanished as well as his flirtatious demeanor. I couldn't sniff a lie. But I knew he meant what he said. I leaned against the wall of lockers and crossed my arms. "Misha, I can't meet your master. And I can't have dinner with you. Aric and I are together now. You have to respect that."

"You dismiss me so easy. Would you have done so if the mongrel failed to hold your interest?"

"Don't call him that."

Misha's stood. His expensive and handmade shoes barely made a sound against the weathered linoleum floor as he marched toward me. He stopped, mere inches from my chest. "You didn't answer my question."

I raked my fingers through my wet hair. "And I won't. It's a moot point, Misha. Aric means everything to me. I can't picture life without him."

My breath caught when Misha yanked me to him, pulling me tight. The tip of a fang scraped my jugular, and his seductive voice whispered against my screaming skin, "Very well, Celia. But remember this, when you tire of playing with beasts and desire the touch of a real man, you know where to find me."

And just like that he was gone.

CHAPTER 18

"What's wrong, Ceel? Did you have a bad day?"

My pulse continued to race long after Misha disappeared. I'd been stupid to think my guardian angel with fangs and I could just be buds. Without thinking, I rubbed my neck where his fang had grazed. Damn. Misha wanted me. Damn.

Most women would fall back squirming with glee if two very hot and very Alpha males desired them. Maybe that remained another virtue that made me "weird." I didn't welcome Misha's touch. In fact, I rather resented it, just as I'd expect Aric to feel if some female tried to seduce him. The tires squeaked as I veered onto the highway. "I just need to get home."

Shayna turned to look at me, and Taran and Emme abruptly stopped talking in the back. I hadn't meant to reveal how upset I was, but my tone gave me away. Shayna rubbed my shoulder. "What happened, Celia?"

"I just didn't have a good day" was the only answer I could manage.

I lowered the window as Tahoe came into view. The sun had begun to set in the horizon, painting the swirling clouds peach, orange, and red while the encroaching night transformed the clear water into a startling midnight blue. Maybe Tahoe knew I needed her tonight. Deep gulps of air soothed and refreshed me with each intake, and her mysticism poured on my body like cream, cooling my frustration, anger, and worry. But I still needed more. I needed Aric's arms around me. And I needed him to erase the insecurities trigged from my interaction with Miguel.

"Do you want to talk about it, sweetie?" Emme asked quietly from the back.

I took another deep breath. "I just need things to be better." No demons. No chastising Elders. No dead bodies. No master vampires in search of a nibble. Was that too much to ask? I thought of where life had taken me thus far. Yeah. Probably.

I pulled into our neighborhood. My spirit leapt from my chest and did a cartwheel when I spotted Koda's Yukon parked behind Aric's Escalade.

Shayna threw her fists in the air. "Woo-hoo. Puppy's home!"

I swerved into the garage. I'd barely set the car in park before Shayna flung open the door and raced up the backstairs. Taran followed behind her, trying not to appear too eager, but her steps were almost as quick. "Go on, Emme." Allowing her ahead of me seemed more polite than knocking the lot of them down and barreling into the house. What can I say? Class is my middle name.

Emme stopped at the top of the landing, her smile faded as she took in what waited inside. "Paul's dead," Koda said from the kitchen. My hand gripped the wooden railing. Paul. Leader of the raccoon gaze was . . .

Oh my God.

Emme passed through the doorway and into the laundry room slowly. I somehow followed, my feet growing heavier with each movement. We entered the kitchen.

Koda, Gemini, and Liam stood with their backs against our polished black and tan granite counter. Silence fell with the weight of an anvil around them. I didn't think any of the wolves were particularly close to Paul. But they'd known him, probably for years. And now he was gone.

Koda's body curled against Shayna's. The way he held her told me more than a friend's death had occurred. I barely spit the words out. "Where's Aric?"

Gemini's strong arms fastened around Taran's back, except instead of directing his attention on her, he focused on me. "He's in your room."

His quiet, troubled tone returned the apprehension Tahoe had lifted from my shoulders. "Is he all right?"

"He'll want you with him," was Gemini's only response.

Aric's muffled voice boomed from the second floor. "I don't know how the hell it happened. Or why he and Talia were alone—" He snarled with frustration. "We'd been tracking in groups of five minimum."

I hurried up the thickly carpet steps.

"Goddamn it, this is not my fault! Paul led his raccoon gaze as he saw fit—I know the kid's dead. The beta. *Paul's* beta is reaching out to the student's family."

I opened the door, my hand shaking as I turned the handle. Aric glanced up at me. "Just be sure they get a proper burial. I'll take care of the rest." He disconnected and tossed his cell phone on the bed.

I shut the door behind me. Aric waited like a knight behind a fortress of rancor and vengeance. My psyche training told me to give him space, that his ire needed to peak before it could begin its descent and allow the comfort of my presence and touch. Except Aric wasn't some volatile stranger, seconds from attacking. He was my love. And he needed me.

I rushed into arms that gripped me as if the fate of the

world depended on our union. My voice shook with grief. Not just for Paul, but for my lover's pain and the implications the *were*s' deaths had brought. "Oh God, Aric. I'm so sorry. How are you holding up?"

"I've been better. This demon shit is out of hand. We're getting nowhere fast, and now we're losing our own."

My hands slipped from his neck to his shoulders. "I want to help. I can't stand that you're out there fighting this thing without me."

Aric didn't hesitate, his response firm and unyielding. "Celia, *no*. It's bad enough you got hurt the first time. Don't worry about me. I'll be fine."

My head fell against his chest. "I always worry about you, wolf." I held him, wanting so much to erase the day and bring him the serenity my beast insisted would only be obtained through the blood of his enemies. "What happened to Paul?"

Aric rubbed his face against mine. "He picked up a fresh scent and located a body floating in Lower Echo Lake. When he *called*, we were at the northern end of Fallen Leaf uncovering four corpses. Paul was supposed to wait for us. He didn't. His tracks indicate he chased something westward." Aric paused. "Or something lured him there."

Death's cold hands inched their way up my spine and sliced like slivers across my shoulder blades. It took a lot to kill a *were*, especially a pureblood like Paul. Aric clutched me tighter, sensing my alarm. *Jesus, what were they hunting?*

"We were about six miles away and arrived less than ten minutes later." Aric swore. "We didn't even have to track them. A trail of blood led us to their bodies. The student accompanying him and Paul's current girlfriend, Talia, had their hearts ripped from their chests. Talia was one of our toughest *pure* females, and the student solid beyond his years. Neither appeared to have put up much of a fight. And Paul? Shit. Whatever got him ripped him to pieces. It took us an hour to locate his fractured skull."

My parents had been murdered. Shot through the chest with sawed-off shotguns by gang members seeking to rob our tiny apartment. I remembered being both horror-struck and mesmerized by the holes where their hearts had beat. And how I tried to shield my sisters from the gruesome chunks of bone and the blood saturating the pullout couch where they'd slept. Evil had taken my parents. Just like it had claimed Paul and his group. I wished I could have spared Aric from finding them. But all I could do was tighten my embrace. "I'm so sorry, Aric," I repeated once more.

"I am, too, baby."

The sun finished setting across the length of our suite, the last bits of light catching the corner of the dresser's mirror and reflecting until the room darkened with nighttime. "What can I do to help?"

Aric's stubbled jaw gently rubbed against my neck. "This." His hands slipped beneath my scrub top to rest against the deep curve of my lower back. "You help by being with me."

"It doesn't seem like enough." A thought occurred to me. "I can organize the funeral arrangements if you'd like. It may help ease the burden of those mourning Paul."

Aric's chest hardened against the side of my face. "Celia, it's best the *weres* handle everything."

"Okay. I understand." I sighed. "Do you know when the funeral is? I have to work on Thursday, but I can ask for the day off."

The sudden strain that beat a space between us halted my words. Aric's hands slid delicately from my back to my hips. And though his touch remained soft, it couldn't suppress the tension firing his stare. "The funeral will be held at the Den's chapel." He paused. "Only *weres* and their mates are permitted on the premises." He pulled me against him when my body unexpectedly slipped from his hold. "Sweetness, don't. I swear I wouldn't attend a Den function without you under different circumstances."

I didn't know Paul well. So Aric's suggestion the *weres* handle the funeral hadn't affected me. As far as the service went, I'd assumed . . . My lid shuts tight, trying to prevent my tears from leaking out. Aric said only mates were permitted on Den grounds. *Mates*. His clarification and my earlier conversation with Miguel told me the thing I'd avoided coming to terms with.

I wasn't Aric's mate. No matter how much I wanted to be.

Pain made me cringe from his gentle strokes. My wolf wouldn't let me go. His lips found mine with desperation. "Don't," he said between breaths. "Don't leave me."

Aric lifted me and carried me to our bed. His heat soldered us together like iron to steel while one of his hands loosened the tie on my pants, giving him ample room to explore. Maybe he needed to feel close to me, to pretend our inevitable end didn't linger in the horizon. And maybe I needed the same. So I didn't leave, and I didn't stop him. I allowed the warmth between us to soar, and fool our aching hearts.

Aric yanked my shirt over my head. His tongue slid from behind my ear to my neck. And then he froze.

He lifted himself from me, anger replacing the scorching passion linking our bodies. "Were you with him?"

I pushed up on my elbows, panting softly. "What?" Understanding raced to the forefront of my mind before the word completely left my mouth. Aric had scented traces of Misha. The weight of his accusation pushed like a palm against my chest. I'd showered again after Misha had left. But it hadn't been enough. Aric's intakes of breath multiplied. And not from passion.

I sat and wiped the tears that hadn't managed to stop in spite of his caresses. "You know I would never do that to you."

Aric's jaw tightened. "Then why is his rancid scent against your skin?"

I reached for my shirt, unable to look at him. The day hadn't started well. Fate had propelled it in a dreadful direction. And now it ended with an insolent slap. I pulled my shirt back on and attempted to bind the pant string. My sobs rested close to the surface, and the lump in my throat ached with a throbbing tightness. My hands trembled so badly I abandoned the ties and buried my face into my palms. Aric didn't trust me. Was he so blind to my love? Couldn't he see that I'd die for him without thinking twice?

"*Celia*. Why do you carry his scent!"

My hands fell away from my face. "Misha came to see me at work today uninvited. He grabbed me against him. I wasn't expecting it—"

"I will *fucking* kill him!"

"No. You won't." I took Aric's hands in mine. "He didn't hurt me, Aric. He just surprised me. I made it clear we were together and that he needed to respect our relationship." My eyes burned and my vision blurred. "I told him that you ... that you mean everything to me. And that I couldn't picture my life without you."

Aric didn't say anything, although I waited. And then finally I couldn't wait anymore. I threw my legs over the side of the bed and curled into my body.

Aric seized me against him. In his arms, against his thrumming heart, I choked on the honesty of my revelation. He murmured to me in French and soft wolfish sounds similar to those that Miguel had used to help Sandra through her torment. There was one major difference between them and us. Miguel and Sandra were forever, whereas I held on to Aric by my bleeding fingertips.

*   *   *

Lights flashed. Again, and again, like an obnoxious strobe light against my tired lids. I sat up abruptly in bed in time to hear something fall off the roof and see Aric's gray wolf form leap through the screen. I scrambled out the window and landed in a crouch on the front lawn.

A midnight wolf soared from Taran's window, followed by a brown one racing from behind the house. They charged through the wooded path where Aric had disappeared. I tore after them, blocking out Koda's deep shout. "Celia, wait!"

The soles of my feet padded through the cold forest floor. I paid no mind to the sharp rocks, bits of bark, or the cold wind biting through my scrubs. The trail led to the main road and also served as a shortcut to the beach. I'd almost reached the end when I encountered Liam, the brown wolf, clenching a camera by the torn strap with his fangs. "Liam, where's Aric?"

He ignored me and then blocked my body with his when I tried to advance. "Fine. We'll do it your way."

I *shifted*, and surfaced behind him, only to have Koda grasp my arm. He wore only jeans. He must have shoved them on before chasing me. I was surprised he also didn't go wolf, but I supposed he didn't want to garner more attention than necessary.

Koda held tight when I tried to shrug him off. I glared at his hand, then at him. The day sucked. And the night hadn't taken a turn for the better. I'd fallen asleep in Aric's arms, exhausted and miserable. I didn't want to fight with Koda, but I needed to ensure Aric's safety. "Koda, let go of me."

Koda shook his head. "Aric wants you to stay put. Don't worry, he's not alone. Gemini's other half is with him."

I jerked my arm free. "Paul wasn't alone, either."

"They're hunting a *were*," Koda said in response. He lifted the camera from Liam's maw and hit a few of the buttons.

I glanced toward where Aric's scent quickly faded in the wind . . . along with the smell of the wereweasal. Oh, *crap*. My head whipped toward the camera. *Shit. Shit. Shit.* The sneaky bastard had photographed us again. My feet dug into the earth, ready to lurch forward and ditch the wolves.

Koda kept me in place through reason I know longer believed I possessed. "Try to understand, Celia. Aric's had a rough day and needs to regain some control." His growl ended the conversation as his tumultuous brown eyes fixed on the camera's digital screen. I stood on my toes and peered over the crook of his arm.

My lids peeled back. Each flick of the button revealed images of me and Aric together—dining at restaurants, standing on the porch the first night we'd made love, walking through Incline Village, jogging along the beach . . . and lying in bed. I stumbled back, shock, humiliation, and anger forcing my fangs to protrude. The number in the corner of the screen stated the camera held sixty-five images. Were they all of me and Aric?

Koda continued to scan through the images. My body shut down. My fangs *changed* back to my human teeth and my arms drooped to my sides. The wind increased in intensity, mussing my hair and flapping the sides of my loose fitting top. I ignored it and Koda's audible protests over the photos. What the hell could this idiot hope to gain? I'd dismissed him as just another supernatural critter interested as to what my sisters and I were, but now I wasn't so sure.

Koda flipped open the tiny compartment housing the memory card and snapped the chip to shards between his large fingers. I stared blankly into the darkness where the last of Aric's aroma dissipated. The *were* hadn't just pushed his way into our lives; he'd violated our privacy. I wanted to scream. But I refused to give the little prick even that. He wouldn't break me. And I'd be damned if I let him dirty the moments Aric and I had shared.

Soft fur found its way beneath my hand. Liam whined and rubbed his side against my ribs. I patted his head. "I'm okay, Liam. Thanks."

He wagged his tail and gave me a wolfish grin, but the arrival of Aric's beast made him immediately back away. Aric's lips peeled back from a mouthful of not-so-inviting sunshine. Koda spoke into his shoulder, carefully avoiding his Alpha's glare. "He's been photographing you and Celia for a while. The images date back to as early as March when you met. Some are of you alone. Others show you sharing more . . . intimate moments. I destroyed the memory card after going through them. No one will see them now."

Aric's snarls ceased and his mouth snapped shut. Yet it was the hatred reflecting in his irises that made him appear more lethal than when he'd protruded his fangs. The wolves, including Gemini, who'd arrived behind Aric, circled out and away from him. I draped myself over his back and hugged his neck. "I'd woken to flashing lights a few times. But I dismissed them as dreams. I didn't think to tell you. I should have known something was up."

Aric curled against me and nudged me with his nose. Koda gave us his back, attempting to give us privacy and a moment for me to help ease Aric's wolf. As the tension beneath Aric's muscles lifted, Koda marched toward our neighborhood, his fist tight around the camera strap. Liam and Gemini flanked our sides. "Come, Celia," Koda said with an edge to his voice. "Aric will do better once you return to the house."

Maybe. The moment I released Aric his protective nature and his agitation returned, boiling over like a tub of acid. I kept my hand on his back. "It's okay, love."

My sisters waited on the front porch with Gemini. Taran tugged her robe tighter around her breasts and followed me into the house. "Son of a bitch. If that asshole shows his goddamn mug here again, you're going to be scraping his charred remains off Mrs. Mancuso's freak-ass lawn ornaments."

Gemini must have updated my sisters on the latest debacle. He held Taran against him, his voice heavy with the credence of my family's distress. "He'd be a fool to return now."

"A dead fool," Koda muttered. No one looked happy. Worry creased Shayna's brow, but the way she clutched the knife at her side also demonstrated that rage didn't linger far behind.

Emme threw her arms around me. "I don't like this, Celia. Not one bit."

"I don't, either," I admitted. My hold around her didn't last. The fur prickling against Aric's neck told me he needed the space that would only come from the sanctity of our bedroom. He trailed me upstairs without a sound from his massive form. I shut the window and the shades tight and drew the heavy drapes I'd never bothered to close.

I padded into the bathroom to wash my sore feet and redressed in a clean tank top and panties. Aric kept his wolf form. In a way I expected it. What I didn't expect was for him to join me in bed as a beast.

I stroked the fur along his back and allowed the motion and his presence to soothe me. Aric typically slept with his back to the window. Not tonight. All four-hundred-plus pounds of him faced the large window, guarding and shielding me from the evils that prowled the night.

CHAPTER 19

"You sure you want to do this?"

It was hard to answer, considering Aric asked while he nibbled on my ear. "Yes, dear. Someone has to show your wolves how it's done."

Koda growled something about a jar of catnip and where I could stick it as he drove his mighty SUV. "Don't you have bunnies to disembowel?" I shot back.

Liam shook his head. "Emme says I'm not allowed to do that anymore."

I shrank back at his comment and glanced out the window while the other wolves barked out laughs. The sloping mountains and forest of Squaw Valley presented the perfect place to build a school for werewolves—and the best place to test their fighting skills. Paul's death and that of the two *weres* demanded blood. Aric, his Warriors, and his Elders wanted to provide that opportunity. But the demon lord remained unknown. So did the extent of his power. Everyone needed to be prepared to fight and kill. Everyone.

Koda veered along the dirt path until the forest became too dense with vegetation to maneuver the vehicle. I hopped out the moment he stopped, and narrowly missed stepping into an overgrowth of ferns. The forest was lush and thick with the scent of magic. The Den students paced close by, their collective excitement and *were* magic piercing through the stratum of the beautiful forest. My tigress stretched within, vitalized by our surroundings.

Thick tree branches blocked most of the sun and infused the air with freshness tangible enough to taste. Aric strode beside me, carrying a box of supplies. We followed the wolves down a winding path that ended at a vast open field surrounded by more forest. I shielded my eyes from the bright sun. The clearing seemed to go on forever.

"Is this private property?" I asked Aric.

"It belongs to us. It's part of the many properties we've acquired for Den use."

We moved forward to where the students assembled in human forms, dressed in their school-issued navy and silver sweats. They parted as we approached. And while I'd initially been eager to meet them, they quickly unnerved me. The crowd of young *weres* scrutinized me with challenging gazes as I passed, some of them snarling. As an outsider, I'd expected some resistance, but not such blatant animosity, especially in Aric's presence.

My tigress chuffed restlessly in anticipation of a fight. Aric dropped the box he carried and let out a growl that made the students immediately lower their gazes. "This is my Celia," he snapped, his eyes sweeping over the crowd. "You *will* respect her."

Aric's declaration flipped my emotions. I went from alert predator to shy tween in under a second. Aric didn't bother to retrieve the box. Instead he took my hand and rubbed my palm with his thumb before leading me through the now quiet crowd.

"You'll also show proper respect to her sisters when they arrive," Koda added, looking meaner than ever. "Now let's begin."

Gemini and Liam divided the students into four groups of varying ages and athletic abilities. Gem had just begun to explain the testing exercises when I spotted my sisters walking toward us on the wooded path. I released a breath I didn't know I was holding. Sisterhood, especially in our respect, truly was powerful.

Taran scraped her sandal on the ground, dragging her foot behind her in an odd way. I wasn't sure why until the breeze carried a foul scent to my nose. She kicked her foot harder. "*Son of a bitch*, I just stepped in deer shit!"

"I think that's chipmunk poop," Emme clarified.

"I don't care what the fu—"

"Woo-hoo! Look, there's Koda. Hi, puppy!" Shayna waved excitedly, then skipped down the small hilltop.

Aric and I exchanged glances and tried not to laugh at her ultracheerleader enthusiasm. His lips tickled my ear. "Being that peppy must be exhausting," he muttered.

Shayna threw her arms around Koda and wrapped her thin legs around his waist. The collection of students gaped at Koda; I'm sure they were surprised he didn't eat her.

Koda nuzzled Shayna's neck. "Hi, baby. I've been worried. Did you get lost?"

"Just a little."

Koda kissed her lips and set her down. Not that the students noticed. Their eyes locked on to Taran's skimpy denim shorts as she sashayed her way to Gemini. She tossed back her ebony waves so they draped over the tiny white T-shirt hugging her breasts, and gave him a "let's have sex against a tree" smile. "What will you have me do?"

Gemini Hamamatsu. Beta wolf. Intelligent. Communicative. Eloquent. Usually. "Ahhh."

The students burst out laughing, but Koda's death glare quickly silenced them like an invisible slap. Despite his cuddly disposition with Shayna seconds before, his ferociousness returned with a vengeance.

Emme blushed sweetly when Liam jogged over and led her to his group. She'd stayed next to me, too timid to confront the crowd by herself.

Aric distributed a flag football belt to each of my sisters, keeping one as he returned to my side. His steel gaze took in the crowd of young *weres*, silencing them and bringing them to attention. "Last month, we lost three strong *weres*." He paused. "This is unacceptable." The wolves growled low in agreement. "We can't bring them back. But we can kill what killed them. We believe a demon lord walks among us and has aligned himself with rogue vampires."

A few students spit on the muddy ground at the word "vampire." Good thing I didn't invite the Catholic schoolgirls along.

Aric continued, his voice growing curt. "Our quandary remains that we don't know where the demon is, or what he can do. We have to prepare for the unknown." He put his arm around me. "Celia and her sisters represent the unknown. Each will wear a belt with two flags attached. To pull a flag represents proximity close enough to the enemy to cast a lethal blow." Aric's face turned fearsome. "I don't have to remind you that these ladies are not the enemy. But I will. If you harm them in any way, you'll have to deal with me."

The students shuddered at his threat and lowered their heads. A wire-thin kid about fourteen raised a shaky hand. "Can we *change*?"

Aric gave a stiff nod. "Except if you're chasing Celia. The belt won't fit her if she's in her other form."

Koda stepped forward. "For those who choose to fight as beasts, no biting or clawing allowed. If we yell, 'Freeze,' everyone must immediately stop. Once we whistle, the exercise is immediately over."

"Do we need both flags?" a big guy with a Mohawk asked.

Gemini came out of his Taran stupor. "No. One will suffice. As an incentive, those who succeed will be exempt from latrine and kitchen duties for the next month. Those who fail to catch a flag have to return to the Den on foot."

An excited murmur spread across the crowd. Nothing like a challenge and a hunt to enthuse a pack of wolves.

Liam smiled down at Emme. "Don't underestimate your opponents," he said to the students. "The girls aren't as innocent as they appear." Emme could've set the field on fire with the heat from her cheeks. Liam laughed. "That's not how I meant it, angel."

Shayna stood apart by a battered lodgepole pine. She carefully scanned the ground before selecting two dead branches. Light flickered from her platinum necklace as she transferred the element into the pieces of muddy wood, transforming them into long silver staffs. She twirled them with the grace and speed of a cheetah, warming up her wrists. A few of the wolves nudged one another and pointed her way. Liam had cautioned them against underestimating our skills. Yet it took a little Shayna action to heed his warning.

Taran stepped along the field, careful to avoid the extra-squishy parts. "Celia, I'm not sitting in the goddamn mud. Do you have something I can use?"

"Take my sweatshirt. I don't need it." No sooner had I pulled it off than Aric had it wrapped back around me.

He zipped up the front. "What are you doing?" he asked firmly.

I zipped it back open. "I'm going to get hot once I start running."

He leaned in close to my ear. "So will I if that's all you wear."

I considered my outfit. It was a perfectly respectable

sports bra and a pair of cotton shorts. Granted my shorts were a little on the small side, but so was I. I laughed. Had I known this would spark Aric's attention, I wouldn't have spent so much on lingerie. I smiled playfully, and spoke just below a whisper. "I'll tell you what, wolf. Pull my flag and I'll wear whatever you want."

I yanked the belt out of his hand and dashed into the woods. What sounded like a herd of elephants charged after me. I cleared a rusting barbed-wire fence with ease while wrapping the belt around my waist. Some of the students weren't so graceful. They swore when they became ensnared in the wire, but I didn't stop. They'd heal fast.

I sprinted amid the trees, weaving to the left before summoning extra speed to cut right. My tigress wanted to tackle and claw, but as her mischievous side spawned, she contentedly leapt and evaded, dodging fallen trees and gorges. I scented sweat, and ambition, decomposing leaves and royal pissed-offness. *Weres* should know better than to believe a tigress easy prey. The awkward clamor of the wolves only lightened my steps, spurring my inner beast to a more graceful, nimble cadence.

I skidded to a stop, allowing the momentum to sweep my hair over my shoulder before doing a little tigresses-rule, wolves-drool dance. My flags rustled and snapped as I surged forward. Judging by the throaty growls, the wolves hadn't appreciated my shimmy.

Five miles later, the odds evened. In true pack formation, the wolves worked collectively, one pursuing me at full speed while the others hung back, and a new leader emerging each quarter mile. I'd known they were finely conditioned and intelligent, but their teamwork impressed me. I panted through a field of waist-high grasses, wondering how much longer I could run at full speed.

Three of them gradually passed me, cutting me off and trying to encircle. I *shifted* before they could strike.

Their breathing hammered loud as thunder and their grunts merged with their pounding feet. They'd begun to tire. Hell, *I* was tired. My hair pasted to my face, my leg muscles threatened to tear off my bones and find a place to nap, and my tigress begged me to just eat one of the students and call it a day. But Aric hadn't stopped the exercise, so we weren't done.

A large stand of tall trees near the far end of the field caught my eye. My strides veered toward the strongest and widest trunk in the cluster. I protruded my front claws and quickly scaled upward, my breath escaping in rapid bursts. I stopped to rest atop a thick branch about halfway up. Below, the small pack of wolves circled the tree, growling in frustration. Some had started to climb, but most fell. *Poor little puppies.*

"Impressive," Aric said, panting next to me.

I jerked back, barely keeping my footing. *Of course wonder boy could scale a tree with his bare hands.* He just missed grabbing my flag when I vaulted away to the closest tree. I continued to spring off branches until I ran out of limbs. When I teetered about fifteen feet from the ground, the students started jumping up at me. Aric chuckled as he got nearer. "Watch out, little kitty. Here comes the wolf."

There was nowhere else to go but down, so I flipped and *shifted* a few feet away from them. The moment I surfaced, I felt a pull on my belt. Aric stood over me, dangling his trophy in my face as he grinned. The look in his eye wasn't that of a wolf who had caught his prey. It was how he looked at me in the bedroom—impish, aroused, and oh so sexy. He cleared his throat before facing his exhausted students. "Haul ass. You have a mountain to conquer."

The students disappeared with a few swears and a lot of grumbling. Aric closed the distance between us and kissed me. His sweet taste demanding that we lie down.

His hands pressed me tighter and tighter until someone yanked my remaining flag. I lurched back, surprised. A scrawny little werewolf danced in circles shaking the flag at us. I recognized him as the young wolf bold enough to ask the first question. "Thanks for distracting her for me!" he said to Aric.

Aric furrowed his brows.

The *were* dropped his head. "You didn't say, 'Freeze,' and you never whistled," he mumbled.

I smiled at Aric. "He's got a point. Good job, little guy."

Aric winked at me, but when he turned back to his student, he was all business. "Fine," he snapped. "John, wait by the car. I'll give you a ride back."

The kid hopped around like a crazed Easter bunny before running off. Aric turned back to me. "As for you, come here." He grabbed the waistband of my shorts and pulled me to him, kissing me softly. "You were amazing. Thank you for doing this."

I immediately lost myself in his gaze. The training had been Aric's way of introducing me to his pack, the equivalent, I gathered, of meeting his family. "Thanks for letting me."

We returned to the training field with our arms around each other, teasing and joking about which of us was bigger and badder. Our good humor faded when we heard a whistle and what sounded like a wolf howling in pain. We raced back at full velocity, stopping when we reached the edge of the clearing where a few wolves had gathered.

Liam's group huddled in a tight cluster, staring at something on the ground. I quickly shoved my way through the group when I couldn't spot Emme. I found her in the center, bent over a large red wolf.

The wolf sprawled in the mud next to a large granite boulder smeared with fresh blood. Emme must have thrown the wolf against the boulder, but I couldn't figure out why she'd reacted so aggressively. The young *were* whimpered and jolted as his ribs realigned beneath his blood-soaked fur. By scent, I recognized him as the big kid with the Mohawk. He'd acted arrogant then. Now he seemed young and helpless.

"Oh, gosh," Emme said quietly. "I'm so sorry. I didn't mean to hurt you."

Liam fumed, majorly pissed. He pulled Emme behind him, his face red and volatile. "Don't apologize. Devin deserves it for the stunt he just pulled." He motioned Aric closer. "He went after Emme with his claws protruded. He wouldn't stop even after I whistled."

Devin cowered at Aric's feet. When he *changed* back to human, Emme and I averted our eyes. "I'm sorry," Devin sputtered. "I lost control."

The students around us let out a collective gasp. Liam growled deeply and took a step forward, but Aric stopped him by putting his hand against Liam's chest. "That was the wrong thing to say, Devin," Aric said. His voice sounded threatening, but with an undertone of concern. "You could have hurt Emme. Your actions are inexcusable. But in the field, against a real foe, you would have been killed." Aric's hard stare brought his students to their knees. "Losing yourself to your beast won't be enough to protect you against what's out there waiting for us. You have to use your heads. You have to stay in control. Paul didn't. And it cost us three lives. Get back to the Den."

Aric turned back to Liam and locked eyes with him, prior to removing his hand from his chest. I guessed it was Aric's way of warning Liam against retaliating against Devin.

Devin took off, glancing nervously over his shoulder. Although his apology sounded sincere, I worried for my other sisters' safety. I chased after him until I reached the area closest to the path. My fears, it seemed, proved ridiculous.

Several wolves surrounded Taran. Some lay on their sides snoring loudly, having been zapped by her sleeping mist. Others whined and paced anxiously, trapped in rings of fire that shot upward to the sky. Taran casually sat on my sweatshirt, leaning back on her hands, legs crossed. She swung her top leg teasingly as she flirted with Gem. I shook my head. I continued to pant, and dripped with perspiration. Meanwhile Taran had spent the past hour sitting on her ass looking like an ad for Viagra.

Shayna, in contrast, was a blur of movement, her light blue T-shirt clinging to her sweaty torso. Mud caked her jeans as she dodged, weaved, and rolled. She twirled her silver staffs like giant batons, hitting any wolf that tried to reach her. With each strike, she knocked her opponents off their feet and maneuvered around them. Her eyes appeared savage, her laugh maniacal, mimicking the persona she embodied behind the wheel. Koda watched her carefully, cautious of anyone who might harm her. He seemed proud, and probably a little turned on.

The wolves obviously weren't getting anywhere alone. A few of them finally realized as much and coordinated their efforts. Four jumped Shayna at once, with one successfully pulling her flag. It was impressive; he managed to hang on to it even after she broke his fingers. Koda whistled, bringing the test to an abrupt end. His group collapsed, clearly exhausted, and probably not looking forward to their hike back up to campus.

Shayna congratulated the flag-wielding wolf when we heard Gemini yell, "Freeze!"

A skinny little guy with bright red hair froze in an awkward position, inches from Taran's flag. He had listened to Gemini's order and stayed put.

Gem examined him closely. "Bryson, how did you manage to jump through fire and not get burned?"

Taran answered for him. "There was no fire, baby. It was an illusion. This kid is the only one who figured it out." She motioned to Bryson and stuck out her hip. "Go on, you can take it." She offered the flag. The love-struck kid reached out, but stopped when Gem glared down at him like he might rip out his spleen. "It's okay," Taran insisted. "You deserve it."

Bryson must have felt Taran's attention was worth dying for, because he grabbed the flag and ran like the dickens. "I got it from the hot chick!" he yelled to the group of students, pumping his fist in the air.

Emme addressed one of Liam's wolves. "You can have one of mine, too," she said softly. "Out of everyone, you worked the hardest, no matter how tired you were."

Liam agreed. "She's right, Nehemiah. You showed tremendous heart and a great deal of skill."

The wolf smiled shyly at Emme and took a flag. "Thanks. You did good, too."

Koda put his arm around Shayna and addressed the remaining students. "Those who have flags, you earned a ride and your privileges. Everyone else, start running. I'll meet you at the Den." He kissed Shayna. "I'll see you back home, baby."

Shayna joined us as we collectively angled toward the path. I couldn't help noticing she lacked a skip to her step, and the sadness that dulled Koda's irises when she left his arms.

"That exercise went well," Gemini said. "It tested their endurance and the skills they learned this past term. I'm impressed that the majority didn't allow their beasts to dominate. That tells me they'll maintain their focus in battle."

Aric nodded. "Everything worked out better than I imagined. Hell, they did amazing considering they didn't know what to expect from our girls." Aric smiled at me. "Celia, maybe we can incorporate your evasive techniques for our graduates next year. You gave everyone a great chase."

Aric said a few more things, but I was still stuck on the "next year" comment. Maybe I wasn't his mate. But he'd introduced me to his pack and he'd refused to let me go.

I just prayed the year he anticipated wouldn't be our last.

CHAPTER 20

I woke up at ten in the morning to an empty bed scattered with pillows and twisted sheets spilling over the sides. The gentle scrape behind the closed bathroom door told me Aric was shaving the beard he'd grown during his past week away from me. I found my discarded shirt and replaced the panties he'd torn off with his teeth. I'd missed him so much. His deep insatiable kisses and our multitude of romps throughout the night confirmed he'd missed me, too.

The blistering July sun brightened the room as I spread the drapes and opened the blinds. I thought to make the bed, but the tap of Aric's razor against the white ceramic sink beckoned me to my wolf. His absence had left me restless and unable to sleep. And it wasn't just because I desired him next to me. I feared what he hunted because of what, and how easily, it could kill.

A trail of bodies had led Aric and neighboring *were* packs as far out as Utah. Maybe I should have felt a sense of relief that the attacks had left the Tahoe region. My tigress warned against it. A demon lord and his vampires lurked somewhere out there. He and his legions continued to stalk, continued to feast. The escalating reports of missing men and women verified as much and promised more death.

I opened the double doors and stepped through, unable to stop the smile my Aric's presence brought me. He was home. At least for the moment. And, more important, he and his Warriors remained safe. So I put aside my reservations and fears and continued toward him.

He grinned when he saw me. "Good morning, beautiful."

My hair was mussed from our antics and my eyes puffy from lack of sleep. Still, I appreciated him believing so. I stepped behind him and hugged his waist. Aric's clean, strong scent at the start of the day was at its most addicting. I kissed along the slope of his spine, making him groan. "Good morning, wolf."

My hands wanted to play. Instead I sashayed to the other sink, adding a little more sway to my naturally exaggerated catwalk. Aric leaned back and locked on to my backside. And that's how he stayed while I brushed my teeth. "I'm going to shower after I finish shaving. Want to join me, baby?"

I rinsed my mouth and pushed out my butt just a little more, swinging it slightly. "Sure, if you want me to."

Aric stopped his razor midstroke. "Well, you know what they say, 'Save water—shower with a werewolf.' "

"Mmm. Yes, your kind is all about saving the environment."

"Damn straight."

I laughed as I dried my hands. Aric lathered his jaw and made quick work with his razor. He scowled at his cell phone when it rang. "Could you tell me who's calling, sweetness?"

I flipped his iPhone over and read the out-of-state number on the screen. Aric wiped his hands and took it out of my hand. He answered with a big, affectionate grin lifting the edges of his mouth. "Hey there, pretty lady."

Pretty lady?

A female responded in a playful voice. "Hello, handsome." She paused. "You were supposed to call when you got back to your place. I was worried."

I stood there with my jaw inches from the russet tiles. *What the hell?*

Aric winked my way. "I got distracted."

"I'm sure you did, but that's no reason to forget about me," she teased.

"How could I ever forget about you?"

I stormed into the bedroom, completely pissed off and ready to set everything Aric owned on fire.

So I'm not the only one. None of this was real. I'm just another one of his freaking playthings. Damn it. DAMN IT!

I opened the window and knocked the screen out, ready to throw Aric's crap on the lawn in true Diary-of-a-Psycho-and-Scorned-Latina-who-can-*change*-into-a-tigress-and-beat-your-ass fashion, when he strolled in and sat on the bed. He did a double take upon catching my tigress eyes blinking back at him and my fangs ready to tear flesh. I thought I saw understanding fill and soften his expression, until the bastard grinned—*grinned*.

He reached out, trying to grab me. I smacked his hand hard, breaking a few of his fingers. "Ouch!" he mumbled, before laughing. His fingers realigned almost immediately, making me want to break them again, along with a few other body parts.

"What's wrong, sweetie?" the hussy asked.

Aric spoke through his increasing chuckles. "Hold on a second." He held the phone out to me. "Celia, my mother is on the phone. Would you like to say hello?"

"Your *mother*?" I asked in a small voice.

Aric lurched off the bed and shoved the phone into

my hand. He snickered and brought it to my ear when I gawked at it like an idiot.

"He-hello?" I dissolved my fangs, though they weren't the cause of my stutter.

"Oh, Celia!" Her voice was warm, and her thrill at speaking to me as clear as if she stood before me. "It's so nice to finally talk with you. I've heard so many wonderful things about you from Aric."

You have? I covered the phone. "Does she know we're living together?" I whispered just above a breath.

Aric tugged off his boxers, not bothering to keep his voice quiet. "That's not all she knows about us, hot stuff." He danced his eyebrows at me.

I reeled away from him, ignoring his come-hither physique, and tried my best to start a half-intelligent conversation with his mother. Aric, of course, just had to seek revenge for his broken fingers. He pushed me onto the bed and held me with one hand, while the other wandered under my shirt.

"I'm looking forward to meeting you, dear. Would you and Aric like to fly out to Colorado and spend Thanksgiving with me?"

I couldn't answer. My free hand was busy trying unsuccessfully to push Aric off me.

Aric's tooth latched onto my nipple. "I think my mother just asked you something, Celia," he muttered through tiny nibbles.

"Um, I don't know." That was me, goddess of wit, charm, and self-control.

Aric yanked off my panties and took in my flushed skin. "Sure, Mom. We'll fly out for the holiday."

I don't think Aric's gruff voice registered with Mama Connor. She continued in that same lovely pitch. "Of course, Aric has explained how close you are with your sisters. They're also welcome. It would be nice to have all the boys home."

I rolled onto my stomach and tried to scramble off the bed when Aric's hands went from daring to downright naughty. "I'll have to ask them about it," I choked.

"Yeah, and maybe you can come spend Christmas in Tahoe," Aric said. He clasped my ankles and yanked me back with one tug. "We have to go, Mom. We'll call you later, okay?"

"Okay, dear. I hope you enjoy the rest of your day."

He pounced on my now naked body. "Oh, we will. Give our love to Aunt Suzie."

Aric disconnected the call and started laughing again. I smacked his shoulder. "I can't believe you just did that while I was on the phone with your mother!"

"And I can't believe you thought there was someone else." His humor ceased and his rough voice deepened. "Damn, Celia. Don't you know how much you mean to me?"

My voice quieted. "I guess I don't."

A bee flew in the window and buzzed around the room. Aric snatched it from the air and tossed it outside. It flew in swirls, temporarily stunned, before disappearing toward Mrs. Mancuso's house. He adjusted his position on top of me. "What the hell happened to the screen?"

"Oh, it's not important." I pulled one of the sheets from the edge of the mattress and fanned it out around us. "Tell me about your parents."

The aroma of Aric's raw need floated into my nose, demanding that I pay attention. "I don't want to think about my parents. I'd rather focus on you."

Aric disappeared beneath the covers, but I pulled him back up before it was too late. "Come on, wolf. I'd like to know more about them."

"Now?" he grumbled.

I batted my eyelashes at him. "Please, baby."

Aric paused, watching me closely as he stroked a few

strands of hair off my cheek. "Okay, but only because I can't resist that face." He kissed my lips so softly I barely felt their gentle sweep. "My parents were mated. But I guess you already knew that."

I nodded. "They connected spiritually."

"Yeah. They sure as hell did." Aric's face reddened. "But it took them years to establish that connection. My father was forty when he realized my mother was his mate, though he'd known her all her life."

My head angled beneath him. "I thought for sure it was a love-at-first-sight moment. You know, staring at each other from across a crowded room and such."

Aric didn't laugh at my humor. Instead he grew serious. "Sometimes it is, but other times it takes a physical act for a wolf to recognize his mate."

I angled an eyebrow. "Dare I ask what kind of physical act took place?"

Aric chuckled. "My mother was twenty-five at the time and had always had a crush on my dad. He considered her his good friend's little sister, so he never paid much attention to her. One day she got mad when she saw him hitting on another *were* at a bar. She went up to him, kicked him in the shins, then kissed him."

"Good for your mom. Was he mad?"

Aric shook his head. He'd probably heard the story of his parents' union a thousand times. Yet he didn't appear tired of it or hesitant to retell the tale. But he did seem a little sad. "The kiss made his wolf identify my mom as their mate. They became inseparable and married days later. Crazy, huh?"

My nails grazed Aric's arms. "I guess." He kissed the knuckles of each hand, then rolled me on top of him. I positioned a pillow behind his head and tucked my head against his shoulder. "When did you come along?"

"Not until my mother was forty-five and Dad turned sixty. Mom had trouble conceiving and maintaining her pregnancies, a rare occurrence when you have two pure-bloods. She lost favor among the *were* elite. The pack Elders encouraged my father to take a mistress."

I stiffened. "Aric, that's horrible."

"It was a difficult time for both of them and one they didn't speak of much. But given that they were mates, Dad refused to have anyone but Mom." Aric adjusted his position so he could see me better. "They had the last laugh, though, when I was born."

"Because you were so damn adorable?"

Aric grinned back at me. "Yeah, that ... and when I proved as an infant to possess the power of an Elder."

My hand slid across his chest to rest against his other shoulder. "How could they know something like that if you were just a baby?" Aric didn't answer, his indecision raking against my skin. "What's wrong, love?"

His fingertips skimmed the edges of my ribs. "I'm going to tell you something about me, but I don't want you to freak out and think I'm weird."

I sighed. "I've split my atoms in front of you and *changed* into a damn chicken." Not that I wanted to remind him of the "feathered ass" incident when we'd first met. "I think it's safe to say I'm the weird one in this relationship."

Aric's hard laugh forced his head back. "Okay. Fair enough." He cleared his throat, trying to quiet. "As *weres*, we're born resembling human babies. We obtain our first *change* during a full moon before our first birthday. The younger we are when we first *change*, the more powerful we'll be as *weres*. The strongest usually *change* between six and nine months of age."

"How old were you when you first *changed*?"

"How old do you think?"

"Considering you'd make the Hulk your bitch? I'll go with not a day past six months." He didn't answer. "Babe, how old were you?"

Aric smirked before answering, "Not even two months old."

I didn't move, or breathe, or blink. "Okay. You are a freak. Welcome to the club. We have a secret handshake."

Aric slid his hands slowly down my back, immediately warming my body. "Can't wait to learn it."

I placed my chin on his chest. "So you really are the big, bad wolf. Aren't you?"

Aric's voice turned distant. "I suppose. But unlike you, my strength didn't come with any special gifts. I'd have given it up for the power to see the future."

I shook my head. "That can be more of a curse than a gift, love."

"Maybe. But at least it would have saved my father." Aric drew me closer. "When I was fifteen, my dad and Martin, our current Alpha, were sent with a team to Africa. Martin's mate, Nala, also accompanied them. Their mission was to dispose of an extremely powerful witch in Lesotho protecting diamond smugglers. In exchange for protection, the smugglers paid her well and gave her sacrifices. When my father and his team caught up with her, they weren't prepared for how powerful she'd become. She bespelled Nala with moon sickness and disappeared."

My stomach churned. Bren once told me moon sickness was the equivalent of bloodlust for *weres*. I didn't want Aric to relive such a tragedy and thought I should interrupt. But he continued. Maybe because he had to.

"My father was one of many *weres* killed that day before Nala was finally destroyed. Martin's strength allowed him to live, and so did his guilt. He felt obligated to raise me since his mate killed my father and because he failed as my dad's Warrior to protect him. My mother didn't fare as well. She was literally on her deathbed the moment she felt my father pass. I kept her alive by making her a foolish promise she continues to expect me to fulfill."

"What did you promise her?"

Aric swallowed hard. "I promised to give her grand-children."

This time it was my turn to tense. "Oh."

We held each other in silence, our beating hearts syncing in strength and rhythm. Birds sang outside and the warm breeze passed hard enough to billow the drapes. In the distance, cars swept along the highway, once, twice, three times before I finally spoke again. "Whatever happened to the witch?"

"I found her six months later. She was my first kill."

CHAPTER 21

I jerked up. Aric had avenged his father at such a young age. Aric sat up, cupping his large hand on my shoulder. "You weren't expecting that, were you?"

"No."

He kissed my forehead. "Don't be afraid. I won't ever hurt you."

"I know," I whispered. My lips met his to prove my lack of fear for him. But then he pulled away and left our bed. He adjusted the vertical blinds so they allowed light in, but veiled us from the outside world.

I adjusted the sheet against my breasts when he returned to bed. He knelt in front of me. "Will you tell me about your first kill?"

I turned my face away from him. "Trust me when I say you don't want to know."

His fingers rubbed the base of my skull, gently playing with the fine hair beneath. "I want to know everything about you. Even the hard times you've endured."

I didn't say anything, choosing to listen to a car pull in next door. Doors flew open and a little girl squealed. Mrs. Mancuso's great-grandchildren had come for a visit. It was the only time she semibehaved around us.

Aric waited patiently for me to speak. He didn't seem to realize how opposed I was to discussing my past, so I offered him an explanation, hoping it would be enough. "Your opinion of me will change if I do."

My reasoning didn't deter Aric like I wished it would. He shook his head. "No. It won't."

"It should." Long drawn-out seconds morphed into agonizing minutes. I finally stole a glance at his eyes. While they maintained the same fire, there was something different about them, a level of compassion I'd yet to discover. I don't know why, but at that moment I felt like I needed to be honest with him. I waited, though, until the last of the children's voices muffled behind the door of Mrs. Mancuso's house. It was silly. It wasn't like they could've heard me, but somehow their innocence made everything I had to tell Aric that much harder.

"I'd accomplished my first *change* a few months before my parents were murdered. But I didn't have any control for a long time. Still my beast waited inside, giving me strength an eight-year-old had no business possessing and heightening my senses to the point I thought I'd go mad." I blew out a breath, willing myself to calm. "I saw the four men who killed my parents standing over their bodies. I could taste the salt of their sweat on my tongue and scent each of their distinguishing odors, even over the blood of my mom and dad. My tigress latched onto their images like three-D photos complete with smells thrown in. And every night for years, she taunted me with their images. I hated her for it."

Aric leaned against the headboard and pulled me against him, wrapping me with the sheet and using the edges to wipe my streaming tears. "Your tigress didn't want to hurt you, Celia. She wanted you to hunt. And she was reminding you of your quarry."

"Like I needed reminding," I said barely above a whisper. I buried my face against Aric's chest to give me the strength to continue. There was no going back now. "I was such an angry kid. But when my hormones kicked in during high school, I pretty much lost it and realized what my tigress was beckoning me to do. I started taking the bus to Plainfield, where my parents were killed, and began my hunt."

"How old were you?"

"Fifteen. Sixteen by the time they were all dead." I couldn't face Aric then. "The first one was the hardest. He pleaded with me not to kill him. After him, it became easy. Too easy."

There was noise outside, I was sure of it. Rain, maybe the kids. But all I heard was the sound of my frantically beating heart.

"How did you feel after it was done?" Aric finally asked.

"It satisfied my tigress, but my human side felt no different. My parents were still dead." I rubbed my eyes. They were sore from crying. "I told my sisters the night after I had killed the last one. They all cried. Finally they felt safe."

"Did you feel safe?"

I focused on the framed photograph Shayna had taken of an ancient tree. He gently turned my cheek to face him. "Celia, did you feel safe?"

My tears threatened to fall once more. "I've only ever felt safe with you."

I couldn't read Aric's expression. He tried to kiss me, but I turned away embarrassed. "How did you feel after your first kill?" The only reason I asked was to shift the attention away from me. Aric wasn't dumb. He knew what I tried to do, but he answered me anyway.

"Celia, we're raised and trained to fight and annihilate evil. We're too connected to our animal side to feel regret. That's what makes us so different from humans. As per *were* laws, your kills were righteous. You avenged your family, just like I avenged my father."

"I guess if I were of your kind, I could live with that. But I'm not." I blinked a few times. "Do you think differently of me?"

Aric's voice dropped several octaves when he lifted me to him. "Nothing's changed between us. And nothing ever will. You're still the best person I know. I just want you to feel safe. Even when I'm not here to hold you."

I locked eyes with him. "Then let me help you hunt the demon lord."

Aric jetted the Jeep Wrangler across the barren terrain, kicking up dry chunks of beaten soil into the hot, sticky air. The packs had tracked the demon's trail to Death Valley. Once again, the irony was not lost. We drove through the sand-filled national park, trying to reach where the latest victims had been unearthed. The four-by-fours were perfect for off-road, except I'd given anything for the closed cabin and air-conditioning of Aric's Escalade.

I'd heard the Valley was a wonder, nature's masterpiece, a rare gem in a world busting with industry and flashy technology. Maybe. But after driving an hour in the one-hundred-plus-degree heat, it more than kind of sucked.

Aric passed me another water bottle. "Drink more," he yelled over the roar of the engine. "We'll have to abandon the Jeeps close to where the last set of bodies were scattered, and hike on foot from there."

I forced down the tepid liquid. Sweat soaked through my white tank and clung to my white cotton bra like a newborn to her mother. "How wide is the perimeter from where the bodies were found?" Danny hollered from the back. His teeth knocked together with every bump and grind.

"About thirty miles," Aric called over his shoulder.

Bren spit out the side of the Jeep, I assumed to rid his mouth from the coat of dust smearing our teeth like old paint. "Shit. That range is too vast even for the number of noses we have to track. Dan, your one-night stands with the Dewey Decimal Dames better pay off. This place blows."

"I'll do my best," Danny muttered.

His apprehension made me turn around. Poor Danny clung to the frayed leather volume in his arms like he held the original Ten Commandments. The "Codex Demon-Summoner" as he called it had come from a "hot" librarian in Ohio. Danny's interest in the Vixens of Microfiche continued to astound me. He'd wanted to help, except his lack of athleticism and his human status seemed to affect his spirits the farther we ventured into the scabrous and desolate park.

Shayna and I were part of Aric's hunting party. Taran and Emme had joined their wolves and another group. They weren't too far from us, but we couldn't exactly count on their immediate help.

Aric had graciously insisted that Bren and Danny ride with us. I could have kissed him for it. His fellow were-beasts didn't like a human tagging along, and resented Bren as a *lone* even more. Aric would help me keep them safe. At least, I hoped.

"We're here, Celia." Aric slowed the Jeep in the middle of stone hill path. The hot air beating against my face dwindled to a stop, exposing us to a layer of ozone so thick it slogged through my lungs. Danny took a few puffs of his inhaler, for all the good it did him. Bren shot him a worried glance before leaping out of the back.

I slid out of my sweat-soaked seat. Dunes stretched out in the horizon, laughing and mocking our withering bodies. Cracks crisscrossed the dry earth, forcing the sunbaked sand to resemble a cobblestone path rather than soil. Yup. Bren was right, this place blew.

"According to the werelion who found the last body, we have to hike about a mile that way." Aric pointed to the dunes. Behind us, three more Jeeps rolled to a stop.

Shayna hurried to me, her pixie face drenched with sweat and bright red from the heat. "Not the best place to track, huh, Ceel?"

"We can handle it," I said, keeping a close eye on the *weres* watching Danny. They laughed when he picked up a crumbling stick.

"What the hell are you doing, Dan?" Bren asked.

"It will help me hike through the tougher terrain."

Bren took it and chucked it behind a large boulder. "Just grab on to my arm. I'll pull you along the rough spots."

"You girls together?" a werebear asked, laughing.

Bren winked and grinned. "Nah, I like banging your sister too damn much to play for the other team."

Aric growled something at the werebear before he could react, cementing him in place. Good for him. I'd already taken a protective stance in front of Danny and Bren. The bear would have to barrel his way through me to get to them. And raging heat or not, I'd kick his ass if he tried to hurt them.

The bear ignored me and narrowed his eyes at Bren. Preternaturals had a tendency to underestimate my petite stature. Stupid mistake on their part.

"*Move*, Carl." Aric's tone broke through the dense air. The bear took the lead without another word or glance back. Aric linked his fingers with mine. "Don't get between two *weres*, Celia. Let me handle things."

"I don't like bullies," I told him, not bothering to keep my voice down.

"And neither do I," Aric answered just as loudly. "Come on, we need to hunt."

We'd trekked along the hard soil less than a mile when Aric's head whipped to the side, two breaths behind Bren. Bren threw Dan over his shoulder and bolted up an incline littered with jagged rocks. Danny held tight to the text despite Bren's spastic movements. Aric and I sprinted after him, leaping over the minilandslide caused by Bren's racing steps.

Bren ran a few more yards toward a cluster of dead branches. The festering smell of meat kicked me in the face.

Bren put Danny down and began tossing the termite-ravaged wood, building a pile on either side of him. Aric joined him until they uncovered two . . . no, two *and a half* men left to rot.

"Fresh kills," Bren said, pointing to the sections of drying blood near one man's cleanly licked femur.

Aric jerked his head to the right. "The scent originated from that gorge."

The pounding of paws and boot-clad feet announced the arrival of the rest of the team. Half of the *weres* had already *changed*; the anticipation of finding their quarry urged their beasts forward.

Danny cleared his throat but couldn't hide his gag. "We should try the summoning spell from the gorge. It's likely where the demon lord cast the lethal blow."

Bren stared at the bodies. "Or where he started munching on these poor bastards."

Danny cleared his throat again. "Ah, yeah. Violence like that can help trigger the spell."

Shayna clutched Koda's neck, turning her head away from the reek of death. Koda patted her leg and adjusted her against his back. I was glad she'd hitched a ride. The climb along the loose and rolling stones could easily have caused a fall or a sprain.

The witch, sent by the oh-so-lovely Genevieve to assist Aric, remained straddled to her werecougar boyfriend. She stroked his fur, scowling at Danny. "Give me the book."

Danny held it protectively against his chest. "Um, it's very delicate. I'll hang on to it until we get to the gorge." He glanced at Aric. "If that's okay with you, I mean."

"No problem," Aric answered. "Let's go."

The witch huffed before her fuzzy method of transportation took off in a dead sprint toward the gorge. Bren lifted Danny again. We barreled through a section of dried bushes, leaping over and across boulders until we reached the rim of the crater. The sides were steep and sharp along the football-field-wide hole. I panted hard, the thick, dry air making it difficult to catch my breath. "You okay?" Aric whispered beside me. His breaths weren't as ragged, but then his *were* lungs were stronger. He kept his voice low so the others wouldn't hear me. He didn't want them to consider me weak. And neither did I.

I held out my hand. "Wanna ride?"

His grin told me he knew what I meant. He clasped my hand and leapt with me. I *shifted* us into the side of the gorge and resurfaced at the center, a few feet in front of the werecougar. The witch on the cougar's back glared at me, with both surprise and apparent anger we'd passed them.

Aric squeezed my hand once before releasing me. "Thanks, sweetness. All right, let's do this."

Bren planted Danny on the ground and stripped before *changing*. Danny adjusted his glasses and turned the worn text over to the witch. "The section is marked with a—"

"I got it. Super thanks," she said, cutting him off in true diva fashion. In high school she would have strutted with, if not led, the "mean girls." My tigress wanted to eat her.

A few of the *weres*, including her boyfriend, formed a ring around her as her eyes skimmed along the frail pieces of parchment. She chanted. Again. And again. And again. The amulet around her neck sparkled from her magic and from the merciless sun roasting our bodies like wieners. She shielded her eyes and looked to the direction of the bodies and then she chanted some more. She waved a hand. She kicked some dirt. And she chanted more and more, this time swearing between chants. She continued. For at least twenty minutes. Her fits growing hairier each time she returned to the start of the page.

"This isn't working!"

Yeah. No kidding, Glinda.

The bitchy witch threw Danny's tattered leather-bound book on the dusty earth. He took a step to retrieve it, but a sneer from the witch and a growl from her werecougar boyfriend halted him midstep.

Bren's colossal beast form bared his fangs and stalked in front of Danny, challenging the cougar for threatening his friend. *"Enough,"* Aric snapped. He rushed between the two from one blink to the next.

The werecougar immediately backed down. In the wild, a cougar would make hamburger out of a wolf. But this wasn't the wild, and they weren't mere animals.

I ambled slowly to retrieve the book, keeping my focal point trained on the witch. Genevieve had sent Miss Personality along to help the *weres*. That didn't mean she'd help me, and it sure as hell didn't mean she wouldn't attack. So I watched and waited for one wrong move.

Sweat dripped in tiny rivers between my breasts and down my belly as I bent to lift the text by its tattered spine. Big mistake. The lexicon filled with old magic spells fell apart and scattered in the sweltering breeze swooping into the gorge. The witch had probably called the breeze just to be spiteful.

She shot me a nasty grin just to prove me right. *Yup, we may have to eat her.*

Danny and Shayna scrambled to snag the floating pages. I would have helped, but the witch's crappy attitude warned me against giving her my back. We had a run-in with a clan of witches when we'd first moved to Tahoe. I hadn't trusted the broom-humpers since.

The witch smirked as another battered piece of parchment floated past her. "Doesn't matter. It was worthless anyway."

I waved my hand to get her attention. "I'm sorry. What's your name?"

"Rita," she said slowly, like it would be too hard for me to pronounce.

"Then shut up, Rita," I snapped.

I'm not sure what she saw in my face. Or Aric's, who'd wandered to my side. But it was enough to make her back the hell away. Fast. "My apologies," she muttered.

"She was saying the words wrong." Danny spoke barely above a whisper, enough for me to hear, but not enough to risk pissing off the witch.

I grabbed a few pages that had swept near my feet and joined him. "Could you read them? Would that work?"

Aric glanced between us when Danny froze. "He's not of magic, Celia."

Danny hurried to organize the pages. "No. But I'm not summoning a demon from hell. I'm summoning him from the immediate vicinity. It should work if it's—I mean, he's close by."

Aric hit Gemini's number on his phone. Scorpions crawled along the ground like ants. The sun cut into our backs like laser beams. We tasted every dry bit of dirt, sand, and disintegrating piece of grass the roasting breeze slapped in our faces. I wanted more water. My beast demanded blood to quench our thirst. Both needs made me cranky as hell. But I refused to gripe. I got what I asked for. I'd joined Aric in his hunt.

"Anything on your end?" Aric said into the phone.

"Son of a *bitch*," Taran shrieked in the background. "Is that a goddamn tarantula?" She must have been standing near Gemini.

I heard a *squish* just before Gem answered, "Ah, nothing here. Should we move inward toward your location?"

Aric let out a breath. "The problem is the perimeter

is just too damn wide. Dan's going to try to read the pages. I'll stay on. Tell me if anything happens." His stare cut to Danny. "You ready?"

Danny shuffled through the pages, his breath panicked enough to steam his Coke-bottle glasses. "Yeah, just give me one . . ." He righted the stack of pages, scribbled with more images than anything that resembled letters. "Got it. I got it right here." He squinted at the unrelenting sun, took two paces back, one forward, and one more to the right after another glance at the paper.

The witch dug her hands in her hair. "What is he doing?"

Danny pointed to the page. "You have to face where the moon might be. It says so right here."

I glanced at the page. All I saw was something shaped like Mrs. Mancuso's lawn jockey and a bird with two beaks. I didn't read old dead languages for fun like Danny. And based on the image of a man with a snake eating his head, I had no desire to learn.

"*Suhaka,*" Danny said, sounding more Jabba the Hutt than Indiana Jones. "*Su. Ha. Ka. Ma nee bo so hee dah. So. Hee. Dah.*"

Danny's words didn't resemble anything close to what the witch had chanted. The snickers among the crowd told me they agreed. Aric's baby browns met mine, flickering with more than a little doubt. His decision to bring me, a *lone* wolf, and a human had been a bold move. And one that could cost him his reputation.

"Don't fuck this up, Dan," Bren had said when Aric first invited them along. I hadn't said anything of the sort. But damn, I was thinking it now.

I moved closer to Danny in a show of support. So did Bren. But the way Bren's tail drooped demonstrated that he, like me, had started to doubt our spindly pal.

"*Hee-ho. Hee-ho. Ha.*" Danny squinted at the sun again and nodded. "There. That should do it."

Aric pinched the bridge of his nose and swore. Twice.

I clutched his arm, red from the sun and just as blistering. "He meant well, Aric. Maybe we could go back to the Jeeps and—"

Thunder shook the gorge despite the lack of clouds and darkness. The dirt in front of Danny spiraled out like a cyclone, sending gravel, sand, and more dried soil to smack and scrape against our exposed skin. Cold burrowed through my bones, chilling me down to the marrow and making me beg for the waves of heat to return. *What the hell?*

Growls spread like wildfire. The dirt funnel widened, overtaking the land around us. "What's happening?" Gemini shouted on the other line.

Aric tossed the phone away from him and shoved me behind him. He *changed* as we retreated from the expanding conduit. My tigress urged me to move closer to the threat, but Aric's beast held me back. Koda grabbed Danny and flung him like a ragdoll behind Bren before his red wolf replaced his human form. Something was coming. And it was pissed we'd called.

The earth blackened and crumbled like charred wood into large chunks. A high-pitched scream burned through my eardrums like liquid fire. Another cloudless crack of thunder broke and shook the earth beneath our feet. Shayna fell on her butt next to me. I quickly hauled her up to stand just as the air imploded in front of us and the demon lord emerged.

Iridescent red scales cloaked his leather body and bat wings. His raptor head whipped my way, followed closely by his four, very developed, very descended testes. His fork-tongue spit out through his needle-thin, yellow fangs. "*Ceeelia,*" it hissed.

Holy shit.

Before me stood the demon lord Misha had warned me about. The one who possessed him. The one who knew who I was. The one who . . . Holy *shit*.

The *weres* pounced on the demon in a massive heap of fur and claws. The creature spun his expanded wings, slicing and cutting into their large bodies. Howls and shrieks erupted and bounced off the dirt walls. The werecougar slammed against the rock slide next to me, his stomach protruding through his skin like a wet tube sock and his head twisted behind him. Wings flapped hard enough to blind us with dirt, and just like that the demon took flight.

He sailed through the air like a massive glider, soaring upward as the *weres* gave chase. Shayna grunted as her thin arms flung her knives with all their might. The blades whistled through the sky and found their mark, piercing through the demon's webbed appendages. The demon screamed again, this time in pain. She'd hurt him, disabling his speed and impeding his ability to climb higher into the sky. Aric and Koda leapt after him, their deadly jaws inches from reaching his talon feet. I started to run, the shock from the demon knowing my name fading fast. But Bren barreled in front of me. I crashed into his side and bounced back. "Bren!"

He sneezed and motioned behind me. Danny's and Shayna's stark white faces kept me from *changing* and scaling the rock hard walls. They were terrified. I couldn't justify leaving them, especially with the amount of backup Aric had.

I retreated hesitantly, and knelt beside the injured cougar. He shook his head and shut his lids tight as he willed his beast to heal him. An ounce of his magic reached my flesh and pricked along my burning skin. I managed not to react when his stomach bobbed back into his body and his head crunched on its return home. Danny couldn't stop his response. He staggered back and tripped over a rock, disturbing a band of scorpions that fortunately chose to scurry in the opposite direction.

The cougar pushed onto his paws. The witch hastened to mount his back. The light from her turquoise amulet turned the cougar's fur blue as he charged to join the other beasts.

I watched diffidently as they faded into the distance with Aric and the rest of the pack. My tigress paced restlessly. She wanted to join the hunt. She wanted to tear evil in two, and give Aric's wolf the other half. But neither Aric nor his wolf needed protecting. Nor did they fear. I couldn't say the same for my little sister and Danny.

"That thing knew your name, Celia."

Shayna's voice shook as if the earth continued to tremble. I tried not to think about what she said. Something from hell itself knowing me by name wasn't just creepy; it numbed and froze my very soul. Bren agreed.

He *changed* behind me, returning to his human form. "Ceel. I gotta give you props. If that mutant freak had called me by name, I would have pissed out a kidney."

The thought had crossed my mind. Good thing my bloodcurdling terror had distracted me.

Taran's swears bellowed near Danny's foot. He picked up Aric's iPhone, while Taran continued to curse. "We succeeded in summoning the demon lord. Aric and the others went after him."

"Where?" Gemini said on the other end.

"East toward Badwater Basin," Bren said without much thought.

"Is it just you and Bren?"

"No, Celia and Shayna are here, too," Danny answered. "Don't worry about us. We're safe and nowhere near the fight."

Danny disconnected the phone prematurely. The cyclone of earth churned once more, bringing forth that biting, unnatural cold.

And another demon lord.

CHAPTER 22

The demon's skin shone lime green. Like his brother, he bore wings the size of sails and clawed hands and feet. Except he had four arms, and four legs, and a tail as thick as a baseball bat. A white stripe of fur covered the top of his wrinkled and turtlelike face. He grinned with four very long and extra-pointy teeth. His tongue slurped across them as if he could already taste our livers. Somehow I thought we'd gotten the short end of the demon stick.

The clang of Shayna's sword as it left its sheath cut through the sounds of Bren's roars. But I paid them no mind. All my thoughts and instincts focused on attacking and making it bleed.

I *changed*, barely feeling my form shred through my clothes and how the tattered bits of sweat-soaked cotton fell against the earth. My tigress made contact first, slamming the demon into the side of the gorge, one paw against his throat while the other ripped an arm free from its socket. My aggression enlivened my beast until the long wet maggots slithering through the amputated limb left the demon and crawled along my back. That's when my inner girl rose to the surface. I jerked back, narrowly missing his seven other angry limbs before Shayna sliced a leg off at the knee and Bren's fangs crunched through the bone of another arm.

More maggotlike entrails exploded out like confetti as the demon shrieked. Dirt coated the insides as they scurried along the ground before quickly shriveling in the baking sun. We gagged like idiots and backed away. But we'd injured the demon. And now he needed to eat to replenish its strength. Like a true predator he picked the weakest among us.

Danny.

The demon tackled him and took flight. Shayna screamed, *"No!"*

Bren and I jetted after him. My claws dug through the hard soil and up the steep incline. I pushed harder and quicker than I'd ever moved, urging my legs to dig deep. Within seconds I passed Bren. He snarled with panic and frustration. He didn't think I could fight this thing alone. And neither did I. But I owed it to Danny to try.

The demon soared higher and faster, his need to escape with his feast making his wings flap harder. I was keeping up, but just barely. He'd soon leave me far behind. I needed to act before he vanished with Danny. Thankfully I spotted a stack of boulders and cut right, passing the demon above me. I clambered up and used my hind legs to propel me forward seconds before the demon veered in the opposite direction. My jaws clenched onto his tail and I jerked my body hard, trying to use my weight to bring the demon down.

The demon tilted upon feeling the mass of my body, but recovered as my back paws hovered inches aboveground. Yet even my hard pulls weren't enough. His wings remained intact and incredibly strong. He flapped them left, right, compensating for the odd angles in which I twisted his body.

The miles passed in a rush below me as we fought.

The demon's remaining limbs expanded their talons and grabbed at my body. I answered with my claws. There was no strategy, no perfect choreographed strikes, no smooth fighting techniques. There was only survival. I batted, I kicked, I scratched, wildly, while holding tight to a mouthful of leathered nastiness my jaws beseeched me to abandon.

My fangs held tight to the demon's tail in order to hang on, but their sharpness eventually sliced through the demon's thick hide. The muscle and tendons split and began to pull from the bone. I *changed*, keeping my claws and using them to scale up his back in human form.

Danny hollered with gut-wrenching terror and agony, "Help me! *Help me!*"

I threw out my arms and pierced my nails through the upper arch of the demon's wings, forcing them to tilt down. The wind slapped at my body and dried my eyes, making it hard to see. He was brutal and attacked any way he could. But, damn it, I was brutal, too. I hung on tight and pulled my legs beneath me so my back claws stabbed into his shoulder blades. I ground my teeth, cursing and grunting until I finally forced his rapid descent.

My long hair belted me in the face and blocked my vision. I threw my head back, allowing the wind to whisk it behind me. I managed just in time to see the mountain of boulders we were about to crash into. I leapt off the demon's back and *shifted* into the earth. The speed plummeted me deep into the mountain. I couldn't slow quickly enough and buried myself deep before I could begin to surface. My lungs shrieked from the pressure and demand for air. I broke through the ground just above my breasts, coughing and wheezing. The stress against my ribs and diaphragm made it hard to draw a breath. I finished my *shift* in short spurts, clawing my way along the searing and jagged rocks.

Oh God. I didn't know where I was—just far, far away from where the demon had first emerged. And crap, the traveling, winged, evil monster assured the *weres* wouldn't be able to track our scent.

I forced myself to a kneeling position, scanning the area in search of the demon. Splattered blood dripped from a collection of boulders high above me. My lids peeled back, hoping my attempt to save Danny hadn't killed him. I staggered to my feet and forced myself to climb, still too oxygen deprived to call forth my beast.

My fingertips were slipping over the first traces of blood when I heard the demon's hiss echo. I clambered faster, ignoring my racing heartbeat and the alarm pooling my palms with sweat. The demon hissed again. It was then that I saw his head jutting into a crack between two boulders. A stick protruded from the small opening and nailed the demon lord in at least three of his testicles.

I launched myself on top of him and ripped off one wing, then the other, before it wrenched me off and threw me against the side of the mountain. My spine cracked like a pile of falling LEGOs. For a moment I thought two demons stalked toward me before my vision merged them into a single, mangled, royally pissed entity.

Shit.

I dug my heels into the rock and tried to rise. The demon was nice enough to help by grabbing me by the throat and hauling me upward. My power had returned enough to *shift* his three legs into the stone. He was trapped up to his knees, enough to momentarily confound him, and prevent him from crushing my larynx.

My limbs flailed wildly and my energy had wavered down to mere trickles when Danny's warrior scream blasted from the crack in the boulders. He rushed out, gripping an old tree branch in his hands, and struck the demon with all his might. The wood splintered in his grasp, but he wouldn't abandon me. He jumped on his shoulders and pounded his angry fists into the demon's head. The demon ignored him. After all, to him, Danny was just another morsel waiting to be eaten.

The red irises of his turtle gaze glowed as his maw opened wide and his tongue slithered out to lick my chin. I ignored his taste, gathered my remaining strength, and punched through his chest. His head lolled forward in shock as his heart pulsed one last time in my hand.

The demon dropped me as his body bopped and rolled like some sinister and twisted Weeble. I landed hard on my side, shaken, severely oxygen deprived but alive. Very, very much alive.

Danny fell backward, groaning when he hit the slab of stone and gagging when the demon burst in an explosion of moving innards. He rolled onto his side and crawled toward me, fighting back his nausea. Maybe I would have had to beat down bile, too, if I hadn't viewed the blast of guts as the equivalent of drop-down balloons to our very nasty, very gruesome victory.

"Oh Gawd. *Gawd*," Danny spit. He trekked across the squirming intestines, slapping a few of the more ornery ones away, until he reached my battered body. He froze, realizing clothing was something my tigress had long since pooh-poohed. I'd crossed my legs and covered my breasts, but that didn't matter, did it? Fact remained, I didn't enjoy anyone but Aric seeing me naked. And hell, I didn't even want him seeing me covered in demon organs.

Danny jerked his body away and yanked the shirt off his lanky frame. "Here. It has some demon snot on it, but I think it's okay."

"Thank you, Danny." I didn't just mean for the shirt. He'd fought for me, despite knowing he might die. I didn't have many friends. But the ones like Danny were worth having.

I sat up and pulled the polo over my head. The shirt

thankfully covered all the important female parts. I leaned against the boulder, trying to ignore the shower of sweat pouring down my body and the blinding pain that leadened my lids. I didn't remember Wonder Woman ever ending up covered in demon bowels. But maybe I'd missed that issue.

Danny inched to my side, panting. The lenses of his glasses spiderwebbed out. It was a wonder he could see at all. "We *asked* to do this," he said with stunned disbelief.

"Yup."

He angled his head. "Do you think Aric will ever let us tag along again?"

I took in the scent of my blood leaking behind my skull, the withered demon parts, the body fluids coating my skin and hair green, and thought about how close we'd come to becoming demon kibble. "Oh, *hell* no."

"Yeah. I didn't think so."

Danny and I stopped moving, stopped speaking, the effort it took to breathe robbing us of our remaining stamina. The sun dragged across the mountain, brightening the rock walls to orange and eventually stealing our shade. *Bastard.* "We need to get back," I mumbled. Too much time had passed. The sun, although grueling, was nothing compared to the chilly desert night that awaited us. And despite the tough exterior with which my tigress blessed me, my injuries needed to be tended to by my youngest sister.

Danny peered over the edge. "How are we going to get down?"

"I'll *shift* us down and *change* at the bottom." At least I'd try. "You can ride me if you'd like."

Danny shook his head. "No way. I'd rather take on another demon lord than risk Aric finding me on top of you."

The sound of roaring engines cut off my laughter.

Danny bolted to his feet and hurried to the ledge. "It's the pack. They must have regrouped and doubled back to the Jeeps. Bren! *Bren!*" He waved his arms.

I scrambled to my feet on wobbly legs, digging my disgusting claws along the indentations of the rock to help me stand. By some miracle my back wasn't broken and my legs still semiworked. But damn, I resembled nothing short of a chiropractor's wet dream.

I ignored my pounding head and focused my topsy-turvy vision on the horizon. Sure enough, the wolves and my sister had arrived. Shayna maneuvered the lead Wrangler. They'd been desperate enough to find us to allow her to drive. She powered through the inclines and ditches, leaving the other Jeeps to trail in the far, far distance. Bren and Aric stood in the backseat, their gazes taking everything in despite the hard jerks and skull-chattering bounces. Bren pointed to us and shouted to Shayna, "Over there. Near those damn rocks!"

Shayna stood in the driver's seat and threw her fists in the air to "Woo-hoo!" before sliding back and taking control of the jolting vehicle. She tore through the underbrush and skidded to a halt at the base of the boulders.

Aric leapt off the Jeep before it completely stopped and scaled to the top within seconds. His hands swept over my face, back, shoulders, and head. When he yanked them back, they were covered with my blood. "*Jesus*, Celia." He pulled me tight. "Stay with me, okay? Emme and Gemini's group are almost here."

I clutched him against me, my body trembling from the adrenaline continuing to ride my body like a bull. "Did you get the other demon?" He nodded but urged me to save my breath. "I'm okay, wolf, just a few bumps and bruises." And possibly some head trauma . . . and tissue damage, and a battered spine.

Bren clambered up next, growling, "Where's the turtle-necked little prick?"

Danny removed his black-framed glasses and wiped the sweat from his eyes. "Gone. Celia pulled out the big guns and killed him."

Aric held me at arm's length, only to cradle me when I wobbled. "You killed the other demon lord?"

A sense of pride warmed my unnerved, and strangely cold, skin. "Yeah. I did."

"Shit, don't you *ever* do anything like that again!" he bit out. He lifted me in his arms and jumped off the cliff. He landed in a crouch and carried me to the Jeep. I didn't complain. Especially since I'd slurred my last words. More Jeeps ground to a stop around us. My sisters rushed me, and the remainder of the pack spilled out of the dusty cars. They raced to us, their chests rumbling, ready to fight, ready to slaughter.

"It's over," Aric told them. "The demon lords are dead."

Silence swallowed all of Death Valley until the howls of triumph broke through, loud enough to collapse its hard walls. Aric's proclamation sent everyone into a frenzy of celebration.

Too bad he was wrong. Dead wrong.

CHAPTER 23

"I love you, Aric."

He stopped caressing my back. The air around us stilled, and his breath barely registered. I kept my cheek against his chest and continued, despite his silence and the tensing muscles beneath me. "I know you're probably used to hearing it, but I want you to know, I'm not used to saying it."

Aric leaned into me, meeting my lips before he spoke. "I have heard it before, but it's never meant anything . . . until now."

Aric's expression lacked the happiness I'd wished for. Only sadness and worry creased the planes of his face. I waited for the words that never came, and that I eventually realized he had no intention of sharing. He didn't move when I inched away from him. So I continued, until I slipped out of bed.

I tugged on a shirt and cotton shorts, not bothering with underwear. Aric sat up and leaned forward, a thick white sheet covering the lower half of his body. "Come back to bed, baby."

My hand rested against the thick footboard, barely

registering the feel of the smooth wood as I stared blankly at the closed window. "I need some water."

I shut the door to our room, but it failed to muffle Aric's curse. My feet moved fast. Too fast. I stumbled over Koda's industrial-size shit-kickers at the bottom of the steps. I picked them up to toss them aside, only to stop and stare at them.

The more I examined Koda's boots, the more my soul hurt. Koda was the scariest thing in a size 17. Yet Shayna had easily won his heart. Perhaps my sisters were wrong, perhaps I wasn't deserving of such love, and all I was capable of waited upstairs in my room.

I filled a glass with water but couldn't bring myself to sip the cold liquid. Without shoes, I hurried out the back door toward the beach and into the warm August night. Tonight I needed Tahoe's magic to hush my inner turmoil and silence my tigress's mournful growls. I only hoped that she'd answer me and grant me the peace I sought.

My fast movements turned into a swift jog. I neglected my worries that someone would see me, and raced along the dirt path and across the road. I stopped at the top of the short wooden pier leading to the beach. The full moon's reflection danced along the waves of the deep blue water, luring me to it, and promising to help me.

My bare feet kicked the sand behind me, my steps urgent as I reached the water's edge. I took a breath, and waited. But all the energy did was bounce off my skin, no longer wanting or needing me.

I waded into the cool water until the soft waves brushed against my thighs. I refused to allow the lake to dismiss me. *Don't you cast me aside, too.*

Tahoe's energy teased around me, not quite touching yet letting its strong presence be known. I bowed my head and hugged my arms, feeling abandoned . . . until Aric's scent stimulated my beast.

Water splashed against my legs as he came up behind me and encircled my waist. He bent and kissed my head. "I wish I could tell you what you want to hear, but I can't."

Despite the stir of the waves, I heard my tears fall against the water.

Aric tightened his hold and whispered words in French. And while I normally would have melted, this time I wouldn't allow myself to be tempted by the softness and fluidity of his words. I broke from his grasp and backed away toward the shore, keeping my arms against me. "I don't want you to say anything you don't feel, but I need you to understand why it hurts me." More tears trickled down my cheeks. "I won't be used, Aric."

Anger and pain flared in Aric's eyes as he advanced toward me. When he reached me, his body trembled violently. "*You* are the most important being in this world to me. More than my brothers, more than my pack. I need you to believe that . . . no matter what happens."

I gasped, unsure and frightened by what he thought the future held. The demons were gone, weren't they? And his Elders . . .

I remained silent. Heat lingered in Aric's gaze, cementing us where we stood. I started to shake, not from fear or cold—something else. Tahoe. Tahoe's energy hit me with one hard sucker punch. It was strong, primal, and my essence welcomed it like a lost loved one.

My back plunged into the quickly warming water and lolled above the surface as if the very lake held me to keep from drowning. When I blinked my eyes open, Aric was carrying me along the wooded path back to our house. Water dripped from his long hair onto his face. His eyes remained fierce, but his focus was unusually distant. "You'll always be mine," he whispered. "And I swear to always be yours."

*   *   *

"Do you want to stop for lunch or keep going?" Koda slipped his arm around Shayna as we continued our hike through Eldorado National Forrest, not the ideal way to trek through the thick vegetated woodlands, but Shayna didn't seem to mind.

Shayna leaned into him. "Let's keep going until we reach the creek. It'll be a nice place to picnic."

The destruction of the demon lords had satisfied the Elders enough to give Aric and his Warriors time off. We'd spent the remainder of the summer at the lake, boating and Jet Ski–ing. I even managed a romantic get-away alone to celebrate Aric's twenty-seventh birthday. I'd kept all my "I love yous" to myself. And while my admission had caused a strain between us, Aric's vigilance, affections, and kindness soon helped repair the hurt he'd caused.

I breathed in the scent of fresh pine, happy with my surroundings and the fact that we weren't competing with the tourists for beach space over the Labor Day week-end. I took in the trees thick with lush green leaves, the small fragrant flowers waiting to be devoured by deer, and the rolling hills littered with stones and wild ferns.

Aric admired his own view behind me. "Damn, sweet-ness. I love the way you walk."

I turned back to grin at him. "My eyes are up here, wolf."

Aric wrapped his arms around me and nibbled on my ear. "I know, but I'm having a hard time getting the image of you naked in the woods out of my mind."

"Well, maybe we can sneak off later," I said quietly.

Aric's entire body stilled. "You mean it?"

Cold and terror suddenly chilled the warmth between us, and goose bumps skittered up my arms like insects on a festering corpse. At first, I thought I was the only one affected until the wolves threw their packs on the ground and surrounded us protectively.

Taran's irises turned almost white. "*Shit*. What the hell is that?"

Emme, who was already shaking, grabbed my arm. "Celia, what's going on? I don't see anything."

"I don't know. Emme, stay close to me. Shayna, grab some wood."

Whatever it was, it was closing in. My hackles rose, and my claws protruded. An unearthly growl escaped my throat just as screeching erupted around us. My heart leapt into my throat as a horde of demon children broke through the surrounding trees. They flew overhead, scurried on the ground on all fours, and crawled on the trunks of trees like creepy toddlers with wings and arachnid legs.

"Celia, get out of here, *now!*" Aric yelled before he and the wolves *changed* and attacked.

I *shifted* the girls the moment they grabbed me, traveling beneath the soil as far and fast as my gift allowed. We surfaced a couple of hundred feet away from the fight. A quick glance back temporarily stunned me. The creatures crawled and flew everywhere, traveling in clumps thick enough to veil our four wolves. *My God*.

The reality of our situation smacked the fear out of me. We hadn't destroyed the demons. We'd only given them time to breed.

A cluster of demon infants attached themselves to the wolves' furry backs, clawing at them mercilessly and saturating the forest floor with their blood. The metallic scent of their essence burned my nose and still Aric and his Warriors shredded through their opponents like paper, seemingly unaffected despite the wicked pain their twitching muscles revealed.

I sprinted back toward the fight. "Shayna, get those things off their backs!"

A stream of long silver needles flew past me. They knocked the creatures off the wolves' backs and impaled them into trees like frogs in biology class.

A demon spotted me. His heavy clawed feet stomped along the soil before he expanded his wings and flew at me with his arms outstretched. I leapt and smashed into his body, twisting him in the air and decapitating him in one smooth move. I crashed to earth and dusted off his crawling remains. I needed to reach the wolves, and none of the damn flying monkeys were going to stop me.

The two Geminis fought a demon well over seven feet tall and almost as wide. Stone gray skin covered his humanoid form and sickly yellow eyes narrowed with challenge. His long leather appendages slapped at Gemini and shielded him from the wolves' snapping jaws. A good offensive maneuver, but not enough to guard his back.

I jumped on his shoulders and *shifted* him up to his neck. He jerked his head around, hissing when saw me. My leg swung back and connected with his head, sending his skull to roll like a soccer ball into the ferns. Wet, pulsating insides spilled from his neck, shriveling once exposed to the fresh breeze.

Three smaller creatures shoved me against a tree. Two held my arms while the third dug his talons into my shoulders. A serpentlike tongue slithered through his fangs and wrapped around my throat, halting my screams and robbing my breath. I gasped from the need for air while his clawed hand yanked at my shorts.

Anger forced me to act. I brought my arms together, slamming the creatures on either side of me into the third. I sliced off the tongue that strangled me with my claws and kicked each in the groin before smashing their heads into the tree like spoiled watermelons.

I drew in ragged breaths as I crushed the heads of small butterfly-size demons crawling along my flesh. *Damn it. Where did they come from?* I scanned the skies. More flew above in a V formation, similar to geese until they dove straight down, landing inches from the battle.

Shayna sliced three into confetti in a whirlwind of swinging blades. Maggotlike intestines littered her face, but she managed to sever the arms of a large demon who'd landed in a squat behind her. Poor Shayna, though, had taken on more than she could handle. The immense creature encircled her wrists with his tongue and dragged her away into the thick brush.

I fought my way through the remaining horde to reach my sister, killing anything that got in my way. When the monster saw me approach, he released her and traded for me. We wrestled, his razor-sharp fangs biting into my shoulder as I attempted to puncture his chest with my claws. I screamed from the pain of his teeth piercing through my bones and gagged from his hot, rotting breath. My head spun as his saliva sizzled against my skin, eating its way through my muscles and tendons. I tore his wings to force his release, only to have him clamp down harder.

Shayna was near, but she didn't seem able to strike. So I continued to roll on the ground while my blood smeared the earth and the creature's tongue eagerly licked my wound. I screamed in agony as flesh tore from my bones. I thought he was eating me alive until the weight lifted off my chest. Above me, Aric held the decapitated head in his hands. He threw it aside, then gingerly pulled me to my feet.

Aric's face shone chalk white. But his obvious worry for me quickly turned to rage. He held tight to my hips. *"What the hell were you thinking? I told you to run!"*

I pushed away, angry at him for yelling at me, only to cringe. My thrust caused a ghastly pain to shoot through me. I hunched over and instinctively grabbed where it hurt. My fingers sank into the large bloody chunk missing from my shoulder. I shouldn't have looked. I really shouldn't have, because the ruptured blood vessels and mangled flesh caused me to become abruptly faint.

Aric caught me before I hit the ground and yelled for Emme. I barely heard the last few splatters of demon remains drench the earth. We'd won the fight. By some miracle, we'd all survived. My sisters hurried over, screaming when they saw my condition. You know you're in bad shape when women who've decapitated vampires can't bear the sight of you. They pleaded with me not to close my eyes, but the horrible ringing in my ears made it hard to understand their speech. My eyelids drooped as if lined with tar, despite my struggles to keep them open.

Aric continued to hold me while Emme touched my skin with trembling hands. "Hang in there, baby," he whispered. "Don't leave me."

Emme's soft yellow light surrounded me. Slowly I regained my strength. My head began to clear, and the horrible pain receded. The moment I healed, I broke free from Aric and put ample space between us. Damn, I was furious. "It's not okay for you to yell at me!"

Aric's expression went from shocked to glaring. He yanked on the shorts Liam tossed him while narrowing his eyes at me. "Those things could have raped or killed you because you didn't listen to me!"

I threw my hands in the air. "Did you honestly expect me to leave you?" He didn't answer. "My God, I don't believe this!"

Gemini interrupted calmly as his other wolf leapt into his back. "The girls were a great help, Aric. They fought well and valiantly."

Gem's words did little to calm Aric. His jaw clenched tighter as he continued to lock eyes with me. "That's not the point."

Koda held Shayna, who leaned heavily against him as if barely able to stand. "Enough of this. We need to get the girls to safety."

I couldn't keep the bite out of my voice as I stalked past Aric. "By the way, you're welcome!"

I stormed off, leaping over the creatures' body parts and limbs that now mimicked dead branches. I paused when I reached the last one. Frustration inveighed me to stomp it to dust. It crumbled easily. Another hour and the remains would probably disintegrate. The knowledge brought me no comfort. More were out there. The attack had proved that much.

My arms crossed as I continued forward. I ignored Aric when he caught up to me. He didn't say anything, and no longer appeared angry, but the anger heating the space between us made it clear neither of us was in the mood for chitchat.

The smell of fear and death stopped me less than a mile from the car. I ran toward the source with Aric at my heels, horror-struck by what awaited beneath a steep incline.

A herd of beautiful deer had been mutilated by those hideous monsters. Some were still alive, twitching and bleating in pain. Others were just chunks of leftover flesh. The bucks had fled, but not the does. They'd apparently chosen to stay with their dying babies. I froze in place, torn between crying and screaming. But it wasn't until Emme and Shayna gasped behind me that I was finally able to pull myself away.

"Koda, don't," Shayna pleaded when he and Liam approached the herd.

"Please, Liam," Emme begged, "I can help them."

The wolves ignored my sisters' desperate pleas and stalked toward the suffering beasts. The bays and whines amplified. The deer had sensed the arrival of new predators and realized their inevitable end. I felt my breath quickening, knowing what was coming and unable to slow my racing pulse.

The sickening crunch of necks being snapped echoed like gunshots in the silence of the forest. I focused on Gemini comforting Taran. She buried her face in his chest and covered her ears. "They're coming for me," she whispered in a trembling voice. "I know they're coming."

Shayna and Emme openly bawled. Aric tried to reach out to me, but I wrenched away from him and moved toward Emme and Shayna. I wrapped my arms around them and led them away from the horror.

No one said anything until we reached the car. But when Koda tried to hold Shayna, she released me and climbed into the backseat with Taran and Gemini. She wouldn't look at Koda. Koda dropped his head and stepped into the driver's seat.

Liam held out his arms to Emme. Emme focused on his large hands, the same ones that had just finished the deer. Koda and Liam had acted in the name of mercy. I knew that, and I was certain my sisters did, too, except that didn't mean their actions were any less disturbing. Brutality and death constantly lingered in the wolves' existence. Not in ours. At least, not now.

"Go to him, Emme," I urged quietly. "None of this is his fault. He did what he had to."

Emme approached Liam slowly. He gathered her in his arms and told her he loved her. And just like that, they were back to their normal selves. Aric and I, not so much.

Aric blocked my way when I attempted to get into the front passenger seat. "You're not sitting with me?"

I met his frown with a glare. "*No.*"

"*Fine,*" he snapped.

"*Fine,*" I snapped right back.

Taran broke the uncomfortable silence on the ride home. "For shit's sake, where the hell did all those demons come from?"

Gemini's tone was dark when he answered, "We didn't destroy all the demon lords. There must have been more."

"No shit," she muttered.

Emme spoke softly. "B-but there haven't been more

bodies—or missing people or anything—since the fight in Death Valley. Even the rogue vampires haven't presented themselves."

Aric answered from the back. It hurt to hear him speak. "They've probably been lying low, especially since they realized we could call them forth. Either that or they'd gathered enough food to last them."

We'd reached the highway. "Pull over, Koda," Taran yelled. "Shayna's going to be sick."

Koda scrambled out of the car with me right behind him. He held back Shayna's hair while a multitude of cars sped past us. When she finished, he took off his shirt and handed it to her.

Shayna's tears streaked her trembling frame. She twisted Koda's shirt between her long fingers. "I'm sorry, puppy. The gore was just too much. And those poor deer, I couldn't take it."

"It's okay, baby. Just don't be afraid of me. I love you. I could never hurt you."

Shayna wrapped her arms around Koda's waist. "I'm not afraid of you," she choked between sobs. "Please don't think that."

Koda picked her up and carried her to the car, tossing Aric the keys along the way. When we climbed back in, Emme switched seats so Koda and Shayna could continue to hold each other. It was such a sweet moment between them. I couldn't help envying their love.

Aric sat next to me and cranked the engine. He glanced my way. I turned to look out the window and rested my forehead against the glass, not ready and not willing to speak to him.

We arrived home to find Danny cooking in our kitchen and Bren lounging on our couch. Bren jumped up, growling, as soon as he got a whiff of us. "What the hell happened? You smell like evil."

I kicked off my shoes and strode into the kitchen to

wash my hands. Yeah, like that did much. "We were attacked by a horde of demon children."

Danny placed the spatula down on the spoon rest and gripped the sides of the counter. "When you say horde ... ?"

"Fifty, maybe sixty," Liam answered. He took a beer out of the fridge, twisted the cap off with his teeth, and chugged it.

"None of this makes sense," Danny said. "It would take an entire army of demons to produce that many offspring, and there are only a few strong enough to leave hell."

Liam stood against the wall with his arms crossed. He glanced over at Emme, who sat on the couch quietly. "I think they were after our girls."

Aric shook his head. "They have no reason to hunt them."

"How can you be sure?" Liam argued. "They've been stealing women for months."

"They've been stealing *human* women for months," Gemini clarified. "The girls smell of magic and power. They're not easy prey. What could they hope to gain by attacking them?"

Aric stood from the kitchen chair, hard enough to make it slide. "I don't know what's happening, but we can't just make assumptions. We have to go to the Den and call a meeting with the Elders."

Koda didn't move right away, despite Aric's direct order. He continued to hold Shayna on his lap as if afraid she wouldn't still be there upon his return. Aric walked over to them. "Koda, the only way to keep them safe is to understand what we're facing. To do so, we must arm ourselves with knowledge and join together as a pack."

Gemini stood and took his place beside Aric. "Don't be afraid, old friend. Bren and Dan will stay and protect them in our absence."

Bren stretched his tensing muscles. "Yeah, don't sweat it, man. I'll protect them, and they can protect Danny."

Normally Bren's comment would have made me laugh. But I wasn't in the mood. I went upstairs before they'd finished speaking.

"Damn it, Aric, just let her go," Taran said behind me. "Celia is still upset. Just like the rest of us."

Aric heeded Taran's advice and left me alone. It was almost midnight when he and the wolves finally returned home. I pretended to sleep when Aric entered our room and continued to do so when he climbed into bed after showering.

He placed his hand on my hip. Even through the sheet, I felt the warmth from his touch. But I didn't move and kept my back to him. "I know you're awake, sweetness," he whispered. "Could you tell me why you're so mad?"

I sighed. Sulking wasn't getting us anywhere; I knew we needed to talk. I arranged my pillows behind me and leaned against them. Aric's hair remained moist from his shower. I could see the dull shine despite the darkness of the room. And I could sense that horrible strain between us. "I don't like the way you yelled at me. It was disrespectful." I paused. There was more I needed to say, except it was hard for me to force the words out. "We're so close in a lot of ways, Aric. But sometimes when we're intimate, you distance yourself from me." I dropped my gaze. "And I'm not talking about when we make love."

I waited for him to respond and watched as he gathered his thoughts. "I don't mean to hurt you or close myself off. And I sure as hell would never intentionally disrespect you. I was angry that you didn't listen when I told you to run."

I pursed my lips tight. "I'm not one of your Warriors to order around, Aric."

"I know you're not. You're something . . . something way deeper than that."

I searched the entirety of his visage—his strong jaw, the gaze that could melt ice during a winter storm, and that mouth that had brought me pleasure and comfort. I searched long and hard for any signs that could reveal some emotion, any emotion that would unleash his thoughts. Yet nothing came, just that whatever he felt was strong. "What am I exactly to you, Aric?"

He closed his eyes. When he opened them, he stared back at me with more force than I'd ever seen. "You're everything to me, Celia. Can't you understand what you mean to me?"

No. I couldn't. I swept his wet hair away from his face. "I fought for you today, Aric. Just as you did for me. And yes, I was injured. But it was worth it, and I would do it again."

Aric slowly shook his head. His eyes swept over where the demon had mutilated my shoulder. He stared at my regenerated skin for a moment before reaching out to me.

His hand gradually ran up my arm, tracing an invisible line along my neck, stopping only to rest against my cheek. I covered his hand with mine, welcoming his touch and the intensity behind his gesture. "Emme may not always be around, Celia," he whispered. He exhaled deeply. "When I saw how injured you were, it infuriated me. But only because losing you is my greatest fear."

Neither of us said anything for several breaths. Aric did appear scared, and disheartened. I came to an understanding about our relationship then. Aric Connor might not have been ready to love me, yet I recognized his feelings for me as very real. And maybe, just maybe, those feelings might someday flourish into love. That hope extinguished any lingering sorrow and replaced it with desire.

I slid onto my knees and pulled off my top seductively. My long hair fell around my breasts. Aric watched me carefully as I then teasingly removed my underwear. But it wasn't until I removed the sheet and climbed on top of him that I realized he hadn't bothered to dress after his shower. My insides ached for his caress. "A little presumptuous, don't you think?"

A small, sultry smile spread across his lips. "No. I just hear make-up sex is hot," he murmured before kissing me wildly.

CHAPTER 24

Aric and I ran fast, slinging the thick mud behind us. The attack the previous day had left our beasts restless. We needed to burn through some energy. Six miles in along the Truckee River, and my tigress had only just begun to settle.

"Are you okay, sweetness? You're moving kind of funny."

"What can I say, wolf? You're too much man for me."

He stopped. "Are you serious?"

I ground to a halt next to him and clutched his arm as I bent to remove my sneaker. "Yes, but actually I think I have a pebble in my shoe."

Aric laughed, only to then shove me abruptly away from him. I looked up from the ground in time to see two wolves tackle him. I lurched to my feet and froze. The wind shifted directions, and oh my God, I could scent them. More beasts waited, in the trees, in the brush, all around me. And I could feel their thirst. I didn't hesitate; I *changed* and ran as fast as I could.

I led them away from Aric. His howl rippled through the air behind me. He knew we were in trouble and *called* forth his Warriors.

Why are wolves attacking us?

I realized too late that it wasn't just wolves after us. A werelion slammed into my side, tackling me down the embankment and into the river. The lion was huge, but I was a tigress, and that made *me* queen of beasts. I dug my claws into his haunches, fear of drowning making my strikes brutal. The freezing water slapped cumbrously against my fur. We clawed and bit each other, but it wasn't until he plunged his fangs deep into my thigh that I felt real pain. My blood mixed with the river water. I knew I had only one choice to survive.

I held my breath and forced myself down to the bottom, dragging my opponent with me. The pull of the water was strong and so was my struggling companion. My frantic movements were less than grateful. My strength, however, seemed to help. Slowly, but surely, I made my way to the bottom.

The force of the current shoved into my nose and against my eyes. I kicked my back legs, the pressure in my lungs building and pleading for release. When I felt his rear claws scrape along the base, I blew out my last bit of air and *shifted* him deep into the mud. Bubbles of his last breath flowed past me seconds before I broke through the water.

I sputtered and choked with every clumsy stroke back to shore, only to encounter more of the werelion's friends. At the edge of the water, eight wolves, four rats, and what appeared to be a deranged-looking squirrel restlessly waited for me.

Shit. Where's Misha when I need him?

I turned and paddled to the opposite shore. Unfortunately rats, it seemed, were pretty decent swimmers. One of them grabbed my hind paw just as I reached the other side. I kicked him in the snout and took off in a mad run. My paws beat hard against the surface, but my mangled thigh caused a painful limp and slowed my speed. Growls and snarls echoed behind me. The bad guys were coming for me and closing in fast.

Just when I thought I was going to die, the cavalry showed up in the form of vampires in Catholic schoolgirl uniforms.

"You rang, kitten?" Misha stood in the center of the path dressed all in black with his arms crossed. His long blond hair whisked against his shoulders from the speed in which his vampires attacked. I turned to help the good Catholics, but Misha grabbed me and yanked me back. "Stop, Celia. You are already wounded. Leave my family to deal with them."

The vamps easily tore the outnumbered *weres* apart, and had fun doing so. Blood splattered against their crisp white shirts. Their elongated nails shred through fur, and their fangs found the perfect veins to puncture and feast from. I *changed* to speak with Misha. At that moment, I was more fearful of Aric's safety than being naked in the arms of a vampire.

"Misha, there are more *weres*. I have to get back to Aric."

"Have you lost weight, my darling? You look thinner."

I shoved myself away from him. "Misha, I'm serious!"

"Very well, Celia. I shall send others after your pet, but you will remain with me."

With just a simple gesture of his hand, half of his vampires took off after Aric. A redhead human with dazed blue eyes appeared carrying clothes. She handed me a dress and some underwear, which I proceeded to don as fast as I could.

My head jerked in the direction the vampires had vanished. "Thank you, Misha."

"You sound surprised that I am a gentleman."

I clasped my injured thigh. "It's not that." I couldn't finish my thought. I was terrified for Aric, and the profuse bleeding seeping through my fingers made my head spin.

"Please sit, Celia, so that I may tend to your wounds."

The redhead spread a blanket on the ground and motioned me to it. I did as Misha asked and positioned myself on the ground, holding tight to my wound. Misha moved my hand with ease and spread my knees apart. Like an idiot, I forgot vampires didn't use first aid kits. A gush of blood spurted out and splattered against the blanket. Misha didn't panic. He bent forward and licked the inside of my thigh very slowly. The wound sealed, but he didn't stop. He continued to lick me in teasing strokes, sending a wave of paralyzing chills up my spine. And call me crazy, but I failed to see how his look of seduction was beneficial to my injury.

"Ah . . . What? . . . I . . ." Words failed me. It took another flick of his tongue to finally jar me out of my shock. I slammed my knees together and quickly scrambled to the edge of the blanket. But I was too late. From nowhere, a snarling wolf appeared at my shoulder.

Aric *changed* back to human. Misha rose to meet him. They stood nose-to-nose. The scent of Aric's fury scorched the air around us. Misha remained blissfully calm. After all, he'd just eaten. Challenging growls and hissing surrounded us as Misha's vampires and Aric's wolves prepared to attack.

I squeezed between them in an attempt to prevent all-out war. *"Aric, stop."* I tried to push him back, yet couldn't even manage to nudge him. Aric typically outmuscled me, but at that moment he was an impenetrable wall of livid energy. I didn't want them to fight, and I sure as hell didn't want anyone to die. So I threw in my only weapon—the weak and helpless card.

"Aric, please, Misha just saved me from a bunch of *weres*."

"I was coming for you!"

"Yes, but you might have been too late. I was already badly wounded, and the *weres* had caught up to me. Misha was just trying to help."

"By trying to seduce you?" Aric's muscles tensed and shook violently beneath my hands.

My breath sputtered as I released it. "I was bleeding from a deep wound in my thigh. All he did was seal it." I glanced back at Misha, hoping he'd back up what I was saying. He didn't. *Bastard.*

Aric ground his teeth. *"What is he even doing here?"*

Misha flashed him one of the wickedest smiles in his arsenal. "Celia was in danger and thought my name. Thus, I responded. And now that I have tasted her blood, our *call* is that much stronger."

Great. More bars, in more places. Having a vampire's digits just got better and better.

Aric went perfectly still. In a way, that was way scarier than the angry, growling, red-faced wolf he'd been seconds before. I swallowed hard. The weak and helpless card clearly wasn't working, so I tried to reason with him. My hand gently touched his face. "Aric, this is not the time. Something terrible is happening. We were attacked by vampires several months back. Yesterday it was a horde of demon children, and today some strange *weres*. What's going to happen tomorrow? Misha isn't the enemy. We have to figure out who is."

Misha whipped his head away from Aric to glare at me. "You were attacked by a *horde* of demon children yesterday? And you did not inform me?"

I threw my hands in the air. *Great, now they're both pissed at me.*

"Your mate is right, boss," said an unfamiliar voice.

The word hit me hard enough to back away from Aric and Misha. I turned to find myself eye level with the biggest set of boobs I'd ever seen. A naked blonde covered in blood had moved to stand beside Aric. *I didn't know Pamela Anderson was a werewolf.*

The blonde smiled and extended her hand. "Hi. I'm Heidi." Her voice was cute and bubbly. Goody for her. I shook her bloody hand and looked at Aric, but he was preoccupied with visions of eating Misha's insides dancing through his head.

Misha motioned his vampires to retreat with a subtle nod. "It appears our clans need to meet and discuss this matter."

"It appears so," Aric answered through clenched teeth. "Heidi, take five wolves with you and escort Celia home. Have Genevieve place a protective ward around her house. *Call me* if you sense any danger. I'm counting on you to keep her safe."

"Okay, boss," Heidi answered cheerfully before *changing* into a beautiful snow white wolf.

Great. Even her wolf form is hot.

Aric turned away from Misha to take my face gently in his hands. "Don't worry. Everything's going to be okay, I promise. I'll be home as soon as I can." He gave me a long, sweet kiss, proving to Misha that he was the one who held my heart.

"They should have called by now." Alayna stared at the phone in her hands. They trembled slightly, but then again we all waited on edge.

"Screw this, I'm calling Gemini."

I placed my hand on her shoulder. "Don't, Taran."

Taran shrugged me off. "Why the hell not? Shit, it's one o'clock in the goddamn morning—"

"Do you really want to interrupt a meeting between a vampire family and a clan of *weres* just because your boyfriend's not home yet?" Bren asked from the couch.

"Screw off, Bren. You don't know what I've seen or felt. You don't know shit!"

Bren narrowed his glare. "And you don't know shit about supernatural politics."

"That's enough." I stood between them. "Your bickering is not helping."

Taran opened her mouth, no doubt to rip into me, when the walls of our house hummed from the ward Aric had asked the witches to place. Something powerful was approaching—fast. Taran's magic ignited, my claws shot out, and a hideous growl thundered from Bren's chest. Shayna raced toward the window with a dagger in her hand. "It's okay, it's okay. They're home now."

Taran released the magic surrounding the house with a charm the witches had provided and threw open the door. "Baby, why—?"

She backed away from the door, allowing the wolves to step slowly into the house. Everyone froze upon seeing their pale and distraught faces. Aric, in particular, appeared devastated beyond words. I hurried toward him, ready to throw my arms around him. He jerked away from me and stepped aside, refusing my touch. I turned to the others, confused by his reaction. The wolves collectively averted their gazes. Koda swore beneath his breath.

A sour sensation effervesced along my back, chilling me instantly. "Aric, what's wrong?"

He kept his head down. "I need to speak to you privately, Celia."

I followed Aric upstairs to our room. The stress and melancholy spilling along his spine reminded me of the funeral march preceding my foster mother's burial. Each step felt more like a walk through quicksand than a stride along a plush carpet. I closed the door behind me and leaned against the dresser, waiting. Aric walked to the window and looked out. He stood with his arms crossed, completely motionless. After what seemed like an eternity, he finally spoke.

"They're dead."

I pushed off the dresser. "Who's dead?"

Aric wouldn't turn away from the window. "My kind. We've been decimated. There were organized attacks yesterday and today. Not just here, but worldwide. They've slaughtered our men, women, and children. They've also targeted the vampires."

I clasped my mouth in horror. "My God. Who—*what* did this?"

"They call themselves the Tribe." Aric scoffed. "We've been such fools, Celia. All these years we've ostracized our kind for being *lones* while the vampires have aimed their wrath on those who dare defy their masters. All it took was an entity smart enough to unite them with the promise of revenge."

Understanding momentarily stopped the knife digging its way into my stomach. "Demons." I almost couldn't say the word.

"Yeah. The demons formed a plan. And a brilliant one at that."

Aric continued to stare outside. "The night Liam and Emme were attacked outside the club, the Tribe had begun to hunt *weres*. Based on the recent deaths, and how aggressive they were in trying to take me, we've surmised the purebloods have been their main objective all along." He glanced over his shoulder. "It's the one way they can guarantee the obliteration of my species."

My lips parted and I shook my head, the deliberation and execution of the demons' tactics too frightening to believe. Aric had lost everything. But he still had me.

I reached out, ready to console him. Again he reeled away. My terror intensified. Why wouldn't he look at me? And why couldn't I touch him? My blood turned to ice and my body trembled. I knew what was coming. "Aric, what aren't you telling me?"

Aric dropped his arms to his sides and let out a deep

breath. "I'm one of the last purebloods left, Celia. I'm being called to fulfill my duties, to continue our race."

The testament of my fears kicked me hard in the stomach. Somehow I ended up sitting on our bed.

Aric covered his eyes with his right hand. His left remained at his side, balled into a fist. I thought he was crying, but I couldn't be sure. "Forgive me, Celia. I never should've let things get this far." He swallowed hard. "I was never supposed to feel this way."

With those final words, he turned and stalked out of our room.

Aric's voice downstairs stung my ears like a swarm of hornets. "I'll expect you back at the Den in an hour."

"Aric, what's wrong?" Taran asked. "And where the hell are you going?"

"Go upstairs. Celia needs you." It was the last thing Aric said before the door slammed behind him.

I scented my sisters, Bren, and Danny entering our room. Shayna's voice echoed in the distance. "What happened, dude?"

Tears slid down my face, blinding me. "He left me," I whispered.

CHAPTER 25

My room became my refuge and my prison. I kept it dark, blocking light by draping a thick blanket over the window and unplugging the lamps. The only light that crept in was from the hall, when some well-meaning soul would open the door to visit.

"Liam and the others are moving out," Emme whispered. I awoke to her gently stroking my hair, unaware if it was night or day, and not caring enough to ask. "He and the remaining *weres* are hunting the Tribe. Th the vampires have joined them on their quest. The witches, too. They're calling themselves the Alliance. It's bad, Celia. Really bad. They realize none will survive without the other." She sighed. "We offered to help, but their Leaders forbid it. I—I—I don't think they trust us. . . ."

"Aric's mother was spared from the attacks, dude," Shayna said one day. "Koda thought you'd want to know." She positioned the tray of food she'd brought on my nightstand when I didn't answer. "Please eat, Celia. You're wasting away."

I'd try to eat the food she'd leave me, but my stomach ached painfully after only a few bites. God, everything hurt. It hurt to breathe, it hurt to simply think. So I didn't do much of anything. Mostly I just cried and slept, haunted by memories that seemed more like impassioned dreams than anything real.

I remembered Taran coming in a few times demanding that I get up, then swearing when I buried myself deeper beneath the covers. And although I often heard the hushed voices of the other wolves, they never came in, only Bren. He and Danny took turns sleeping with me at night. I think they were afraid to leave me alone. It wasn't necessary; no one was worth killing myself over, not even someone like Aric.

I stumbled out of bed one morning to use the bathroom. When I looked in the mirror, I barely recognized the pathetic mess staring back at me. My long waves were little more than greasy knots and my eyes bloodshot and swollen. I ran my hands down my emaciated form. My shirt hung loose, despite the stretchy fabric. Maybe that's what it took. Maybe I just needed to see what I'd become. I was done crying. Crying made me feel weak and vulnerable, and I refused to be either. Ever again.

I brushed my teeth and spit out blood from the force I had used. My glare fixed back at me in the mirror. I no longer felt depressed; I was *pissed*.

I lurched toward the shower and turned the water on, only to turn it off again. My breath quickened, and the beat of my racing heart pulsed in my ears. I marched back into my bedroom—*our bedroom*. The same room we'd made love in so many times.

I made the mistake of looking around. My eyes wandered to the bed, the place I'd bared my soul to him over and over again. I turned my scowl on the dresser, where I'd posed the night I seduced him. It seemed empty, but I wasn't sure why. Then it hit me—the pictures of us were gone. Someone must have removed them. The one taken of us at a restaurant captured a loving moment between us; the other Shayna had snapped of us on the couch downstairs. Aric had sat behind me with his arms wrapped around my waist. I was laughing in it. He was smiling and nuzzling my neck. Aric had placed both in beautiful and expensive frames, gifts from him, back when I thought he gave a damn.

"Liar."

Bren sat up in bed, rubbing his eyes. "Did you say something, Ceel?"

I kicked open the door to my closet, only to be smacked in the face by Aric's scent. It clung to every last stitch of clothing still hanging neatly along the racks. I couldn't get dressed or shove sneakers on fast enough. His aroma overwhelmed me with a barrage of feelings too raw to deal with. I bolted from the room and down the stairs. "Celia, wait!" Bren called.

"Dude, what are you doing?"

"Shit, go after her!"

I dashed into the greenbelt behind our house. Bren, Koda, and Liam beat feet after me, forcing me to sprint faster. My beast possessed me, fleeing as if wounded and trying to outrun the agony. She busted across streams to hide our scent and circled trees to confuse our pursuers. She succeeded, losing them within miles. Except my human side couldn't escape our pain, our anger, our sense of betrayal.

"Liar."

Aric had lied to me with his body. He'd lied to me with his words.

"You're beautiful."

"Liar."

"You're the best thing in my life."

"Liar!"

Aric's words reverberated in my mind as I raced farther up the mountain. *"Can't you understand what you mean to me? Losing you is my greatest fear."*

"*Liar!*"

"*Don't be afraid. I won't ever hurt you.*"

"LIAR!"

My thighs burned, but I pushed on, forcing my legs to move faster. The forest became a blur as some of his last words rang through my head.

"*You'll always be mine. And I swear to always be yours.*"

"*You goddamn liar!*"

Hours passed before my legs finally gave out. I collapsed on a bed of thick ferns, screaming until my voice turned to roars, roaring until my throat burned with the acid from my shriveled stomach. My body was done, beaten physically and emotionally into submission.

And yet it was all my fault.

I'd never mourned my parents' deaths, though my tiny heart had beat because they'd given me life and a love without prejudice. My sisters were young, Emme barely five. They sought me out to help them through their grief. How could I be selfish, when they needed my courage so desperately? When our foster mother died, again there was no time to wallow in my emotions. I had family to take care of and support. So instead of tears, cement and steel took over my soul, building up the walls I needed to survive.

Then Aric came into my world. He demolished my barriers with his kind words, his protection, and his touch. Like a fool, I allowed him into my heart and into my bed, permitting the happiness he bestowed on me and begging for his pleasure. I should have known better. Freaks like me didn't get a happily ever after. *This* was all I'd ever know.

I swayed to my feet, covered in dirt—empty, numb, and once again alone.

Shit.

The return trip took hours, although I scarcely noticed. I stumbled up my front steps on wobbly legs, barely managing to stay upright. When I pushed open the door, all eyes locked on me.

Emme appeared out of her mind with worry. She tripped over her feet as she hurried toward me from the kitchen. "*Celia!* We've been searching everywhere for you—" She stopped short, clasping her hand over her mouth. Her eyes widened as she took in my scraggy and taciturn form. She wheeled from me, her voice strained. "I—I—I'll let Bren and Misha know you're home."

Taran met me with a glare, and her phone glued to the ear. "It's okay, baby," she muttered into the phone. "She's back now . . . No. *Don't.* That son of a bitch doesn't need to know anything."

I expected my sisters' stress to morph into anger. Instead they regarded me with pity. I scoffed. Their fury would have been more welcoming.

Shayna approached me slowly. "How are you, Ceel?"

My expression didn't waver. "Hungry."

Danny rose from the kitchen stool and walked over to me. He sighed before taking my hand and leading me to the table. I followed him almost blindly, looking at everything without really seeing.

My sisters dispersed one by one, busying themselves in the kitchen and piling a week's worth of food in front of me. I ate until I thought I'd burst, but somehow I still felt barren on the inside. Without a word, I headed upstairs to finally shower.

I returned to work the next day, embracing the distraction the stress of my job provided. Shayna had been calling me out sick, claiming I had the stomach flu. By the way the other nurses reacted when they saw me, it seemed no one doubted my fake illness. "Oh my," I overheard one of my coworkers whisper. "Celia looks like hell." She was right. But slowly my appetite bounced back, helping my physical self to rejuvenate and to camouflage my vacant spirit.

I remained unusually quiet, not wanting to talk to anyone, including my sisters. And while I had started to run again, it was more from a desire to be alone than to return to something I'd once enjoyed. I ran midday in the busy streets of Incline Village, instead of early morning along the desolate Tahoe beaches, deliberate attempts to thwart a potential attack, and to avoid seeing Aric. The Alliance believed the Tribe had abandoned the area. The absence of local activity suggested as much. But after I'd been jumped by evildoers galore, no way was I taking any chances.

Aric had returned for his belongings one day while I was at work. I'd come home to a half-empty bedroom, his key on my dresser, and his aroma lingering. Instinctively I took a deep breath, only to be sideswiped with memories induced by his scent. My head spun with images of our time together. I toppled back, clinging to the dresser for balance until my eyes finally focused upon the key.

I stared at it for a long while, wondering if Aric had hesitated, felt regret—felt *anything* at all. I pushed away from the dresser resentfully, deciding it was best not to know.

The *weres* remained unclear of where the demon lords leading the Tribe harbored their secret lairs. Each time a captured Tribesman divulged any information, he'd explode. Just like the wereraccoon had done on my doorstep.

"It's probably some kind of internal spell, or curse, to ensure Tribe secrets and loyalty," Danny rationalized. "I think the wereraccoon knew what was happening. From what Koda has said, the Tribe's recruiting methods are very cultlike. They target *lones*, using their isolation and bitterness to lure them into joining. Maybe that guy got sucked in. And maybe he didn't like what he saw."

"You think he was trying to warn me?"

Danny nodded. "You or Aric. Based on the picture Liam found, the raccoon realized you knew him. Why else would he have run to your house?"

It made sense. I'd scared the raccoon off a few times, but I'd never given him a reason to want me dead. In looking back, he'd seemed so feeble and frightened. It would have been easy for someone like him to get in over his head. "He didn't reveal anything, though. Not one word. Why would he just explode like that?"

Danny removed his glasses and cleaned them against his shirt. "Look at this way. If you planned to take over the earth, would you risk leaving any trace of evidence that could possibly implicate you? Or warn the good guys?"

I honestly never thought to make the world my playground. Yet I knew what Danny meant. "No. I guess not."

I shuddered. It was a frightening time. The world as I'd known it had become a hellish nightmare almost overnight. Not only did humans continue to disappear, but many powerful witches had gone missing, and *were* numbers persistently dwindled. In response, Elders nationally expanded their Dens to become safe havens for the remaining *weres* and their families, while head witches grouped their covens.

The wolves never discussed the details of Alliance missions, but my sisters and I knew their assignments were explicitly dangerous. After all, *weres* as young as fourteen were being used as assassins. Some didn't make it back.

CHAPTER 26

"Get the hell out of my house!" Taran screamed.

Gemini's tone carried the hurt Taran's words had caused him. "Taran, tell me what's wrong."

"Just leave. You're going to do it anyway. You might as well do it now!"

I hurried down from my bedroom, confused and worried about what could have caused her to react so viciously. The wolves had returned after an almost-two-week absence. Taran and Gemini should have been locked in her room, not fighting in the kitchen.

Gemini had his arms around Taran. She shoved against his broad chest, trying uselessly to push him away. "I won't leave you, Taran," he said gently. "I love you."

Taran stopped struggling and sobbed into her hands. "It doesn't mean shit. You're going to dump me, just like that asshole dumped her!"

Gemini tucked Taran into his shoulder and stroked back her dark hair. "No. I won't," he promised.

Taran continued to cry in his arms. I was going to return to my room when her retort halted my steps. "He broke her heart," she whimpered.

Gemini looked up at me then. "I know."

I could have picked up the house and thrown it at them, sick of their relentless pity.

I'd started to growl when Liam bounded down the stairs. "Hey, Ceel," he said, oblivious of the fact that I was about to gnaw on Gemini's eyeballs. "We just ordered food from Lakeside Pizza. Come with me to pick it up."

I didn't want to go with Liam, but begrudgingly agreed so not to upset Emme or crush Liam's feelings. My loneliness made it difficult to be around my sisters and their wolves. I found excuses to leave the house when they were around. My actions upset my family and had strained our relationship. They probably thought I was incapable of being happy for them, but they were wrong. The wolves were just a constant reminder of what I'd had and lost.

Liam drove with the windows down, allowing the unusually warm October breeze to hit our faces. We were waiting for our pizzas when the door opened, and I was struck by a scent that threatened to stop my heart.

Aric froze the moment he saw me. Only at the insistence of the gorgeous blond *were* clutching his arm did he slowly move toward us. It was the first time I'd seen Aric since he'd left me and, my God, it hurt to see him with *her*.

She was tall, almost as tall as Aric. Cascading waves of shimmering blond hair swept down to her elbows, while her short red dress showed off her ridiculously sensual curves. As for me, I still wore my sports bra and shorts from my earlier run and hadn't showered.

The *were* bitch pretended I wasn't there. "Hi, Liam," she said.

Liam stiffened and answered with a nod. Aric continued to stare at me, just as he had from the moment he walked in. "Hello, Celia," he said.

At the sound of my name, the blonde tightened her

grip on Aric's arm and finally acknowledged me. Oh yeah, I had her attention then. The scowl she initially greeted me with was quickly replaced by a condescending little grin. "I'm Barbara." She paused to lick her lips. "Aric's fiancée."

Aric closed his eyes and let out a pained breath. But you know what? It couldn't have possibly compared to the pain I felt. The crumbled remains of my heart sank to my stomach. "Of course you are," I said through gritted teeth.

I stalked out the door and into the parking lot, stopping only to dent the mailbox in with my fist. *Fiancée.* Aric had a *fiancée* after only a few weeks. We'd been a couple for more than *five months!*

Rage and grief sent a tidal wave of tremors up my body. My encounter with Aric and his fiancée had torn the scab off my emotional wounds. I had tried not to picture him with anyone else. But now I knew, knew what she looked like, knew what she smelled like, knew that she now shared his bed.

I turned when I heard Liam. He fumbled with his car keys while juggling eight pizzas in his left arm. "I'm sorry, Celia. I'm so, so sorry. I had no idea they'd be here."

Liam apologized the entire way home. I was too busy fuming to talk. As soon as we arrived at the house, I stormed up the stairs.

"What happened, Lee?" I heard Emme ask. "Why is Celia so upset?"

"We ran into Aric and Barbara," Liam muttered.

"Who the hell is Barbara?" Taran asked.

"Aric's fiancée!" I screamed at the top of my lungs.

"Dude! He has a fiancée?"

"That son of a bitch."

"Oh, gosh, Liam. Why didn't you tell me?"

"Yeah, Koda. You must have known. We could have told Celia gently. It didn't have to be like this, dude!"

"Stupid, insensitive bastard."

"What were you boys thinking?"

"Angel, Aric asked us not to say anything," Liam said.

"So you just listened to him?" Shayna argued. "This is Celia we're talking about, not some stranger. Didn't you think she had a right to know?"

Apparently not.

I fell back onto the bed, draped an arm over my eyes, and firmly reminded myself that I was done crying. Downstairs, Taran had momentarily stopped swearing. I could almost picture her glaring at the lot of them when she spoke again. "Well, it's pretty damn obvious where your loyalties lie, right, boys?"

"Taran, please calm down," Gemini said. "Aric didn't want to hurt Celia more. He's been waiting for the right time to tell her."

"There is no right time!" Taran was officially screaming. "Shit, after what he did to her, he's a goddamn coward for not telling her to her face!"

"Do you think this has been any easier on Aric?" Koda growled. "If you only knew how he felt."

"I don't give a damn how he feels," Taran shot back, "*He* walked away from *her*, not the other way around."

"She's right, puppy," Shayna said, a little more calmly. "Not to mention he's got that fiancée of his to make him feel better. Who does Celia have?"

"She has us," Emme said gently.

Emme was wrong. My connection to my sisters was waning, in part because I no longer felt needed. They had their wolves to keep them safe and to be strong for them. But I did have someone else, someone with a presence too commanding to ignore.

I rolled toward the nightstand and reached for my cell phone. Misha had begun calling a few days after Aric left. When I first spoke to him, it was during my angry phase. I yelled at him for tasting my blood. Instead of becoming defensive, Misha merely stated that my gruff voice sounded sexy. His retort had stunned me like usual. And while I knew I should keep my distance, my loneliness had made it impossible.

Out of all my sisters, Shayna was the most disappointed by my reconnection with Misha. Koda had her convinced that vampires, especially Misha, shouldn't be trusted. Misha's true intentions remained to be seen. Yet I looked forward to our talks and our interludes at the local ice cream shop. It was the only time my mind wasn't flooded with thoughts of Aric. It also helped my fragile self-esteem to know someone wanted me, even if Misha didn't precisely need me.

I hit the speed dial, ignoring the escalating argument downstairs. "Have dinner with me tonight."

Misha paused before answering, "I take it you have learned of the mongrel's engagement?"

Why am I the last to know? I ran my fingers irritably through my hair. "Does it matter?"

"No. Expect me at seven." Misha disconnected.

I went downstairs and snagged an entire pizza for myself. No one attempted to speak to me. They watched, and waited, for my much-anticipated meltdown. I took a huge bite and swallowed.

"If you'd like, I can probably smash some dishes or boil a bunny in a pot."

That was their clue to look elsewhere.

I finished my snack and went upstairs. After I showered, I called my sisters to my room.

They entered slowly when they saw me wrapped in a towel with my arms crossed. "I'm going out with Misha tonight. Will you help me get ready?"

Taran's face lit up. "You're damn right I will." Her heels pounded down the stairs on her way to raid her closet.

Shayna let out a disappointed sigh. "Is this really what you want?"

"No, but I can't have what I want, can I?"

Shayna averted her gaze. Perhaps the hurt and anger in my eyes were too much for her. Emme placed her hand on my shoulder. "We'll support you," she said quietly. "Here, I'll help you straighten your hair."

She led me to the bed and plugged in the flatiron. With gentle sweeps of a brush she dried my hair to silky perfection. Taran returned with an extremely sexy and revealing outfit for me. She slipped me into a silky black dress that plunged low in the front and back, making it impossible to wear a bra.

I fidgeted and fumbled with the cleavage, debating whether I had the ovaries to wear something so daring. Taran raised her brows upon taking in my hesitation. "Does it really matter if you go braless?" she asked.

I glanced at the floor for a moment, thinking about who was taking me out. "No. I guess not."

Emme finished straightening my hair and Taran applied my makeup. What little I allowed her to add brought out my green eyes and full lips. Shayna didn't participate, but she did smile and pinch my backside when she saw me. "You look hot."

I glanced in the mirror while putting on the diamond earrings Misha had given me. *Okay, maybe not hot, but definitely vampy.*

I walked downstairs just before seven. The wolves did a double take. Liam outright gawked. "Going out tonight, Celia?"

I played with the fastener on my earring. "Mm-hmm."

Koda frowned. "And exactly who are you going out with?"

"With anyone she damn well pleases," Taran countered.

Gemini hurried over to me. Seeing as how males didn't

exactly beat down my door to date me, he knew precisely whom I intended to meet. "Celia, please don't do this." His uneasy expression implored me to reconsider. "It would devastate Aric to know you were with Misha."

My lips parted. I couldn't believe Gemini had brought up Aric. And I especially couldn't believe he tried to guilt me into sparing his feelings. "Aric doesn't have to know about this. I'm not meeting Misha to hurt him." It was the truth. I wasn't a petty or vengeful person. I was just a person with a broken heart, and one who needed to forget the memories that ailed me.

"He'll know," Gemini answered.

I frowned. "I don't want him to."

"He has a right to know!" Koda snapped. "Shit, Celia. Aric *hates* him!"

I threw a palm out. "Why? Because Misha is a vampire? Or is it because he's a male who desires my company?" The wolves collectively tightened their jaws, giving me hard stares, but refusing to answer. Something was up. And damn it, I needed to know what. I met their judgmental glares with equal frustration, my tigress giving my tone an extra boost. *"Just tell me."*

Koda leaned back on his heels and crossed his arms. It was clear he didn't want to say anything, but he finally did. "Misha hurt someone Aric cared about deeply. He's never forgiven him for what he did to her."

My back stiffened. So Aric had cared for someone else. No wonder he'd abandoned me so easily. The jealousy that seared to my bones made me defensive. "That has nothing to do with me. I'm not that girl."

Koda's furrowed eyebrows relaxed. "No, you're not," he admitted. "She's dead."

My sisters gasped behind. I remained still as stone.

"M-Misha killed her?" Emme sputtered.

Koda watched me carefully before answering, "Aric blames him for her death."

"That's not the same thing as murdering someone, Koda." I spoke with conviction, and Koda didn't deny it. In truth, I didn't know. Misha was a vampire, one with enough clout to easily kill or order someone's death. Except more than once I'd seen the man behind the fangs, the arrogance, and the sin. No, Misha hadn't killed Aric's love. This, I was absolutely sure of.

Liam dropped his head, low enough for me to count all the spikes in his rock star hairstyle. "Celia, please don't do this to Aric."

My bruised heart throbbed cruelly. How had I come out the bad guy?

Taran stomped to my side, jabbing her finger in the air at the wolves. "Forget Aric and his goddamn feelings. *He* left *her!*" She released her rage. The flowers in the vases ignited in blue and white flames, boiling the water so hot the vases shattered.

Shayna's head whipped to Taran. "Dude, calm down!"

Taran's blue irises paled to white, her face barren of any reason. "Don't tell me to calm down!"

I raced into the kitchen, grabbed the fire extinguisher, and sprinted back into the family room. Koda growled in wolf. I'm not sure what he said, but the charred smell of his anger coated my tongue like ash. The others were finishing batting out the flames on the couch and failed to recognize his rising fury.

Thunder exploded outside, shaking the entire house. Taran's ire had reached a climactic crescendo, with no descent in sight. Koda stormed toward Taran and clasped her shoulders. "*Stop*. You need to stop *now*."

Taran's white irises locked on his turbulent browns. "You're telling me Aric can screw who he wants, marry who he wants, and love who he wants, but Celia is denied that right!"

Koda's eyes flared just as blue and white flames shot like a rocket up our fireplace and heated the entire room.

"I won't pretend to know what Celia is going through, but don't you assume Aric is not suffering in his own personal hell."

Taran quirked a dark eyebrow, making her stare appear more crazed. "How hot is it getting in hell with that blonde?"

"Let her go. *Now*." Gemini dropped the blanket he'd been using to beat the flames and instinctively darted to Taran's side, bringing with him the strong aroma of werewolf magic.

Koda dropped his hands and stepped into Shayna's startled arms, proving why Gemini had been chosen over him as Beta. "Forgive me, Tomo. I meant no disrespect against yours." He'd used Gemini's given name. That in itself was a bad sign. Some furious, scary, werewolf, mojo thing had just happened. I didn't understand it and I wanted it gone. I placed the fire extinguisher on the floor and slumped on the couch that had been spared from Taran's fury. I glanced at the clock, hoping Misha would arrive soon and take me away from the madness I blamed myself for causing.

Gemini's wrath lessened as he continued to watch Koda and Shayna holding each other. Gemini nodded once before slipping his arms protectively around Taran. Her eyes slowly regained their normal shade of blue. Yet her voice remained sharp. "Keep Aric and his bitch fiancée away from Celia. If they so much as hold hands around her, he'll never use his penis again."

Emme used her *force* to sweep up the mess. The soft brush of the broom broke up the unpleasant quiet of the room. But that's about all it did. If it wasn't for the doorbell ringing, I would have bolted away from the lot of them.

Emme glanced nervously at the wolves before opening the front door. "Hello, Misha."

"Good evening, sweet Emme."

Emme shuffled her feet. "Um. Thank you for taking Celia out, but I'd like your word that you'll be a perfect gentleman."

I think Emme would have liked living at the North Pole with Rudolph.

Misha regarded me as I uncrossed my legs and stood. "I am truly sorry, my dear, but I am not accustomed to making promises I cannot keep."

The wolves responded by clenching their fists, puffing out their chests, and growling. Gemini appeared especially menacing, the extent of his boiling point continuing to linger. In an effort to avoid more drama, I thought it best to leave.

Misha greeted me with a sensual smile. "You look stunning. Are you ready for me?"

His voice dripped so much sexual connotation that I had to take a deep breath before answering, "Yes, Misha. I'm ready."

I *was* ready—to forget about Aric. And Misha was the only one capable of distracting me.

We shared a nice dinner, and I enjoyed our time together. Misha even succeeded in getting me to laugh. It was a hell of an accomplishment, considering the day I'd had. Still, I couldn't help feeling sad. A heavy sense of bereavement wouldn't leave me. It wasn't until dessert arrived that I realized I mourned the loss of hope that Aric would come back to me.

"I do not understand how someone so lovely can appear so miserable," Misha said while we waited for his car.

"I'm sorry, Misha. The last few weeks have been horrible. I don't mean to be such a lousy date."

Misha pressed me against a wall in the shadows of the building. His large hands held my waist, and his breath was warm against my jaw. "Perhaps what you need is something to occupy your mind," he murmured.

I trembled when his lips skimmed across my neck. My God, it felt so good to be touched. I hadn't fathomed the extent of my loneliness until Misha's caress awakened the sensuality buried deep within my body's memory.

I shoved away the grief generated from the strokes of unfamiliar hands, and forced myself to feel the tantalizing effect of Misha's contact. *This will end the hurt and numb the pain,* I reminded myself. *If only for a little while . . .*

Misha kissed me. My lips parted as I welcomed him deep into my mouth. He tasted delicious and decadent like the most tempting and sinful of desserts. My body sank into his, my arms linked around his neck, and my fingers tugged his long, gorgeous hair.

Our kisses increased in fervor. His hands wandered up my dress, exploring my body in a rough, seductive massage. But as a long, deep moan escaped my lips, he vanished, except for the strands of his hair entangled between my fingers.

A horrible crash made me lurch to the side. Misha lay sprawled with his body embedded in the building across the street. Crumbling chunks of brick peppered the sidewalk as he stirred. I took a step in his direction, confused as to what happened. "Misha—"

That's when I smelled *him*. The scent of water crashing over stones mixed with the smell of fury. *Aric* stood in the street, facing Misha. The guttural rumble in which he spoke burned me to the core. "Get up, you goddamn leech. I'm going to rip you to pieces. *You* don't touch *her!*"

Misha extracted himself from the building in one hard pull. He dusted off like he'd just rolled in the hay, but calmness had clearly left him. He reminded me of a venomous snake, a pissed-off and hungry venomous snake coiling to strike. "I've waited a long time for this, *boy*."

Misha launched himself at Aric, but they never made contact. Wolves and vampires surged out of nowhere and grabbed them. Koda, Gemini, Liam, and even Bren were among the wolves trying to stop Aric, yet despite their united effort, they couldn't hold him back. "Aric, don't do this," Koda urged. "We have an agreement."

Misha's bodyguards and some of his family also tried unsuccessfully to restrain Misha. "Master, please," Agnes begged. "Think of the treaty!"

Emme ran to me, her face pale with fright. "Oh my God, Celia. They're going to kill each other."

That was all I needed to hear to pull me out of my stupor. I sprinted forward, grabbing Aric and Misha seconds before they connected and *shifted* them into the road. I surfaced, leaving them embedded from their shoulder blades down. *"Enough,"* I hissed as they struggled. "That's *enough!"*

Ragged breaths filled the quiet street. I ignored the stares the vampires, the wolves, and my sisters trained on me. All I cared about was putting miles between Aric and Misha. Cracks split the street from their struggles and the pounding of their efforts shook my feet. They'd be free soon. And no one would be able to stop them.

I bent forward to face Misha. "I'll let you up if you promise to walk away."

The edges of his lips curved with wicked hunger. He looked right at Aric when he answered me. "Only if you walk away with me, kitten."

I nodded, knowing what he meant. "Yes, I'll go with you, Misha."

Aric's struggles grew more violent. A block of asphalt broke near his right shoulder as he swore at and threatened Misha. We were running out of time. I grabbed Misha's exposed hand and *shifted* him up to the street. He immediately snaked his arm around my waist. I placed my arm against his lower back, trying to hurry him toward his awaiting vehicle.

Taran bespelled a bunch of onlookers, convincing them that an earthquake had caused the damage, and imploring them to return to their homes. I didn't look back after that. I climbed into Misha's Hummer limo, and we drove away.

Despair squeezed my throat like a vise. My personal life was in an emotional tailspin. I'd emerged from my depressive state only to dive back in again.

Misha put his arm around me and smoothed my hair. He held me with kindness unbefitting a vampire of his caliber and any vampire in general. No. This wasn't a master capable of murdering a young female. No matter what the wolves believed. "Aric blames you for killing someone he loved," I said quietly.

A flicker of recognition played briefly in his expression. "He does."

"But you didn't kill her."

Misha leaned back, waiting for me to say more. My comment wasn't a question. He heard my acceptance of his innocence in my voice.

"What did happen, Misha?"

He patted his knee as if bored, taking his time to answer. "My master, Uri, and I visited the lupines years ago at their sacred Den in Colorado. A young pureblood there demonstrated an interest in me. When I refused to entertain her company following our night together, she took her life." The hand at his knee clenched into a tight fist. "Had I recognized her fragile state, I wouldn't have allowed her in my quarters. In his grief, your wolf sought to cast blame. As vampire, I of course became his obvious target."

I bit back my sorrow, threatening to unravel like a tightly bound cord. "That's why Aric's so angry at finding us together. I remind him of his girlfriend who he loved and lost."

Misha watched me closely. "The she-wolf was a relation of his, Celia. One he regarded like a sister." His face hardened. "That mongrel has never loved."

Yeah. Maybe you're right. Tears streaked down my face, ruining Taran's cosmetic efforts. Misha didn't seem to mind. He lifted my chin and wiped my eyes with a silk handkerchief. "You will not join me in bed tonight, will you?"

He knew I was going to refuse him, yet he wasn't angry or hurtful or proud. He was simply Misha, the man I'd come to know.

I blinked a few times, taking in every ounce of his enticing features, from his godlike face, to the impenetrable wall of muscle surrounding his tall frame. Good Lord, Misha was masculine beauty molded to perfection.

And yet not the one who I desired.

"I'm sorry, Misha. You deserve better than what I can offer."

"Somehow I doubt that," he said almost silently. For the second time since I'd met him, Misha's eyes lost their sting. There was no hint of a wicked smile or of the ruthless master that terrified his keep. At that moment, Misha seemed more human than the day I'd returned his soul.

Instead of taking me to his house, Misha ordered Hank to turn the BYTE ME mobile around. I didn't know what he planned until the limo pulled up in front of the ice cream parlor we'd frequented. When Hank opened the door, Misha stepped out and offered me his hand. I took it. Then we walked inside to drown my sorrows.

A strange sense of quiet surrounded my neighborhood and thickened as Misha and I sauntered up the front steps. I didn't know why until I opened the door. Aric stood in the middle of our family room with his fists clenched, his face red, and his wolf on the verge of attacking. Taran must have placed a silencing charm around the house to contain his growls. He lunged at Misha the moment he saw us. The wolves barely jumped on him in time.

"I'll kill you! I'll tear out your goddamn throat!"

Emme tried to help hold Aric with her *force*. Shayna quickly manipulated the fire poker into restraints. Taran stepped in front of me and gathered her magic to stun him.

Although Misha remained calm, I didn't want to risk another confrontation. I shut the door and led him back to the limo. "I'm sorry for everything, Misha. Thank you for your friendship tonight. I would have been lost without it."

"It is not your friendship that I seek, my beautiful kitten. But it will do for now." With that he kissed my lips and left.

Everything stopped when I entered the house. Their combined strength had succeeded in restraining Aric.

I scoffed, disgusted, and moved toward the stairs.

"Release me *now*." Aric's command sounded more animal than human.

As soon as they did, Aric scrambled to his feet. "I'd lay down my life for you to be happy, Celia," he said behind me. "With anyone but *him*."

Aric's words hit me like a tangible force. I dropped my purse and slowly turned to face him, meeting his anger with my own. "*You* walked out on me without looking back." The lump in my throat ached when I swallowed it back. "*You* don't get to decide who makes *me* happy!"

There was more I wanted to say, but it was torturous to stand there and look into those brown eyes I had once cherished. I moved quickly and reached for the railing.

Aric grabbed my arm before I could take the first step. The moment I felt his skin against mine, that familiar warmth I'd longed for spread throughout my body, making me shudder. When I met his eyes, his anger was gone. Only the tenderness I knew so well remained.

I ripped my arm away from him. *"Don't you touch me!"* I sobbed at him. *"Don't you ever touch me again!"*

Aric's face and voice were nothing short of an agonized mess. "Celia . . . *Mon âme fait mal sans toi.*"

I fled. I couldn't take more of his games. When I reached my bed, I collapsed, crying. Emme and Shayna tried to soothe me, but the pain was too overpowering to suppress.

"You *asshole*!" Taran screamed downstairs. "Can't you see what you're doing to her?"

I presumed Aric could, because I heard him leave. It sounded like Koda and Liam followed him.

"What the hell did he say to her anyway?" Taran asked Gemini, her voice cracking from her rising emotions.

Gemini let out a sigh before he spoke. "He said, 'Celia . . . my soul hurts without you.' "

CHAPTER 27

Sleep evaded me that night. A million thoughts raced through my head, but the emotions remained the same. Aric's actions had pummeled me back into despair and left me angry and confused.

Does he still want me? Or does he just not want Misha to have me?

Regardless, I still wanted him. And while I knew I loved him, my tigress would never have allowed me to beg or plead with him to stay. No matter how much my human side wanted to.

Around seven in the morning, I sluggishly crawled out of bed and made breakfast. My sisters and their wolves emerged from their bedrooms one by one. No one spoke, and no one appeared to have slept all night. I loaded their plates with the mountain of food I'd prepared. My sisters regarded me with empathy. The wolves kept looking at me like I might snap. Maybe I should have. But then maybe I already had.

"How did Aric find me last night?" I finally asked.

Liam brought his chair closer to the table, staring at his plate before answering, "He came by shortly after

Misha picked you up. I guess he wanted to talk to you about what happened at the pizza place."

Koda put his fork down. "Aric was pissed the moment he smelled Misha in the doorway. When he realized you'd left together, he went crazy."

You think?

"Aric tracked you to the restaurant, and we tracked him," Gemini said quietly. "We called everyone, knowing Aric wouldn't hesitate to attack Misha."

"We tried calling you, dude. But you didn't take your phone." Shayna reached into the back pocket of her jeans and placed my cell phone on the table. "When I used your phone to call Misha, the vampire who answered refused to put me through. She said he didn't want to be disturbed for the rest of the night."

Liam wasn't eating. He pushed his plate away, worry wrinkling his brow. "When Aric saw you and Misha all over each other, he completely lost it." He shook his head. "I've never seen him like that. He's always had such control. Then he met you. And everything changed."

I covered my head with my hands, wanting to scream. "I didn't do anything to him. He's the one who left me. We're not together anymore."

"No, but he'll always belong to you, Celia," Gemini added gently.

Taran stood so fast she knocked her chair over. "Like hell!"

My arms dropped to the side with defeat. Nothing I said seemed to get through to the wolves. Their loyalties to Aric blinded them. He was their friend and hero. "I can't believe you would say this to me, Gemini. Aric is not mine. He's marrying someone else. She's the one who gets him forever. I don't have that option."

"Barbara may be his fiancée." Koda paused. "But, Celia, *you're* Aric's mate."

Of all the things Koda might have said, nothing could have hurt me more. I gripped the counter tightly. "That's not true."

Koda exchanged glances with Gemini, who took a deep breath and reached for my hand. "Celia, Aric has known you're his mate since the first time he saw you. I think he's tried to suppress his feelings to spare you both. Our Elders . . . they never wanted you together. Perhaps he's always known he'd have to leave you."

A strange shiver crept up my spine despite the warmth in the kitchen. I could barely breathe. "Did he tell you this?"

Koda mimicked a statue, hard and barely moving. "No, but as his Warriors, we sensed your bond the night you claimed each other as mates."

I blinked back at Koda, certain I'd misheard. He dropped his eyes and glanced around awkwardly. "Koda . . . I don't understand what you're talking about."

Liam smiled. "Celia, the moment you and Aric accepted the claim, our connection to him linked us to you. That's how we know. And that's why we'll always protect you, just like we're duty-bound to protect him."

Shayna appeared as confused as I felt. "Okay, so you're all connected to Celia. But what's a claim, and how do you make one?"

Liam and Koda looked right at Gemini, with the expectation, it seemed, that he would elaborate. Gemini didn't appear eager to do so. In fact, his head shot to the nearest exit. "I don't feel it's my place to discuss this."

Koda grew impatient, and so did his tone. "Don't be such a wimp. You're Aric's *Beta*. This is your territory."

Gem scowled. "My duties do not oblige me to explain delicate matters to my Alpha's mate."

I turned to Taran. She got the hint right away. A slow, seductive smile spread across her face. She danced her fingertips up his arm and whispered closely in his ear,

"Please, baby. We'd like to understand more about your ways."

Gem's eyes followed her hand, before he cleared his throat. "Celia, do you remember a time when Aric asked you during your, uh, lovemaking if you wanted him?"

My body grew warmer, and my cheeks immediately flushed. "Um, yeah, a few times."

He fidgeted in his chair, glancing back at Taran before continuing. "Did he also ask if he could have you?"

I thought back to the night I'd posed for Aric and nodded.

"And at the time, was there a, um, barrier, when he, ah, finished?"

I shook my head no. That was the first night we'd made love without a condom.

Gemini clasped his hands together and rubbed them. "Well, then, that was the night you claimed each other as mates and consummated your union."

"But Aric's wolf recognized you as his mate before then," Liam explained. "The claim is performed after the human side accepts what the beast already knew. It's the official way of becoming mated."

"The claim only works if both partners feel the same way," Koda added when he saw my blatant disbelief. "Otherwise, it would have failed."

I gaped at the faces staring back at me, not knowing what to think or do. Then I remembered Heidi had referred to me as Aric's mate a few weeks back. "Gemini, is Heidi also one of Aric's Warriors?"

He nodded. "Yes, but she's not close to him like we are."

Yeah, sure she's not. I stood there, dumbfounded. *Why would Aric keep this from me?*

Shayna practically glowed. She draped her arms around Koda's neck and smiled. "Is this what you were trying to talk to me about the other night?"

Koda returned her smile and stroked her cheek. "Yes. There's no doubt in my mind," he answered softly.

Shayna rested her cheek against Koda's massive chest. I didn't remember ever seeing her so happy.

Taran turned the color of sand. "Oh, *shit*," she whispered.

Gemini gathered her in his arms and pulled her close. "It's okay," he told her patiently. "We'll wait until you're ready."

Two of my sisters were next in line to be "claimed" and "mated." But when Emme faced Liam expectantly, his head dropped and he let out a weary breath. Her cheeks flushed and she turned to Gem. "Now that Aric is with someone else, will he remove his claim on Celia?" When she saw the hurt on my face, she quickly explained, "So Celia can move on, I mean."

"It doesn't work that way, Emme," Koda replied, holding tight to Shayna. "Even if Aric never claimed Celia—oh, hell, even if they'd never *met*—she would still be his mate." He offered me a sad, sympathetic smile. "She's the one. He'll never love another."

My escalating frustration caused my hands to tremble. "But then how could he leave me?"

Gemini rubbed his goatee, searching for the right words to say. "Celia, you can't fathom how much Aric is struggling. All he's ever known is conflict with what he feels for you. Believe me, there's nothing he wants more than to be at your side. But he's bound by blood and obligation to our pack. It's his duty to ensure our survival."

My stomach twisted uncomfortably. As much as I wanted to believe I was Aric's mate, I couldn't. After all, he never admitted to loving me, even after knowing that I loved him.

I left them in silence and returned to my room, with the realization Gemini was right: Aric had to help continue his race. Without the *weres*, our world would perish. So as much as I wanted to hate him, I couldn't. How could I hate someone who would put the world's needs before his own?

"This is stupid. Why are they having sex if the psycho with the machete is after them?"

Bren tore his eyes from his flat-screen just to roll them at me. "Ceel, graphic nudity in slasher flicks gives the viewer a chance to breathe before the next set of limbs gets hacked. Everyone knows that." He shrugged. "Besides, the blonde has awesome hooters."

"I thought they were designed to warn teens against having sex?"

"Hooters?"

"No, Bren. You know, slasher movies?"

Bren shook his head. "I don't think so. I lost my virginity while watching *Halloween*."

I rubbed my eyes, though I shouldn't have been surprised. When the blonde with the awesome hooters arched her back during the "act," the psycho in the mask stabbed her in the chest. The tip of his machete pushed her still-beating heart out through her back in pure slasher-flick glory. I knew how she felt. I rubbed at my own chest, still sore from crying.

Bren's phone rang. "Yeah?"

Taran screamed over the phone. "Tribesmen attacked Emme and Liam. Emme's hurt and she's not waking up."

Bren scrambled to his feet. "Where are you?"

"The Den. Please hurry."

"We're on our way, Taran," Bren promised.

I bolted after him. "Bren, *wait*. I don't know how to get there."

"I'll show you."

We raced down his apartment stairs and into my car. I started the engine. "How do you know where the Den is?"

"Aric offered me asylum there once we became aware of the Tribe. Take Eighty-nine to Squaw Valley." He frowned. "How come you don't know where it is?"

I thought back to Paul's funeral. "I've never been there. Only *weres* are allowed through the gates."

Bren scoffed. "What a bunch of snobs, just one more reason not to belong to a pack. I tell you, the day I *call* one of them is the day hell freezes over."

I drove fast, worried about Emme and uneasy about what would happen once I reached the Den. Would I have to fight my way in?

Bren interrupted my thoughts. "You and Aric were pretty serious, weren't you? I mean, it wasn't just physical?"

I had the impression Bren had been watching me closely. "I thought so."

"Did you ever meet his parents?"

"I spoke to his mother a few times on the phone, but his father died on a mission when Aric was fifteen." I became quiet. Eliza Connor had thankfully survived the attacks.

"What is it, Ceel?"

"Nothing. It's just that his mother had invited us for Thanksgiving. I was supposed to meet her then, but of course that's no longer possible."

His eyes softened before he turned back to face the road. "Sorry I brought it up, babe."

Bren gave me more specific directions when we arrived at Squaw Valley. He had me turn onto a winding dirt path that led up a steep mountain. It made sense why the wolves owned SUVs; the stomach-churning drive up the path took almost fifteen minutes. I rolled down the window, hoping the magic of the area would settle my nerves. The Jeffrey and ponderosa pines and California red firs added a fresh aroma. Yet the growing scent of *were* magic fed my anxiety. Unlike the bewitching power of Tahoe, the divination of the mountain told me I wasn't welcome. And that only danger waited.

"Do you feel that?" I asked Bren.

"Huh?"

I shuddered. "Never mind."

We veered onto a paved private road and approached a colossal wrought-iron gate. My shoulders relaxed slightly when a familiar figure stepped out, smiling. "Hi, Celia, it's nice to see you. Come on in."

"Thank you, Heidi."

Bren gawked at her as we pulled away. "Are those real?"

I glared at him. "How the hell would I know?"

Bren lowered the window and placed an arm against the doorframe. His laid-back demeanor dissolved as he took in the campus. "You know, this place sits on over a hundred acres. With so much land, I never understood why Aric ran at Tahoe. I'd think his wolf would prefer the rugged terrain."

"Aric was out exploring the area the day we met. The beach was close to the lodge where he and the other wolves were staying. They liked Tahoe and thought they'd find a place around the lake." My tigress paced inside me, vigilant of the danger we continued to perceive.

"But then they moved in with all of you."

I continued to take everything in. "Yes."

"Makes sense," Bren said.

"Why?"

"Wolves are pack animals, Ceel. In becoming their girlfriends, you became part of their pack."

I thought about us all living under one roof. How easily we'd grown accustomed to their presence and how we had depended on one another. "I guess you're right."

The trees cleared. Rows of beautiful, three-story lodges simulating a majestic ski resort occupied the clearing. Each building, while unique, was adorned with stone steps and railings leading to sweeping wraparound porches with stout granite pillars and outdoor fireplaces. The landscaping consisted of strategically placed shrubs, trees, and plants that intermingled with sculptures designed from boulders and petrified wood. The Den didn't so much resemble a school, but rather a vacation spot that catered to the ridiculously wealthy and the power elite.

I stopped the car in front of one of the larger structures and jumped out. Bren and I wandered down the stone-paved road trying to figure out where to go. I feared the worst when I dialed Taran and my call went straight to voice mail.

"Hi, Celia. Aric is in the main building over there." The little wolf who snagged my flag pointed to a building across the street.

I looked at the building, then back at him. "Hi, John. I'm not looking for Aric. I need to find my sister."

"Oh, the little blonde who was hurt? She's there, too. Follow me."

The building John led us to was at least three times the size of the other lodges. He had us wait in the massive foyer while he jogged up the steps of a sprawling wooden staircase. Moments later, everyone, including Emme, appeared at the top of the stairs.

I sprinted up the stairs, grabbing Emme in a tight embrace when I reached her. "I'm okay, Celia, really. It just took me a little while to heal," she said.

I released her slowly and hugged my other sisters before addressing their wolves. Worry and anger shadowed Liam's boyish features. "She was knocked unconscious, Celia. I thought she was gone."

Rage prickled my skin. My baby sister had almost died at the hands of those bastards. "Did you kill them, Liam?"

He turned back to Emme. "Of course I did. I—"

A ripple of strength and authority swept in, similar to the small waves before the tsunami hits. In the arched doorway, Aric stood with two men and a woman. My tigress recognized them as the pack Elders; their power was unmistakable.

Liam and Gemini took Emme and Taran and hurried toward them. Koda grabbed Shayna and me and followed them with Bren at our heels. Koda released me only when Aric came to stand by my side.

The larger and most commanding of the two male Elders examined me closely. He was a tall, African-American with broad shoulders and bulging muscles, despite his advanced age. Gray touched his short black hair, and deep-set wrinkles framed his eyes. His gaze didn't appear challenging, yet he seemed to expect something of me.

Aric nodded slightly and moved close enough that I felt his body heat. The fondness he'd demonstrated to the Elder in that subtle gesture made me realize I'd just met Martin Lockwood, the pack Alpha.

CHAPTER 28

I stepped away. It hurt too much to have Aric near and know we could no longer touch. Martin pursed his lips. A small motion, but I noticed it anyway.

Aric didn't attempt to close the distance between us. Instead he mirrored his Warriors, who had bowed their heads.

The remaining male Elder stepped forward. He was Native American with waist-length black hair streaked with silver. Unlike Martin, whose expression I couldn't read, this guy was clearly ticked. "Explain yourselves," he snapped, unleashing a deep growl.

"Anara, calm," said the Native American woman behind him. Her pure white hair flowed behind her like a veil. She was petite and slight of figure, but stood strong. And although I placed her at about eighty, her only wrinkles fell along her laugh lines, leaving me the impression she'd smiled a great deal throughout her life. She touched Anara's shoulder, soothing him and silencing his growls. It was only then the wolves dared speak.

Gemini stepped forward. "Ladies, may I present our distinguished Elders, Martin Lockwood, Anara Running

Bear, and Makawee Light-Feather. Honorable Elders, this is—"

"We know who they are," Anara said tightly. "The question is, why are they here?"

"I allowed them to come, Anara," Aric interrupted.

Anara's thick brows appeared menacing enough to crawl off his face and slap me. "Aric, your lapse in judgment astounds me. First last night's exploits and now this? They need to leave." He trained his glare specifically at me. "You don't need any more distractions."

I glared right back. "We were just leaving."

Aric stepped in front of me so fast the breeze from his speed pushed my hair back. Bren gave my arm a warning squeeze. Everyone tensed. I realized too late that mouthing off to a pack Elder was probably not the smartest thing to do.

"Then do so *now*," Anara snapped.

The Warriors quickly escorted us outside. Someone had already parked our other car in front of the building, no doubt to expedite our departure. Emme and Taran drove off after some hurried encouragement from Liam and Gemini. Shayna chose to ride with me. She climbed into the back of our SUV. Bren took the front. I could feel the Elders continuing to watch us. I wanted to leave just as badly as they wanted me gone, but when I tried to open the driver's-side door, Aric stopped me.

"Please, wait. I want to talk to you."

Anara's voice imitated that of a beast. "Aric. Let her go and return to my office *now*."

Makawee interrupted in a serene whisper. "Anara, allow him a moment with Celia."

I turned to her, puzzled that she knew my name. She greeted me with a small smile. "Yes, child, I know who you are. I recognize your aroma from scenting it on Aric."

Makawee's smile widened at my blush. "Anara," she

continued, "you were young once. Let Aric say good-bye."

Anara didn't argue. He followed Makawee up the stone steps, stopping once to glare at Aric and me before entering the building. I didn't see Martin. Yet I sensed his essence all around me.

I turned to Aric. It was the first time I'd allowed myself to really look at him since arriving at the Den. Deep shadows collected beneath his eyes, while lines bracketed the corners. His jaw bore heavy stubble. I couldn't get over how hard he appeared; it was as if he no longer slept, and no longer cared about anything. He stepped closer to me. "Celia, may I hold your hands?"

Aric's request aggravated the tension between us. It reminded me that I'd told him never to touch me again. My God, so much had changed. Just a few weeks prior we had slept in each other's arms. And now . . .

Aric took my hands into his when I nodded. And just like that, the familiar feeling of warmth encompassed us. He let out a deep sigh. "Celia, things are so broken between us. I just wish I knew how to make them right."

"You can't, Aric." My face cracked into a million pieces. "Look, I don't like what you're doing, but I realize you don't have a choice."

Aric didn't say anything; instead he squeezed my hands tighter, regarding me with apparent sorrow. I allowed the heat we shared to comfort me one last time before pulling away. The moment we separated, loneliness consumed me. "Good-bye, Aric."

I slipped into the SUV before I did something stupid. I wanted to kiss him, to beg him not to let me go, to tell him I'd be willing to share him with Barbara. But my tigress managed to hang on to our self-respect. She knew, like I did, that I wanted and deserved more.

My hands trembled badly. It took me several tries to push the key into the ignition and I almost broke the key in the process. I peeled away, raw emotion stirring every nerve in my body.

"Damn. That sucked." Bren drummed his hand against the armrest. "I mean, it was like a scene right out of *Titanic*."

I gripped the steering wheel firmly and tried to focus ahead. A loud crushing sound caused me to glance in the rearview mirror. The lump in my throat grew tighter. Aric stood next to a cracked granite pillar, blood spilling from his knuckles. Yet instead of staring at the destruction, his gaze fixed on my car.

"Oh, shit!" Bren said, looking back. "I hope that was just decorative. You know what, Ceel? I think Aric loves you."

I tried to stifle a sob. Shayna reached around the front to tug Bren's arm. "Dude, knock it off. You're making her feel worse." Her voice softened to plead with me. "Ceel, please don't cry. It's going to be all right, I know it is. Hang in there, tiger."

I took a few calming breaths, but I couldn't stop shaking. The road blurred in front of me, and I felt the car swerve off the road. Bren grabbed the wheel and jerked it to the left. I took it back and yanked it away from him. "Celia. Stop the car."

"No," I growled at him.

"Damn it, you almost hit a fountain. Stop the car now!"

My foot stomped on the brake. I glared at him when he came around the driver's side.

"Get out. You're in no condition to drive."

I didn't move. My eyes closed and reached into my inner beast. She alone had kept us safe when we found the bleeding corpses of our beloved mother and father. She had been my strength through our terrifying abuse. She kept us functioning when Ana Lisa's body failed her. She would help me survive without Aric. Because as much as we hurt, and as much as our loneliness threatened to smother us, we refused to lie down and die.

When my eyes open, Bren frowned back at me, more with worry than the anger he'd held moments before. "My world is shit, Bren. Get back in the car, and allow me some control."

Shayna stepped out of the car and placed her hand on Bren's arm. Her eyes glistened with tears. "Please, dude. Just let her drive."

Bren leaned toward me. I thought at first to haul my ass out. I tightened my hold on the steering wheel hard enough to bend it. Bren surprised me by kissing my cheek. "You're going to be okay, kid."

I couldn't sniff lies. Yet I knew Bren didn't believe his own words. He ambled around the car, his head lower than usual. The moment he buckled in, I sped off, probably a little too fast. Taran and Emme idled at the gate. Taran rolled down the window when she saw me. "You all right?"

I nodded.

She scowled. "Forget him, Celia. Time to get the hell out of Wolf Central."

The more I drove down the snaking road, the more I felt my control breaking away. My tigress was strong, but even she would need time to cope without Aric's wolf. I angled the car to the side, ready to let Bren drive, when a frigid cold struck my body all at once.

Hordes of demon children swept down from the sky and surrounded us. The biggest one I'd ever seen landed on Taran's sedan and tore into the roof. She slammed down on the accelerator and tried to shake it, but the creature dug his back claws into the metal and continued its rampage, peeling the exterior like layers of foil.

Bren scrambled out the window. "Get me close!"

I remained at least ten feet away when Bren propelled himself off my hood. He *changed* midjump and tackled the creature. They toppled off the car and into the thick underbrush. I couldn't see what happened next. All I heard were Bren's growls as he fought and my sisters screaming for him.

Two others landed on Taran's roof and finished breaking through. She jerked the car right and left, and back again, barely keeping the car from veering off the jutted road. I thought her maneuvers would knock them off, but when they started grabbing for my sisters, I was forced to articulate the unthinkable.

"Shayna, *drive!*"

Shayna climbed to the front and smoothly took over as I crept out. I leapt onto Taran's mangled car and flung the closest demon against a large tree trunk. It exploded like a piñata, spraying the car behind me.

I went after the other as it pulled Emme, shrieking, out of the damaged roof. I tore off his wings before he could take flight, then jumped on his back and ripped off his head. The demon's claws abruptly released Emme. I barely managed to grab on to the side of the car and catch her before she toppled onto the road.

Hell must have frozen over because in the distance Bren *called* for the pack. Farther away, a wolf answered his howl, then another, and another.

My glance shot toward Bren's call. More demons swooped down from the sky, all large, all strong, all hungry. Drool glistened their yellow fangs, red irises fired with gluttony. Their numbers so vast, their wings and bodies collided against one another as they barreled toward us.

I shoved Emme through the window. "Taran, *go*. They're coming, Taran. *They're coming!*"

Emme was halfway in when a demon swept down and dug his clawed feet into my shoulders. The stabbing pain rippled across the length of my arms in agonizing spasms. I pushed Emme through before he took flight, thrashing violently, but the demon wouldn't let me go. He drove his claws deeper into my skin, impeding my movements.

My feet slapped along the treetops when a bolt of lightning sizzled past me and struck the demon. It dropped me in a combustion of limbs. The world spun as my body plummeted to the ground. Emme tried to catch me with her *force*, but my weight and speed seemed too much for her. I landed hard on my stomach, losing the air in my lungs in one, long, painful exhale.

Sharp stones and pieces of broken branches pierced into my flesh. I struggled to regain my breath, frantically searching for my family. Taran's car remained lodged between two trees. My car angled next to hers. Chunks of demon parts slithered out from beneath the tires from where Shayna had crashed into them.

My sisters stood in the middle of the road, fighting for their lives. Taran blasted everything she could with her fire, her hair whipping in the breeze as she reeled to face the advancing scourge. Emme launched a hailstorm of jagged stones, puncturing through their chests and slashing through their scaled hides. Shayna had transformed the car antenna into a rapier and sliced off heads and limbs. But there were too many of them, and not enough of us.

Deep within the forest, the pounding of massive paws against the earth announced the wolves' approach. I growled with frustration. They were still far away. No way would they reach us in time.

I forced myself to stand, only to stagger backward when the strong aroma of vampire reached my nose. They stalked through the trees armed with rifles and dressed in tattered clothing. "Oh my God," I gasped. *They're not the ones on our side.*

My fear turned into panic when a redheaded vamp lifted the barrel and pointed it at Emme. I ran toward her as fast as I could, yelling her name. Another vamp saw me coming and shot me in the collarbone. The force knocked me against the graveled dirt. I roared in agony. I'd never been shot before; the pain was unbearable.

I wrenched myself to my feet. Another bullet struck me in my thigh. Horrible burning spread, but it was quickly replaced by a strange numbness. My limbs failed me, and my breathing slowed. From the hard ground, I watched the same vamp fire at Shayna.

Shayna fell limp and unmoving. The vampire who shot her approached, laughing. He cocked the rifle and aimed for her head, but he never got the chance to shoot.

Bren sprinted out of the trees and tore the vamp's head off in one ferocious bite. He continued his vicious killing spree while I tried in vain to *change*. My tigress failed to respond. She tumbled deep within me, clawing with the need to hang on. Tears burned my eyes as the strength of her power receded. She left me. My God, *she left me*.

My muscles turned flaccid and weak, except I couldn't understand why. It was more than just blood loss and loss of my beast. Something felt *different*, and everything around me slowed like a snail's journey across a ravine.

Another shot was fired, this time hitting Emme. She collapsed, crying out in an earsplitting holler. A demon grabbed her around the waist and took flight while another lifted Shayna's lifeless body in his arms. His bat wings extended like giant kites. He smiled, clutching Shayna eagerly against him. I tried rolling. My vision doubled from the effort and my heart rate slowed to a weak thud.

Two smaller demons dragged Taran away, each clenching an arm. "Celia, *Celia!*" She swore when she spotted my unmoving form. Her body thrashed violently and her pale skin dripped with the cold sweat of her terror. Her nightmare had come true. The demons had us, and they weren't letting go.

Taran tried to gather her magic. A faint brush of her dwindling power raked against my failing senses. One of the monsters halted her efforts by crushing her wrist. As numb as I felt, her wails of pain sent a spear of ice down my spine. They launched into flight with her at the same moment my body left the ground. Below me Bren fought six demons in his desperate effort to reach us.

We soared upward, the flap of the demons' wings a faint whisper in my ears. Taran unleashed a guttural scream. My eyes burned as blue and white light exploded out of her. The creatures holding her burst into nasty bits while she remained suspended above the treetops. Poor Emme used the last of her strength to keep Taran from falling.

Emme's hand quivered and her lids fluttered. She was losing her hold. Taran's body bounced and twitched in the air as the first of the wolf pack arrived. Heidi clawed her way up the nearest tree and leapt off a thick branch, fastening her powerful jaws on to the waist of Taran's jeans. She ricocheted from tree trunk to tree trunk until she brought my sister safely to the ground.

Tears drenched my cheeks, knowing at least Taran had been spared.

My vision clouded as I scanned the forest floor. What seemed like the entire pack chased us. Aric and Koda thundered in the lead, growling with murderous fury. But I realized their efforts were hopeless as the demons lifted us higher into the darkening sky.

Misha, Misha, please find us.

And then the world went black.

CHAPTER 29

The sound of clanking steel gradually stirred me. At first, I thought I was home, waking to an earthquake. But instead of warm sheets, only cold metal chilled my back.

Metal?

I pried my eyes open. My vision blurred, and the pounding in my head intensified. Every part of my body felt stiff and sore, yet I couldn't remember why. Then, slowly and painfully, my eyes cleared and the memories rushed back.

I sat up abruptly, only to pitch sideways and curse when every one of my injuries screeched. *Shit.* My chest, and my right hip and thigh throbbed mercilessly, while a burning sensation coursed through the deep gashes in my shoulders.

When I tried to move again, I realized my wrists were bound behind me. My tigress freaked. I thrashed like a caged beast and dug my nails into the rope. But it was useless. I couldn't tear free.

"Celia. Celia, *stop*!"

My growls drowned most of Shayna's hoarse calls. I searched around anxiously but couldn't immediately spot her. That's when it hit me; the heightened senses my tigress gave me were gone, even though her presence had returned.

I was . . . *human*. And it scared the hell out of me.

I shook my head, disoriented. My weakened gaze slowly adjusted and focused on my sisters, slumped and bound across from me. God, they'd taken a beating. Cuts and bruises covered their bodies, but what distressed me most were their bullet wounds.

A tear streaked down Shayna's dirty face. "We're in the back of a semi, dude. Tell me you're okay."

I couldn't tell her what she wanted to hear. None of us were okay. Just alive. For the moment.

A million thoughts scrambled through my brain, but as I continued to stare at their injuries, something didn't make sense. I cleared my throat to speak, further irritating the harsh dryness. "Why haven't you healed?"

Emme's face crumbled. "I can't, Celia. Our powers are gone."

That horrible dread found its way back into my bones. "What's happened? The last thing I remember is the demons flying us out of the Den."

Emme bowed her head, sobs shaking her slight form. Shayna took a calming breath, then another, before finally speaking for her. "The demons carried us to an industrial park, Celia. You were still unconscious, but when they tried to bind your wrists, you woke up and started slaughtering them. You did a lot of damage, and at first I thought we were going to escape. . . ." She shuddered and grimaced into her shoulder.

I didn't understand her reaction until Emme focused her bloodshot eyes on me. "They shot you four times, Celia. I don't know how you're alive." Fresh tears streamed down her face and she curled into a tight ball.

My lack of memory told me two things. One, my tigress had regained consciousness before I had. And two, she'd woke fighting. Good. That's what we needed.

Emme choked on a sob. I inched toward her and so did Shayna. We lay against her, trying to keep her body warm with ours. Shayna blew out a shaky breath. "It's worse than we thought, Ceel. The Tribe recruited a band of dark witches. One of them possesses the ability to bespell the bullets to block our powers—or at least she did possess." Shayna tried to swallow except the effort seemed too cumbersome. "The Tribesmen bragged about giving her to their Tribemaster once she'd exhausted her use."

"Tribemaster?" I asked, despite knowing what she meant.

"The demon lord, Ceel. The real one." She shook her head. "I don't think the creatures we fought at Death Valley were it. I think we'd fought . . . his babies."

My body scorched with newfound pain as my pulse raced. If Shayna was right, we fared far worse than I could have imagined. The demons Danny had called forth tossed the *weres* around like pillows and almost killed us. No way did I want to meet Papa.

Emme sealed her lids tight. "What do you think they're going to do to us? They're hungry, I can see it. But they haven't . . ."

Tried to eat us? Emme had a point. Why wait? The Tribe had a plan for us. But what did we have that they could want? I didn't want to find out. I scanned our dirty metal cave. A single bulb dully lit the area around us. Otherwise, the compartment was dark and empty, and reeked of rust and garbage. I pushed up to a standing position. "Any idea where we are or how long we've been driving?"

"No," Shayna answered.

I spit some blood onto the filthy floor. "Well, screw this. Come on."

I shimmied against the sides. Shayna and Emme grunted, barely able to roll. Emme shook her head. "We can't, Celia. Maybe it's your metabolism burning through the magic of the bullets. But you're in better shape than we are."

My brain hammered against my skull, and blood continued to pool in my mouth. My sisters could barely crawl. Dear Lord, how was I going to get us out of here? "Just try, okay? I'm going to play with the door to see if I can get it open. If we're on an open highway, maybe someone will see us."

I reached the roll-up door and anchored my foot beneath a metal latch. The semi clashed in a percussion of steady bounces, sending me sprawling into my sisters. I twisted forward again, banging into the door when the truck came to an abrupt halt.

The air brakes had barely stopped screeching when the trailer door swung open, momentarily blinding me with bright sunlight. Before I could react, two demon children dragged me out of the semi with their clawed hands. I flinched away from their serpentine tongues licking my face and squinted wildly, trying to keep a position on my sisters.

Emme cowered and cried harder. Shayna kicked and flailed, making the Tribesmen holding her laugh. I decided not to fight. No, not yet. I needed to conserve my remaining energy. If Emme was right, I'd get my strength back somehow.

Misha, Misha, where are you?

Even as I *called* Misha, I thought of Aric, hoping he and the other wolves were tracking us. The thought of what might happen in the meantime, though, made me panic, so I willed myself to relax. My sisters needed me, and I needed a plan.

I took in my surroundings, trying to figure out where the hell we were. Before us stood an imposing building resembling a castle, its high walls and towers fashioned from tan and gray brick. At first, I thought we were someplace foreign, until a large sign in front of the building gave away our exact location.

The Old Idaho Penitentiary
Tours Sunday through Saturday, 12 p.m. to 5 p.m.

I focused hard on the sign and thought of Misha, hoping our *call* would somehow transfer the information.

I hadn't concentrated long before our demon captors hauled us through the gate and into a large courtyard where a slew of Tribesmen awaited us. The courtyard mimicked a well-manicured and surprisingly pretty park, unlike the lockdown unit we entered next.

Tribesmen crammed the unit. The former prison had become their lair. As we were dragged through, *weres* and vampires catcalled and whistled while demons greedily licked their fangs. They taunted in an obvious attempt to frighten us. It worked. I tried to edge away from their unnerving stares only to encounter disturbing visions that sent my heart fluttering into a frenzy.

Hundreds of cells, each housing one nightmare after the next, lined the three-story-high enclosure. Naked women in varying stages of pregnancy crammed several cells nearest to us. A few of these broken souls curled on the filthy floor, quiet and still, reeking of urine and feces. Others cackled in hysteria, clawing at their bodies or pounding their heads viciously against the cinder block walls. Worse yet were the parasites that crawled beneath the surface of their bellies. I shuddered, understanding then what had become of the women who'd disappeared. The slaughtered men had gotten off easy.

Emme and Shayna shut their eyes, but I couldn't do the same. I needed to know everything we faced. But then I saw her. The awkward young woman from the club the night we were attacked. The one ignored by the males who'd flirted with her friends. My God, I hadn't realized she'd been one of those missing. I searched her face for any signs of verve or hope. Only to have her dead eyes stare past me, an empty shell of what once held promise.

The demon wrenched me away before I could pledge to help her. But as the being stealing her life squirmed the length of her protruding stomach, I knew nothing could spare her now.

About halfway down the cement corridor, the Tribesmen stopped unexpectedly. Inside the adjacent cell lay a pregnant woman screaming and convulsing violently. It was hard to watch the suffering, mostly because there wasn't a damn thing I could do about it.

What happened next, though, proved more than I could bear. The woman's stomach erupted like a bloody volcano, splattering the paint-chipped bars and cracked floor with nauseating fluid. From her remains, a demon child's head emerged. His clawed hands carved open the rest of her body. His tongue eagerly lapped the blood caking his face. Once free, he jumped against the bars, making the vampire and werebear holding me shudder. They gagged as his revolting and putrid-smelling form writhed next to us. I vomited uncontrollably, unable to take the gore.

One of the larger demons opened the cage and grabbed the newborn by the throat. He tossed him in the adjacent cell, then flung the woman's lifeless body into the heap. That cell housed a flock of them, happily munching away on what remained of their mothers.

The next block contained about thirty vampires in the late phases of bloodlust, chained at their necks and waists to the rear walls. Judging by their size and degree of starvation, the bars alone wouldn't have held them. As we passed, it became apparent that even the chains weren't enough. One of the bloodlusters broke free and took hold of the werebear through the bars. The bloodluster tore into the bear's throat and drained him in a matter of seconds.

A horde of demon children serving as guards tried to contain her as the others hauled ass to our final destination. A vampire yanked open a large metal door, with a tiny window, leading to the prison's former death row. Death row. Awesome. Irony had a way of spitting in my face. I only wished I could punch back.

Only four cells and a short hallway composed death row. Our captors shoved us into one cell together, but they didn't shut the barred door right away. One of the werewolves lugged me to my feet by the front of my T-shirt. He sniffed my neck in a way that made my stomach roil.

"Leave her alone!" Shayna screamed.

"No! Please no!" Emme begged.

I was too scared to move.

"What are you doing, Bryan?" one of the vamps asked.

The wolf's breath was hot and nasty. "I want to taste Aric's whore."

Terror gripped me when he licked my neck, and I began to hyperventilate. But when he groped my breasts, my fear turned to rage. I swore once I'd never let anyone hurt me that way again, so I leaned back and slammed my head hard into his face.

Blood spurted from his nose like a jet stream. His fist drew back, but my dulled reflexes slowed my response. His blow launched me into the cinder block wall, where stars exploded in my vision and my body collapsed like sand.

A sick throbbing sound pulsated behind my left ear before a rush of fluid seeped out. I tried to stand when I saw him coming, only to immediately topple over. Shayna and Emme scrambled in front of me in a pathetic attempt to shield me. But I knew they were powerless to stop him.

Just when I thought he would kill us, the vampire twisted the *were*'s arm behind his back and pulled him away. "Tribemaster wants them alive," he told the *were*.

The *were* growled. *"That whore is mine! No one hits me and lives."*

The vampire rolled his eyes. "Relax, idiot, you're already healing. Besides, do you really want to be fed to the demons over this stupid bitch?"

The *were* stormed away, foaming at the mouth and swearing. The threat of death by hungry demons proved a suitable deterrent. The others followed, slamming the metal door behind them.

The bleakness of our situation hit Emme and Shayna all at once. They collapsed against each other and sobbed. The room swayed and turned repulsing colors, yet my sisters' despair compelled me to gather my senses.

I scooted toward them, although my body begged me not to move. "I have a plan."

"What?" Shayna stammered.

"We're going to cut these ropes. Shayna, you have to sharpen something—anything—no matter how small."

Shayna let out a shaky breath. "I don't know if I can. I'm so busted up."

"Emme suspended Taran in midair after being shot. You can do this. I know you can. Start looking for anything you might be able to transform." I turned to Emme, sounding more optimistic than I felt. "Can you use your *force* to manipulate the locking mechanism?"

"I'll try." She shook her head. "But, Celia, what good will that do? There are hundreds of Tribesmen and only three of us. We'll be slaughtered."

"There won't be just three of us, Emme." I swallowed more pooling liquid in my mouth. "You see, we're going to release the infected vampires."

CHAPTER 30

Shayna went to work following her initial shock. She tried a faucet from the old broken sink and the chains supporting the beds, but the alloys proved too thick and she remained too weak to transform them. Emme thought to use a piece of broken bedspring. I pried it loose and dropped it in her hands. After several efforts to draw her power, Shayna's gift triggered and released between her fingers. A glimmer of light spiraled along the metal, changing its shape into a tiny sword, slightly larger than the plastic kind used in cocktails and with a blade thick and deadly enough to slice through stone. *Yes, that will do.*

Shayna panted and paled, immediately slicing the ropes that bound my wrists. I freed her and Emme, and then Emme unlocked our cell. Their efforts wiped them out, but there was no time to waste. We hugged each other quickly and headed for the door leading out of death row.

I peered through the small window. Only four vampires stood guard by the door. The lockdown unit boomed loudly with manic cackles and famished hisses, loud enough to distract the vamps from noticing me. Uncertainty punctured through to my skull until I spotted the locking mechanism closest to where the infected vampires were housed.

Emme stood at my urging and nodded when I pointed to her target. I held my breath and watched, praying she had enough strength left. Her face reddened from her grueling effort, but the latch did move, inch by agonizing inch. Finally she gave one last mental heave and about thirty cells popped open.

For a moment, everything went quiet. But then the bloodlusters recognized their golden opportunity. And took full advantage.

They broke through their chains and out of their cells, turning the unit into an all-you-can-eat buffet. Mayhem erupted. I grabbed my sisters and hauled them along. It was hard. I limped badly, but still fared better than Emme. She barely managed to stay on her feet. We crept along the walls until we snuck behind a huge werebison pummeling his way toward the exit.

Misha, if you're coming, now would be a good time to show up.

No one noticed our escape at first. I'd just caught the first whiff of fresh air when a werecat clinging to the rafters yelled and pointed our way. By chance, the only attention he received was from a charging bloodluster. He tackled the werecat and brought him down to the cracked concrete, cutting off the cat's gurgled screech in one voracious bite.

We hit the yard and I immediately dragged my sisters behind a row of bushes. The expanse was too open to cross without being seen, so we adhered to the shadows and shrubbery along the building until we reached the rear of the prison. I peeked around the bushes. No one seemed to be around, but my senses remained too dulled for me to be certain.

I tried *shifting* into the ground, hoping to transport us

beneath the wall and away from this nightmare. Except my body remained stubbornly aboveground, and my head pounded from the effort. I gathered my prowess and turned to my sisters. "Okay, you're going over the wall. Stand on my hands and I'll throw you to the top." I knelt by Emme and cupped my hands to show her. "Try to roll as you land. It'll help absorb the impact and prevent you from getting hurt."

Emme glanced toward the high wall. "What about you? How will you get over?"

Emme's eyes widened the longer it took me to answer. Shayna grabbed my arm. "You aren't coming with us, are you?"

"I can't, Shayna."

Her breaths released in short, horrified bursts. "Is it because of Aric?"

"No. It's because I want you to live." I swallowed hard. "It won't take the Tribe long to discover we're gone. If I can distract them from finding you, I will."

Emme flung her arms around my neck. "Celia, we can't leave you."

"You have to." I ripped Emme off and held her away. "Just go. Misha will find me in time." I dragged them to the wall before they could argue.

Tears slicked Shayna's face. "What if Misha doesn't show?"

I stilled, knowing Misha might not arrive in time. "Then don't let me die in vain."

Shayna allowed me to toss her, though she continued to openly weep. In my weakened state, I barely managed to get her to the ledge. She hung on with her good arm and used her legs to climb the rest of the way. Her thighs straddled the wall as she waited for Emme.

I sent Emme soaring, only to have a demon child catch her midair while another swooped down and captured Shayna. We had come so close!

"Going somewhere?" a grotesque voice gurgled behind me.

I spun around. A clawed hoof caught me in the chest and shoved me to the ground. To my right, demon children restrained Emme and Shayna. They cried when the creatures hissed menacingly and snapped at them with their fangs.

The demon that held me dug his dagger-sharp nails deeper to gain my attention. I let out a pained grunt. "I am Matar, the Tribemaster," he said. "Father of your unborn children."

Chills pelted my body like sleet. Matar's voice triggered a memory I'd long since suppressed. I'd been wrong. The demon Aric fought in Death Valley had not been the one to possess Misha. That one, and the one I'd killed, had lacked the speech capacity and the shrewd gleam dominating the demon lord that held me. The Death Valley demons had been more hungry carnivores, in search of food. Matar . . . his red eyes blinked back at me with the keen intelligence of a true predator.

Jesus.

Matar towered eight feet above me. Hideous yellow fangs glowed against his silver-scaled body and wings, wrinkling in the grooves of his face and giving him a scarred appearance. And to complete the scary-monster-from-hell look, he flaunted a snakelike tail that whipped around to caress my cheek. "I've been watching you since first learning of your exoneration from vampire court." Matar motioned to the side, where the damned wereweasel who'd photographed Aric and me snickered. If I wasn't pinned down and terrified, I would have killed the shifty bastard.

My head angled back to face off with my captor. Aric feared his presence would place me in danger. Here, I'd managed to do that on my own. Yet I failed to feel regret just then. What I did feel was resentment, and hate.

Matar and his band of goddamn misfits had tortured, kidnapped, killed, and raped, spilling enough blood and horror to overflow a river. My jaw clenched. "What the hell do you want with me?"

"I told you. I want to breed with you, Celia. And your sisters." Matar's voice reverberated with desire. His clawed fingers tugged the waistband of my jeans. "The problem was stealing you from those who guard you. I tired of waiting and ordered my tribe to take you yesterday. No matter the price." Matar's face twisted into a gruesome smile. "I'm only disappointed they failed to obtain your other sister. She sounds delicious."

Matar's sentence structure was casual, very unlike the sinister tone of his voice, which rumbled as if he gargled with broken glass. God, he literally looked and sounded like hell.

I tried to squirm, but couldn't budge under the weight of his foot. "Why us?" I choked.

The claw on Matar's big toe poked my already injured shoulder. I gasped, biting back a scream. He frowned, displeased by my lack of suffering. "Like all my brothers, I am the product of a demon father and a witch mother. Our mothers' magical strength makes us indestructible and allows us to spend unlimited time on earth."

Matar's head tilted to the side as his toe dug deeper into my flesh. This time I couldn't squash my shriek. Matar smiled, satisfied. "Powerful magic wielders are scarce, Celia. We've fertilized mostly humans, giving us spawn, but none that matched our power. Then you and your sisters came to my attention." His body shuddered with obvious arousal. "With your magic, and my spores, the unimaginable will rise from your wombs."

"Oh my God," Emme whimpered behind me.

I knew how she felt. Every hair on my body stood at attention and begged for a quick death. "Why destroy the *weres* and the vamps?" I asked in hope of distracting him from our apparently enticing wombs. It didn't work. The scent of his increasing arousal reached my human nose and clenched my bowels.

"We can't conquer the world without killing those who guard it. And the vampires will never bow down to us." He let out a ghostly eerie cackle, flapping his wings with apparent delight. "Ironic, isn't it? Their own outcasts will aid us in their destruction."

"Excuse me for interrupting, Tribemaster." A trembling vampire knelt beside Matar, his head bowed low enough to touch the ground. I recognized him as one of the vampires guarding the entrance to death row.

Matar licked his fangs, refusing to turn from me. "What is it?"

"The escape of these women cost us."

Matar growled. "How many Tribesmen did we lose?"

Rivers of sweat drenched his flimsy white shirt. "Including half the bloodlust population we were forced to kill? Ah, over two hundred, sire."

"I see." With a flick of his tail, Matar decapitated the vampire. Blood and ash spewed across Matar's back, but he didn't appear to mind. He slid his giant tail across the grass, wiping off the excess goo. "Celia, in the past two days, you and your allies have destroyed more than a third of my Tribesmen. While your cunning demonstrates potential for our offspring, you *will* be punished." Matar motioned another vampire forward. "Take them back to their cell."

Matar licked my face with a tongue that slithered out of his tail. At least, that's what I hoped it was. You know things are bad when you're praying a demon tongue is the only thing touching you.

The vamps dragged us back to death row. This time, they didn't abandon us to our cell. Nor did they bind our limbs. After all, there was no place to run, and our weakened and terrified states rendered us powerless. My only sparkle of hope remained in Matar's words. "Powerful magic wielders are scarce," he'd said. That meant there couldn't be many of him in existence. In time, maybe the Alliance would destroy them all.

Emme and Shayna cried. We slumped on the floor, speaking only to pray and comfort one another. Night draped the horizon. That's when Matar appeared. My heartbeat raced into my throat at the sight of him. God, I was so scared, but I rose to stand in front of my sisters.

Matar loomed over me. "I've decided how to punish you."

I dodged his tail when it reached for my face, believing he meant to strike. He laughed at my trembling form. "Physical torture alone won't satisfy my vengeance, my pet." He shook his head almost regrettably. "You're just too strong. Your heart, however, is easily crippled."

His gaze leered behind me and still I flinched from its pure viciousness. "It's time to destroy your spirit, Celia. Your sister Shayna will make a delightful meal for my hungry children. Tribesmen, take her."

Tribesmen piled on me and Emme, hog-tying our wrists and ankles. Two more dove for Shayna. I thrashed and roared, lashing out brutally and throwing most of them off me. *"No! Don't touch her! Get off her, get off her!"*

No one noticed Shayna drop her miniscule sword beside me as they dragged her away. I snatched it quickly, concealing it between my hands before a *were* yanked me back by my hair. Shayna's horrified screeching echoed the length of the hallway. Emme's sobs teetered on the verge of hysteria. I breathed heavily, inundated by a strange sense of calm cooling my bruised skin.

Matar watched me, expecting me to cry, I supposed. But I wouldn't. *"I'm going to kill you,"* I promised through gritted teeth. "I swear to God, I will *annihilate* you!"

Matar smiled. "Your spirit requires more of a beating." He sniffed the air around us, only to shoot me an embittered look. "My spores are precious, Celia. If I scented the ripeness of your womb, I'd take you now." He looked to the werewolf next to him. "But Bryan has plenty to spare."

Emme choked on her screams. "Take your time with her," Matar told Bryan on his way out. "If she fails to satisfy you, you may have the other one next. Come, my Tribesmen, there is much to be done."

Bryan tore off my shirt before the door leading out slammed shut. Emme jerked and struggled to get to me while I methodically adjusted the tiny weapon between my fingers.

Bryan sneered with anticipation but never got the chance to grope me. I rammed the tiny sword into his eye and twisted. He collapsed to the floor, unconscious and barely breathing.

Emme stilled with apparent shock as I cut through her restraints. But when I slipped Shayna's weapon into her hands, she didn't hesitate to free me.

"Emme, listen to me. I'm going to cut the bullet out of your leg so you can heal. Go ahead and scream. The others will just assume Bryan is hurting us." I placed her on her side for better access to the wound. "When I'm done, you have to do the same for me. We need our powers back. It's the only way."

Emme nodded and closed her eyes. I worked fast, the stress of the situation making me brutal. I ignored her agonized cries, and within just a few minutes, dug the bullet out.

Emme's pale yellow light stuttered, surrounding her in barrages rather than encasing her smoothly. The feel also lacked its usual intensity, and her healing seemed unusually slow. She failed to notice, or least chose not to, and began to cut into my skin with our makeshift scalpel. The urgency made her physical motions quick. She removed the first two bullets with a surgeon's ease, allowing the start of my strength and senses to return. The last two were harder, and took more time than we had. One lodged deep in my thigh; the other, in my hip. She tried to distract me by talking, but I didn't like what she had to say. "Celia, promise me if we're caught again, you'll kill me."

"What?" I gritted as she twisted the blade deeper.

"Promise you'll kill me. I don't want those creatures to touch me. I don't want to bear one of those *things*. You have to kill me, *promise*."

"But then who'll kill me?" I asked, not wanting to answer her.

Emme locked eyes with mine, revealing a fierceness I'd never seen. "You're going to live, Celia. You're going to make it. There is no doubt in my mind."

With that, she pried the last bullet out.

My unholy scream caused the Tribesmen outside to break out with laughter. Jesus, no way could we have pulled this off earlier.

Bryan stirred beside us, snarling and reaching for his injured eye. I tackled him hard and ripped his head off with ease. And absolutely no regret. It rolled into the corner, colliding against the dusty cinder block.

Bryan's death at my hands empowered me. My tigress returned full force, thirsting for blood and desperate for vengeance. I hauled Emme to her feet. "Let's get out of here."

We rushed to the small window and peered out. A giggle escaped my lips. I clasped my mouth to suppress another, and another one after that. It seemed strange to laugh, but I instinctively knew why.

I beamed at Emme. She gaped at me like I'd finally snapped. Her hands reached to touch my face. "I need to heal you," she whispered.

I grasped her wrists, my grin widening. "There's no time, Emme. Misha's here."

CHAPTER 31

Massive explosions shook the prison. The lights flickered. A deep crack emerged in the wall next to us, quickly branching upward toward the ceiling. I threw myself on Emme, knocking her to the floor and shielding her with my body as chunks of concrete rained down. Echoes of pained howls and vicious roars pounded against the door. Emme remained beneath me, covering her head. A primal scream from what sounded like a woman made me lurch off her and scramble to the window.

Danny teetered on the third-floor landing, screeching in soprano and wielding a massive machine gun. He fired. The kickback knocked him on his ass. Two levels below him, Alliance members in their animal forms tore into Tribesmen visibly caught by surprise.

Blood splashed the small window, hindering my view, but enticing my beast to take action. I kicked open the door, protruding my claws and severing the throats of the closest Tribesmen.

Emme raced behind me, using her *force* to launch several Tribe *weres* into the cinder block walls, crushing their skulls and killing them instantly. She was a different

Emme now, one hell-bent on surviving and vested by fear.

Blue and white lightning bolts slashed through the thick dusty air. I nudged Emme and pointed to the three-story ceiling. Taran levitated in a trance, a cast encasing her arm. Yet it didn't hinder her. Her eyes blanched to white as she unleashed her fury on the demon children flying overhead. We were showered with their nasty remains. I brushed them off, my focus remaining on finding Shayna.

"Come on, Emme." I started to run, but Emme didn't follow. She froze, staring blankly ahead. Something held her attention. At first, I didn't care enough to see what it was. I grabbed her arm and shook her. "Emme, we have to move now!"

I yanked her along only to stop short when I spotted Aric down the long corridor. His huge gray wolf form advanced deliberately toward me, viciously mutilating everything in his path. Tribesmen attempted to scramble away, only to be ripped into bloody chunks by the wolves directly behind him.

Aric bolted the last few feet and *changed*. His expression darkened as his gaze swept over my beaten form. Never had he been so fierce.

My initial reaction was to comfort Aric, to assure him I was all right. But my relief at seeing him brought the horrors I'd endured to the forefront of my mind, forcing my words back down and rendering me speechless.

"I thought I'd lost you," he whispered with barely controlled rage.

I collapsed against Aric's chest. Except I couldn't find the peace I sought in his strong embrace. Emme's loud sobs drew my attention. No matter how much I needed him to comfort me, my sisters needed me more.

Liam held her a few feet away. Taran had descended to the floor. She stroked Emme's hair, crying hard enough to make her shoulders tremble. Danny and our other wolves, now in human form, gathered around and formed a defensive ring as the bloodshed moved to the rear of the prison.

Taran screamed when she saw me. My battered appearance must have been shocking; even the males jumped back in alarm. Koda gawked at me before kicking the door to death row off its hinges and racing in. He scrambled out seconds later, thunderstruck with dread. *"Where's Shayna?"*

"We don't know." I took a shaky breath. "Matar, the demon lord, took her to feed to his children."

The color drained from Koda's face. Aric squeezed me tighter. "Koda, Gemini, Liam, I'm releasing you from your duties. Find Shayna. *Find her now!*"

The Warriors *changed* and took off, Koda leading the way.

Aric kissed my forehead and stepped away. "Stay with the others," he said in a low voice. "I'll come back to you when I'm done."

He stalked toward the large opening in the wall. I didn't want him to leave. "Aric, where are you going?"

Every muscle and bone on Aric's broad back stiffened. His voice deepened to a growl. "To kill Matar." He *changed*, not bothering to glance back, and disappeared into the darkness.

I peeled the remains of my shirt away from my sports bra and faced the others. "We have to find Shayna. You four finish searching here." No one moved. "Go! I'll check the other buildings."

Bren pointed his finger in my face. "You've had the unholy shit beaten out of you. No way am I leaving you alone!"

"They need your nose to pick up Shayna's scent. If we split up, the search will go faster." Bren didn't budge. "Damn it, Bren, there's no time to waste!"

Bren reluctantly *changed* back to wolf, roaring as I sped off without them. I barreled through the exit, leaping over the remains of the dead.

Outside, Alliance members and Tribesmen continued to battle. Dark clouds churned overhead and thunder shook the ground as witches cast their deadly curses. Flesh and ash saturated the earth where *weres* and vampires fought the enemy with fangs, claws, and all the viciousness of preternatural beings. I shoved my way through the maze of bodies, killing when I needed to, but mostly trying to move forward. It wasn't until I came upon an opening that I stopped.

The Elders' power and that of Misha's master, Uri, hit me like a rush of wind, forcing me to stagger back. They, along with Aric and Misha, attacked Matar and the bloodlust vampires protecting him. Yet I feared their combined magic wouldn't be enough.

Matar stood another three feet taller, his muscles resembling small boulders. His tail whipped viciously, filleting half of Uri's face while crushing Anara's back into powder. Uri was a Grandmaster, Anara a pack Elder; Matar shouldn't have crippled them with such ease.

Martin and Makawee fought two infected vampires. To my astonishment, Aric and Misha worked together to take down the third. Misha's head snapped toward me. He must have caught my scent. His eyes widened when he saw my condition, but then he flashed me one of his wicked smiles. He nodded toward the vamp and grinned, pulling an arm while Aric clamped onto the other. No further explanation needed. I *changed* and sprinted toward them, slicing through the bloodluster's neck with my fangs.

Aric leapt into the fray the moment the vamp fell limp. Misha forced his hand through the decapitated vamp's chest and ripped out his heart. "I knew you would survive, kitten."

That made one of us.

Bits of cinder block exploded like shrapnel as Matar embedded Uri and Anara into the retaining wall. His daggerlike claws pierced through Martin's and Makawee's larynxes, and out the base of their skulls. Aric's chest rumbled in challenge, attacking his serpent tail and distracting Matar from completing his decapitation of the Elders.

I charged Matar, knowing they needed help. Misha sped close behind me. We hit him at once, me slamming him with the full impact of my body and Misha jumping on his shoulders, trying to sever his head. Matar didn't budge, despite our powerful strikes. I attempted to *shift* him into the earth. It was like trying to force a brick through steel. He was too big and I remained too weak. So I clawed and bit through his thick hide, desperate to bring him down.

Revulsion swept through my body. Matar *tasted* evil. I ignored my instincts to stop biting him, thinking of Shayna and every bit of suffering this bastard had caused.

Matar flung the listless bodies of the Elders and turned his freed claws on us. One went into Misha's chest and the other rammed into my left side. We let out unearthly roars of agony as he suspended us in the air. When his claws penetrated deeper, the torture became unbearable. I lost my focus and *changed* back. I thought I was going to die, only to have Matar howl in pain and drop us.

Aric held Matar's severed tail between his deadly fangs. It jerked violently like a separate entity despite the necrosis setting in. Matar bellowed with fury and kicked Aric in the chest, breaking his ribs in a heart-clenching crunch and launching him into the prison's outer wall. Aric yelped upon impact, then collapsed, unmoving.

I struggled to stand, barely able to move. Misha

lunged to his feet and hurtled his body against Matar. To my horror Matar grabbed Misha's arms and ripped them off his body. Misha dropped to the ground, bleeding and screaming.

Aric woke with a start and catapulted into Matar's chest, knocking him over. His potent jaws crushed Matar's sternum, breaking through the bone and opening the cavity. Aric was going to kill him. There was no doubt in my mind, until Matar nailed Aric across the muzzle, snapping it in half.

Matar stabbed his claws through Aric's underbelly. Aric thrashed violently, trying to break Matar's grip. Matar's body jerked from Aric's rough motions, and his hard breaths filled the night. He stumbled to a kneeling position, lifting Aric's huge wolf form over his head.

A long silver spike jetted out from Matar's knee. My eyes widened, knowing he meant it for Aric's heart. Matar smiled at my terror. "Aric, be sure to tell Shayna that Celia says hello."

I *shifted* underground faster than ever before, *resurfacing* in a high leap behind Matar. With all I had left, I punched through the back of his skull and grabbed his brain. Out it came, along with most of his spinal column.

My feet hit the ground in sync with Matar's lifeless form. "Get up from that, *asshole!*"

The thunder stopped and the clouds dissipated, revealing a clear night sky full of shimmering stars. All was quiet except for the sound of labored breathing from those struggling to rise to their feet. I rushed to Aric, panting on the ground. He met my gaze and *changed*, holding me against him while the broken bones of his face realigned and healed.

Weres, vampires, and witches from the Alliance encircled us. So did the Elders, resuming their human forms. To my relief, Misha also rose to his feet. His arms remained scattered somewhere in the yard, but he had stopped bleeding, thanks in part to the charitable tongues of the Catholic schoolgirls.

Aric released me as Uri and Anara extracted their bloodied and battered figures from the wall and limped toward us. Uri smiled at me pleasantly, an impressive feat considering part of his face was still at large. "Well done, Celia," he said, with a slight nod.

Makawee and Martin also approached, smiling. Martin's deep baritone rang out. "You were right, Aric. Celia is a formidable warrior."

"Yes," interrupted Anara. "A pity she's not one of us."

My head dropped. After all this madness, I still didn't rank on the "Worthy Females" list. I bent and lifted Matar's leftovers. And threw them in Anara's face. "Fuck you, if you don't think I'm good enough!"

I ignored the gasps from the crowd, and the approving nods from the vampires. All I cared about was finding Shayna. I *changed* and bolted, not knowing where to begin, yet knowing I couldn't stop until I found her.

Aric caught up to me in wolf form, ignoring Anara's commands to return. We'd rounded the first building when Taran screamed my name. Harrowing fear spread through my soul. We sprinted toward her voice. It led us to an old gymnasium where remnants of the last of the demons scattered in the evening wind. There, in the basement, we located Taran and the others kneeling with their backs to us.

I *changed* back to human and approached, trembling. They'd found Shayna. Aric placed his arm around me, but it did little to soothe me. I muffled back a scream when I saw what remained of my beautiful sister.

Chunks of Shayna's body were missing where the demons had feasted. Yet I could still see her struggling to breathe.

Emme convulsed, desperately trying to heal Shayna. Taran cried uncontrollably into her hands. "Emme, please help her," she begged between hysterical sobs. "Please, Emme!"

Koda wept and rocked Shayna's limp body against him. "Baby, don't leave me. I'm nothing without you," he whispered.

Shayna's glazed eyes stared blindly at Koda. She attempted to speak, but words failed her. I wanted to cover my ears from their cries and shield my eyes from the torture. But I didn't, I watched and heard it all.

God, no. Please no.

Emme's nose bled and her arms quivered. Her normally effervescent aura sizzled in and out. She screamed, whether in frustration or to boost her power, momentarily blinding us with her glow.

Emme's light receded, turning her skin a sickly gray. It was no use; Shayna's body was too broken. Her wounds sealed briefly, only to tear back open with a nauseating clatter. At last the strain became too much. Emme released Shayna, collapsing against Bren.

"No! No! No!" Taran screamed.

Koda unleashed a mournful howl, calling forth the powerful rays of pack magic. It saturated the basement, compelling the fangs of his beast to appear. He pulled Shayna closer, plunging his sharp canines deep into her heart. *Oh my God.*

In his desperation to spare Shayna's life, Koda attempted to *turn* her *were*, risking his life in the process. Except how could I blame him? He and Shayna were true mates. Neither would survive without the other.

Aric lunged at him. *"Koda, no!"*

Koda swept up Shayna and barreled out the door with my sister draped lifelessly across his arms. The remaining wolves intercepted Aric as he gave chase. "Let him go, Aric," Gemini said quietly. "There's nothing you can do for them. The process has already begun."

Aric roared. "But we'll lose them *both*!"

Emme's and Taran's hysterical cries filled the room. The wolves and Danny bowed their heads, tears splitting their faces in streaks. I didn't cry. I just sat there. Everyone seemed to be moving farther from me. I thought I felt someone shake me, but I wasn't sure.

Bren's deep voice resonated from somewhere far away. "Celia. *Celia!*"

Danny's words sounded rushed. "She's going into shock. We need to keep her warm."

I don't recall much. Things sort of went blank. It seemed to take forever to pull out of my haze. At first I was only aware of a soft yellow light. Then sounds of terrible cries filled my ears. It took a moment to realize they came from me.

"Stop her before she takes the plane down!" Uri yelled.

Strong arms grabbed my upper body and legs.

Taran pleaded with me over Emme's frantic weeping. "It's okay, Celia. It's okay. You're safe now. Emme was just trying to heal you. Please calm down, honey,"

"Misha, put her to sleep," Danny whispered. "You'll be able to in the state she's in."

Aric's deep warning growl filled my ears as I sensed Misha's approach. "Silence, wolf," Misha snapped. "You know I will not harm her."

"Aric, quit playing jealous boyfriend and let him help her," Bren urged at my feet.

Misha's scent filled my lungs and spread through my body. My muscles relaxed and the pounding in my ears faded. A yawn escaped my lips just before I succumbed to a deep sleep.

I awoke, surrounded by my soft, warm sheets. I was finally home, in my room, in my bed. Aric lay beside me, watching me with sad, tired eyes. "Are you all right?" he asked gently.

My eyes stung before I could speak. "No," I whispered.

I cried for all we'd endured and for everything yet to come. And I cried for the arms that held me close, that would soon leave me forever.

But Aric didn't leave me. At least, not right away. He stayed with me all night. He stroked my hair, kissed my face, and whispered words of comfort.

CHAPTER 32

I heard only half of the clergyman's words. They almost didn't matter. Time continued to pass slowly as I stared at Shayna. She reminded me of a statue, serene and beautiful. Around us, people wiped their eyes and sniffled, while I continued to stare at my sister's lovely face.

The clergyman finished his prayer with an "amen" and smiled before motioning to the bride and groom. "And now the vows."

Shayna passed Emme her flowers so she could clutch her mate's hands. Koda spoke first. And I knew his words would be the ones to release my tears.

"Shayna, I wasn't complete until I met you," he began, the depths of his emotions running rivers down his cheeks. "You were the only one who ever saw past the anger and hurt and chose to love me. You'll always be my best friend and soul mate. I promise to love you forever."

Shayna grinned, crying as she spoke. "Koda, you're my heart, my soul, my pure joy. Thank you for being my strength when I had none. Thank you for being my spirit when mine failed me. Thank you for loving me with all of your being. I promise to love you forever."

White petals from the wedding arch they stood beneath fell like large snowflakes as the late-October breeze swept across the lake. Tahoe, it seemed, approved of my sister's union. It didn't matter that she and Koda hadn't known each other long. Their love had already proved its strength by surviving the *turning* process.

Aric and his Warriors had discovered Shayna and Koda days after they'd disappeared. The wolves had expected to find their corpses—not a happy couple ready to sprint to the nearest altar. We didn't yet know if Shayna had been transformed into a werewolf. We only cared that the attempt had healed her completely.

Aric watched me during their vows. I adjusted the wrap of my midnight blue bridesmaid's dress, both to shield me from the chill and to give me an excuse not to look at him. It just hurt too damn much. He stood as a groomsman beside Gemini, Bren, Danny, and Liam, the best man. My eyes wandered back to Koda and Shayna, just in time for their kiss. The small group of guests stood and applauded. After the kiss to end all kisses, Shayna skipped down the aisle, easily keeping up with her mate's long strides. They were followed by Liam and Emme, then Aric, Taran, and Gemini.

Aric glanced at the newlyweds before meeting my eyes as he'd done so many times. He couldn't hear my thoughts. But he knew my heart. Knew I loved him. Knew I always would. And it still didn't matter. The demon lord's destruction hadn't dissolved the strain between us. It had only solidified Aric's place in the resurrection of his kind.

My tears dripped faster as Aric followed the happy couple inside the château, where the reception was about to begin. I didn't want to know a life without him. I didn't want to wake without those powerful arms swathing me in protection. And I didn't want a day to pass without meeting his grin with mine. But I would. Because I had no choice, and neither did he.

Danny squeezed my hand and kissed my cheek. He was gentle and sweet, unlike Bren, who grabbed me in a choke hold and dragged me down the aisle. "Come on, Ceel. Time to have fun!"

"If Helen of Troy's face launched a thousand ships, Koda's mug sank them."

My muffled laughter joined the rest around the hall. Liam continued his toast unaffected, despite Koda's narrowing eyes. "Koda was the baddest wolf around, well— next to me, of course." Liam hiked up his pants before pointing around the room. "And Aric, and Gemini, and Heidi . . ." He rubbed his chin thoughtfully. "Oh! and maybe that little girl in the pink dress in the back."

Even Koda chuckled at that comment.

Liam's eyes darted over to Shayna, his voice growing soft. "Then he meets this little thing who forever changed his world. Shayna, you smiled and skipped your way into his heart. And that is where you will remain for eternity. Thank you for coming into his life. . . ." He sighed and covered his eyes. "But most of all, thank you for finally getting him housebroken."

Shayna's kiss to her groom was probably the only thing that saved Liam's ass. The couple had abandoned their seats at the head table to hang with us. We laughed a lot. It was just like the great moments we'd had at our house . . . once upon a time when Aric and I were still together.

I'd sat on Bren's lap after Shayna and Koda chose my seat to make out on. They hadn't been able to keep their hands off each other. I supposed their near-death experience had brought them ever closer.

"You do realize the honeymoon hasn't officially started?" Liam joked.

Koda growled at him, but then ignored him to continue kissing Shayna. From the bar, Heidi waved enthusiastically, happy to have been invited to the wedding. But how could we not have? After all, she'd saved Taran's life.

"I'd like to butter her bun," Bren muttered as he took a bite out of his roll.

"I think she can hear you," Danny warned.

Bren rolled his eyes. "That's the point, man." He finished his meal, then hauled me onto the floor to slow-dance. We'd barely taken two steps when Aric asked to cut in. Bren shoved me into Aric's arms when I hesitated. He also slapped my butt for good measure. I growled at him. He'd pay for that.

When Aric first held me, it felt awkward. It was like being thirteen at the seventh grade dance again. But as the familiar warmth encompassed us, I relaxed into his arms. I kept thinking we'd just dance until a fast song played. But then another slow song came on, followed by a few more. I used it as an excuse to hold Aric one last time. I guessed his thoughts mimicked mine, because he pulled me closer and caressed my back. Peace and security filled my soul once more, until one of the servers approached. "Excuse me, sir. There's a woman outside who wants to see you. She claims to be your fiancée."

I braced myself against Aric's chest, waiting for him to release me for the last time. He continued to hold me as if the server hadn't interrupted our dance, speaking in a soft murmur that carried the weight of our regret. "I never apologized to you about Barbara."

I cringed from the sudden stab in my heart. "Aric, please don't say her name. Knowing you're with her every night is killing me."

"Celia, I swear I haven't touched her." He closed his eyes and sighed deeply, placing his forehead gently against mine. "How can I make you understand?" he whispered. "I'm with her only because I have to be. I don't get a choice. If I did, I'd choose you." His lips brushed over mine. "You're the one I want to marry.

You're the one I want to bear my children. You're the one I want to grow old with. I love you, sweetness. I always have. I just can't actually *have* you."

And at those words my tigress wept. Aric's tears fell on my cheeks, mixing with mine. I didn't think the pain could get any worse, but then he kissed me.

What started out slow and tender quickly turned passionate and desperate.

"Aric!" Barbara yelled from the front of the hall.

I tried to pull away, but his grip tightened, and our kiss intensified.

"Excuse me. This is a private party, and you are not invited," Emme scolded.

"Get out of my way, little girl," Barbara warned.

High heels stormed across the dance floor. I knew they were Taran's even before she wigged out. "Wag more, bark less, *bitch*!"

Gemini spoke calmly. "Barbara, Aric is busy at the moment. I'm sure he'll be with you soon enough."

"I can see he's busy, Gemini!"

I tried to pull away, not wanting a fight to break out at my sister's wedding. Aric realized we couldn't be together. And I did, too. This was our moment of weakness, one I clung to as long as I could. But now it was time to let go.

I broke away from his grasp and stepped back, though my arms ached with the need to hold him. "Things have changed, Aric. Not just for you, but for me as well." I shuddered, dreading what I had to say. "I've made a decision. One I hope you'll respect, and one I hope you'll someday forgive me for."

His ardor fused me in place while he struggled to control his ragged breaths. "What did you do?"

I stepped forward to touch his face. "I can't explain it all now. Just know that I love you, no matter what happens."

I kissed his lips quickly and *shifted* before he could

stop me. I surfaced in the coat closet, although not alone. Heidi was there, naked. And so was Danny.

I slapped my hands over my eyes. Damn. She wasn't even a librarian.

"Oh. Hi, Celia," Heidi mumbled.

"Um, it's not what you think," Danny stammered.

"Oh, I think it is." I bolted, not bothering to wait for Heidi to rise from her knees. The hostess grabbed me when she caught me sprinting red-faced from the closet.

"Eh, um. It is time for the bride and groom's departure."

I waved in acknowledgment and rushed outside, with Danny and Heidi tugging on their clothes behind me.

The guests had gathered on the front lawn. Shayna smiled upon seeing me and jumped into my arms. Her voice shook when she told me she loved me. As the oldest, I knew I should have told her something meaningful, but I couldn't gather a single thought. Instead I simply told her I loved her, too.

Koda bent to kiss my cheek when I released her. I ambled back into Emme's and Taran's awaiting arms. Together we watched the ivory limo disappear past the swan-shaped bushes and into the late October sunset.

I kept my gaze ahead, trying my best to avoid eye contact with Aric, despite feeling the strong presence of his aura behind me. The moment had arrived. And though I'd asked Aric to forgive me, I knew he never would. Nor did I know whether I could forgive myself.

A black Hummer limo pulled in along the circled drive. Misha stepped out, strands of his long mane falling over sensual gray eyes. He leaned his newly regenerated arms on the doorframe. "Are you ready, kitten?"

I nodded and gave my teary sisters one last hug. There was scuffling behind me as the wolves struggled to hold back Aric. He called to me, but I couldn't turn back. So instead I hurried into the limo to begin my new life with Misha.

Read on for a look at the next novel
in the Weird Girls series by Cecy Robson,

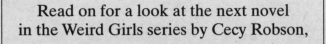

Cursed by Destiny

Available from Signet Eclipse in print
and e-book in January 2014

Tahoe City, California

"Are you ready, Celia?"

Misha's voice was nothing more than a seductive whisper. It made me breathless. "Yes."

His gray eyes wandered down my body. "Are you sure you can handle it?"

"Yes."

"*All* of it?"

I shot him an exasperated look. "We're no longer talking about the scrimmage, are we?"

He let out a deep sigh. "No, but perhaps we should continue."

Misha gave the order in the form of a subtle nod. Ten of his vampires attacked me, the thirst of the hunt shadowing their overly eager faces. It was hard not to rely on my claws. The vamps fought dirty, and they didn't hold back, but, hell, neither did I. My body was sliding lithely across the hardwood floor of the dojang when two vamps tried to tackle me. They slammed into each other—hard, like two boulders colliding.

The moment I kipped up to my feet, three more advanced. I punched, kicked, and maneuvered my way around them. It was grueling, and my animal instincts propelled me into overdrive. Yet my innate need to survive and the long months of extensive martial arts training paid off. The two overly obnoxious and excessively tanned vampires dropped with a skull-pounding crunch against the hard floor while I continued to hold my own against the rest. It wasn't easy. Liz, Maria, Edith Anne, and Agnes Concepción were especially vicious. For she-vamps who bounced around in Catholic schoolgirl uniforms all day, they sure were a mean bunch.

Maria threw back her dark hair, her Brazilian accent thick and dripping with spite. "Did you get an invitation to Aric and Barbara's wedding, little tigress?"

That was low, even for Maria. "That's none of your business." She hadn't even hit me yet, but I knocked her out with an uppercut to the chin just for being a bitch.

Liz jumped over Maria's body, pouting her perfectly plump bottom lip as she advanced with all the grace of a starving cheetah. "What's the matter, Celia? Are you mad that you're not good enough to marry that were-wolf?"

My hackles rose. Liz had hit a raw nerve. "Mention Aric one more time and you'll be gumming your next meal."

Liz smiled, peering down her nose at me. "*Aric*. There, now what—"

Liz's fangs landed somewhere near Misha's feet. He rolled his eyes. A vamp silently appeared and swept the pointy canines into a pan.

Edith Anne crouched into an attack stance. "Damn. You're an angry little shit."

I growled at Edith, blocked her strike, and wrenched her arm behind her back. She hissed and snapped her fangs at me. I silenced her with an elbow to her temple. The sickening snap almost made me feel bad. Almost.

Maria stirred as she regained consciousness. I was still ticked at her for mentioning Aric's wedding, so I knocked her out again with a kick to her face. My sudden bitterness overwhelmed me and made me lash out at two male vamps who'd struggled to their feet.

My foot nailed the first vamp in the jaw, but his pal struck me across the face before I was able to plant both feet. I whirled in the air three times before crashing onto my back. *Crap.* He leapt into the air with his fist held back. I rolled away—*fast.* He grunted upon impact, lodging his hand through the floor. My heel found the back of his neck before he could jerk his arm free. The pop of his vertebrae and limp form told me he wouldn't be getting up anytime soon.

I panted and spun around, swearing under my breath. The vamp could have easily busted my jaw. I knew it, and so did the next two vamps who rushed me.

I couldn't heal like *weres*, but damn it, I was just as strong and just a little faster. And unlike *weres*, I could *shift* underground and come up completely unscathed. I spat out some blood and used my resentment against the remaining opponents.

I held Agnes and Edith with my feet pressed against their throats, taking care not to protrude my back claws when they grabbed my ankles and tossed me. I flipped back and landed in a crouch. Maria regained consciousness, again, and tackled me from behind. I yelped when fangs dug into my skin, piercing my flesh like sets of scorching needles. The scrimmage ended and the pain receded before I could tear the Prada-worshipping leeches off.

Edith and Agnes visibly shook as Misha laid into them. "Celia belongs to *me*," he hissed. "You are never to taste her."

I frowned. "I'm not yours."

The vamps ignored me. "I didn't drink her blood, Master. I swear it," Edith Anne whimpered.

Agnes cowered at his feet. "Neither did I, Master. Not even a lick."

I rubbed my face. The Catholic schoolgirls and I weren't exactly buddies. In fact, we barely tolerated one another. Still, I didn't want them turned into clumps of dust. I strode to Misha's side and grasped his elbow, halting his tirade. "Misha, it's fine. They only bit me. On the shoulder and . . ." I turned to look at my backside. "Damn it, Edith, you bit my ass?"

Edith shuffled back and forth, looking at her feet. "Sorry, Celia. It was an accident."

Her wicked smile and flirty wink told me otherwise. Misha glared with the might of his master badass-ness. "Leave *now*."

The so-called Prince of Darkness knew how to clear a room. There was a slight breeze and the whole lot of them vanished—as in hauled serious supernatural ass. I tried to leave, too, but Misha grabbed my hand. "Wait. I must heal you."

The smoldering look Misha gave me told me exactly what he meant. "That's okay—they're only puncture wounds. I'll see Emme tomorrow. She'll fix me right up."

Misha closed the distance between us. "They left deep marks. You should not wait to tend to them."

"Misha . . ."

Chills spread through my body as Misha licked my shoulder to seal the wound. His tongue and breath felt warm against my skin. Misha had been around for more than a hundred and forty years; he'd had plenty of time to learn how to touch a woman. He continued on, even though the bites had closed after the first flick of his tongue.

I broke his hold and backed away. "Misha, don't." Misha was a thrill ride I didn't want to straddle. My loneliness had become unbearable; every part of me longed to be touched. But it wasn't his hands my body craved.

Misha's heated gaze promised me hours of pleasure. "I'm not done yet, kitten."

My mouth went dry. This was a problem; when it came to fighting, I'd take on anyone, anytime, anywhere. When it came to males, I *changed* into the superhero of dorks, a big ole D blazed across my chest and an army of pocket-protector worshipping fiends bowed at my feet. Any able-bodied female in my situation would have taken control and made Misha beg for pleasure. Where were these able-bodied females when I needed one?

I inched my way back, laughing a little too hysterically for my taste. "You don't really want to kiss my butt, do you? What will people think?"

A wicked smile spread slowly across his strong, masculine face. As if on cue, a gust appeared despite the closed windows and fanned Misha's long blond mane in perfect supermodel fashion. "Do I strike you as someone who cares what others think?"

My eyes darted around, searching for the source of the breeze. My eyebrows knitted tight. "Did you just do that on purpose?" The gleam in his "come hither and do naughty things to me" expression affirmed my suspicions. My gulp dissolved my frown. I'd already backed into the bamboo walls. Misha continued to stalk toward me. His smoldering gray eyes accelerated my pulse, and my forlorn female parts screamed to give in, and my hands itched to take off my clothes. Thank God, my mind still functioned reasonably. "Misha, under no circumstances will your tongue *or* lips touch my backside."

He placed his palms on either side of my head and regarded me with growing desire. "As you wish."

My shoulders slumped with relief . . . until I realized I hadn't been specific enough. Misha grabbed the two fingers of my right hand and placed them in his hot mouth, instantly spiking my body temperature ten degrees. I was so distracted that I didn't notice him yanking my yoga pants down to my ankles. By some lingerie miracle, my thong remained in place. He pulled my delighted fingers out of his mouth and smoothed them over my remaining marks. I swallowed hard while he held my gaze. My body was literally shaking with need. No man had touched me like that since Aric. . . .

Aric.

I jumped out of Misha's grasp, only to land on my face and scramble away like a damn epileptic inchworm.

Misha sighed when I managed to stand and yank up my pants. "Kitten, why must you make things so difficult?"

"Misha, I don't want this. I told you that before I moved in."

Misha leaned against the wall and quirked an eyebrow. "It didn't appear that way a moment ago."

My hands dropped to my sides in frustration. "I know, and I'm sorry. But I can't stay here if this is what you'll expect of me. You promised you'd keep your hands to yourself."

Misha pushed himself off the wall and, in a blink, faced me. "I promised to make you the perfect weapon, one that could help us defeat the Tribe." He licked his lips and focused on mine. "I also promised not to do more than you would allow between us."

"There is no *us*, Misha. I can't allow our relationship to go further."

Misha flashed me another wicked grin before he gave me his usual line. "We'll see."

Did you miss the first book in
the Weird Girls series?
Read on for an excerpt from

Sealed with a Curse

Available now in print and e-book

Sacramento, California

The courthouse doors crashed open as I led my three sisters into the large foyer. I didn't mean to push so hard, but hell, I was mad and worried about being eaten. The cool spring breeze slapped at my back as I stepped inside, yet it did little to cool my temper or my nerves.

My nose scented the vampires before my eyes caught them emerging from the shadows. There were six of them, wearing dark suits, Ray-Bans, and obnoxious little grins. Two bolted the doors tight behind us, while the others frisked us for weapons.

I can't believe we're in vampire court. So much for avoiding the perilous world of the supernatural.

Emme trembled beside me. She had every right to be scared. We were strong, but our combined abilities couldn't trump a roomful of bloodsucking beasts. "Celia," she whispered, her voice shaking. "Maybe we shouldn't have come."

Like we had a choice. "Just stay close to me, Emme." My muscles tensed as the vampire's hands swept the length of my body and through my long curls. I didn't like him touching me, and neither did my inner tigress. My fingers itched with the need to protrude my claws.

When he finally released me, I stepped closer to Emme while I scanned the foyer for a possible escape route. Next to me, the vampire searching Taran got a little daring with his pat-down. But he was messing with the wrong sister.

"If you touch my ass one more time, fang boy, I swear to God I'll light you on fire." The vampire quickly removed his hands when a spark of blue flame ignited from Taran's fingertips.

Shayna, conversely, flashed a lively smile when the vampire searching her found her toothpicks. Her grin widened when he returned her seemingly harmless little sticks, unaware of how deadly they were in her hands. "Thanks, dude." She shoved the box back into the pocket of her slacks.

"They're clear." The guard grinned at Emme and licked his lips. "This way." He motioned her to follow. Emme cowered. Taran showed no fear and plowed ahead. She tossed her dark, wavy hair and strutted into the courtroom like the diva she was, wearing a tiny white minidress that contrasted with her deep olive skin. I didn't fail to notice the guards' gazes glued to Taran's shapely figure. Nor did I miss when their incisors lengthened, ready to bite.

I urged Emme and Shayna forward. "Go. I'll watch your backs." I whipped around to snarl at the guards. The vampires' smiles faltered when they saw *my* fangs protrude. Like most beings, they probably didn't know what I was, but they seemed to recognize I was potentially lethal, despite my petite frame.

I followed my sisters into the large courtroom. The place reminded me of a picture I'd seen of the Salem witch trials. Rows of dark wood pews lined the center aisle, and wide rustic planks comprised the floor. Unlike the photo I recalled, every window was boarded shut, and paintings of vampires hung on every inch of available wall space. One particular image epitomized the vampire stereotype perfectly. It showed a male vampire entwined with two naked women on a bed of roses and jewels. The women appeared completely enamored of the vampire, even while blood dripped from their necks.

The vampire spectators scrutinized us as we approached along the center aisle. Many had accessorized their expensive attire with diamond jewelry and watches that probably cost more than my car. Their glares told me they didn't appreciate my cotton T-shirt, peasant skirt, and flip-flops. I was twenty-five years old; it's not like I didn't know how to dress. But, hell, other fabrics and shoes were way more expensive to replace when I *changed* into my other form.

I spotted our accuser as we stalked our way to the front of the assembly. Even in a courtroom crammed with young and sexy vampires, Misha Aleksandr stood out. His tall, muscular frame filled his fitted suit, and his long blond hair brushed against his shoulders. Death, it seemed, looked damn good. Yet it wasn't his height or his wealth or even his striking features that captivated me. He possessed a fierce presence that commanded the room. Misha Aleksandr was a force to be reckoned with, but, strangely enough, so was I.

Misha had "requested" our presence in Sacramento after charging us with the murder of one of his family members. We had two choices: appear in court or be hunted for the rest of our lives. The whole situation sucked. We'd stayed hidden from the supernatural world for so long. Now not only had we been forced into the limelight, but we also faced the possibility of dying some twisted, Rob Zombie–inspired death.

Of course, God forbid that would make Taran shut her trap. She leaned in close to me. "Celia, how about I gather some magic-borne sunlight and fry these assholes?" she whispered in Spanish.

A few of the vampires behind us muttered and hissed, causing uproar among the rest. If they didn't like us before, they sure as hell hated us then.

Shayna laughed nervously, but maintained her perky demeanor. "I think some of them understand the lingo, dude."

I recognized Taran's desire to burn the vamps to blood and ash, but I didn't agree with it. Conjuring such power would leave her drained and vulnerable, easy prey for the master vampires, who would be immune to her sunlight. Besides, we were already in trouble with one master for killing his keep. We didn't need to be hunted by the entire leeching species.

The procession halted in a strangely wide-open area before a raised dais. There were no chairs or tables, nothing we could use as weapons against the judges or the angry mob amassed behind us.

My eyes focused on one of the boarded windows. The light honey-colored wood frame didn't match the darker boards. I guessed the last defendant had tried to escape. Judging from the claw marks running from beneath the frame to where I stood, he, she, or *it* hadn't made it.

I looked up from the deeply scratched floor to find Misha's intense gaze on me. We locked eyes, predator to predator, neither of us the type to back down. *You're trying to intimidate the wrong gal, pretty boy. I don't scare easily.*

Shayna slapped her hand over her face and shook her head, her long black ponytail waving behind her. "For Pete's sake, Celia, can't you be a little friendlier?" She flashed Misha a grin that made her blue eyes sparkle. "How's it going, dude?"

Shayna said "dude" a lot, ever since dating some idiot

claiming to be a professional surfer. The term fit her sunny personality and eventually grew on us.

Misha didn't appear taken by her charm. He eyed her as if she'd asked him to make her a garlic pizza in the shape of a cross. I laughed; I couldn't help it. *Leave it to Shayna to try to befriend the guy who'll probably suck us dry by sundown.*

At the sound of my chuckle, Misha regarded me slowly. His head tilted slightly as his full lips curved into a sensual smile. I would have preferred a vicious stare — I knew how to deal with those. For a moment, I thought he'd somehow made my clothes disappear and I was standing there like the bleeding hoochies in that awful painting.

The judges' sudden arrival gave me an excuse to glance away. There were four, each wearing a formal robe of red velvet with an elaborate powdered wig. They were probably several centuries old, but like all vampires, they didn't appear a day over thirty. Their splendor easily surpassed the beauty of any mere mortal. I guessed the whole "sucky, sucky, me love you all night" lifestyle paid off for them.

The judges regally assumed their places on the raised dais. Behind them hung a giant plasma screen, which appeared out of place in this century-old building. Did they plan to watch a movie while they decided how best to disembowel us?

A female judge motioned Misha forward with a Queen Elizabeth hand wave. A long, thick scar angled from the corner of her left jaw across her throat. Someone had tried to behead her. To scar a vampire like that, the culprit had likely used a gold blade reinforced with lethal magic. Apparently, even that blade hadn't been enough. I gathered she commanded the fang-fest Parliament, since her marble nameplate read, CHIEF JUSTICE

Antoinette Malika. Judge Malika didn't strike me as the warm and cuddly sort. Her lips pursed into a tight line and her elongating fangs locked over her lower lip. I only hoped she'd snacked before her arrival.

At a nod from Judge Malika, Misha began. "Members of the High Court, I thank you for your audience." A Russian accent underscored his deep voice. "I hereby charge Celia, Taran, Shayna, and Emme Wird with the murder of my family member, David Geller."

"Wird? More like *Weird*," a vamp in the audience mumbled. The smaller vamp next to him adjusted his bow tie nervously when I snarled.

Oh, yeah, like we've never heard that before, jerk.

The sole male judge slapped a heavy leather-bound book on the long table and whipped out a feather quill. "Celia Wird. State your position."

Position?

I exchanged glances with my sisters; they didn't seem to know what Captain Pointy Teeth meant either. Taran shrugged. "Who gives a shit? Just say something."

I waved a hand. "Um. Registered Nurse?"

Judging by his "please don't make me eat you before the proceedings" scowl, and the snickering behind us, I hadn't provided him with the appropriate response.

He enunciated every word carefully and slowly so as not to further confuse my obviously feeble and inferior mind. "Position in the supernatural world."

"We've tried to avoid your world." I gave Taran the evil eye. "For the most part. But if you must know, I'm a tigress."

"Weretigress," he said as he wrote.

"I'm not a *were*," I interjected defensively.

He huffed. "Can you *change* into a tigress or not?"

"Well, yes. But that doesn't make me a *were*."

The vamps behind us buzzed with feverish whispers while the judges' eyes narrowed suspiciously. Not knowing what we were made them nervous. A nervous vamp was a dangerous vamp. And the room burst with them.

"What I mean is, unlike a *were*, I can *change* parts of my body without turning into my beast completely." And unlike anything else on earth, I could also *shift*—disappear under and across solid ground and resurface unscathed. But they didn't need to know that little tidbit. Nor did they need to know I couldn't heal my injuries. If it weren't for Emme's unique ability to heal herself and others, my sisters and I would have died long ago.

"Fascinating," he said in a way that clearly meant I wasn't. The feather quill didn't come with an eraser. And the judge obviously didn't appreciate my making him mess up his book. He dipped his pen into his little inkwell and scribbled out what he'd just written before addressing Taran. "Taran Wird, position?"

"I can release magic into the forms of fire and lightning—"

"Very well, witch." The vamp scrawled.

"I'm not a witch, asshole."

The judge threw his plume on the table, agitated. Judge Malika fixed her frown on Taran. "What did you say?"

Nobody flashed a vixen grin better than Taran. "I said, 'I'm not a witch. Ass. Hole.'"

Emme whimpered, ready to hurl from the stress. Shayna giggled and threw an arm around Taran. "She's just kidding, dude!"

No. Taran didn't kid. Hell, she didn't even know any knock-knock jokes. She shrugged off Shayna, unwilling to back down. She wouldn't listen to Shayna. But she would listen to me.

"Just answer the question, Taran."

The muscles on Taran's jaw tightened, but she did as I asked. "I make fire, light—"

"Fire-breather." Captain Personality wrote quickly.

"I'm not a—"

He cut her off. "Shayna Wird?"

"Well, dude, I throw knives—"

"Knife thrower," he said, ready to get this little meet-and-greet over and done with.

Shayna did throw knives. That was true. She could also transform pieces of wood into razor-sharp weapons and manipulate alloys. All she needed was metal somewhere on her body and a little focus. For her safety, though, "knife thrower" seemed less threatening.

"And you, Emme Wird?"

"Um. Ah. I can move things with my mind—"

"Gypsy," the half-wit interpreted.

I supposed "telekinetic" was too big a word for this idiot. Then again, unlike typical telekinetics, Emme could do more than bend a few forks. I sighed. *Tigress, fire-breather, knife thrower, and Gypsy.* We sounded like the headliners for a freak show. All we needed was a bearded lady. *That's what happens when you're the bizarre products of a backfired curse.*